DOWN THE LONG VALLEY

The Old Man's Gift

Book 4

Home on the Range Series

Rosie Bosse lives and writes on a ranch in northeast Kansas with her best friend and husband of many years. She was once told, "If you can't find the books you want to read, write them." She is doing just that.

Enjoy this fourth historical novel in Rosie's eleven-book Home on the Range series. The series spans twenty years from 1868 to1888. Immerse yourself in these adventures and experience the Old West. You'll share joys and triumphs as well as laughter and heartaches with characters who will become your friends.

Be sure to check out Rosie's children's books and her Uncivil War series too. Here is to attention-grabbers and books that are worth losing sleep to read!

DOWN THE LONG VALLEY

The Old Man's Gift

Rosie Bosse

ISBN: Soft Cover –978-1-958227-28-2
ISBN: eBook – 978-1-958227-25-1
Second Edition
First printed 2021, Second Edition published 2025

**POST ROCK
PUBLISHING**

Post Rock Publishing
17055 Day Rd.
Onaga, KS 66521

www.rosiebosse.com

In memory of Sue Slate who gave me inspiration
and ideas with lots of laughs along the way.

WELLS FARGO RULES
FOR RIDING THE STAGECOACH

Adherence to the Following Rules Will Insure a Pleasant Trip for All

1. Abstinence from liquor is requested, but if you must drink, share the bottle. To do otherwise makes you appear selfish and unneighborly.

2. If ladies are present, gentlemen are urged to forego smoking cigars and pipes as the odor of same is repugnant to the Gentle Sex. Chewing tobacco is permitted, but spit WITH the wind, not against it.

3. Gentlemen must refrain from the use of rough language in the presence of ladies and children.

4. Buffalo robes are provided for your comfort during cold weather. Hogging robes will not be tolerated and the offender will be made to ride with the driver.

5. Don't snore loudly while sleeping or use your fellow passenger's shoulder for a pillow; he or she may not understand and friction may result.

6. Firearms may be kept on your person for use in emergencies. Do not fire them for pleasure or shoot at wild animals as the sound riles the horses.

7. In the event of runaway horses, remain calm. Leaping from the coach in panic will leave you injured, at the mercy of the elements, hostile Indians and hungry wolves.

8. Forbidden topics of discussion are stagecoach robberies and Indian uprisings.

9. Gents guilty of unchivalrous behavior toward lady passengers will be put off the stage. It's a long walk back. A word to the wise is sufficient.

PROLOGUE

Down the Long Valley, the Old Man's Gift is the fourth novel in my Home on the Range series. The setting is in the Bitterroot Valley, Montana Territory. This valley is on the southwestern edge of the state and is bordered on either side by mountain ranges. The Bitterroot River runs the full length of the valley. It is one of those rare rivers that runs south to north.

This prologue includes the history and some physical background on the Bitterroot Valley. Enjoy these tidbits and see how they intertwine through the fiction of this novel.

Bitterroot Valley in Montana

The Bitterroot Valley of Montana has been a home for the Indians of the area as well as a major travel corridor for many years.

Moist air from the Pacific coast is pushed east, funneling between the two mountain ranges that define this valley. This allows for more precipitation here than in many other parts of Montana. Its north end begins with the city of Missoula and follows the Bitterroot River nearly one hundred miles south to Lost Trail Pass at the end of the valley.

The Sapphire Mountain Range rises to heights of seven thousand feet on the east side and the Bitterroot Mountains form a barrier to the west with heights just over ten thousand feet. The valley is mostly flat and is known for its more moderate temperatures as well as its fertility.

Although not all are navigational in bad weather, five passes lead out of the valley. Lost Trail Pass allows passage into northern Idaho while Chief Joseph and Gibbons Passes cross over the Continental Divide on the southeast end. They form a wishbone shape as they merge and drop into Big Hole Valley. Lolo Pass gives access to the west across the Bitterroot Mountains. All four of these passes are very steep and provide scenic drives in or out of the southern end of this beautiful valley.

Skalkaho Pass crosses the Sapphire Mountains about three miles south of Hamilton. It connects the towns of Hamilton in the Bitterroot Valley to Phillipsburg in the Flint Creek Valley. It is considered a primitive and seasonal road. To this day, it is the only direct route between those two important agricultural areas.

The Bitterroot Valley is the ancestral home of the Salish people, but it was not to be their home forever. In 1891, the United State Government moved them north to the Flathead Reservation. They were joined with the Kootenai to form the Confederated Salish and Kootenai tribes.

Bitterroot Flower

The Bitterroot Valley was named by the Indians after the bitterroot plant. The Salish called it "Spet-Im" which meant "plant with bitter-tasting root."

The bitterroot is a small, low-growing plant. It begins to grow with the fall rains, and the little perennial remains alive beneath the snow.

Leaves appear soon after the snow melts, usually in April. This is a sign that the roots are tender and nutritious. They are now at peak time for harvesting. However, the plant cannot be pulled. The soil must be loosened, allowing the entire plant to be lifted from the ground.

When the long, cylinder-shaped buds appear, they begin to pull starch from the root. This causes the dark bark on the root to become harder.

As the flower buds develop, the leaves begin to shrink. By the time the plant blooms in late May or early June, the leaves are completely gone leaving only the small pink flower. Each flower will stay open for two to three days making its pollination time extremely short. After the color fades, the petals begin to dry and blow away. Soon, a tiny, cone-shaped package of black seeds will be the only thing left visible to the eye. Those small seeds are now ready to be blown far and wide by the wind. By July, there will be no trace of the now dormant plant.

In native Indian culture, the bitterroot plant may not be harvested until the elder women of the tribe conduct their First Roots ceremony. One or two bushels of fresh roots are enough to last an Indian family until the next year. After harvesting, the roots are spread in the sun to dry. Salish, Kootenai, Shoshone, and Nez Perce all have a reverent regard for the small, tubular plant.

Before the twentieth century, these amazing roots were a major food source for the Indians of this area, particularly, the Salish tribes. The roots can regenerate after being dried even when they appear to be dead. They may be consumed but not in large amounts. They are usually mixed with other ingredients to form pemmican. The starchy plant also works well as a thickener in soup, but its bitterness makes the plant an acquired taste.

Historically, bitterroot has been used to increase the flow of milk in nursing mothers, to relieve sore throats, calm poison ivy rash, and even suppress diabetes symptoms. However, the reverence with which it is regarded may have more to do with the plant itself in relation to birth, death, and new life.

The bitterroot flower was officially designated Montana's state flower in 1895. It handily won over thirty-one other contenders.

Lewis and Clark Expedition

Captain Merriweather Lewis and William Clark documented the first white exploration of the Bitterroot Valley in 1805. They entered from the south through Lost Trail Pass. The valley was mostly unsettled.

On their return trip, they rested at Travellers Rest (now spelled Traveler's Rest) on July 3, 1806, at the eastern end of Lolo Trail. The expedition then split their company.

Lewis traveled east while Clark traversed the valley before he continued south. He crossed the Continental Divide on a popular Indian road through what became known as Gibbons' Pass and descended into Big Hole Valley.

During this time, a sack of dried bitterroot could be traded for a well-trained horse.

St. Mary's Mission and The Jesuits Who Built It

Twenty-four Iroquois Indians arrived in the valley from the Northwest sometime before 1823. Twelve of these braves remained. They married Salish women and were adopted into the tribe.

The Iroquois had had been introduced to Christianity nearly two hundred years earlier, and they brought that faith with them. Their talk around the campfires at night about white men who wore long black robes intrigued the Salish and their neighbors, the Nez Perce. The two tribes sent three delegations thirteen hundred miles to St. Louis, Missouri, between 1831 and 1837. They wanted a Black Robe to come and live among them to teach them the things the Iroquois talked of. In 1839, a fourth delegation was en route to St. Louis. They stopped to rest with the Potawatomi tribe near present-day Council Bluffs, Iowa. There they met Father DeSmet.

Father Pierre Jean DeSmet arrived in the Bitter Root Valley on September 24, 1841, with two other priests and three lay brothers. They brought their personal items and supplies in three carts and a wagon. Those were the first vehicles to arrive in the valley.

The Jesuits established Saint Mary's Mission on the east bank of the river and immediately began construction. It was the first pioneer settlement in what was to become the state of Montana and was built just west of the present town of Stevensville. The Jesuits named the river and the tallest mountain peak to the west St. Mary's.

The first chapel, built in 1841, was twenty-five by thirty-three feet with room to accommodate the entire Salish tribe. It was the first church in the Pacific Northwest. In 1842, due to the popularity of the Black Robes, a larger chapel was built. This one was thirty feet by sixty feet. It was built about two hundred yards east of St. Mary's River. Father DeSmet then journeyed to Fort Vancouver on the West Coast to purchase livestock. He brought back with him Montana's first cattle, swine, and poultry.

Father Anthony Ravalli arrived at St. Mary's Mission in November of 1845. He was Montana's first physician, surgeon, and pharmacist. He was also an architect, an engineer, an artist, and a sculptor. He oversaw the building of the first gristmill and sawmill.

Religion classes were taught twice daily as well as instruction in reading, writing, and arithmetic. Teaching was done in the Salish language. Those who were interested were also taught to farm and harvest crops as well as how to tend livestock. The Mission even had its own brand ⊥ which was read as "Cross on a Hill." It was one of the first brands used in the future state of Montana and is still registered to St. Mary's Mission. The first irrigation and water rights in Montana are also associated with the mission.

By 1846, an even larger church was under construction. However, problems with the Blackfeet, the Salish's traditional enemies, forced the closure of the Mission in 1850. This closure was intended to be temporary. That same year, John Owen, a former army sutler, purchased the land and the mills for $250 in a Conditional Bill of Sale. If the Jesuits returned in two years, all would revert back to them.

Unfortunately, it was sixteen years before the priests returned. During that time, the little mission became a trading post which John Owen renamed Fort Owen. He became known as Major Owen even though he had never been in the military. He expanded the mills and developed a successful business.

When the Jesuits heard that John Owen was using the church as a saloon and dispensing whiskey over the altar, they asked that the church be burned to avoid further sacrilege. Owen complied, and St. Mary's Mission was no longer.

The Black Robes were missed by the Salish people and the other Indians. They worked hard to bring Father Ravalli back.

In 1866, Father Ravalli and Brother William Claessens were called back to the valley. They arrived there with their superior, Father Joseph Giorda. Brother Claessens built the fourth chapel shown on the cover of this book. This one was built about a mile from Fort Owen. The priests also built an attached study, dining room, kitchen, and barn. In 1879, an addition to the front of the church doubled the size of the chapel. A choir loft was also added.

The priests constructed everything they used and decorated the interior of their little chapel with what they had on hand. Tin can lids were even soldered to make silver decorations.

The original colors used inside the chapel were colors symbolic to the local Indian tribes. Indigo was used to make the blue color, and vermillion clay made the red. The yellow color was made from mineral pigments and plants. The robe of the Blessed Mother was made blue with berry juice.

The original wooden candlesticks, altar, and baptismal font were made by Father Ravalli. He used the metal band from a wagon wheel to make his first saw.

Father Ravalli's pharmacy had a ride-up window where he dispensed the drugs he made and gave advice. He was also a skilled craftsman. The rocking chair I mention in this book, along with the rosary, were made by him and given to special friends.

The talented priest signed none of his creations, but a picture of the Blessed Mother has been credited to him. It was removed from St. Mary's Mission in 1888 and placed in St. Francis Xavier Church in Missoula. Father Ravalli also sculpted the statues that still stand today in the little chapel.

The Blessed Mother appeared twice to children in the valley—once before the priests arrived and a second time after their arrival.

The first appearance was to a young girl who was dying. Before her death, she predicted the coming of the "Black Coats."

The second time was to Little Paul. He was a boy of about twelve. He had learning problems which affected his ability to memorize his prayers. A beautiful woman appeared to him on Christmas Eve in 1841, and on Christmas Day, he was able to recite his prayers perfectly. He was baptized that day. Although documented, neither of these miracles have been verified.

Father Ravalli's pharmacy has been restored along with the chapel and two priest residences. Chief Victor's cabin is now a Salish museum.

If you would like more information on St. Mary's Mission as well as the Indians and priests who helped to build it, I recommend Lucylle Evans' book, *Good Samaritan of the Northwest*. It offers an in-depth picture of Father Ravalli and is fascinating. You will see much of Father Ravalli in this novel as well.

The Forest Service renamed St. Mary's River the Bitter Root River in 1898. In 1908, they changed the spelling of Bitter Root to one word,

Bitterroot. Because my book is based in the 1870's, you will see the river called the St. Mary's River and Bitter Root spelled as two words.

The story of St. Mary's Mission and the priests/laymen who helped build it was a favorite part of my research for this book. It was exciting to learn about these brave and talented men, and the story of the Indians who begged them to come.

Stevensville, Montana Territory

When he arrived in the Bitter Root Valley in 1841, Father DeSmet called the little settlement he built St. Mary's. It was built near the location of present-day Stevensville. The name of the vibrant settlement was changed from St. Mary's to Stevensville in 1864 to honor the territorial governor, Isaac Stevens. General Stevens had overseen Indian affairs and military operations in the Northwest Territory for the past year. When Stevens moved his government and military attachments to Fort Owen in 1853, he expected to see a fort, not a trading post.

In 1858, Stevens was called back into active duty to serve with the Union Army. He was one of the early casualties of the Civil War, dying in 1862 at Chantilly, Virginia.

The townsite of Stevensville was formed about one mile south of Fort Owen in 1863 when John Houk and John Winslett started the first general mercantile store. Numerous fires destroyed most of the early buildings. However, many of those early businesses rebuilt and continued to thrive well into the twentieth century.

Apple orchards played a large part in the history of Stevensville and the surrounding area. The first apple orchard in the Bitter Root Valley was planted at St. Mary's Mission in 1867. A second orchard was started in Stevensville in the mid-1870s. A single old tree is all that is left of the Mission's once-large orchard.

Today, Stevensville is a quiet town with population around two thousand. It is a delightful place to visit with lots of history and friendly people. Ruins are all that are left of Fort Owen, but St. Mary's Mission has been preserved. Be sure to take a tour and look inside St. Mary's Chapel. Maybe even take home a "branded" item. The old "Cross on a Hill" brand lives on.

John and Nancy Owen

In the winter of 1849 and 1850, a 31-year-old army sutler by the name of John Owen traveled west on the Oregon Trail with a regiment of soldiers. The soldiers were to build a string of military posts through the unsettled Northwest. They wintered on the Snake River in what was known as Oregon Country, six miles above Fort Hall. When the army moved on in the spring of 1850, John relinquished his sutlership and stayed. He traded there with the emigrants bound for California and Oregon. His plan was to buy their worn-down oxen which would be fattened and rested for a year. He intended to sell them to travelers the following spring. However, he didn't remain long enough to put that plan to work.

It was during his time near Fort Hall that he met his future wife, Nancy. She was a twenty-six-year-old Shoshone woman. Owen soon took her as his common-law wife and lived with her family for a short time.

Little is known about Nancy's family although many relatives visited the couple between 1850 and 1868 at Fort Owen. We do know that she was an accomplished fisherman. She also knew how to find her way in the wild and often picked berries. She could cook but cooking was not something Nancy enjoyed.

John knew of the Bitter Root Valley and believed the location had potential importance as a trading center. In the fall of 1850, Nancy, John, and John's brother, Frank, set out on a difficult journey by oxcart for the valley. There they befriended the Jesuits at St. Mary's Mission.

Owen's conditional purchase contract of St. Mary's Mission for $250 was the first official land transaction in the future state of Montana as well as the first legal document to be recorded there. John immediately began to develop the property into one of the most important commercial centers in the Northwest.

John Owen married Nancy in 1858 in one of the first legal unions of a white man to an Indian woman before western Montana was even a territory. John often referred to her in his journals as his "old wife," but they were devoted to each other.

Between 1851 and 1864, the couple traveled over twenty-three thousand miles by horseback and mule to obtain trade goods. Owen was a savvy businessman, but he was not good at navigation. Luckily for him, that was one of Nancy's skillsets.

John studied the Salish language. He even wrote a dictionary and phrase book to help him to communicate better with his customers and friends. He also kept precise weather reports between 1852 and 1871 which are still referred to today.

Nancy died in 1868, and John Owen's life began to spiral downward. He soon lost Fort Owen and was declared legally insane in 1874. He died in Philadelphia, Pennsylvania, in 1889.

Even though Nancy died and Fort Owen was sold before the timeline of this novel, I did make John and Nancy Owen part of my story. I also gave them children. While the Owens had no biological children, they took in several Shoshone children and raised them as their own. Their personalities here are what I see them to be. History shows them as upstanding citizens and assets to the community.

Missoula, Montana Territory

The city of Missoula received its beginnings as a trading post called Hellgate Village. It was established in 1860 by C.P. Higgins and Francis Worden about five miles west of the city's current location. This location was chosen based on the expectation that the Mullan Road and future rail traffic would pass through that area.

The first settlement was moved upstream to Missoula's current location in 1864 to achieve easy access to water. This ready water supply was needed to grind the grain into flour in the gristmill the founders planned to build. Both a gristmill and a sawmill were added quickly, and settlers soon called the area Missoula Mills. A hospital was added in 1873. The completion of the Mullan Road allowed the army to establish Fort Missoula in 1877. Missoula quickly became an important travel and trade hub in western Montana.

A Horse Name Comanche:
The Only Cavalry Survivor of Custer's Last Stand

Comanche was purchased for $90 from horse traders by the United States Cavalry on April 3, 1868, in St. Louis, Missouri. The horse was then sent to Fort Leavenworth in Kansas by rail. Lieutenant Tom Custer, brother of General George Armstrong Custer, was sent to Leavenworth to procure new horses since battles with the Indians had depleted their supply. The lieutenant returned by train to the 7th Cavalry's camp near Fort Hays in western Kansas with forty-one horses. One of them was the soon-to-be famous horse named Comanche.

Captain Miles Keogh of the 7th Cavalry, an experienced soldier and veteran of the Civil War, liked one of the new horses and began to ride it regularly. The horse was injured on September 13, 1868, in a skirmish with Comanches in Kansas. One of the soldiers told Keogh that the horse screamed "like a Comanche" when it was struck with an arrow. From that day on, Keogh called the horse Comanche.

Comanche stood fifteen hands tall and has been described in color from bay to dun to chestnut to claybank. The quote below was taken from a paper printed two years after the Battle of Little Big Horn and is a quiet compliment to a brave horse.

Bismark Tribune, May 10, 1878:

Comanche was a veteran, 21 years old, and had been with the 7th Cavalry since its Organization in '66…He was found by Sergeant DeLacey in a ravine where he had crawled, there to die and feed the Crows. He was raised up and tenderly cared for. His wounds were serious, but not necessarily fatal if properly looked after…He carries seven scars from as many bullet wounds. There are four back of the foreshoulder, one through a hoof, and one on either hind leg. On the Custer battlefield three of the balls were extracted from his body and the last one was not taken out until April '77…Comanche is not a great horse, physically talking: he is of medium size, neatly put up, but quite noble looking. He is very gentle. His color is 'claybank.' He could make a handsome carriage horse…

The horse was found two days after the Battle of Little Big Horn where Custer and two hundred sixty-four of his men died. During that battle, Comanche suffered at least seven wounds, and three of those were severe. A correction to the above article stated that three of the bullets from that battle were removed at Fort Abraham Lincoln in the Dakota Territory, not on the battlefield.

Comanche was walked fifteen miles from the battlefield to the steamer, *Far West*. From there, he and fifty-two soldiers in Major Reno's command were taken down the Missouri River to Fort Lincoln near present day Bismarck, North Dakota. This is the post where Custer lived with his wife, Libbie, at the time of his death.

After Comanche's recovery, Colonel Samuel D. Sturgis issued an order in April of 1878 for Comanche to never again be ridden. In parades, he was saddled but marched riderless with his soldiers.

Comanche was taken to Fort Meade near Deadwood in Dakota Territory in June of 1879. There, he was officially retired with military honors. He was treated honorably and remained at that post until 1887. He was then moved to Fort Riley, Kansas, where he was made the "Second Commanding Officer" of the 7th Cavalry. He was treated like a pet and sometimes led parades. It was at Fort Riley where Comanche developed a predilection for beer!

The famous horse died at Fort Riley of colic on November 7, 1891. Although his actual age was unknown, he was believed to be around twenty-nine years old. He is one of two horses to be given full military honors upon his death.

Professor Lewis Lindsay Dyche agreed to preserve and mount the famous horse at the request of the 7th Cavalry officers. He offered to waive his $400 fee if Kansas University in Lawrence, Kansas, was allowed to keep the mount.

The original mount was made of wood, wire, and clay. The horse's skin was stretched over the man-made structure. Comanche is still on display at the Kansas University Natural History Museum in a climate-controlled glass case. Only verbal and other non-official records remain of Dyche's agreement with the 7th Cavalry officers.

I have long loved the story of Comanche and was excited to work him into this book. Since his ancestry and birth date are not known, I created that for him. You will see him linked in this story to one of the main characters.

Helena, Montana Territory

The original name of Helena in current-day Montana was Last Chance Gulch. The mining camp was founded after four Georgians discovered gold there on July 14, 1864. The camp grew quickly, and by fall, the population was over two hundred.

Some of the citizens thought the name Last Chance was too rough. On October 30, 1864, five months after Montana became a territory, a group of self-appointed citizens met to choose a new name. After many suggestions, Helena was chosen. There was an ongoing disagreement as to how it should be pronounced though. The southern pronunciation with the emphasis on the first syllable won and is still used today.

Last Chance Gulch would come to be the second largest placer gold deposit in the new territory, producing over $19 million in gold. Even after the gold ran out four short years later, Helena survived due to its location. It was on several major transportation routes, was close to mining towns, and was well supplied with agricultural products from a nearby valley.

Five Sisters of Charity from Leavenworth, Kansas, arrived by stagecoach in 1869 at the invitation of Father DeSmet. Their three-fold mission included teaching, caring for the orphans, and ministering to the sick. They founded St. John's Hospital in 1869, the first Catholic hospital in the territory, and were Montana's first trained nurses. The sisters also cared for the mentally ill until 1877 when another facility was made available. In 1881, the sisters founded St. Joseph's Home. It was the first orphanage in Montana Territory. Protestant matrons and Catholic mother superiors worked together to care for fallen women, children, and pregnant girls.

By 1888, around fifty millionaires lived in Helena, more than any city in the world at that time. Their fortunes were made with gold. Of course, this large concentration of wealth brought in those who wanted a share in that fortune including the development of a thriving red-light district. Helena's brothels were solid and successful well into the 1900s. They ended with the death of the last madam, Big Dorothy Baker, in 1973.

I modeled the house where my character, Clare, and her son lived after the Caretaker's House listed on Helena's Women's Tour. The cabin was basically a shack with a dirt roof. By the mid-1880s, this cabin had become the southern boundary of the lower end of the red-light district where cabins and cribs stretched north of the library. It would have housed the lowest-paid prostitutes. The original cabin was rehabilitated in the late 1930s and is the only nineteenth-century brothel still standing in Helena.

Big Dorothy was a benevolent madam in Helena from the 1950s to 1973. Her facility included seven bedrooms and five sitting rooms. Brothels were illegal after 1917, but "working women" after that time used what was referred to as "furnished rooms." Customers entered through Big Dorothy's back gate and went down steps to reach the back door.

The madam's back door was well known to those who made deliveries. Five dollar tips were common. Children selling products also knew they could count on a sale if they stopped at Big Dorothy's. The madam made countless donations to charities and supported the local schools.

Even though Big Dorothy operated after the timeline of this novel, I did incorporate her in my story. It was not uncommon for the early madams to support the communities and the churches through their donations, both publicly and in secret. Big Dorothy was part of that group.

Early Livestock Production

Blue grama, buffalo grass, needle-and-thread grass, western wheatgrass, and other native species of grass are all abundant in Montana. These grasses cure standing up, so the winter snows do not flatten them. That fact, along with the many streams that thread through Montana, made the new territory a cattleman's paradise. Once the Indian tribes were forcibly moved to reservations, the land was free to the settlers for the taking.

Cattle first came to Montana in 1842 when they were brought to St. Mary's Mission. When gold was discovered, the population exploded. Since all those new residents needed to eat, ranching and cattle production grew quickly to fill that need. One of those early ranchers was Conrad Kohrs.

Kohrs was a German immigrant who came to Montana in 1866. He grew his land holdings over the years to eventually control over a million acres of land. His location gave him an advantage since he was close to the early mining towns where he was a primary supplier of beef. He also shipped nearly ten thousand head of cattle annually to the Chicago Stockyards. Kohrs is known as Montana's Cattle King.

Many Montana ranches in the late 1800s ran breeding stock of Hereford, Angus, and Shorthorn cattle. Often, those early herds were brought in from the east or the west. However, some longhorn herds were moved north.

Nelson Story, a miner from Montana Territory, used his profits from the gold fields to move six hundred head of longhorns north from Texas. He pushed through Colorado and Wyoming Territories, and on into Montana Territory following the Bozeman Trail.

In 1880, nearly eleven years after the first transcontinental train crossed the United States, the railroad reached Montana Territory. The first train steamed north over Monida Pass, crossing the Continental Divide between Montana and Idaho Territories. Rail transportation in Montana Territory from east to west did not arrive for another six years.

Bringing cattle into the Bitter Root Valley would have been especially challenging for the early ranchers due to the mountain ranges on either side. Most herds were brought in from the north, past Missoula, and trailed down the valley to where they needed to go.

Angus Cattle in the United States

The first Angus cattle were raised in northeastern Scotland where they were native in the counties of Aberdeenshire and Angus. There they were called Aberdeen Angus or Angus doddies. In the United States, the name was shortened to Angus.

Angus cattle are naturally polled meaning they have no horns. Their native color is black. Today, Red Angus is a popular breed as well. In the United States, we consider the two colors of Angus to be two separate breeds.

The environment in Scotland is harsh. Because of this, the breed adapted well in the West. Angus cattle were and are often added to a herd because they usually birth smaller calves. This makes calving easier. Since most cattle were birthed on the range, this trait would have been desirable to early beef producers.

The first Angus cattle in the United States were brought to Victoria, Kansas, on May 17, 1873. George Grant of that area brought in four Angus bulls. No cows were purchased at that time. Of course, the neighbors were all curious as to how the new bulls would adapt to Kansas weather, as well as what kind of calves they would produce when crossed with Grant's longhorn cow herd. The results were positive, and Angus cattle of both sexes began to arrive in the United States.

The small town of Victoria, Kansas, is located about a mile south of Interstate 70 as you head west through Kansas toward Hays. To the south of the Catholic cemetery stands the Basilica of St. Fidelis also known as the "Cathedral of the Plains." It is a huge, historic Catholic church. The beautiful church was built over one hundred years ago in just three years by the local community. Also explore the old cemetery where the tombstones are metal scrolls and listen for the voices of the past.

Early Trails

The Bozeman Trail was originally called the Road to Montana. It was an overland route that connected the gold fields in Montana Territory with the Oregon Trail. John Bozeman was credited with creating the trail after he scouted a shortcut that saved nearly five hundred miles. Unfortunately, his route illegally crossed treatied Indian lands. This caused uprisings by the affected tribes.

While it was rough and dangerous, Bozeman's trail was easier to navigate. It avoided the mountain ranges as much as possible and crossed Wyoming Territory at an angle from southeast to northwest. It passed into Montana Territory southeast of current-day Bozeman.

The trail was already in use before the discovery of gold in 1862 on Grasshopper Creek in Montana Territory. However, the ensuing gold rush caused traffic to increase. It increased again after the end of the Civil War in 1865.

New treaties with the affected Indian tribes shut down travel across their reservations and hunting grounds. As a result, Bozeman's cutoff was used for less than five years. Nearly thirty-five hundred emigrants traveled the dangerous trail for the few years it was open.

The Mullan Wagon Road was the first wagon road to cross the Rocky Mountains into Montana Territory. While it was never heavily used by the military, it was an important civilian route and promoted settlement in the Northwest. Captain John Mullan constructed the six-hundred-twenty-four-mile road between 1855 and 1862. It connected Fort Benton in central Montana Territory to Fort Walla Walla, Washington, on the Columbia River.

Construction of the road was a difficult job. During and after its completion, large parts were destroyed by rain and flooding. Those sections had to be moved and/or be rebuilt. In addition, there were many Indian difficulties. Still, it opened that area to travel for settlers as well as for the army.

In its day, the Mullan Road was the fastest land-water route across the continent. Travelers were on the road for forty-seven days, but they could board a steamboat at either end.

Much of the original route of the Mullan Road is in use today when one travels west across Montana to Spokane, Washington. Most early roads followed animal and Indian trails because they were the easiest routes. Today, our highway system follows many of those same trails.

One of the things that was most amazing to me as I researched this book was how difficult travel was for early settlers, not only in the Bitter Root Valley but in all of Montana. No stagecoaches ran the full length of the Bitter Root Valley nor throughout Montana Territory.

The population could not support them. For the early residents of the Bitter Root Valley, that meant all travel in or out would have been by wagon or on horseback. The passes are high and difficult today. They would have been even more treacherous in the 1800s. Combine those travel issues with rail travel that was sketchy and incomplete at best. I am reminded once again of the strength and tenacity of those who have gone before me.

I would like to thank Colleen and Jay Meyer of Stevensville, Montana, for all their help with the logistics of this book, as well as for opening their home to my husband and me when we visited.

A thank you also goes out to Roy and Sue Slate for helping me choose the location for this story. Thanks especially for allowing me to use their names as part of the fabric of this novel. One of the stories in this novel was based on an actual incident told to me by Sue…except it was a cow that was throttled instead of a donkey!

And finally, thank you to you for choosing my book—may it be all you hoped it would be and more. All my novels and children's books are available through your local bookstore, your library, and various online providers. They may also be ordered on my website listed below.

Rosie Bosse, Author
Living and Writing in the Middle of Nowhere
rosiebosse.com

Bitter Root Valley
Montana Territory
May 15, 1871

CHAPTER 1

DARBY McCune

THE OLD MAN LAY ON A BUNK IN HIS SMALL CABIN. HIS gnarled hand held an old pistol that pointed at the door. Brass bullet casings were scattered on the floor beside him. The wolves outside snarled as they darted by the open door and quickly disappeared.

"Well, ya didn't git me yet. Ya think ya cin hold out till I fall asleep, but I'm tougher than ya think." He flipped open the chamber of his gun and checked the cartridges.

"Three bullets left an' then you'll have me, ya blood suckers. But I won't go easy. I'll take at least one of ya with me, mebbie two when I poke ya with this here pigsticker." He held a large knife in his left hand with the cutting edge up. "Never been a McCune yet what went easy when the chips was down."

The old man tried to shift his legs and grimaced with pain.

"I sure hope my Jenny is all right. She carried me home an' dumped me at my own door. I crawled in here an' passed out. Now she's in the barn, an' I hope she pulled that door closed so's those wolves cain't pull her or my little mare down."

A large shadow passed briefly in front of the door, and the old man cocked his gun as he hollered, "Ya big cowards! Ain't brave 'nough ta take me on yur own, are ya? Ya need a whole pack ta take down one crippled ol' man."

The grizzled old man thought about the accident that left him in this condition. He rubbed his eyes to keep them open.

"Durned eyes. Cain't see much no more, 'specially when they's shadows 'round." He groaned as he shifted his leg and added, "Was a time when three shots woulda taken all three a them wolves down."

The tree that fell on him had crushed his leg. He had been busy clearing brush around his creek and didn't see the broken trunk until the tree came down. He jumped out of the way of the large trunk, but a heavy branch hit him and knocked him out.

He lifted his blanket and stared at his bloody leg. He cursed softly and shook his head. "Ya jist never know when yur time is up."

The old-timer smiled briefly as he watched the door. The sun was shining brightly outside, and shafts of light filled the doorway. His smile faded when flitting shadows blocked the sun.

"Yep, those wolves follered my blood trail back here. Sure am glad my Jenny come when I whistled. She's afeard a wolves, but she stood still an' let me drag myself on 'er. Another half hour an' I wouldn't a had the strength."

His eyes slowly closed, and the gun almost slipped out of his hand. As it bumped his finger, the old man woke up and stared at the snarling wolf leaning in his door. He pointed his gun and fired. The wolf yelped as it swerved away. It backed out of the doorway, still snarling.

"This here's yur last ride, Darby. Ya better git ready ta meet yur maker. When them wolves come in, they's a goin' ta be comin' fast." He looked around the small cabin and softly added, "An' when they do, there won't be many folks what will miss me neither. Sure hope it won't be little Suzanna what finds me. She's a sweet little gal, an' she don't need no memories like that."

CHAPTER 2

A Cattleman's Dream

ROCK BECKLER RESTED HIS MUSTANG JUST OVER THE crest of a hill and stared down into the valley below. It was May of 1871, and he was twenty-four years old. He had left his foreman job just south of Fort Benton in northern Montana Territory about a week before. It was a pretty place, and he got along well with the men. He didn't see eye to eye with the boss though. It was easier to ride away than to argue every day with a tinhorn. He had ridden southwest. When he reached the Sapphire Mountains, he slowed down. He'd been riding through them for the last two days just taking his time and looking around. The grassland rolled between the trees and stretched as far as his eyes could see. *It looks like the trees just spread apart to let the grass escape.*

He could see the Bitter Root Mountains on the other side of St. Mary's River. The river was a shimmering ribbon as it curled its way around and down to the south end of the valley. Of course, that was misleading since St. Mary's River ran north as it wound its way between the two mountain ranges. Rock grinned and shook his head.

"You never know what tricks nature tries to play on folks."

Wind lifted the wide brim of his Stetson and ruffled the bandana around his neck. He pulled off the beat-up black hat, and the wind sifted through his short, curly hair.

When his hair was long, reddish-brown curls covered his head. Rock frowned as he ran his fingers through the curly mess. He had never been impressed with his hair. Besides, women seemed to be attracted to curly hair, so he liked to keep it short.

Red stubble covered the hard planes of his face, and laugh wrinkles showed around his eyes. Rock shifted in his saddle. His long legs hung down on the sides of the large stallion, and his wide shoulders rippled under his thick shirt.

"Bitter Root Valley, Red. One of the prettiest places in Montana Territory." Red's ears flicked back and forth as he listened to his rider.

Rock swung one long leg over the saddle and hooked it around the saddle horn. His green eyes glinted with pleasure and sheer enjoyment of the morning. The valley was long, nearly one hundred miles, and reached north almost to Missoula. If he had figured correctly, Stevensville was somewhere to the north of him. He could see St. Mary's Mountain across the river to his right, and Lost Trail Pass was to his south. The entire valley was a cattleman's dream.

"If I was going to start my own place, Red, this is where I would like to settle. Good grass, lots of cover for winter grazing, plentiful water, and milder temperatures. Sounds like a little piece of Heaven." His mouth lifted in a sardonic smile as he looked at the small mule beside him.

"Georgia, I know you don't think much of being used as a pack mule. You're not big enough for me to ride though, and Red here can't carry me and my pack." Georgia snorted as she stamped her small feet. She was nearly three years old but was small for her age.

Rock looked at the donkey following behind. "And Gomer's not good for much of anything." The old burro had followed him when he'd left one of his riding jobs. He seemed to think he was part of Rock's family.

Red flicked his ears again as he looked around at his rider and Rock laughed.

"All right, Red. We'll get a move on. I don't think I have ever seen a horse that liked to stay on the move as much as you." Gomer moved up beside Red, and Rock grinned as he thought of how the little donkey had come to be with him.

Red and Rock had signed on with the Three T up by Helmville four years ago. The boss was pleased with Rock's cattle knowledge. Besides, he was handy with horses. Everything was going smoothly—for a time anyway.

Then, one cold December night, Red kicked in the door of the barn to get acquainted with a fancy little mare that had come in heat. Rock caught Red before he could get inside, but he didn't see Gomer. There were quite a few stray burros in their area because of the mining boom, and Gomer had adopted the ranch even though the boss didn't want him around. The little burro crawled under the boards and made his way into the mare's stall. He spent the entire night with her. Gomer was much smaller than the dapple-gray mare, but by morning, she was bred and Gomer was pleased.

When Old Man Slate opened the stall the next morning, Gomer raced out of the barn.

Rock laughed out loud as he remembered the shouting and the colorful words that had come from the barn that morning.

The boss caught Gomer with his bare hands and tried to throttle him. The men were staring as Old Man Slate and the burro went round and round in front of the barn. The little burro finally bit him and broke free. As the scruffy donkey raced for the hills, Old Man Slate chased him shouting, "Shoot that durn donkey! He molested my Estelle!"

The men didn't know their boss could run, but he almost caught the little donkey. Gomer looked back, kicked both of his feet backwards, and farted right in Old Man Slate's face before he disappeared in the trees.

The cowhands almost collapsed as they laughed. However, the laughing ended when their boss turned around. Now that they knew how fast he could run *and* that he would throttle a donkey, all the riders were on their best behavior. Besides, the boss was in a sour mood all day, so everyone trod lightly.

Georgia was the result of Gomer's tryst that night. To say her owner was not impressed was an understatement. To make matters worse, when Georgia was born, both Estelle and the little molly mule almost died. Rock saved them both along with several other mares and foals that season.

Old Man Slate was convinced that Rock had something to do with the donkey getting into the barn. He asked the hands, but they were overly innocent. No one shared any information with the boss, and Rock certainly didn't tell him that Red was the one who had broken the barn door. Still, he thought it might be a good idea to move on. He repaired the barn door and told the boss he would be leaving in the spring. Even though he was a top hand, the boss hadn't argued.

The boss had a cute little daughter. While his wife liked Rock, Old Man Slate made it clear that his foreman wasn't welcome at the main house. Rock didn't think a pretty girl was worth all the problems she could cause him. He left when winter broke.

"That little molly mule is so puny that she won't make it to her first birthday. You just take her when you leave," the boss said, "and I hope that dadgum donkey follows you too. In fact, if he doesn't, I'm going to shoot him. I'm tired of him hanging around here trying to breed my mares."

Neither the mare nor her foal was pleased with the boss's decision, but Rock left with a six-month-old mule filly trailing behind his stud horse—and Gomer decided to follow as well.

Black was his partner at the time. Rock chuckled as he thought about how innocent Black had acted and answered when the boss had questioned him. Black *wanted* to marry the boss's daughter, but he was right behind Rock when the snow cleared. She was a nice little gal, but Black said he wasn't going to trade his best pard for a woman even if she did come with a ranch. Of course, the boss threatened to shoot them both if Black didn't follow Rock down the trail.

Their ranch work for the next year was determined by whether the boss would allow a mule filly on the place. Rock didn't mention Gomer. After all, he didn't own the little donkey—it had just adopted him. Besides, Gomer came and went as he pleased.

Rock shook his head as he thought of Black. South of Helena, the rancher's sixteen-year-old daughter fell in love with Georgia and was casting eyes at Rock as well. As ornery as he was in the bunkhouse, Rock was afraid of women, especially the bold ones. He didn't think the passes would ever open that spring, and he was the first hand to leave with snow still on the ground. Black wanted to stay but Rock was determined to go. Black followed, be it unwillingly.

"I keep ridin' with you an' I'll never get married. Yore plumb scared of women. Next time you cut out on a ridin' job, I'm goin' to stay."

Rock looked up and scowled as he thought about Black. "You just had to go bad, didn't you, Black?" He reached down and rubbed Georgia. "Greed causes all kinds of trouble. And women too. Isn't that right, Georgia?"

The little filly nuzzled Rock's hand with her soft nose and snorted again. She was the color of her mother and had the lines of a thoroughbred, but Gomer had contributed to her size. Georgia was small, but she was a beautiful little filly with a loving nature. She was timid around crowds, but she loved Red and Gomer.

Rock pulled an apple out of his saddle bag and broke it in half. He gave the pieces to Red and Georgia. Gomer pushed forward and stuck his nose in Rock's saddle bag. He knew where the extras were carried, and he helped himself. The little donkey rose up on his back legs and walked that way to dig in the saddle bag since he was too short to reach it.

Rock looked down at Gomer and shook his head. "Gomer, you don't even belong to me, but you think you run this show.

"Well, Red, let's mosey on down this hill and see what waits for us in this valley."

Red was eager to push on and started down the hill briskly, maneuvering around the rocks and downed trees. Rock looped Georgia's lead rope around her saddle horn, and she picked her way carefully behind them.

Gomer raced ahead, dodging the boulders, and jumping over the downed trees. He brayed as he ran just for pure enjoyment.

They were almost to the bottom of the hill when they heard a gunshot followed by the loud howling of wolves.

CHAPTER 3

WOLVES!

ROCK GRABBED GEORGIA'S LEAD ROPE AND SPURRED Red as they raced toward the sound of the howling. Gomer moved close to Red's side and followed cautiously.

As they broke into a small clearing, three wolves charged the little cabin. The door was open, and a gun fired from the inside.

Rock pulled out his rifle, aimed, and knocked down a large wolf. The other two wolves turned at the sound of the gun and charged Red. Georgia jerked lose and ran back up the trail. As Rock tried to aim at the second one, the largest wolf jumped toward Red's throat. The stallion reared and thrashed his front legs. He spun and his kick knocked the wolf rolling. Rock dropped the rifle and grabbed his Colt. He shot the rolling wolf while Red spun to attack the remaining one. It was the smallest of the three. As it slid away, Red reared and charged with his mouth open. His huge front feet came down on the small wolf and continued to stomp it long after it was dead. Gomer sniffed the dead wolves' bodies and kicked each of them one more time just to show that he was as tough as the mustang.

The stallion was trembling and blowing as it continued to snort and paw. It only calmed down when Rock dismounted and led it away from the wolves. His heart was pounding almost as hard as Red's. He looked in the direction Georgia had run and whistled loudly.

"Georgia! Come, girl!" Picking up his rifle, he turned Red loose. "Go find Georgia," he ordered as he headed toward the cabin.

"Hello, the cabin! You alright in there?"

A man's weak voice answered, "You'ins shore 'nough come along at the right time."

Rock stepped through the door. He could smell the infection before he saw the man's wound. He walked closer to the old man and pulled back the blanket. A festering leg wound showed through the rough bandage. Rock studied the wound before he looked up at the old-timer.

The man's grizzled face was twisted in pain. The gun he held was old and the floor was covered with bullet casings. He grinned up at Rock even as pain showed in his drawn face.

"Tree falled on me. It were my own durn fault—I warn't payin' attention ta nothin' but the tree I was cuttin' on, an' when she come down, the branches brought down a dead tree ta the side. I didn't git outa the way in time, an' a big branch landed on me. Tore me up purty good. My ol' Jenny let me climb up on 'er. She dropped me off at that there door, but I didn't git it barred. The wolves found me last night." He glanced toward the open doorway and added grimly, "Ya come jist in time. I had plumb run outa bullets." He waved his hand in disgust toward the floor.

"I cain't see worth a durn or I'd a had 'em when they first showed up."

Rock studied the old man's face as he nodded slowly. "Give me a little time here and then I'll have a look at that leg."

He turned to the fireplace and banked the wood for a fire. The wood and the kindling were both dry, and he was able to start a fire quickly. The well was close to the house, and Rock soon had water heating in the pot that hung on a hook over the fire. He returned to the old man's side.

"Does your donkey need water? I might turn her loose unless you think she needs to be hobbled. "

The old man grimaced as he moved his leg. "Jist turn 'er lose. We get lions up here from time ta time, so I always lock 'er up at night. She runs loose durin' the day though. There's a nice little mare in the barn jist 'bout ready ta foal if ya'd check on 'er." He grinned up at Rock.

"They's a rope tied inside the barn door. Jenny cin pull the door shut but she cain't get it open. Works purty good an' I shore hope she's in there.

"They'll both be thirsty. They been in there fer over two days now."

Rock headed for the barn. Red was coming down the trail followed by a skittish Georgia. He waited until the two animals came up to him. He gave Red a sugar cube.

"You're a good old boy, Red. And you, Georgia. What do you think you're doing, running off like that?"

The little filly studied Rock with her velvety eyes and tossed her head. He rubbed her neck as he opened the barn door.

Gomer ignored everyone and appeared to be sleeping in the sun as he stood with his head hanging down.

A small burro almost knocked Rock down as it charged out of the barn. It raced toward the house, braying and bucking with each step. Gomer's head flew up and he snorted as he followed the little jenny. Rock looked back at Gomer and shook his head as he went into the barn.

The little mare was lying down, and she rolled her eyes at him. He talked quietly to her. She stood and drank thirstily when Rock filled her water pan. He gave her some oats before he closed the barn door.

Rock pulled the saddles off both Red and Georgia and stashed them in the barn. He carried his saddle bags and pack into the house. The old man's burro was standing in the doorway and showed no inclination to move as Rock walked around her. She wobbled her lips at him, and Rock scratched her head as he walked by.

"Do you have any corn liquor or alcohol of any kind?" Rock asked.

The old man pointed at a lower cabinet and Rock pulled out a jug.

He looked seriously at the old man. "I need to clean that wound and see what is going on. It doesn't smell good to me. If it's rotten, your

leg is going to have to come off." He grinned at the old man as he held
out his hand.

"The name is Rock Beckler. You probably ought to know the name
of the feller who is going to be cutting on you."

The old-timer took his hand. "Jack's the name, Jack McCune, but
folks here jist call me Darby. Now I seen a bottle of good stuff in yur
bag an' if'n ya let me dose myself, I think I cin jist go ta sleep whilst
you'ins work on that leg."

Rock laughed as he pulled the bottle out of his bag. It *was* good stuff
and was about a third full. He handed it to Darby. "Drink up. I'm not
sure there is enough in there to knock you out but go ahead and try."

The old man tipped the bottle up and drained it in just a few seconds.
As his eyes began to glaze, he told Rock, "Do what ya have ta do. I
reckon I cin live with one leg if that's all the Good Lord thinks I need."

CHAPTER 4

Let's Look At That Leg

ROCK PULLED A PACKET OF HERBS FROM HIS saddlebag and mashed some of them in hot water. He lifted Darby's leg out of the blanket and cleaned the wound. The skin around the wound was discolored and Rock cut around it until fresh blood showed. Darby's toes and feet were still warm so he was hoping he could save the old man's leg. When he poured the corn whiskey into the open wound, the old man groaned. The young cowboy made a poultice of steeped herbs and applied it to the wound. When he finished, he sat back in his chair and shook his head.

"That's a nasty wound, Darby, and it festered for a time. I hope it heals." Rock dug around until he found some clean rags on a shelf. He wrapped the old man's leg before he felt around the bone.

"I don't feel a break but that doesn't mean the bone's not cracked." Rock wiped his hands on another rag and stood up. "We'll have to wait a day or two to see if this works." He patted the old man's shoulder. "I am going to look for some moss to put on that wound."

Rock picked up his rifle and studied the yard before he stepped through the door. Both Red and Georgia were grazing, and Rock petted them as he walked by.

The May air was cool and crisp. Spring in Montana didn't arrive as quickly as it did farther south, and there was still scattered snow at the bases of the trees. Rock was able to find quite a bit of moss though. He carried it back to the house. Darby was still passed out when he removed the rag and applied the moss. The old man stirred a little when Rock rewrapped the leg, but his eyes were still closed. Rock burned the dirty rags and eyed the old man's meager food supply.

"I'm short on food and it doesn't look like you have much. Maybe, between the two of us, I can make a little dinner."

Rock pulled half of his meager supply of salt pork from his pack. With the beans he found in a crate, he soon had soup simmering over the fire.

When it was just past noon, Rock slipped back into the barn to check on the mare. She was up and moving around, so Rock filled a bucket with more water.

"I hope you get this show on the road, girl," he told the mare as he petted her and left her stall. He didn't want to put any of the livestock in the barn until the mare foaled.

Darby was still asleep, and the soup wasn't quite done. Rock smelled the old man's leg before he strolled outside and looked for things to fix. He nailed up several boards in the corral and then stared at the front step. The top board was broken, and the ground beneath it showed through the large hole.

"A man could almost lose a foot there if he didn't pay attention," he muttered to himself as he added a new board.

Rock finished around two that afternoon. He pulled the soup off the hook just as the old man began to stir. He ladled some soup into a bowl and carried it over to Darby.

"Feel like eating? I make a mean bean soup."

Darby lifted the rag and stared at the moss covering his wound.

"I see I still have a leg. How bad were she?"

Rock shrugged.

"I've seen worse. You'll live and you might even keep your leg. That rot around your wound is probably what brought the wolves in. Nothing like blood and a little smell of sickness to get them excited."

The old man dragged himself up and began to eat. Rock chuckled as he refilled the bowl twice. "Guess it didn't affect your appetite any."

Darby swallowed the last of the bean soup. He grinned as he lay back on his cot and rubbed his belly.

"You'ins plan ta settle 'round here? If'n ya do, I hope you's close. I jist might join ya fer meals on a regular basis," Darby commented dryly as he winked at Rock.

The two men visited a time before Darby drifted off to sleep.

Not a man to sit around, Rock went to work on the wood pile. He chopped and split the large, cut logs that were near to the house. An hour's work took care of the logs, and he stacked the split wood against the house. He flexed his shoulders and grinned. "Feels good to be working. I think I've bummed long enough."

He rebuilt Darby's fire and made some biscuits to go along with the rest of the soup. While the biscuits were baking, he sniffed Darby's leg again and changed the moss.

Around five, Rock checked on the mare again. He could see one leg out but nothing else, so he pushed the mare until she stood. Then he walked her around. She was restless, and he slipped out of the stall.

Rock walked to the corral and stared off down the little valley. The grass looked good from where he stood and the cowman in him became excited.

As he studied the buildings, he could see that everything was built to last. The old man had put down roots and had made this isolated place his home. Rock felt an aching in his chest, but he pushed it away.

"You're just a durn tumbleweed, Rock. Don't go pining away over something you'll never have," he muttered as he grinned at his shadow on the ground. He checked the mare again. She had finally foaled, and the colt was up. He was a strong little fellow and was trying to nurse. Rock refilled the mare's food pan and brought her more water.

"Good girl. You have a nice little horse colt. Old Darby will be happy to know that."

Red and Georgia were drinking. When they finished, Rock opened the barn door and led them into the barn. He put Red in a stall by himself, away from the little mare. He let Georgia and the little burro roam inside the barn. Gomer refused to go in and Rock grinned.

"You're on your own, Gomer. You might change your mind after one night here though. There aren't any folks around, and those wolves have friends. They might decide to make a meal out of a fat little donkey like you." Gomer ignored him and the cowboy laughed.

Rock didn't worry much about Gomer. The little burro had lived on his own for a long time and seemed to know how to survive. Besides, he was like a dog. He brayed if he heard anything out of the ordinary. If Rock didn't respond, the little donkey would pull his blanket off and stand over him, breathing heavily in his face.

Darby was still sleeping when Rock ate his biscuits and a little of the soup. He rolled his bed out on the floor and was softly snoring by seven.

It was nearly dark when Darby awoke. He could smell the biscuits and the bean soup, but Rock was asleep. He smiled and closed his eyes. His sleep was restful, and his dreams were sweet ones.

CHAPTER 5

"Who is That Tall Man?"

ROCK WAS UP EARLY THE NEXT MORNING. HE MADE more biscuits and fried the last of his pork. The gravy was thickening when Darby opened his eyes.

"Yur mama teach ya ta cook or did ya jist pick this up on yur own?"

Rock grinned as he piled some biscuits and gravy on the old man's plate.

"I learned on my own. It was learn to cook or starve. My ma died when I was just a little tyke, and my pa didn't cook much." Rock frowned as he looked at his pack. He added, "I am low on supplies though, and you don't have much here. What direction is the closest town? I might ride down and pick a few things up."

Darby waved his hand toward the north.

"Jist foller the river north. St. Mary's be 'bout twenty-five miles from here. 'Course they's a callin' that town Stevensville now. Started out as a mission but she's a growin'." Darby snorted. "Renamed our little town after a durn politician, an' mighty few politicians deserve ta be remembered. It be what it be though.

"They's a dry goods store in town, an' I have an account with 'em. If'n you'ins cin reach me some paper an' that there stub pencil, I'll write a list of what I need."

Rock was ready to leave for Stevensville about an hour later. The mare and her foal were up and looking good, so he led her out of the barn. He debated hobbling her but decided to turn her loose with the donkey.

Red and Georgia were ready to go, and they arrived in Stevensville around nine. When Rock reached Murphy's Dry Goods, he sat on his horse and stared. A young woman was sweeping the walk and humming to herself. She had a wealth of blonde hair piled on top of her head and her small body was moving quickly with the movement of the broom. She was the prettiest girl Rock had ever seen. Not that he would ever talk to her—he just liked to look.

The young lady felt someone's eyes on her. She stopped sweeping, placed her hands on her hips, and looked the cowboy directly in his eyes. "Well, did you ride all this way to stare, or is there something you are wanting to purchase?" She tossed her head and turned quickly into the store.

Rock was grinning as he dismounted. *Well, isn't she a sassy little thing!* He walked up to the counter and handed the older woman both lists. "That second list is for Darby McCune. He said to tell you to put it on his account."

She stared at the stranger for a moment before she asked, "Is Darby all right? His writing looks a little shaky."

The cowboy was startled but he nodded. "I think he will be. He had a little accident, but he seems to be doing better." He glanced behind him and added, "I want to have the smithy check my horses' feet. I'll be back for those orders when I'm done."

Rock looked around for the young blonde woman, but she was nowhere to be seen. He thanked the older woman and turned toward the door. His tall frame filled the doorway as he left, and he walked easily in his tall cowboy boots. He talked to his horses, and they followed him across the street.

Suzanna came to the front of the store and watched the stranger saunter down the street. "Who is that tall man?" she asked her Aunt Maggie as she looked over her shoulder.

Maggie Murphy smiled. "Just a rider passing through although it looks like maybe he stopped to help Darby." She frowned. "I have told Darby many times that he shouldn't be staying out there alone. Now he went and got himself hurt. Stubborn old coot."

CHAPTER 6

Maggie Murphy

AXEL O'CONNOR, MAGGIE'S FATHER, RAN A DRY GOODS store in St. Louis, Missouri, from the time the town was founded in 1823. Maggie was ten when they arrived. Her mother had died birthing her little brother, and baby Knox died the next day.

Even as a child, Maggie's bright red hair matched her fiery disposition. She was seventeen years old when Paddy Murphy came into their store to buy some thread. Now Paddy had no idea how to sew nor did he know how much thread one should buy at a time. However, he had heard that there was a beautiful Irish maiden who worked in her father's store, and he was determined to meet her.

His friends warned him, "Aye, she's a pretty lass, but her father's as big as an ox. I'd be careful around that one!"

Maggie looked up when she heard the bell shake on the door. Paddy's red hair caught the sun, and his broad shoulders were just a little wider than his smile. When the fair lass smiled at him, Paddy knew he would be returning for more thread. He stood there for a moment to stare.

Maggie's father looked up with a scowl. He stepped between the young soldier and his daughter.

"What will ya be needin', laddie? And if yur eyes be for my daughter, she's a'ready spoken for."

Maggie snorted as she stepped around her father. "And I told you, Daidi, that when I marry, it will be for love and not for the 'mighty dollar.'" She smiled again at the soldier.

"Will ya be needin' a needle for your thread as well?" Maggie could tell that the young man had no idea how to sew or mend anything, but she was certainly pleased when he came back fifteen times in the next six weeks for more thread. She married the young Irishman two months later, just before his company was transferred to the West.

Axel O'Connor wasn't happy about their courtship. He was hoping Maggie would marry a prosperous young farmer outside of town, but Maggie had her heart set on Paddy. Her father gave in.

It was a bittersweet moment for Maggie when her father gave her in marriage and bid her goodbye the same day. They both knew they would likely never see each other again. Axel O'Connor shed some large tears as Maggie's new husband lifted her into the army wagon.

Over the next twenty-plus years, Paddy was stationed all over the West, and Maggie went with him to every post. St. Mary's Mission in Oregon Territory was the farthest north either of them had been, but they liked the area. They made friends quickly around the little mission.

John Owen resigned from his position as a licensed military trader or sutler in the winter of 1849—around the same time he met his future wife, Nancy. They came to the Bitter Root Valley in 1850 with a regiment of soldiers who were to establish a string of military posts. Sergeant Paddy Murphy was one of those soldiers.

The regiment set up camp north of St. Mary's Mission. That same year, trouble with the Blackfeet forced the missionaries to leave the Mission. John Owen bought the land and facilities with a conditional bill of sale for $250. The contract stated if the missionaries returned within three years, everything reverted to them. However, if they didn't, the Mission and all its buildings would belong to him.

The missionaries didn't return for sixteen years. During that time, "Fort Owen" as John called his trading post, grew in size and profitability. It served the settlers, Indians, trappers, and miners—and John's Indian wife, Nancy, helped him to run it in every capacity. The customers began calling John "Major Owen" even though he never been in the military.

When Paddy Murphy saw that John Owen was using the altar in the abandoned Mission church as a bar, he was angry. "Why, that's just wrong," he told Maggie. "St. Peter himself will come down and smite us all dead."

Paddy was an altar boy as a youngster, and even though he rarely attended Mass as a soldier, he wasn't going to tolerate a church being desecrated. He and some other soldiers burned the church to the ground. Major Owen was angrier about losing his whiskey stockpile than the loss of the church building. However, business was brisk, and he quickly recovered.

Maggie Murphy hired on at the trading post and became good friends with Nancy Owen. She and Sergeant Murphy had no children, so Maggie enjoyed working there as well as helping Nancy with her busy family.

Paddy mustered out of military service in 1854 to work with John Owen. The Jesuit priests had built lumber and gristmills before they left, and John was in the process of expanding those. His business was growing, and he needed help.

Paddy became not only a valued employee but also a great friend. When Nancy and John married in 1858 in one of the first legal unions of a white man to an Indian woman in western Montana, the Murphys stood up with them.

Maggie and Paddy had been married thirty-three years when Paddy passed in 1863. "Healthy as a horse, he was," Maggie said, "until one day, he just didn't wake up."

Nancy encouraged Maggie to stay at the trading post. "You will always have a place here, my good friend. Stay and live with us." Lots of little voices joined the chorus, "Please, Auntie Maggie! Stay here and play with us!"

The new widow shook her head. Her strong Irish upbringing wouldn't allow her to depend on her good friends. She kissed the children and promised to visit. "I won't be far—I will still be in St. Mary's, so we will see much of each other." Being the strong woman she was, Maggie squared her shoulders and marched into the next phase of her life.

About four months after Paddy's passing, Maggie opened Murphy's Dry Goods Store. It was much smaller than the trading post but was a perfect size for her. She catered to the townspeople and the ranchers of the area. Her store was well-stocked and included specialty items not available at the trading post. Because of her many years of experience and extensive contacts in the mercantile business, she could also find hard-to-get items.

Maggie smiled as she pushed back her hair. It seemed like a lifetime of years ago when she left her father in St. Louis. Now here she was in what folks back home called the "Wild West," running a dry goods store by herself. She frowned and shook her head. "Even the name of our little town has changed. St. Mary's is now to be called Stevensville, and by a decree of the president himself."

She looked around at the full shelves in her busy store and smiled again. Her life as the wife of a soldier had been difficult, but her years with Paddy had been happy ones. Even though they were never blessed with any children of their own, Maggie had no regrets.

"My father never told me when he became ill. He just sold his store and sent the bank draft to me. By the time I received his letter, Daidi had been gone for nearly a month. That was just a year before Paddy died." Maggie's bright eyes clouded with tears. She wiped at them and smiled wistfully. "And that bank draft paid for this store. I owe you so much, Daidi." She breathed deeply and whispered. "No need to cry over loved ones passing on to a better life,"

Now, it was 1870, nearly seven years since Paddy's passing. Maggie wiped her eyes. She kissed her fingers and touched the picture of Paddy and her on their wedding day. Her father had sent it to her as a gift about a year after she married. She had no pictures of her parents, but she held them in her heart.

"Aye, I've had a good life. And my little store is busier than ever. In fact, it is so busy that I'm thinking of hiring someone to help me."

CHAPTER 7

SUZANNA

WHEN MAGGIE RECEIVED WORD THAT BOTH HER younger sister and her husband died of cholera in Texas, she invited Suzanna, their youngest daughter, to live with her. Suzanna had always been strong-willed and independent, much to her mother's dismay. Maggie admired those qualities in her niece though. She sent Suzanna a quick note.

April 6, 1870

Dear Suzanna,

I would like to invite you to come live with me in Montana Territory. It is a strong land filled with strong people. Here in Stevensville, I have a small dry goods store. You may work with me if you'd like. We also have a wonderful priest at the Mission who is a doctor and an excellent surgeon if you would like to study medicine or pharmaceuticals with him.

My home is open to you. You may stay forever or until you get your feet under you, whichever you choose. I am including money for your trip. I know it will be a long and difficult journey. Do bring some warm clothes and plan to leave immediately as the areas you will travel through must be passed in warm weather.

Love, Aunt Maggie

Nearly two months later, a letter arrived from Texas.

May 10, 1870

Dear Aunt Maggie,

Thank you for the invitation! I have checked into routes. There are no trains that connect me to large towns here in Texas, so I am going east to the Mississippi River. It will take me several days to get to the nearest harbor in Louisiana. I will be able to travel by steamboat from New Orleans to St. Louis, Missouri. From there I will take a train to Kansas City on the Missouri side. A ferry will take me over the Missouri River and then I'll take another train north to Omaha, Nebraska. From there, I can take the new Overland Route or the Pacific Railroad as some folks call it. It runs west all the way over to the Utah Territory.

One of my friends here suggested, as a woman traveling alone, that I stay out of Corinne in Utah Territory and instead travel north from Salt Lake City as far as I can by rail. I will be able to catch a stagecoach north over the Montana Trail to Salmon, Utah, and then a stage or a wagon the rest of the way. I am leaving on May 10th, so I will be well on my way when you receive this. Sláinte!

Your niece,

Suzanna.

Maggie smiled as she remembered the day Suzanna had arrived that warm day last June. The young woman was eighteen years old and beautiful, so she caused quite a stir. Of course, women of any age were scarce in Montana Territory in 1870 and certainly young women as pretty as Suzanna.

"Aye, conversation stopped when little Suzanna was helped down from the wagon, but a mob of young men soon rushed to help her carry her bags.

"She smiled prettily at all of them, thanked them, and hurried across the street to my store leaving those men and boys to argue over who would carry her bag and small trunk."

Maggie rushed out of the store to hug her niece. "Suzanna! I am so happy to see you. I know your trip was long and hard. Would you like to lie down for a bit or are you hungry?"

Suzanna hugged this aunt whom she had always loved. When Uncle Paddy's regiment was posted in Texas, Aunt Maggie came and stayed with them. She came other times to visit too but not since they had moved so far north. Suzanna understood why after her own journey.

It *was* quite the trip from Texas. The train ride from Corrine was slow, and the Overland Stage ride was both long and rough. However, the last one hundred fourteen miles of that five-hundred-mile trip north from Salt Lake City were the hardest. The stage north of Salmon handed the passengers off to a mule train, and Suzanna rode in a wagon the rest of the way. That was the slowest and the roughest part of the entire journey.

"I'm glad you told me to bring a coat. I brought a quilt too and I was glad for both. The evenings were cold even when the days were warm. And I'm done sleeping on the ground!" Still, the weather had been good most of the way.

"Did anyone bother you? I have been so worried. It is so far up here!" exclaimed Aunt Maggie.

"The trip was fine. I only encountered one rude man. We were on the stage north of Salmon, and he just talked all the time. He was a drummer of some kind and tried to sell everyone on that stage some kind of tonic. They were all tired of him even before he began to bother me.

"He kept trying to scoot closer and closer to me. I finally slapped him." Suzanna giggled and added, "He was thrown off the stage in the middle of nowhere and they *left* him. The door was opened, and he was tossed out. The stage didn't even stop! No one seemed to be too worried if he lived let alone if he made it to the next settlement.

"One of the cowboys told me that there were rules regarding men's behavior on stagecoaches as well as the way women were to be treated. He said, 'Ma'am, we plumb apologize. That feller's behavior don't speak fer all of us on this coach.' The rest of the men did their best to make my travel comfortable." When she finished talking about her trip, she leaned toward Aunt Maggie. Suzanna's eyes sparkled as she whispered, "Some of them even asked to come and see me."

Maggie smiled again as she wiped off the counter in front of her. "Aye, that was nearly a year ago. Now it is May of 1871, and I would be lost without Suzanna."

Suzanna had adjusted well. She enjoyed the small but busy little community. The ratio of men to women was quite high so she didn't have many women friends. Still, the community was a friendly one, and Aunt Maggie seemed to know everyone. She even took Suzanna out to the trading post to meet the Owens and their little family.

Of course, male traffic in the store picked up after Suzanna arrived. They had men in their store every day who didn't need a thing. Each bought a small item of some kind so he had an excuse to talk to Suzanna.

Suzanna just laughed. She was a friendly young woman and was used to male attention. She was careful of her reputation as a lady though. She danced with all the young men at the weekly dances throughout the summer and fall, but she never went riding with any of them.

Now, the banker's son was back from school in the East, and he was pursuing Suzanna quite openly. She just tossed her blonde curls and rolled her blue eyes. Johnny Whipple didn't impress her even if his daddy was the richest man in town.

Horseshoes and Conversation

ROCK WANTED THE SMITHY TO CHECK BOTH OF HIS horses. He had shoed them himself at the last ranch, but he had no way to do that now.

Georgia and Red followed him across the street without being led, and the smithy looked up in surprise.

"You have yourself some well-trained stock there, stranger."

Rock grinned and agreed.

"Do you have time to check their shoes? Or if you don't, do you mind if I check them over here? I can shoe them myself if you don't have time."

The smithy rubbed his chin. "I can't get to them today, but you are welcome to check them over. No charge unless you need new shoes."

Rock agreed. Both horses needed their feet trimmed so Rock pulled the old shoes off. He was hammering in the nails in Georgia's last shoe when the pretty little gal from the mercantile arrived. She had lunch for the smithy.

The blacksmith smiled as he took it from her. "Thank you, Suzanna. I hope you brought me more of your meatloaf today." They visited a little more before Suzanna glanced back where Rock was working.

"Hire yourself a new farrier, Joe?"

Joe laughed and shook his head. "Nope, but maybe I should. He seems to know what he's doing."

Rock dropped the horse's foot. "I owe you for forty-eight nails. I was able to reuse the shoes."

"Two bits and just take the rest of that box. Then you will have them for next time," the smithy replied.

Rock dropped twenty-five cents on the counter. He nodded at Suzanna, thanked the smithy, and led his mounts outside.

Suzanna fell in step beside him.

When Rock looked down at her in surprise, she rolled her eyes. "Don't compliment yourself. I just want to know how Darby is. He's a nice old man, and I've been worried about him." She smiled up at Rock before she added, "I'm Suzanna."

Rock grinned down at Suzanna and almost forgot he was shy. He tipped his hat. "The name is Rock Beckler, and I will sure tell Darby you were asking about him.

"He seems to be doing better. He dropped a tree on his leg, and it gave him a nasty wound. I think it's healing now although I was a little worried he might lose his leg when I found him yesterday."

Suzanna nodded. "Please tell him that I will ride out and check on him later this week."

Rock looked at her carefully. "You'd better head out early. Give yourself time to get there and back in the daylight. I killed three wolves right up by his house, so you sure don't want to be out there at night."

Suzanna glanced up at the stranger in surprise but said nothing. Rock held the door to the mercantile for her and stopped at the counter to pick up his supplies. He added a dozen apples to his list and paid quickly. He tipped his hat to Suzanna again before he headed out the door.

A company of soldiers was riding into town led by a striking man with long, blond hair. Rock looked closer and scowled. He had first met

Lieutenant Colonel Custer at Fort Benton and hadn't been impressed with the man.

As the 7th Cavalry moved by, a horse nickered at Rock and pushed out of formation. Captain Miles Keogh grinned at Rock as the horse excitedly nuzzled the man.

"Hello, Comanche. I see you haven't forgotten me." Rock handed the horse one of the apples he had just purchased.

Custer swung his mount around and ordered, "Back in formation, Captain! And you on the ground—do not feed our military mounts. You civilians know nothing about horses."

Rock patted Comanche as the captain turned him away.

"Good to see you, Captain." As he stared after Custer, he muttered under his breath, "That arrogant fool is going to pick a fight where he shouldn't someday. I just hope he doesn't get anyone killed in the process."

Rock turned back to where his animals were tied and broke a second apple in half. He gave half to each and talked to them as he tied his supplies on Georgia. When he looked up and saw Suzanna standing in the door watching him, he grinned.

She stepped out of the store and gestured toward the line of soldiers. "That horse seemed to know you."

Rock chuckled. "He should. I helped birth him. His mother shouldn't have been bred and certainly not to the stud she was paired with. Lucky for her, Comanche wasn't a large foal. It was kind of touchy for a bit but they both made it. That horse has a staying power. He's a tough fellow.

"My boss sold him to a horse trader who was visiting from Saint Louis. I guess that fellow sold him to the United States Army because that horse is back in Montana Territory." Rock paused and watched the column of soldiers move through town.

"Captain Keogh is a good man and treats his mounts well. We called that claybank Rusty, but Keogh calls him Comanche. He carried

Keogh through a battle after being wounded. They were fighting some Comanches down in Kansas."

Suzanna looked puzzled. "Claybank?"

Rock nodded and pointed toward the horse. "Claybank is his color. He's a red dun. See how he is a reddish tan? That stripe down his back and the markings on his head and legs make him a dun. When those markings are red instead of black, the horse is called a claybank."

Rock mounted his horse and touched his hat. "Ma'am."

He was smiling as he left town. *Picking up supplies here could be fun if I get to see that sassy little gal each time*, he thought with a grin.

Suzanna stared after Rock's departing back. She finally turned to walk back inside the mercantile. She ignored Johnny Whipple when he came into the store and shut herself in the storage cave until he left.

CHAPTER 9

BUSHWHACKERS!

RED SNORTED SUDDENLY AND PRICKED HIS EARS forward. Rock looked around carefully. They weren't too far from Darby's cabin. He pulled Red to a stop and listened closely. When he heard gunfire, he dropped Georgia's lead rope and charged his horse down the hill into the little valley.

Three horses were ground-tied outside the cabin, and two men were dragging Darby between them.

Rock raced Red toward the cabin, guiding him with his knees as he shot first one and then the other.

Darby shouted as he fell, "There's one more inside!"

Rock turned Red toward the back of the cabin and slid off, holding his rifle as he hit the ground.

All was quiet in the little clearing except for Darby's labored breathing.

A man's head appeared briefly in the window of the cabin. When no shot was fired, he showed himself in the doorway. Then he stepped outside and ran for his horse.

Rock stepped around the corner of the cabin.

"Lose those guns or I'll drop you where you stand."

The small man pivoted and tried to aim. Rock shot the gun out of his hands, grazing the man's shoulder. He walked toward the moaning outlaw. The man was down and curled up.

Rock grabbed the small man by the collar and dragged him towards Darby. He jerked his hat off and stared when a girl's face was exposed.

"What the…! Darby, do you know this gal?"

Darby stared and slowly shook his head.

The girl looked up at Rock and screamed, "Ya killed 'em! Ya killed my brothers! My Pappy 'ill come fer ya!"

Rock glared at her. He dropped her and turned his attention to Darby. "Were you shot? Let me look at you."

Darby was holding his side. When Rock gently moved his hand away, he saw an ugly wound down low and through the old man's stomach.

He rocked back on his feet and muttered a low curse. He could feel the anger growing in him as he looked around at the girl. The outlaws had shot Darby's old jenny mule too, probably because she tried to protect Darby. He didn't see the mare, but Darby was dying.

Darby looked up. "Don't look good, does it? I think they got me good."

The girl was crawling toward the gun she had dropped, and Rock kicked it way from her. Taking a piggin' string off his saddle, he tied her like he would tie a calf but bent her legs and arms backwards behind her body. She screamed at him and cursed, using words that made his neck turn red.

Rock left her a short distance away and turned his attention back to Darby. He gently lifted the old man and carried him into the cabin.

Darby was struggling to breathe. "Git me some paper, boy. Folks need ta know that it warn't you what done this."

Rock's face was angry. He cursed quietly as he dug out more paper and the stub of a pencil.

The old man wrote,

Bushwakers done it. I giv it al ta Rock Bekler.   Darby McCune

Rock looked at the note and shook his head. "You don't have to do this, Darby. We barely know each other. Besides, I did what any man would do. A man shouldn't get paid for doing what's right."

The old man shook his head. "Ain't no one else. Got no wife or kids, jist this little spread." He paused and looked up at Rock with pleading eyes. "Can ya check on my little mare an' her foal? I was a sittin' outside watchin' 'em when them fellers rode in the yard." He frowned and added disgustedly, "I didn't even take my durn rifle. It was in here by the bed. I tried to crawl back inside an' they shot me. I couldn't get ta my gun 'fore they was on me." He looked toward the cursing girl and added bitterly, "An' she was 'most as mean as they was. They kept a kickin' my bad leg, an' she jist stood there whilst they done it."

Darby hollered at the girl, "You shet yur mean mouth. My brother 'ill be coming along here soon an' I'll have 'im sic his mule on yur whole durn family."

Rock stared at the old man in surprise. "If you have a brother, Darby, don't you want to leave your ranch to him?" Rock asked as he tried to hand the paper back.

Darby shook his head. "Naa. He's a wealthy feller." He grinned up at Rock. "Them bushwhackers thought I was too, but they didn't find nothin'."

Rock leaned back on his haunches and patted the old man's arm. "I'll find your mare. How do you call her?"

"Jist give a couple a short whistles an' she should come. Her name is Lady. I ain't named the foal." He grabbed Rock's arm as the younger man started to stand. "There's a little gal in town by the name a Suzanna. I promised 'er that foal. She comes out now an' then to look in on me." He grinned at Rock through his pain. "You might want ta git ta know 'er. She's a spunky little thing."

Rock squatted down again by the old man and asked, "Does she work in the dry goods store? If that's the one, she said to tell you that she would be riding out this week. Said to tell you hello."

Darby closed his eyes. "That's the one. She's a sassy little filly but she has a good heart." He opened his eyes again. "Now you'ins go find my hosses."

Rock stepped to the door and gave two shrill whistles. Red looked up and stared at him. He snorted and continued to watch his owner.

"Not you, Red. We need to find that little mare and her colt." He grabbed a lead rope that was hanging by the door and stepped outside.

Red raised his head and whinnied loudly, looking toward the trees to the east of the clearing.

Rock grinned at him and began to walk that way, talking softly.

The little mare was standing in some trees. The colt was next to her and neither seemed to be injured. Rock walked toward her, holding an apple. He heard a nicker behind him and Red pushed his big head over Rock's shoulder, trying to grab the apple.

"Now, Red, you just share. This little gal has had a couple of hard days, and she's a little skittish."

The mare walked slowly toward Rock, and Red nickered at her softly. She paused and then came forward, letting Rock slip the rope around her neck.

Rock broke the apple in half and gave part to the mare and the rest to Red. He led her up to the house and she stepped right into the doorway.

Darby opened his eyes and smiled as Rock knelt beside him.

His voice was barely more than a whisper and it cracked as he spoke to Rock. "Ya found her. Now you'ins take good care a this place, Rock. I have 'bout twelve thousand acres in here—I own the land on this here side a the river north towards Stevensville an' south a ways too. I never stocked it so that is up ta you'ins. I always enjoyed minin' more than runnin' cows, so I let the neighbors use my land." His mouth twisted into an ornery grin, and he tried to wink. "They think it's open range.

'Course they think I'm a poor feller too." His grin became bigger for a moment before his face twisted in pain.

He gasped, "The map ta my mine is over there 'bove the fireplace. Ya jist pull out two a those bricks an' you'ins cin see it there. The deed ta this place is in there too."

Darby's voice was growing weaker and Rock leaned closer.

The old man's voice broke as he stared up at Rock. "Shore wish I coulda knowed ya better, Rock. I think yur a good man, an' we'd a been friends."

Rock took the old man's grizzled hand in his big one. "We are friends, Darby. It's been my pleasure," he told the man softly as his eyes turned a little red.

Darby died with a smile on his face, and Rock's heart twisted at the senseless loss of a good man.

CHAPTER 10

"She Ain't Exactly a Lady"

ROCK GLARED TOWARD THE DOOR AS HE REMEMBERED the girl tied outside. He squeezed Darby's hands and rose to his feet. He whistled for his horses and took the pack off Georgia. Grabbing the girl, he untied her and threw her in the saddle. Her hands were quickly tied to the saddle horn, and her feet were bound together beneath the mule's belly.

"You just sit there and contemplate your life while I bury this good man," Rock growled at her as he turned toward the house.

He wrapped Darby's body in a blanket and laid him on the ground by a big tree. He dug a hole under the tree with an old shovel he found and gently placed the old man in it.

He removed his hat and began to recite Psalm 23. The girl stopped cursing and stared at Rock as his voice carried across the small clearing.

"...Yea, though I walk through the valley of the shadow of death, I fear no evil; for Thou art with me; thy rod and thy staff, they comfort me..."

When Rock finished, he walked back to the cabin without speaking to the girl.

She called after him, "My hands is goin' numb an' my shoulder hurts where ya shot me. Ya nearly killed me, ya know. Loosen up these here ropes."

Rock appeared in the doorway. His voice was hard when he spoke.

"I know where I shot you. I rarely miss what I intend to kill. And I'm inclined to let you sit there all day mean as you are, but I like my little filly too much to do that to her."

Red came when Rock whistled, and he adjusted the cinch on the stallion. Red didn't know where they were going but he was ready to go.

Rock pulled the cabin door closed. His eyes rested on the two dead men. Since he didn't have any way to haul them to town, he dragged them to the barn. He locked Lady and her colt in her stall. He checked her feed bucket and forked some hay before he filled her water bucket. He strode back to the house and grabbed the small piece of paper where Darby had scratched his will. As he stared at the simple statement, Rock again felt a sense of loss for the old man, and anger at the men who had done it.

"And that girl too," he muttered under his breath as he shoved the paper into his saddle bag.

"Let's go, Red. We need to get this gal to the sheriff's office, and I sure hope I can find my way back up here after dark." The girl was quiet on the trip to Stevensville, and Rock saw no need to talk to her.

As they rode down the main street, people came out and stared at them. The muttering was getting angry since tying a woman onto a horse was not considered acceptable behavior. Rock could feel his neck turning red, but he ignored the stares. He stopped in front of the sign that said "SHERIFF."

He left both mounts ground tied and walked inside.

The sheriff glanced up as the big man stepped through the doorway. Rock didn't introduce himself. He just pointed behind him.

"I have a backshooter outside. She and her two brothers cut down Darby McCune this morning. I buried him under his big tree. The other two bushwhackers are in his barn, and they won't be going anywhere."

The sheriff's eyes opened wide when Rock said *she*. He stood as he craned his neck to see out the window.

"Why she's barely more than a girl!" the sheriff exclaimed.

Rock looked hard at the man.

"She was big enough to help kill a wounded man and shoot at me. I don't think age really matters."

The townspeople were gathering in the street, and the murmur of voices was increasing in volume. Suzanna came out of the dry goods store. She stood at the back of the crowd and said nothing as she listened.

The sheriff stepped outside and signaled for the people to listen while Rock leaned silently against the doorjamb.

"Ma'am, this man says you were part of a gang who killed Darby McCune. What do you have to say for yourself?"

The girl sat up straighter in her saddle and gave the sheriff a sweet smile. Rock snorted and she glared at him before she answered.

"I shot at him 'cause he scared me. We was jist visitin' with that old—with Darby when *that man*," and she pointed at Rock, "come racin' in the yard. He cut down on my brothers 'fore they could fire a shot, an' he tried to kill me!" She dabbed her eyes and pretended to cry, sniffling loudly.

Rock stared at her incredulously.

The girl smirked at him before she continued her charade.

"I think he cut that old man down fer his money. He just didn't want nobody else hornin' in on his deal."

As the muttering from the crowd grew louder, the sheriff turned to Rock.

Before he could speak, Suzanna pushed through the crowd.

"Sheriff, this man was in town this morning. He told me that Darby had been injured in a tree-cutting accident. This man treated him and probably saved his life. He had a supply list written in Darby's hand that he filled and took back with him." She pointed at the blacksmith.

"Joe can verify that he was here as well as my aunt. Why would a fellow intent on killing an old man ride over two hours to show his face to an entire town and then ride back out to kill a man? And for what money? Darby doesn't have any money!"

The sheriff looked back at Rock, and the big man shrugged his shoulders.

"The lady pretty much covered it."

The sheriff didn't reply. He pulled his knife and strode toward Georgia to cut the ropes on the girl.

Rock stepped forward. "Those are slipknots, Sheriff. I don't intend to lose a good rope on this gal."

He pulled the knots loose and the girl swayed in the saddle until the sheriff put out his arms. She toppled off the horse, crying as he lifted her down.

Rock shook his head as he tied his rope onto his horse.

He mounted Red and picked up Georgia's lead rope. As he turned to ride out of town, he nodded at Suzanna.

"I do thank you, ma'am," he called softly. He tipped his hat and rode down the street.

The sheriff called after him, "I need to see those bodies!"

Rock turned in his saddle. "They will be in the barn until noon tomorrow. Then, I am going to bury them. By that time, they'll stink more than they do now."

The girl dropped out of the sheriff's arms and began to scream at Rock. The volume and kinds of words she called him would have blistered the ears of a sailor.

The townspeople gaped at her.

"She ain't exactly a lady, you see," Rock stated with a grin.

CHAPTER 11

CLAREY

THE SHERIFF GRABBED THE GIRL'S ARM AND BEGAN TO drag her toward the jail. She hit him and tried to bite him as she turned her wrath on the surprised man. The smithy stepped forward to help, and it took both of them to get her into a cell.

Joe grinned at the sheriff. "I think I understand why that feller tied her to his mule!"

Sheriff Hawkins' face was pale as he agreed.

"I need to find out who she is. She's just a darn kid. Why, I doubt she's over fourteen. And what kind of upbringing has she had to be talking like that?"

Suzanna stared from the young woman to Rock's departing back. As she thought of Darby, her eyes began to water. She wiped them hurriedly and rushed back to her aunt's dry goods store.

"Aunt Maggie, I am going to the jail to talk to that girl," she called to her aunt before she hurried across the street.

"Sheriff Hawkins, may I talk to the prisoner? I will try to find out who she is."

The sheriff studied Suzanna's face, and he slowly smiled. Everyone in town liked Suzanna—the town ladies as well as all the young men who wanted to court her.

"That would be fine, Suzanna. Just don't get too close to the bars. She's a little unpredictable."

Suzanna walked back to the cell. The young girl was curled up on the cot with her face to the wall. She was sobbing and muttering to herself. Suzanna could see blood on the shoulder of her dirty jacket.

"Are you okay?" she asked softly.

The crying immediately stopped, and no sound came from the cot.

"We need to know who you are so we can contact your parents," Suzanna continued.

"I ain't got no ma an' my pappy 'ill whup me fer gettin' caught. I have four more brothers to home, an' they'll cut that man down fer killin' our kin."

Suzanna was quiet a moment and then asked, "What is your name?"

The girl rolled over and stared sullenly at Suzanna for a moment before she finally answered.

"My name is Clare, Clare Ann Childs, but Pappy calls me Clarey. We have us a little shack a couple a hours west of that ol' man's place. We was goin' fer supplies last week when we seen 'im come out of a hole in the mountain some ways off. We figgered he had 'im a mine back in there. We couldn't find the openin' so we follered 'im back to his place." She paused and looked hard at Suzanna. "He carried somethin' outa that mine. He's got gold stashed somewhere. That's why my brothers decided to pay 'im a little visit today, an' they brung me along."

Suzanna could feel anger surge through her body, but she tried to keep herself calm.

"How old are you, Clarey?"

Clarey peered at Suzanna before she shifted her eyes to the door leading out of the cell area.

She shrugged before she answered. "I don't rightly know. My pappy says I'm old 'nough to marry, but I ain't got Mother Nature's Gift yet. I have to git that first. I don't know what he's talkin' 'bout though.

"There ain't no boys 'round nohow. Jist a buncha ol' men an' my brothers." Her forehead puckered as she frowned. "Pappy said Mama died when I was borned, an' her tombstone has 1 8 5 8 carved into it."

Suzanna stared at Clarey in horror.

"Why, Clarey, you are thirteen years old and that is way too young to marry. You should be going to school and playing with other kids!" She paused a moment and then asked, "Have you ever gone to school?"

Clarey shook her head. "I never been. My pappy an' my brothers ain't never been neither. Pappy said girls don't need to know nothin' but to cook an' have babies. An' do what they's told."

She stared at Suzanna and then slowly walked across the cell floor. She reached through the bars to feel Suzanna's dress. "I ain't never had a dress before," Clarey whispered. "We take baths in the creek sometimes. I ain't never had a bath in a tub but I've heard talk of it."

Suzanna's blue eyes flashed with anger.

"Clarey, I am going to see if we can arrange for you to take a bath in a real tub with hot water. Then we are going to brush your hair to get rid of those tangles. I will try to find a dress for you too. It may take me a little time, but I'll be back soon."

She spun around and marched out to where the sheriff was sitting at his desk.

"Sheriff Hawkins, that girl is only thirteen years old. I am going to talk to Pastor Mack. I want to see if he and his wife will take her in. She has never been to school and should never go back to her family. In addition, she's way too young to be in this jail!"

The sheriff's face showed his surprise. When Suzanna finished speaking, he slowly nodded.

"I knew she was young," he agreed. "If you can find someplace for her to stay, I will let her out of jail," he promised.

Suzanna hurried down the street to the little house that served as the parsonage. Pastor Mack had come to Stevensville about a year ago. The Macks had no children but seemed to be a kindly couple. She hoped they would be willing to take Clarey in.

Rebecca Mack opened the door with a smile when she heard Suzanna's knock.

"Well, good afternoon, Suzanna. What a pleasant surprise. Would you like a cup of tea, or do you need to talk to John?"

Suzanna smiled at Mrs. Mack. Rebecca was a kindly woman in her fifties. When she helped the younger women with their children, she told them how lucky they were to have little feet in their homes. Pastor Mack agreed. He told his little congregation to bring their children to church.

"Don't stay home because you think your children might disrupt the service. Children are like flowers, and you can never have too many flowers."

Suzanna took a deep breath. "Actually, I would like to talk to both of you if you have time."

Pastor Mack heard his wife invite Suzanna in, but he didn't hear Suzanna's response. He stepped out of his office and smiled as he greeted the young woman.

"Hello, Suzanna. What brings you out this afternoon?"

"Pastor, Rebecca—there is a thirteen-year-old girl in jail as we speak. Her brothers were shot this morning out at Darby's place. The man who was helping Darby tied her to a horse and brought her to the sheriff's office. She is dirty, wounded, and she should never go back to her home. Can you help her?"

Pastor Mack was stunned. As he stared at Suzanna, Rebecca whispered, "I will get us some tea."

She hurried into the kitchen while Pastor Mack led Suzanna into their sitting room.

He was silent for a moment, but he smiled at Suzanna.

"You have a kind heart, Suzanna. Perhaps when Rebecca comes back, you can tell us a longer version of what you just shared."

Rebecca hurried in with the tea. She set a cup down for each of them and nodded. "Yes, tell us the whole story."

"I really don't know much more than I just told you. I only know if she goes back home, her father intends to marry her off. She is certainly too young for that," Suzanna replied with a frown.

Suzanna blushed as she added with a giggle, "She has a colorful vocabulary and can make a grown man's ears burn. She has never been to school either. Sheriff Hawkins said she could be released from the jail if she had some place to go." Suzanna's face clouded and she continued softly, "She has never had a bath except in the creek and has never worn a dress." She looked at both of them intently. "Can you take her in? She has nowhere to go."

Pastor Mack frowned as he listened to Suzanna. He glanced over at his wife. Rebecca's eyes were full of tears, but they were shining with hope as well. He nodded slowly.

"We will offer to take her in, but that doesn't always work, you know. She may decide she doesn't want to live with us. She could even run off."

Suzanna slowly nodded. "I realize that, but when I told her I was going to try to find her someplace to stay, she didn't argue with me. She knows her future is bleak at home. I believe if we can get her into school and surround her with people who are good—people who love her—she just might grow into a fine young woman."

Rebecca was smiling as she looked at her husband.

"Oh, John. It will be so wonderful to have a child in our home. I'm sure we will have some bumps in the road, but I believe the Good Lord sent that child here. We need to help her."

Suzanna let out a long breath. She jumped up excitedly and smiled as she rushed toward the door.

"I am going to try to find her a dress. Do you want me to tell her that we found her a home, or do you want to tell her yourselves?"

Pastor Mack squeezed his wife's hand. "We will meet you at the jail in about fifteen minutes. She can take a bath and clean up here if you want to help Rebecca with that. She might be more comfortable with you around."

Suzanna hugged them and hurried out the door. She raced back to her aunt's store.

"Aunt Maggie, do we have a dress that will fit Clarey?"

When her aunt stared in confusion, Suzanna explained, "The young girl who is in jail. Do we have a dress here that we could give her?"

Maggie smiled as she looked down at her niece. She nodded slowly and disappeared into the back of the store. She pulled a new dress out of a trunk and shook it out, holding it up for Suzanna to see.

"After you wrote that you were coming, I had this made. In my mind, you were still a little girl. The beautiful young lady who arrived though was too old for this small dress. I tucked it in my trunk and forgot all about it until now." Aunt Maggie handed the dress to Suzanna. "You go ahead and give this to her. I am pleased it will have a good purpose."

Suzanna held the dress up. It was light pink with small roses embroidered in the bodice. It had a large ruffle around the bottom. A tiny border of lace trimmed the neckline as well as the bottom of the short sleeves.

"Aunt Maggie, it is beautiful," Suzanna whispered as she wrapped her aunt up in a hug.

They didn't have time to iron it, but the two women laid it out on the counter and finger pressed as many of the wrinkles as they could from the soft cotton fabric.

Suzanna was leaving her aunt's store just as the Macks entered the sheriff's office. She hurried to join them.

Sheriff Hawkins stood and greeted the Macks as they entered. He smiled at Suzanna as she hurried in behind them.

"I see you didn't waste any time," he drawled as his eyes twinkled. "When Suzanna is on a mission, just get out of the way or plan to get plumb run over!"

He lifted the keys from the wall and led the three people back to the small cell where Clarey was huddled against the wall. She had drawn her knees up against her chest and her dirty face was covered with tear tracks.

Clarey looked up as they entered. Her eyes darted from one person to the next, finally coming to rest on Suzanna. She stood and stared at the dress Suzanna was carrying before she walked cautiously toward her.

"Is that fer me?" she asked hopefully.

Suzanna smiled and held the dress toward Clarey for her to feel. "Yes, it is but you get to take a bath before you try it on. My aunt bought it for me when I came here to live, but it was too small.

"It is a new dress, Clarey. You will be the first to wear it!"

CHAPTER 12

A New Life

THE MACKS WERE SMILING, AND SUZANNA POINTED toward them. "Clarey, these people would like you to come and live with them. They are Rebecca and John Mack. John is the pastor here."

Clarey's eyes narrowed as she stared at the couple. "Need a girl worker, do ya? Well, I cin work all right, but I ain't gonna call ya Mama an' Papa."

Rebecca was surprised, but she smiled.

"You will have chores, Clarey, but we will work them around your schooling. Your education is most important right now."

Clarey's eyes opened wide. "You want me to go to school? An' I cin learn to read? When do I start?" Her eyes were sparkling with excitement as she gripped the bars of the cell.

Rebecca smiled with delight as she answered, "Why, we will start tomorrow. Tonight, you will take a bath and try on your new dress. Then we will eat supper as a family. We have a small room ready for you. We will order a bed this week, so you don't have to sleep on the cot."

Clarey stared at them suspiciously. "Why ya want to be nice to me? Ya don't even know me." She glared from Pastor Mack to Suzanna and then back to the man.

Pastor Mack smiled kindly at her. "Because that is what Jesus would want us to do. He runs this big wide world, and sometimes, he drops folks in places they didn't plan to go just to make things better for them." He put his hand through the cell door. "It's very nice to meet you, Clarey. Rebecca and I would love to have you live with us and be part of our family."

Clarey was quiet as she stared at the smiling couple. She slowly nodded her head as she touched his hand.

"I reckon I cin try it fer a week or so. But I ain't a gonna eat skunk. I told my pappy that I was tired a cleanin' an' eatin' skunk an' I ain't a gonna do it no more."

Rebecca looked horrified, but Pastor Mack's eyes glinted with humor. He nodded somberly.

"That will be just fine with me, Clarey. I don't like skunk either. Besides, I'm quite sure Rebecca would make me clean it myself if I brought one home for supper!"

Sheriff Hawkins cleared his throat and stated gruffly, "Here, let me open this cell so this young lady can take a bath and eat some supper."

He opened the cell door and stood back as Clarey slowly walked out. Her eyes darted from the Macks to front door of the jail. Suzanna could see panic flood through her.

"I'll walk with you down to the Macks, Clarey. I can even show you how to scrub if you want me to." She lifted a tangled lock of Clarey's reddish-brown hair and smiled at her. "Your hair is so thick. It will be beautiful once we get it all brushed out." She reached for Clarey's hand, and the young girl followed her cautiously out of the sheriff's office.

"Cin I carry my dress?" she whispered, and Suzanna handed her the new dress.

Clarey stared at it almost reverently. "I sure never thought I'd ever have a dress as purty as this one," she commented softly.

When they arrived at the parsonage, Pastor Mack opened the door. He stepped back for the women to enter first.

Clarey stared from him to the open door.

"Why'd he not go on in? He was the first one an' he didn't have to wait fer us. What's in there he don't like?" she whispered loudly to Suzanna.

Suzanna whispered back, "Because we are women, and men are supposed to let women enter a room first. That is considered good manners." She added, "They help you in and out of wagons, up steps, and even on and off your horse."

Clarey stared at Suzanna and snorted.

"I never saw no man ever act that way. I have to fight fer a place to sit at the table an' I only eat what the menfolk don't want 'cause my arms ain't as long."

Suzanna frowned slightly as she patted Clarey's arm.

"Things will be different for you here, Clarey. Be nice to the Macks. They are good people, and they will treat you like the special person you are," she whispered. "I'm glad you came to Stevensville. I know you will be happy here, and I am excited to have a new friend."

CHAPTER 13

"Who Is That Girl?"

JOHN CARRIED THE WATER FOR CLAREY'S FIRST TUB bath. Then he went into his office and closed the door. He could hear the laughing and giggling in the kitchen as the two women helped the young girl to bathe. Not only had she never taken a tub bath before, Clarey also didn't know what soap was. She was amazed by the suds and how slick her clean skin felt. She didn't like the water being poured over her head, but she was surprised at how long her hair was when the tangles were combed out.

Once Clarey had taken off her bulky men's clothing, Rebecca and Suzanna could see how thin she was. Her ribs were visible under her skin. All three were amazed at how much soap it took to wash thirteen years of grime off Clarey's dirty body.

Rebecca's lips trembled as she carefully washed the bruises on the young girl. She thought about asking who hit her but changed her mind. *Maybe she will tell me in time. Poor little thing.*

Rock's bullet had just notched the flesh on top of Clarey's shoulder, and the dried blood stuck to her clothes. Removing her dirty shirt opened the wound again, so Rebecca applied some horse ointment after Clarey's bath. There wasn't a good way to bandage it, but she laid a small piece of cloth over the ointment before Clarey put on her dress.

The new dress was large on Clarey. Rebecca pulled the waist tight with the large sash and tied it in the back. She handed Clarey a mirror so she could see herself.

Clarey stared at the mirror and then at the two women. She pointed at each of them.

"I see you and you in here, but who is that girl?"

Rebecca kissed Clarey's cheek. "Why, that's you, Clarey. You are a beautiful girl," she told her softly.

Clarey touched her cheek where Rebecca had kissed her. She stared at the woman, and her chin started to tremble.

"I ain't had no mama kiss me in a mighty long time," she whispered as tears leaked out of her eyes.

Rebecca pulled Clarey close and hugged her. She whispered into her hair, "I love to give kisses, Clarey. If you like them, you will get lots of kisses in this house."

She hugged Clarey again before she looked over at Suzanna.

"Suzanna, will you call John? Please tell him we can eat as soon as I get this water mopped up."

John carried the bath water outside and dumped it around their small trees. Once the garden was planted, they would pour the wash water on that as well. It worked well not only for watering but for insect control too. He shook his head at the filthy water.

"That little gal has just been neglected," he muttered to himself with a frown.

Clarey kept touching her new dress. Once, when she looked up, Rebecca smiled at her. She gave the woman a small smile in return.

Suzanna excused herself when the family sat down to eat. Clarey watched her with worried eyes, but her new friend patted her hand.

"I'm sure I will see you tomorrow," she told Clarey with a smile. Then she leaned over and whispered, "Maybe you can come down to the store after your schoolwork is done. We'll let you taste some hard candy!"

Clarey was barely listening as she stared at the food.

John filled Clarey's plate as Suzanna slipped out the door. When Clarey just stared at it, John told her, "Eat up, Clarey. There is more where that came from. We don't want you to leave the table hungry."

Clarey grabbed handfuls of food and shoved them into her mouth. Neither Rebecca nor John corrected her as they used their eating utensils.

When she stopped and watched them, John touched her fork. "Hold it like this, Clarey. And no one is going to take your plate away. You may eat slower if you'd like."

After supper, the Macks showed Clarey where she would be sleeping. She stared at the cot as she looked around the room.

"Who else is sleepin' in here with me?" she demanded.

Rebecca smiled. "Just you, Clarey, but if you become frightened, our room is just down the hall."

Clarey frowned. "I ain't no baby!" Her frown became a glare as she looked from the bed to the door.

"That door ain't got no lock an' there ain't nothin' in here to stack against it. How do I keep menfolk from comin' in?"

Rebecca's face turned pale, but she shook her head.

"No one will bother you here, Clarey—I promise. John and I sleep down the hall, and we are the only ones here. This room is all yours."

Clarey stared at Rebecca suspiciously. She finally climbed onto the cot, new dress and all. Rebecca had a bed shirt for her, but the young girl was asleep before she could even unfold it.

The Macks stood and looked down at Clarey.

"I am so thankful the Good Lord brought her to our home, John," Rebecca whispered.

John smiled at his wife. *Things are certainly going to be different around here, but it will be nice to have a child in the house.*

After the kitchen was cleaned, Rebecca pulled out some schoolbooks and prepared a short lesson for Clarey. She helped teach in some of the towns where John served, and she was looking forward to working with Clarey.

CHAPTER 14

"Why You Care?"

CLAREY AWAKENED EARLY THE NEXT MORNING. NO one was stirring and the house was still dark. She slipped off the cot and tried her door to see if it was locked. It wasn't. She looked around furtively as she opened the front door.

Stevensville was just coming to life at five-thirty. Clarey sat on the porch stoop in the dark and waited for the sun to come up. This had always been her favorite time of day—when the sun came out of hiding and dropped color all over the sky.

She was still sitting there at six-thirty when John came outside and sat down beside her.

"Sunrise has always been one of my favorite times of the day too. Did you know that the sun rises at different times in different places? Even the seasons of the year are affected by the sun. That is why our days in the winter are so much shorter than our days here in the summer."

As Clarey stared at him, he continued, "The earth is round so it makes sense that people see the sun come up at different times of the morning depending on where they live."

Clarey turned her face to look at the sky and stated quietly, "My Pappy will be comin' fer me. He'll go to Mr. Darby's first an' kill that man what killed my brothers. Then he'll come here an' drag me back home with 'im." She added in a whisper, "An' he'll whup me fer not runnin' away."

John stared at the sunrise a little longer before he answered.

"Do you want to go back home?"

Clarey looked at him in surprise and frowned.

"I don't reckon I have a choice."

John put his arm around Clarey's small shoulders and gave her a hug.

"Clarey, Rebecca and I would love for you to stay with us. We would like to raise you as our own daughter. I know that won't always be easy for you, but right now, I think you will be safer away from your family. I'm not sure they have your best interest in mind."

Clarey pulled her knees a little closer to her chest as she looked out of the side of her eye at John.

She finally answered in a rough voice, "Why you care what happens to me? We ain't kin an' ya barely know me."

John felt his heart tighten. He nodded as he tried to keep his voice even.

"We are all children of God, Clarey. I know you may not understand that right now, but He created all of this." John swept his hand across in front of them to take in the mountains and the forest, now awash with color. "Mankind can build the wagons on the street and the buildings sitting there, but we can't create the trees and horses or the colors in the sunrise. Look at those mountains and the snow up there on top. God created that and He created you."

He looked down at her and smiled. "I believe the Good Lord has special chores for each of us that we need to do before we die. Sometimes those chores are easy to figure out, and sometimes they are as hard to track as a beetle running circles in the dirt."

John patted her hand. He stood and reached down to help Clarey up.

"I believe the Good Lord wants Rebecca and me to help you, and that is a chore I would very much like to do. Welcome to Stevensville, Clarey, and welcome to our home."

Clarey was quiet through breakfast. She tried hard to mimic how the Macks used their eating utensils. She wiggled a little when Rebecca brushed her hair, and she stared at herself in surprise when she was shown how she looked in braids.

Rebecca handed her the hairbrush. It was pearly white and smelled good. Clarey took it reverently.

"You have lovely hair, Clarey, and hair likes to be brushed. Try to brush it all over one hundred times per day."

As Clarey stared at her in confusion, Rebecca laughed. "Don't worry, we will have you counting to one hundred very soon. Now let us start your school lessons. John offered to clean up today so we can get an early start!"

Rebecca showed Clarey where to wash before and after meals. Then she led her into the sitting room. She had the schoolbooks laid out, and the lessons for Clarey's first day of school were ready.

CHAPTER 15

DARBY'S BROTHER

ROCK WAS WORKING ON THE ROOF OF THE BARN when he spotted an old man on a large mule coming up the lane toward the house. He climbed down and casually leaned against the barn with the rifle in his right hand. He wore two guns, and both were tied down. His black cowhide vest and britches were dusty and worn. However, his shirt was clean, and the little spread was tidy.

The old man pulled up and looked around with approval.

"Howdy. The name's McCune. I be lookin' fer my brother. Darby be his name."

Rock straightened and moved forward with an outstretched hand.

"Rock Beckler is my name, Mr. McCune. Climb on down and have some dinner with me. I decided to fix this roof right away this morning," he commented as he waved his hand toward the barn, "but I put on a pot of Mexican strawberries and side pork before I started. They should be done about now."

The old man dismounted spryly, and the mule wobbled his lips at Rock.

Rock pulled a sugar cube out of his pocket.

"Does your mule like sugar?" he asked as the mule lifted it out of his hand.

"Shore now, that mule likes to chaw on all kinds a things. Sugar, hay, grass, apples, bad folks, outlaws…"

When Rock looked at him in surprise, the old man laughed again, and his ornery eyes twinkled.

"Jist call me Badger." He pointed at his mule. "This here feller be Mule. We rode up from Wyomin' Territory." Badger glanced toward the house. "I'm a guessin' Darby ain't 'round or I'd a heard 'im by now."

Rock led the way to the small graveyard under the big tree. He had put up a marker and built a little fence around the grave site.

"Darby died a couple of months ago. I came up on this place by accident and shot some wolves that intended to take him down. He had an accident cutting trees. He was inside the house and was in a bad way. They must have smelled the blood and followed his trail."

Rock paused and added softly, "I only knew Darby a few days. I worked on his leg and then headed to Stevensville the next day to get supplies. When I came back, some fellows had bushwhacked him. I shot two of them and winged the girl.

"Darby didn't last long. After he passed, I buried him here and took the girl down to the sheriff in Stevensville. She was young, but she was a little wildcat."

Badger studied the grave and the big man beside him. "Darby musta liked ya since ya stayed on."

Rock's neck turned a deep red. "Darby left this place to me. I told him he should give it to you when he said he had a brother, but he insisted I take it. I have his will if you need to see it." Rock looked away briefly before he stated softly, "But I sure won't fight you for it if you are wanting to stay."

Badger waved his hands. "Naa. We talked a while back an' discussed what we'd do with our places." He waved his hand and grinned at Rock as his bright eyes twinkled. "Shore now, ol' Darby thought 'nough of ya ta give you'ins this here ranch. Reckon he sawed somethin' in you'ins that he liked. Nope, this place be yurs."

Badger squinted his eyes as he stared across the valley. "Ya 'spectin' company? Three fellers is a tryin' ta ease up here, ridin' kinda sneaky like."

Rock stared and shook his head. He could barely see movement, so he wasn't sure what Badger had seen.

"Not anyone friendly. I've wondered if the kin to those fellows I shot might not show up here. It'd been long enough now that I was beginning to question if they were coming."

"Oh, they's a comin' an' they's loaded fer bear. 'Fact, I think they's more in their party than the three we cin see. We best git ready fer trouble." He quickly pulled the saddle and bridle off his mule. He took the mule's head in his hands and talked to him before he turned him loose.

The big buffalo gun Badger carried was almost as tall as he was, but he handled it with ease. His bowed legs bent the tall boots he wore to the sides, and everything about him looked old. However, he didn't move like he was old, and his bright blue eyes didn't miss a single detail.

"How you'ins want ta handle this here deal, boy? I figger they'll split up, an' I ain't so comfortable stuck in a cabin as outside where I cin move 'round."

Rock agreed and the two men split up—one on either side of the barn and back in the trees. It wasn't long before three men rode in. They looked around as they stopped in front of the house.

"Looks empty, Pappy. Mebbie that there feller done left."

The old man he was talking to looked around and spat. Then he shook his head. "Naw. Somebody's been workin' 'round here." He hollered, "Hello, the house!"

Neither Rock nor Badger responded, but Mule raised his head. He walked slowly toward the men.

One of the younger men dismounted. "Look here, Pappy. They done turned this here mule loose. We cin shore take 'im with us when we leave."

The older man spat again. "You boys get off'n them hosses an' check that cabin. I know that old man were minin' fer gold. It has ta be 'round here somewhere. Tear that there house apart. If'n we don't find it in one a these here sheds, we'll burn the whole place jist fer spite."

Rock stepped away from the barn. His rifle covered the old man. The two younger men were turned sideways making it difficult for them to see him. "You boys get back on your horses and get on out of here. No one is going in that cabin."

The old man looked unperturbed, and Rock felt the hair come up on his back. He knew there was another man behind him, but he couldn't turn to look.

"You must be the feller what shot down my boys an' runned off with my gurl."

Rock stared at the man with cold eyes. "Your boys shot an unarmed old man. As for your girl, I turned her over to the sheriff in Stevensville."

A twig snapped behind Rock and he threw himself to the side as he pulled his handgun. He continued to roll before he shot toward the man behind him.

The big buffalo gun boomed from the other side of the clearing. The old man grabbed his leg as he fell, screaming curse words every bit as colorful as his daughter's.

The downed man in the bushes was groaning, but Rock didn't think he was much more than winged. He stayed down and waited for the man to expose his location.

Badger hollered from across the clearing, "Ya boys drop them thar guns an' raise up yur hands. I'm a tolerable peaceful man but I done runned out a peacefulness jist now."

Mule suddenly pricked its ears up and charged toward the bushes behind Badger. A man screamed once but his voice was cut off as the sound of thrashing came from the trees.

Badger barely moved.

"Whoever were behind me ain't there no more. Now I'm a tellin' ya fer the last time ta drop those guns, an' that goes for the skinny feller too, the one over there 'hind my friend."

The moaning stopped behind Rock. All was silent as the three men in the yard dropped their weapons. The mule came out of the trees and stood quietly beside Badger. The old man was sitting on the ground, holding his leg when one of his hands started moving up toward his neck.

Badger spoke softly, "Mister, if'n ya think you'ins cin pull that pigsticker faster than I cin shoot, ya jist go right ahead an' try." He glanced toward Rock and added, "Boy, ya shoot jist ta the right a that there big rock 'hind ya. Shoot 'bout waist-high an' see if'n you'ins cin hit that feller squattin' there."

Rock moved the muzzle of his gun and the man behind him stood. He held his pistol with the trigger guard looped over his finger as he raised his hand.

"I'm a comin' out. Don't shoot!" As the man behind Rock stepped into the open, the two younger men in the yard dropped to the ground and grabbed for their guns. Badger whistled and Mule charged the three men. He stomped the two that were raising their guns and kicked the old man. He was racing for the fourth man when Badger whistled again.

The mule stopped. It reached out and grabbed the man's shoulder with its open mouth and tossed him into the air.

The man landed hard and was screaming as he tried to scoot away from the mule.

Badger walked toward the downed men. The two younger ones were dead. The older man had been kicked hard and was unconscious. The fourth man was still screaming.

Badger grabbed the screaming man by his collar and jerked him to his feet. "I'm a guessin' that you'ins be kin ta the boys what killed ol' Darby. An' jist so you'ins know, Darby were my baby brother."

The man became quiet.

Badger's blue eyes looked like ice chips as he glared at the wounded man. "Now here's how this is goin' ta be. You'ins is a goin' ta load up yur kin there on the ground an' that thar ol' man. Ya ride outa here an' don't even look back oncet, 'cause if'n ya does, I'm goin' ta turn my mule loose again. An' next time, I won't be a stoppin' 'im. Ya boys come here lookin' ta rob an' kill a second time, an' I don't take kindly ta that."

The wounded man stood and walked over to the mangled bodies on the ground. He tried to lift them onto their horses but moaned as he moved his wounded shoulder.

"I cain't lift with this bum shoulder," he whined.

Badger spat. "Figger it out, boy. You'ins be a runnin' outa time."

The fourth man finally had both of his brothers laid over their saddles. He tried to help the old man up. The old man's eyes were still glassy. He staggered as he tried to stand. He was still able to curse though.

Badger hollered at them as they moved back down the lane, "An' don't ya go a lookin' fer yur little sis. No gurl should have ta grow up 'round fellers like you'ins,"

Rock stared from the departing men to Mule and then at Badger. "What about the fifth man there in the trees behind you?"

Badger gave Rock an evil grin. "Guess they knowed he wouldn't load too good." He slapped Rock on the back. "Now let's go eat them thar beans you'ins promised me whilst we talk 'bout this here spread."

THOSE LITTLE JOBS

Rock lifted the bean pot off the hook and set it on the rough table. He spooned some beans into each of their bowls and set the rest of the breakfast biscuits he made on the table.

Badger grinned at him and began to sop his biscuit in the bean soup. "So ya been out ta the mine yet?

Rock shook his head. "No, I've been fixing this place up. I replaced lots of corral boards and just started on the barn roof. I ride out every day to look more of the ground over. I want to see how many cattle Darby's land will support." He pulled the plat map out from behind the bricks and showed it to Badger.

"We are here but it looks like there are little creeks just about everywhere. I can't tell from the map what the grass is like. I've ridden out every day though and know there is some good grazing around here. I thought I would talk to the neighboring ranchers this week to let them know I will be running my own cattle this year. Then I need to talk a bank into giving me credit so I can stock this place."

Badger grinned at him before he shoveled another spoonful of beans into his mouth. He stomped his foot on the floor, and the old boards creaked and swayed. "Mebbie the next repair job you'ins should do is ta fix this here floor."

Rock laughed and agreed. "Yeah, that needs done, but I can deal with a bad floor for a while. I think some of these other jobs are more important."

Badger studied the younger man. "Tell ya what. I'll jist help you'ins replace this here floor whilst I'm here. I ain't goin' ta climb up on that barn, an' it looks like the corral is in purty good shape now. Let's work on this here floor an' I'll tell you'ins some stories 'bout Darby whilst we work.

"Any new planks in the barn we cin put back down here?" Badger asked with a grin.

Rock looked at the old man in surprise and slowly nodded his head.

The two men finished their dinner and headed to the barn. Pine planks were stacked neatly by the wall in one of the stalls, and they carried them up to the house. Rock found a crowbar, saw, and a claw hammer along with some new nails. He began to pull the floor up while Badger pulled out the old nails. The old floorboards would be cut up for kindling, and they didn't want any nails left in the wood. The table, chairs, and bed were already set outside. Little else was in the small house.

Badger pulled a tape measure out of his saddle bags and began to mark the planks for cutting. As they moved closer to the middle of the floor, the boards were looser. The ones in the middle didn't seem to have any nails holding them down at all. When Rock pulled the loose boards up, he saw bags stacked between the floor joists. Frowning, he lifted one out and opened it. Gold dust and nuggets poured into his hand as he stared.

Rock raised his shocked eyes to look at Badger, and the old man began laughing.

"Sometimes them little jobs is the most important ones of all!" the old man chortled as his bright eyes sparkled.

The two men lifted the bags out of the floor. There were forty-eight bags of various sizes. Rock was stunned. "Did you know he stashed gold in the floor?" he asked in surprise.

Badger shrugged. "I guessed he did. I knowed he had it here somewhere, an' that's where I'd a put it. The question now is, where do *you'ins* want ta put it?"

Rock stared at the bags as he rocked back on his feet. "Darby worked hard for this gold. Surely, he knew someone better than me who should have it."

Badger shrugged his shoulders as he tried not to smile. *Darby picked a good one. He found an honest man 'fore he died an' one who'll use his money ta benefit more than jist hisself.* He scratched his chin.

"Wahl, did he mention anyone else when ya talked? Mebbie someone in town?"

Rock smiled as he thought about Suzanna. "There is a little gal in town who helped him out some. She works in her aunt's dry goods store. He mentioned her several times. In fact, he wanted that little horse colt out there to go to her. I reckon I could split this with her. Maybe I could use some to stock this place with cattle and then split the rest with Suzanna." Then he frowned. "I don't know a thing about gold or how it converts to cash money. How much do you reckon is here?"

Badger hefted several bags. "I reckon most of these weigh between six an' ten pounds. Some likely be heavier. They weigh gold a little different than most things, but I'd say each a those bags should be worth over $1,300. Mebbie $2,000 or even more dependin' on the weight." He grinned at the younger man. "I believe ya jist become a wealthy feller, Rock!"

Rock stared at the gold in the floor and then at Badger. He shook his head and frowned. "I didn't help him get this gold. Darby surely had some purpose for it. He was saving it for something."

Badger slapped Rock's back. "I reckon he left that up ta you'ins. Now let's git this here floor finished so's I cin sleep on a floor tonight an' not on them durn joists."

Rock lifted the bags out of the floor. He put eight of the smallest ones behind the loose rocks above the fireplace. Fifteen more went under a loose board below one window which he nailed down. He pulled up the board on the second window and placed thirteen more in that cavity. Eight went back into the floor, and the four largest ones went into his saddle bags.

"I reckon I will get started buying cattle now!" he exclaimed as he grinned at the older man.

Badger's old eyes twinkled as he nodded somberly.

"Yep, an' ya better talk ta that little yellow-haired gal while you'ins be at it."

Red slowly moved up Rock's neck before he grinned. "Tomorrow might be a good day for both," he agreed.

The two men finished the floor, and Rock fixed venison stew for supper. They fed and penned their livestock before dark and visited until the sun went down. The stew was thick and the meat tender when Rock pulled it off the fire.

Badger smacked his lips as he ate with delight. "Shore now, you'ins be a good cooker. I don't know I ever ate food this good cooked by a durn cowboy!"

The two men decided to ride down to Stevensville in the morning. Badger knew the priest at St. Mary's Mission and wanted to talk to him before he left town. He looked at Rock and grinned.

"Had that there priest paint me a picture of ol' Mule here. This here mule's 'most like kin ta me.

"Ol' Darby give the Mission a little gold now an' then. That padre offered ta paint a picture fer 'im as his way a sayin' thanks. 'Course, Darby didn't have no one he needed a picture of, so that priest asked me. I pointed ta Mule an' he agreed." Badger's grin became wider as he added, "I like that padre. He's a smart feller. He told me ta stop in the next time I was up, an' he'd have it ready fer me. I reckon I'll stop there on my way outa this here town. Then, I'll ride on south ta Salmon in the Idaho Territory an' catch me a stage there."

Rock nodded toward Mule. "What are you going to do with your mule?"

Badger winked at Rock. "Oh, he jist follers along at his own speed. When he gets tired, I stop awhile an' rest up. Mule's a travelin' feller though. He goes a far piece 'fore he wears down. I'll catch the train when I git farther south, an' we'll ride the cars to Cheyenne."

Rock stared at the old man to see if he was teasing, but behind the grin, Badger seemed serious. Still, that was a lot of running in one day for any animal.

He looked over at Gomer and the scruffy donkey yawned. Rock laughed and pointed at him. "That lazy feller adopted me, but he's not good for much of anything…other than breeding fancy horses and stealing apples."

CHAPTER 17

A Ride and a Picnic

THE TWO MEN WERE UP EARLY. ROCK FED AND watered the little mare before locking both her and her colt in the barn.

Neither horse was happy about it, and both were nickering when Rock led Georgia down the lane. Gomer watched them go. He brayed a couple of times but appeared to go to sleep.

Suzanna was crossing the street when she saw Rock and the old man ride into town. Her heart began to beat heavy in her chest as she hurried into the dry goods store.

Maggie saw Suzanna's flushed face and started to question her when she saw a tall cowboy stop at the hitching rail in front of her store. He visited with the old man beside him for a moment. They shook hands and the old man turned his mule down the street. Maggie coughed to hide the smile on her face.

The cowboy dismounted slowly and talked to both animals before he opened the door. He scanned the store and tried to keep the disappointment off his face when he didn't see Suzanna. When he stepped toward the counter, Suzanna appeared, slipping easily in front of Maggie to help him. Rock's grin showed his pleasure, and Suzanna blushed as he laughed.

"Well, do you have a list or are you just going to stand there and stare again?"

He looked at her somberly and slowly nodded his head. The list was in his pocket, but as he pondered, he realized there were other things he needed. He pointed at some items under a low shelf behind the counter, and several things Suzanna had to stretch to reach.

When Suzanna set them on the counter, Rock's grin grew bigger. He started to point at another high shelf, but she interrupted him.

"Let me see your list. I don't believe you even needed those items, but since you enjoyed yourself so thoroughly watching me retrieve them, I am going to make you buy them!"

Rock grinned and tried to look confused, but he couldn't help laughing.

When he finally took his list from his pocket to check it, Suzanna plucked it out of his hand. She scanned it quickly. None of the items on the counter were listed. *The nerve of the man!*

"Did you enjoy yourself, Mr. Beckler? I believe I know what your motive was!"

Rock grinned at her. He tried to look confused but he was smiling too big. "Motives? I only came to town to buy supplies—and to ask you if you would like to come riding with me. Maybe we could pack a lunch and eat under a tree somewhere."

Suzanna stared at him and cocked her head. "And what do you intend to eat? Or should I prepare this meal you are going to share with me?"

"Nope, Mrs. Barry over at the eating house will fix me a pack of food to take with me. But if you have a blanket, you can bring that. How about I pick you up in about twenty minutes?"

Suzanna stared at him. "It took you over two months to ask me out, and I am supposed to be ready in twenty minutes?"

As Rock grinned at her, Suzanna laughed and added, "Why come back? I will grab my cloak and come with you now."

It was Rock's turn to be surprised. Suzanna smiled up at him sweetly as she took his arm.

"And just where are you taking me, Mr. Beckler?"

Rock grinned and his green eyes sparkled. He drawled, "I have this place I take all the gals—it's by a—"

Suzanna jabbed his ribs with her elbow, and Rock started laughing. "Miss Suzanna, you sure are fun to tease!"

Rock was going to leave Georgia in the livery. However, she became so anxious that he relented and let her come along.

"What is your mule's name?" Suzanna asked as she patted the skittish little filly.

"I call her Georgia. Her mother was a dapple-gray thoroughbred, and her daddy was a knot-headed little burro that followed me all the way down here. She kind of reminds me of a little gal I once knew. Her name was Georgia. She was flighty, stubborn, and mighty pretty—almost as pretty as you but not so sassy."

As two red dots appeared in Suzanna's cheeks again, Rock grinned and added, "I sure miss my little sister."

Suzanna was surprised, but she laughed along with him.

The location Rock picked was a pretty one beneath a large tree. It was cool there, and the picnic meal was delicious. They visited right through the noon hour. Soon, it was after two.

Rock stood and helped Suzanna to her feet. "Miss Suzanna, I sure enjoyed my meal with you. You are about the easiest person to talk to that I ever did meet."

Suzanna smiled. She didn't know how to respond. This man kept her off-balance, and he didn't even try.

He gave her a leg up onto her horse, and they rode toward town. Rock was quiet, and Suzanna was trying to come up with the words she wanted to say. Finally, she reined her horse in.

"Rock, I have something to ask you. There is a Ladies' Choice Dance on Saturday night. I was wondering if you would like to go with me."

As Rock stared at her in surprise, Suzanna's face paled a little. "I know it is forward of me to ask but—"

"I'd love to, Suzanna. What time would you like me to come by?"

Suzanna's heart was beating heavy again in her chest. "Why don't you come by around six and we will eat with my Aunt Maggie before we go."

Rock was watching Suzanna intently as he listened. He reined Red closer to her mount.

"Miss Suzanna, would it be all right with you if I kissed you?" he asked softly. "I have never kissed a girl before, but I would sure like to kiss you."

Suzanna's eyes were large as she nodded.

Rock lifted her off her horse and across his saddle. He kissed her gently and studied her face. "That was mighty pleasant, Miss Suzanna. I think I could get used to that." Then he carefully placed her back on her own horse and they continued on to Stevensville.

When they arrived at the mercantile, Rock dismounted. He put his hands around Suzanna's waist. His green eyes were dark, but his hands were gentle as he placed her on the ground. He stood looking down at her for a moment before he remounted. He was smiling as he rode away. When he turned to look back, Suzanna waved to him.

Rock tipped his hat, and Suzanna knew her heart would never again belong to only her.

SLASH B RANCH
STEVENSVILLE
MONTANA TERRITORY
MAY 6, 1878

CHAPTER 18

MEMORIES

ROCK BECKLER LEANED AGAINST THE DOORJAMB OF the ranch headquarters and stared across the yard toward the valley below. Spring was just coming to the Bitter Root Valley, and even though it was May, there was still snow on the mountains.

His cattle were scattered across the valley and were eating contentedly on the rich grass that was just coming up. The previous eight months had produced quite a bit of snow, and with all the moisture, the grass was going to be good this year.

Rock's eyes followed on around until they came to rest on the big Ponderosa pine tree a few hundred yards from the house. The smile slowly left his face as he stared at the tombstone beneath it.

"Ah, Suzanna, if only you were here to enjoy this morning with me. We only had three years together, but they were the best three years of my life.

A pensive smile crossed his face as the remembered the first time he saw her.

"I just sat on old Red and stared while you swung that broom. You finally turned full around to face me, placed your hands on your hips, and asked if I rode all that way to stare or if there was something I needed."

Rock laughed as he remembered Suzanna's sassy face and the way she tossed her head.

"And when I did go into the store, you were nowhere to be seen. I stalled as long as I could, but you never showed your face. You caught me as I was leaving town though, and we talked a little.

"I rode home that day and dreamed about you for the next two months."

A woman's voice called from inside the house and broke Rock's reverie.

"Breakfast is ready, and you have a wee one who is calling for her daddy!"

Rock's face broke into a smile as he appeared in the doorway.

"Good morning, Maggie. Today is going to be a beautiful day." His smile became bigger as he gave her a quick peck on her cheek.

Maggie smiled at this man who was more like a son than her employer. "That it is, and a fine bit of work you have to get done before the spring gather."

Rock didn't answer as he moved toward the small room where his daughter was calling him.

"Papa, I'm ready to get up!"

Rock stuck his head in the door. "And why can't you get up? Don't your legs work?"

An impish little face beamed at him from the small bed. "Papa, you know my legs never work in the morning! You *always* have to pick me up."

Rock sat down on the bed beside his four-year-old daughter and smiled at her. "And what about when you get so big that I won't be able to pick you up?"

Annie smiled at him as she held out her arms. "Little girls never get too big to hug their papas!"

Rock scooped Annie up and held her close. Her dark curls tumbled around her face, and her blue eyes sparkled just like her mother's.

"Annie, you are as pretty as your mama," Rock whispered into her hair.

"Papa, can you tell me a story about Mama? Tell me about the first time you heard her laugh."

Maggie spoke from the doorway, "How about the two of you come out to breakfast, and I will tell you the story of how your mama came all the way up here from Texas."

Annie slid off Rock's lap and raced toward Maggie.

"Auntie, did you know Mama *before* Papa knew her?"

"I sure did, sweetheart. Now you wash your hands and your face so we can eat breakfast."

Rock followed the little girl out of the bedroom as she chattered. She was Suzanna's last gift to him and to Maggie as well. He glanced toward the big tree one more time before he sat down at the table.

Annie rushed back to the table with a wet face and dripping hands. She folded her hands solemnly in her lap and squeezed her eyes shut as she began the prayer she had said every morning since she could talk.

"Dear Jesus, thank you for breakfast and Papa and Auntie. Thank you for my mama out there under the dirt, and please bring me a new mama someday. Amen." She opened her eyes and leaned forward excitedly. "Now tell me that story about my mama!"

Rock smiled at his daughter as he cut her meat and placed an egg on her plate. Maggie's face took on a far-off look as she began.

"Your mama was only eighteen years old when both her mommy and daddy died. Lots of folks were getting sick and many died. Your grandmother, Suzanna's mother, was one of the last healthy ones. She took care of everyone in their town who came down with that sickness until it finally overtook her too.

"She sent your mama out to the country to stay with some friends early on. She wanted your grandfather to go as well but he refused. When your grandmother became ill, he took care of her. He stayed by her side until she passed. He died shortly after he buried her.

"Your mama went from a warm and comfortable home and a loving family to no family and no home—no home because there was no one to work the land or take care of the livestock. Your grandmother was my sister, and when folks became ill, she wrote and asked me to take your mama in." Maggie smiled sadly as she remembered, but her smile became joyful when she looked at Annie.

"I remember when your mama stepped out of that wagon the day she arrived in Stevensville. Every young man in town was fighting to help carry her bags. She was sweet, but she was a sassy one too—kind of like a little girl I know."

Annie grinned as she shoved some meat into her mouth. Rock's breakfast was untouched as he listened to Maggie's story.

"She looked around at the group of young men falling all over each other to walk beside her. She said, 'Boys, I am in town to stay. It's not like I'm leaving tomorrow.' Then she marched across the street to my store and left them to argue amongst themselves." Maggie laughed and her eyes crinkled as she added, "And we had young men calling almost every night. Your mama was nice and sweet, but she wasn't interested in any man—until your papa rode into town."

Annie beamed at her father, and Rock's throat caught. He put a spoonful of cold eggs in his mouth and chewed just to keep his mouth busy.

Maggie looked over Annie's head and smiled at Rock. "When you left town that first day, Suzanna went to the door and watched you ride away. She asked, 'Who was that tall man, Auntie? Does he live close?'" Maggie smiled again at Annie.

"Then, when the Ladies' Choice Dance came around several months later, she told me she was going to ask your daddy." Maggie looked away and was quiet for a moment as she remembered.

"After her horseback ride and picnic with your papa, she came back to town on cloud nine. She knew your papa's name, what he liked and disliked, *and* she had a date for that dance."

Rock laughed and shook his head. "Good thing she asked me because she was way out of this cowboy's loop. It might have taken me another two months to work up the courage to ask her on a second date."

Annie was quiet for a moment as she thought. She looked seriously at her father and said, "I like it when you tell stories about mama. I think you liked my mama a lot."

Rock scooped up his daughter and swung her around. "I liked your mama every bit as much as I like you, and that means I loved her to the moon and back. Now you had better finish your breakfast if you want to go riding with me today."

He squeezed Maggie's shoulder and strolled toward the corrals. When he whistled, a sorrel mustang threw up his head and nickered as it trotted toward him.

"Good morning, Red. Ready to go for a ride today?" Rock rubbed the horse and talked to it as it followed him into the barn. A small Shetland was running loose. It ran to him when he shook the bucket he was holding. He caught and saddled it as well. He led the two horses to the house and tied them to the hitching rail.

The sun caught the side of Rock's face as he turned his head. Tiny laugh wrinkles showed around the corners of his green eyes. Dark hair curled out from under his black Stetson, and there was no gray in his sideburns. His mouth turned up at the corners in a half smile, and the planes of his face were strong. Long legs fit into the tall cowboy boots, and a single gun was tied down on his left side. The bright red bandana was a contrast to his faded shirt and dusty black vest.

Rock Beckler was all about utility. If it didn't have a purpose, he probably didn't own it, and he certainly wouldn't wear it.

Annie came running out of the house. Her hair was in two little fluffy pigtails, and the pink shirt her auntie made was embroidered with horses and dogs. Her britches were too large for her small body, so Maggie cinched them up at the waist with a little piece of rope. Rock grabbed the jacket she was carrying and stuffed it in his saddlebag. Annie clambered onto her pony and began talking to him.

"Steed, we are going on a ride today, and you must keep up. No lollygagging around now or I'll have to use my spurs—and you know you don't like my spurs."

Rock smiled as he watched his daughter. Her spurs were little wooden rollers attached to a leather strap she had hooked around her boots. She wanted spurs so Rock made her a pair that wouldn't hurt her pony in case she was too aggressive.

Maggie watched them go with a smile on her face. "Aye, it's a fine thing to see that man smile again." She hummed to herself as she readied her kitchen for another day.

"I believe I will make some bear sign today. We haven't had any of those little fried doughballs in quite some time."

Annie talked steadily for nearly two hours. When she became quiet, Rock lifted her off her horse and placed her in front of him. He looped Steed's reins over the saddle horn and turned the pony loose to follow.

Rock smiled. He still had a few creeks to check but he didn't mind. It was a fine morning for a ride. It was nearly noon when they returned. Annie had been asleep for over an hour, and Rock was humming, "The Streets of Laredo" as they rode into the yard.

"Maggie, we have a tired little girl here," Rock called as he rode up to the house. He handed Annie down, and Maggie carried her into the house, whispering to her when she stirred.

Helena
Montana Territory
May 15, 1878

CHAPTER 19

THE DEATH OF JOHNNY BRAXTON

BENTON AVENUE CEMETERY WAS A SIMPLE ONE. THE graves were laid out haphazardly, and many had no markers. A few wildflowers bobbed their heads around some of the tombstones, but most were as bare as Johnny's new grave.

Clare Braxton stared at the pine box as the men from town lowered it into the cold, hard ground. She had cried when she received the news of Johnny's death, but she couldn't bring herself to cry anymore. Even then, her tears were from fear, not from the pain of losing someone she loved.

Johnny, we came here three and a half years ago so you could mine for the gold that was discovered here in 1864. I wanted you to take a riding job, but you said mining would be easier. It was hard though, and you didn't like it. After just four months, you told me, 'Why should I work that hard? I can gamble. It's easier to take the money other folks make.'

That was the beginning of your drinking and gambling. You couldn't hold your liquor, and you were a terrible gambler when you drank. Now you are gone, shot down for cheating in a card game, and I am terrified as to how I will support my son on my own. Not that you were much help these last six months but at least you gave me a few dollars here and there.

I am angry, Johnny. I am angry at myself for marrying a boy who offered to give me and my six-month-old son a home. I am angry at you for never growing up—and that's certainly not fair. You should never have married me and taken on the responsibility of husband and father. You had no idea how hard it would be…and I should never have married for security.

You left us alone and spent all your time in the saloons. When you did win a little, you bought drinks for everyone.

Clare pulled Zeke closer, and she smiled through her anger. She remembered how Johnny played with Zeke and how her son loved him. *You tried to be a father when you were here, Johnny. You were such a kid yourself that playing with Zeke came easy for you.*

Liquor took you away from us. I think you knew that I didn't love you enough even though I tried. And I really did try. I did everything a good wife should do, but I just couldn't love you the way you wanted me to. You told me once when you were drunk that you didn't like how I saw you when you looked in my eyes. A lump formed in Clare's throat. *I'm sorry for that, Johnny. I was wrong to marry you. You married for fun, and I married out of fear. In the end, both of us were sad and disappointed.*

A man touched her arm. "Mrs. Braxton, may I walk you back to your home? This wind is chilly today, and there is no need for you to stay longer."

Clare looked past him as several men began to fill in the grave. She nodded and gave him her arm. "Thank you, Mr. Cole. I would appreciate that."

Leonard Cole was quiet as they walked down the hill toward Clare's little shack. Finally, he stopped and looked down at the young widow. "Mrs. Braxton, Colonel Black just opened an eating house in the Pacific Hotel, and he is wanting to hire a couple of young women to wait tables." His face colored a little as Clare looked up, and he looked away. When he looked back, his eyes were sincere. "I just thought maybe you could use a job."

Clare felt a surge of hope, and she gave him a quick smile. "Thank you, Mr. Cole. I will speak to him tomorrow. And thank you as well for walking me home."

Leonard waited until Clare opened her door. He tipped his hat and frowned as he walked away. "Johnny Braxton ran up bills all over this town in the last year. He won just enough for businesses to think he was good for it. Now he's gone and left his wife and young son alone. They live in a shack with a dirt floor and a sod roof.

"Clare has no idea how much money he owes. Why if the man was alive, I'd punch him myself."

Leonard had just discussed Johnny Braxton and his young family with his missus a few days before. Nettie Cole was never one to be shy with words. She shook her head.

"I've half a mind to call that young man out. I don't think he has a clue how hard life is for his wife and son when he gambles day and night. And poorly too. How Clare stretches the small amount of money Johnny gives her is beyond me.

"And she is such a beautiful girl. Smart too. I just don't understand what she saw in that man."

Nettie refused to go to Johnny's funeral, but Leonard went. He didn't go for Johnny—he went for Clare. "Clare is a hard worker, and she is too proud to ask for help. I'm going to see if she would like a job," he told his wife.

Colonel Black owned the nicest hotel in town and had been planning to add an eating establishment for some time. It had opened the day before, and business was brisk.

"I will stop by the Pacific Hotel on my way home and put in a good word for that girl. She could use a hand up."

CHAPTER 20

A New Start

CLARE WOKE EARLY THE NEXT MORNING. SHE STARED at the small amount of oatmeal left in the jar. She opened the can where she kept her grocery money and stared at the few remaining coins. When they were gone, she and Zeke would be out of money. She sat down at the rickety table and cried.

When Zeke awoke rubbing his eyes, Clare kissed him and pointed at his bowl with a smile. "Your oatmeal is hot, Zeke. I put a few dried apples in there, just like you like it." Zeke was only four. He had no idea the number of meals his mother skipped to make sure he had enough to eat. He clambered off the blankets laid over the dirt floor and climbed onto his chair.

"Let's say a prayer of thanksgiving for this meal, and as soon as you finish, we are going to walk uptown. I am going to talk to a nice man about working for him. If I get the job, maybe we will be able to afford some milk to go with your oatmeal."

Zeke's big brown eyes lit up as he smiled at his mother, and Clare's heart melted. She kissed his head and hurried to change. She had pressed her only good dress the night before as well as a clean shirt for Zeke and his best britches. She didn't know what she would do with her son during the day while she worked. The idea of entrusting him to someone else terrified her.

Both the Pacific Hotel and Delmonico's Restaurant were busy when Clare and Zeke arrived at seven that morning. Colonel Black glanced their way and looked again.

"Leonard didn't tell me that the widow woman he was sending down here was a real looker. If she can work, this just might work out well for both of us."

He rushed toward the young woman with a smile on his face. "You must be Clare. I'm Colonel Black. And who is this fine young man?"

Clare smiled proudly as she held Zeke's shoulders, but the little boy ducked behind his mother. "His name is Zeke. He just turned four this summer."

Colonel Black felt a pang of sympathy for the young mother, but he was too busy to think long. "Clare, the job is yours if you can start now. The Sisters of Charity have a house just across the street, and they are willing to watch your son while you work. I have a small room here that you can use at no charge if you would be willing to help with the milking and the chicken chores. We are open from six in the morning until ten at night. You will work from six until two or three in the afternoon. That will give you a little break before you start chores at five.

"I will pay you $20 per month, and you will work six days a week. Chores, including milking the cows, will be your responsibility every evening. On your day off, you will do morning and evening chores. If you need a day off for anything, you will need to talk to me at least a week in advance." He paused and smiled at her. "I'm sorry that I don't have time for a proper interview, but as you can see, I am short on help. So, what do you say? Do you want the job?

"Oh, and your noon meal will be eaten when you have time. You can take leftover food home in the afternoon to eat for supper. The room I am offering you here doesn't have a cookstove."

Clare's eyes were shining. "That sounds wonderful, Mr. Black. If the Sisters can watch Zeke today, I will start immediately."

"Just call me Colonel. I was a colonel in several wars, and that is all anyone knows me by now." He rushed off and left a surprised Clare standing by the door.

"Come, Zeke. We need to go see some nice ladies. They are going to let you play with their kids while Mommy works."

A nun in a long, black habit with a large string of beads at her waist opened the door. Her hair wasn't visible behind the black veil that trailed past her waist, but her face was joyful. She smiled at Clare before she looked down at Zeke. "My name is Sister Casimir. You must be Zeke. How about you stay with us today while your mommy works? We are just getting ready to eat breakfast if you are hungry."

Clare followed the nun as she swished into the dining room where eight children of various ages were just beginning to eat. A short nun with a jolly face scooped Zeke up. "You sit here on my lap, and I'll introduce you to the rest of these kids." She smiled at Clare and whispered, "My name is Sister Rudolph, and he will be fine. You go on now. We will see you this afternoon."

Panic began to rise in Clare's chest. "I—I have never left him," she gasped as her face paled.

The sisters both smiled and nodded as Sister Casimir pointed at the little boy. He had already slid off Sister Rudolph's knee and was climbing up to the table to sit in front of an unclaimed plate of bacon and eggs. "He will be fine," she whispered, and Clare backed out of the room.

She rushed across the street and the colonel smiled at her as he handed her a pad of paper, a pencil, and an apron. "The menu is written on that slate board over there. We have two choices for each meal. Drinks are coffee, tea, milk or water. The prices are on the board. Take their order and then hook it on one of those clothespins there by the kitchen. Be sure to put your name on it and mark it in some way so you know what table it is. Good luck!"

Clare tied on her apron, took a deep breath and stepped into a new phase in her life.

CHAPTER 21

A BOLD OFFER

CLARE AND ZEKE THRIVED WITH THE CHANGE IN their lives. They were now eating on a regular basis, and both laughed more often.

Zeke's cough that had been with him since he'd started crawling went away, and his legs became strong from running. Clare gave the kindly nuns her tip money, but as it increased, they gave some of it back. "You don't need to give us all your tips, Clare. If you can spare a dollar or two per month, that is plenty."

Clare soon convinced the colonel to skim the cream off the top of the milk instead of stirring it in. "That way, we can make more of our own butter as well as other desserts. Your three Jersey cows produce lots of cream, and we just as well be using it."

It wasn't long before Colonel Black hired a young man to do the chores full time. He sent Clare back to help the cook after she finished her morning shift. Everyone liked her tasty desserts, and her pie sold out quickly.

After just two months of employment, Clare was making $30 per month including tips. That was more money than she had ever seen. She smiled contentedly as she hurried toward the dining room. Even though the work was hard, the customers and staff were friendly. Some of the girls thought the colonel was too demanding, but Clare enjoyed working with him. He was abrupt and blunt, but he had a tender heart under all his abruptness.

Today was July 3. Johnny had died almost two months ago, and Clare was happier than she had been in a long time. She had a place to live, food for Zeke, and steady income. "I am blessed," she whispered as she tied her apron on.

The colonel looked up and nodded a greeting. He shoved an envelope toward her.

"George Fox dropped this off last night. He's the president of People's National Bank here in town. He said to make sure you received it right away." The colonel's serious face broke into a grin.

"I sure hope he isn't trying to hire you away from me. You are an asset to this eating house, Clare. In fact, I just don't know what I'd do without you."

Clare smiled but she was a little apprehensive. She had no bank account and was confused as to why the banker would need to see her. She turned away from the customers and tore the envelope open.

Mrs. Braxton, Please stop by the People's National Bank at your earliest convenience.
  George Fox

"Why—why would he want me to come by? I don't understand." As she stared at the note, she covered her mouth and her face became pale.

"Johnny owes money!" Clare knew how Johnny spent money, especially when he won a little. "Oh, Dear Lord, please don't let it be very much." She stuffed the note in her apron pocket and whispered, "I will have to run up there tomorrow afternoon before I start the pies for supper." She took a deep breath and turned to face the room full of customers.

She smiled at a group of cowboys who were seated by the window. They were young, rowdy, and looking for fun.

The bravest one winked at Clare as he rocked his chair back with the front legs off the floor. He grinned and drawled, "Yore a mighty good-lookin' gal. How about y'all run away with me? My name is Brazos, and my hoss is right outside."

The other cowboys were smiling. They all chuckled and bumped each other as they waited for her response.

Clare acted surprised and excited.

"Today? You want to run away today! Oh, that sounds like fun!" Her brow puckered for a moment before she asked, "But how many horses do you have? I would need at least eight."

Brazos dropped all four chair legs on the floor as he stared at Clare.

"Eight! Why in the world would we need eight hosses to go for a little ride?"

"You said run away, and if I do that, I have to take all my children." She pointed across the street where lots of children were playing. Most were dirty and several had their faces pressed against the fence. They waved excitedly when Clare tapped the window and waved at them.

All the cowboys swiveled their heads to stare across the street. The table became quiet as they looked back at her. The youngest one asked softly, "Jist how many kids do y'all have?"

"There are eleven over there but several of them can ride together." She pointed at the big clock on the wall. "I am off at three, but I can leave early. I can have all of them ready to go in half hour since we don't own much of anything. That still gives you plenty of time to eat. Don't plan to ride too fast though. They aren't very good riders. Besides, they will have to stop often to go to the bathroom."

Brazo turned red and began to stutter while his friends laughed.

"Ol' Brazos is usually purty slick with the ladies. He thinks he's a smooth one, but he put his hair in the butter this time!" one of his friends commented.

"Did you change your mind, Brazos? Oh well." Clare smiled and shrugged. "There's always tomorrow."

The cowboys didn't know what to say. Even though they were confused, they were laughing. Brazos even chuckled a little.

"Ya called my bluff, lady. I have to hand it to ya. That don't happen often—an' I still ain't shore if yore bein' truthful!"

Clare laughed as she looked around the table. "Be careful what you ask for, fellas. You might bite off more than you can chew. Now, tell me which meal choice you want today."

George Spurlach, or Spur, as his friends called him, was seated several tables away. He rode for Rowdy Rankin down in Wyoming Territory and was on one of his long horse-buying trips. He planned to eat a warm meal before he headed home.

He listened to the entire conversation and chuckled as he shook his head.

"She had those fellers goin'. 'Course I know the mamas of most of those kids, so I know they ain't *all* hers. She's too young to have that many kids anyway, but she shore made those boys eat crow."

Spur was still grinning when Clare stopped at his table.

"That's a passel of kids for one little mama, but I'll take that ride if you'll go. I just happen to have ten horses down at the livery."

Clare wrote quickly on her pad as red moved up her neck. She looked at the bold rider cooly.

"I only accept offers once a day, and you missed your chance. Now, do you want dessert with your meal?"

Spur grinned and nodded.

Clare muttered under her breath as she hurried to the kitchen.

"Men! They all think they are so funny. And he didn't say what he wanted so I'll choose for him." She stuck the order on a clothespin and was smiling again when she greeted the next table of hungry customers.

CHAPTER 22

A Trip to Helena

ROCK RODE RED INTO THE CITY OF HELENA ON JULY 4, a little after two in the afternoon. He looked around the town in surprise. It seemed like every year he made this trip, more buildings were added, and more businesses were open.

He always stayed at the Pacific Hotel, and even it had changed. Now there was a bustling restaurant inside its lobby. He studied the board, and a young waitress arrived quickly to take his order.

"Do you have any pie?"

"No, but we will for supper if you want to come back. Clare will start them around four today."

Rock nodded as he grinned. "Bring me whatever meal you have left, and I'll have some pie this evening with my supper. Thank you, ma'am."

He ate quickly and rode up to the People's National Bank of Helena. He had deposited Darby's gold in this bank in 1871. From the first day he walked in, George Fox had been his banker. While Rock didn't have to borrow money, he enjoyed talking to George about investments, what cattle were available, and marketing trends. He didn't have any business with the banker today, but he always made a point to stop in when he was in town.

The two men visited for a time. Both were smiling when Rock stood. As he glanced down at George's desk, he noticed a letter addressed to Clare Braxton. He pointed at the letter in surprise.

"Does Clare Braxton live in Helena? She used to live in Stevensville and was my wife's best friend."

Fox scowled as he looked down at the letter. His eyes were full of remorse when he looked up. "How well did you know her husband?"

Rock shrugged his shoulders. "Johnny was a rider for me off and on. He was always a wild kid. I was surprised when the two of them married. Why?"

George studied Rock's face. His frown was still in place when he opened the envelope and dumped the contents on his desk. Rock stared as he read the promissory notes. They were for amounts of $10 up to $100 owed to eight different saloons in town as well as the dry goods store.

Shock registered on Rock's face as he looked from the pile of notes to his friend. "He ran up all those? Why don't you go after him? He didn't run off and leave Clare and little Zeke, did he?"

George's face pulled down in tight lines. "No, he was shot back in May for cheating in a card game.

"Clare and that little boy about starved to death while he was alive. He just kept drinking more and more, staying out all night.

"Colonel Black opened an eating house in the Pacific Hotel several months ago. He calls it Delmonico's. Clare has been working there ever since Johnny died. I didn't realize how thin she and Zeke were. Now that I see her nearly every day, I am almost ashamed of myself for not noticing.

"The Sisters of Charity watch Zeke during the day so Clare can work. She is just getting back on her feet and now this."

Rock picked up the notes and studied them for a moment before he stuffed them in his pocket.

"I'll take care of these. Clare stayed with us some to help out when my wife was pregnant with our little girl. She came out again after Suzanna died and helped care for Annie. I owe her this and more."

George's eyebrows arched a little and he laughed. "You flummox me, Rock. You drive a hard bargain in your business deals and are so tight you squeak. Then you just go and give money away."

Rock grinned and shrugged as he looked out the window into the street. His face was serious when he looked again at the banker.

"I will pay them before I leave town." He frowned and added, "I don't want Clare to know about any of this though. She would never accept charity."

He studied the envelope with Clare's name before he took $50 out of his wallet. He placed it in the envelope. As he sealed it, he grinned again at George.

"Tell her a fellow who owed Johnny money stopped by to pay him. When he found out Johnny had died, he said to give it to his widow."

George nodded slowly and stood to shake Rock's hand. "Rock, we are all better off for you helping old Darby. It has been my pleasure to work with you these seven years."

Rock blushed and muttered. Finally, he looked up at George and grinned. "I had better get back down to the Pacific and get a room. They might sell out if I'm not careful. Besides, I have my heart set on pie tonight."

He shook George's hand and strolled out of the banker's office. When he reached the door, he turned around. "I'm looking at O'Malley's cattle in the morning. I'll eat dinner at Delmonico's around noon and then head south of town to look at Moser's and Klaussen's cattle if you want to come along."

George paused and then nodded. "I think afternoon might work. I'll stop in while you are eating breakfast and let you know. Will you eat earlier than seven?"

"Naw, seven is good. I don't want to get out there too early." The two men shook hands again, and Rock walked out of the bank. He pulled the promissory notes out of his pocket and cursed under his breath as he studied the name on each one.

"Darn your hide, Johnny. What were you thinking?"

CHAPTER 23

A Secret Gift

CLARE RUSHED TO PICK UP ZEKE AFTER SHE FINISHED her shift. The colonel let her leave a little before two even though the restaurant was still full. She had shown him the note from the bank on one of her breaks, and he frowned.

"You go ahead and take care of that right away, Clare. Just remember that I need you in here to start on pies by four if we are going to have them ready for the supper rush."

Zeke was still asleep, and the good sisters told her they would bring him over to Delmonico's when he awoke.

"Let the little fellow sleep, Clare. He is a growing boy, and it takes a lot of energy to grow and play."

Clare nodded. She smoothed her hair and brushed off her dress. She took a deep breath as she hurried up the street to the bank.

The receptionist knocked on Mr. Fox's door and the bank president invited Clare in with a smile. "Thank you for coming by so quickly, Mrs. Braxton. I'm sorry if I made it sound as if it was an emergency."

Clare's breath was coming quickly. "How much money does Johnny owe? I am guessing he somehow managed to charge drinks at several of the saloons, and they are tired of carrying his credit."

George could feel heat climb up his neck, but he smiled and shook his head. "No, a young fellow stopped in here. He was looking for Johnny. Seems Johnny loaned him some money, and he wanted to pay him back. When he heard Johnny had died, he asked me to give this to you." George handed Clare the envelope, and she opened it with trembling hands.

Clare stared in surprise as she lifted out a $50 bill. Her hands shook as she stared at the bill. Then she placed the money back in the envelope and tried to hand it back to George.

"There must be a mistake. Johnny never had money to loan to anyone—he spent every penny he ever made. I think perhaps your rider remembered incorrectly."

George Fox shook his head and wrapped Clare's hand around the envelope. "No mistake, Mrs. Braxton. I am telling you what I was told. That money was left here for you. The man who left it was not from around here, but he was adamant. He didn't say when the loan took place, but there is no mistake."

Clare's breath was coming quickly as she clutched the envelope. When she finally looked up, she took a deep breath. She smoothed her dress and smiled at George Fox.

"In that case, I would like to make a deposit. I would like to take Zeke to Stevensville next summer, and this will help to pay for the stage ride. Thank you, Mr. Fox."

Clare left the bank with a smile on her face. As she rushed back to Delmonico's, she didn't notice the tall cowboy across the street. He paused on the boardwalk and stared at the papers in his hand before he moved down the street to another saloon.

It took Rock nearly two hours to make his rounds to the various saloons and pay the notes. He didn't say who he was. He just asked to see the owner in each establishment and paid the amount listed. Rock had each man sign the note where he had written, "Paid in full."

The note for $80 at the dry goods store was his last stop. Leonard Cole looked up from the counter with a smile on his face when Rock walked in. It drew into a frown when Rock laid the note on his counter. His face turned red and he tried to tear it up.

Rock kept the note pressed on the counter. "What was this for? Surely it wasn't for groceries."

Cole shook his head as he frowned. "I was gone one afternoon and had a young man helping me out. Johnny came in and bought a whole new outfit—britches, shirt, vest, boots, hat—the works. If I'd been here, I wouldn't have sold him anything but food. His wife was barely eating. She and that little boy were surviving on next to nothing for income. That young man didn't know though.

"I asked the banker to take it out of Johnny's account the next time he was paid for anything, and then he died. Mrs. Braxton never said a word through the entire service. She buried him in those fancy clothes and went home to her shack." Cole's face turned red as he added, "I would never ask Mrs. Braxton to pay this. I had forgotten that I gave it to George Fox. I was mad the day I did that. Johnny was still alive, and I was furious that he charged clothes at my store. Mostly though, I was angry for how he treated his wife." He reached for the note again. "Let me have that, and I'll tear it up."

Rock shook his head. "No, I'll pay it. Mrs. Braxton helped my wife out when she was sick, and I can do this for her." He frowned as he added, "I knew Johnny was a little irresponsible, but I thought marrying would grow him up. Guess I was wrong." He looked around the store. "Do you have any hats that would fit Clare's little fellow? I'll take one of those if you have one."

Cole grabbed a small hat with a wide brim and set it on the counter in front of Rock. He looked at the man with friendly eyes. "No charge for that. It should fit Zeke. He sure is a sweet little boy."

CHAPTER 24

AN OLD FRIEND

ROCK CHECKED INTO THE PACIFIC. HE RODE DOWN to the bath area for a long, soaking bath before he turned Red over to the hostler. He felt like a new man when he walked into Delmonico's for supper.

The restaurant was busy at six-thirty, and two young women were taking orders. He squeezed into a corner of the busy room and took the last small table. As he leaned back in his chair, he studied the waitresses. He recognized Clare immediately.

The blue dress she wore brought out the shades of blue in her eyes. She laughed easily with the customers and was efficient. Her thick reddish-brown hair was pinned on top of her head and small curls hung down around her face. The patrons seemed to like her, and she was friendly to everyone.

Four cowboys were at the table next to him, and Rock could hear their conversation. "Good thing ya knowed which table to pick. Here comes that young widow woman now. She sure is a looker, but the word is she won't walk out with nobody."

Clare stopped at their table with a smile on her face. "Good evening, fellows. What can I bring you this evening?"

All four of the young men appeared to be tongue-tied. When she glanced up from her pad and looked at each of them, they just stared at her. Finally, the oldest of the four stuttered out their order, and she hurried on to the next table.

Rock grinned despite himself. "You fellows forgot to order pie. You had better get that done."

The cowboys laughed along with Rock. When Clare rushed back with their milk, they gave her their pie order.

"Better take this feller's order behind us. He might want a little pie too."

Clare looked toward Rock's table with a smile. Her face froze as she stared at him.

"Rock? What are you doing here?" Her surprise changed to pleasure and her face lit up with pure joy at seeing him.

Rock stood and Clare gave him a quick hug. She stepped back a little breathlessly and smoothed her hair.

"Are you here on business? I'm sorry I don't have time to talk now, but I would love to catch up. I'll be off around eight if you will still be around. Meatloaf?"

Rock nodded as he laughed. He sat down, and the four cowboys looked at him mournfully. One finally spoke.

"Well, durn. We was goin' to ask her if we could walk her to the fireworks. Shoot. Y'all said nothin' an' already have a date for the night."

Rock grinned at them. "I have an inside edge on you boys. I have known her since she was just a girl. My wife was her best friend."

Clare was back quickly with food for all five of them. She set a piece of chocolate pie in front of Rock. "I hope you like chocolate. That was the last piece of pie, and I know how you like pie." She gave him a quick smile before she hurried off to wait on other customers.

Rock ate slowly. He wasn't a big fan of crowds, but it was good to see Clare. She looked happier than he had ever seen her. *I'm glad you are doing well here, Clare. Life has dealt you some hard knocks. It's about time your path was a little easier.*

The other young waitress was waiting on a table of loud men, and one was being rude. Rock didn't hear what the man said, but the young woman's face became pale, and the other men at the table laughed loudly. Rock could feel irritation rising in him as he continued to eat.

The rude man stood and tried to grab the waitress's arm. "Come on now, Kit. Why don't ya take me back to yore room an' we can roll around a little before my food gets here."

Before she could answer, Rock kicked the chair opposite him. It slammed into the man's leg and knocked him sideways. The man staggered and almost fell. He caught himself and glared at Rock.

"What did ya do that for? I was jist funnin' her."

"Rudeness to women is not tolerated here. You know that. Now apologize to the lady so we can eat this meal in peace."

The man snorted and pointed at Kit. "Her a lady? I'd never apologize to her. Why she's nothin' but a two-bit tramp!"

Rock's left hook landed solidly on the man's chin, and the rude stranger hit the floor with a crash. Rock rubbed his knuckles and grinned at the other three men.

"Now, all he had to do was apologize. Reckon you boys had better drag him out of here. Of course, if you want to take this discussion up outside, I'll be happy to accommodate you—as soon as I finish my supper. It would be a shame to waste food this good."

Two of the men dragged their friend outside and dropped him on the boardwalk beside the door. They came back in and cast furtive glances at Rock before they sat down.

Kit's cheeks were pink as she stepped up to their table. The shortest man of the three cleared his throat and spoke haltingly.

"Ma'am, we want to apologize for our friend. He had no call to talk that way. We've been up in the mountains for nearly three weeks and stopped at the saloon for some drinks before we came here. Cal was a little drunk. Still, we was all rude, and we do apologize."

Kit murmured a thank you. She took their orders quickly and rushed to turn them in.

People were waiting to get in the door, and Rock finally stood. He laid his money down and wove his way through the tables toward the stairway. He caught Clare's eye and waved.

"I'll be back around eight," he called before he started up the stairs. When he reached the top and looked down, he could see Clare carrying large plates of food from the kitchen. The table where he had been seated now had two miners squeezed against it. Rock shook his head. "Busy place."

He lay down on the bed. He was tired but he didn't want to sleep. He swung his legs to the floor as he checked his pocket watch. "Seven-fifteen. I think I'll have a beer and listen for a little while."

He chose the only saloon where Johnny hadn't run up a bill and leaned against the bar. The Indian fight at Little Big Horn had taken place almost two years ago. Custer's Last Stand, or The Battle of the Greasy Grass according to the Indians, had taken place on June 25, 1876, and it seemed to be the topic of conversation that July evening.

"The 7th Cavalry had some tough boys. Too bad they all died. That durn Custer just couldn't wait to start a fight, and now the only survivor is a horse."

The battle had taken place about three hundred miles east of Helena. Rock had heard quite a few rumors about the battle, including one that a horse had survived. He continued to listen quietly.

"Yep, it was Keogh's horse. I think he called it Comanchero or Kiowa or something. He loved that horse. Reno's boys found it half dead in a gulley. Shot seven times. The word is that the cavalry is retiring that horse. Why if horses could talk, we might know what happened out there. Hard to know for sure when one side is all dead and the other side would soon as kill a feller as look at him. Besides, those braves are scattered to the wind. They will only be seen if and when they want.

"The Indians won that battle, but the brass has brought the full force of the soldier boys down on them. Won't be long before all the Indians are on reservations. 'Course, the ones who are there are starving. Their kids are hungry, and the young braves want to fight. Cain't rightly say as I blame them. Heck of a way to live."

Rock frowned. *I always knew that man would get someone killed. He was just brash. Rushed into fights without considering all the things that could go wrong. I think maybe I will ride through Missoula on the way home. I came across the Sapphire Mountains on the way up here, but I'd like to put a little more distance between me and any small bands of braves who might be roaming around. They just might be a little too eager to fight.* He drained his beer and dropped some money on the table. He checked his pocket watch. *Not quite eight.* He glanced up the street.

Delmonico's was still busy, so Rock wandered down to the livery. The hostler was gone, but he found a brush and a currycomb. He began to work on Red, talking softly to the horse as he brushed him.

"It was sure a surprise to see Clare here. I'm glad she is doing well. I thought about asking her to come back to Stevensville, but it looks like she has quite a few friends here as well as a job she likes. It will be nice to spend some time with her though."

Red blew through his nose as Rock talked, and the tall man laughed. "You are the best listener I know, Red. You get some sleep now. We have some ranches to visit tomorrow, and we will be leaving the next day for home." He paused and blushed a little as he asked, "Think I should ask Clare if she wants to ride with me tomorrow?" Red snorted and Rock nodded. "Yeah, you're probably right. I'm guessing she has to work. See you in the morning, old fellow."

CHAPTER 25

FIREWORKS AND CONVERSATION

ROCK STROLLED BACK TO DELMONICO'S. IT WAS right at eight, but he didn't see Clare anywhere. The young waitress from earlier hurried over to his table, and he ordered a cup of coffee.

When she brought his coffee, she asked with a smile, "Are you Mr. Beckler? Clare went to get Zeke and will be back here in a bit. We both had to work longer today since it is a holiday."

"My name is Kit." Her face turned pale as she added, "I want to thank you for what you did today. No man has ever demanded that I be treated like a lady. I guess I have become used to some men's rudeness."

Rock answered quietly, "I reckon every woman deserves to be treated like a lady." His face colored and he grinned as he added, "Although Clare has some stories about me that might show me in another light!" He nodded around the room. "Been working here long?"

"Clare found this job for me. The other waitress left to marry, and Clare asked the colonel to hire me." Kit looked down and took a deep breath before she lifted her head to look at Rock directly.

"I was working for Big Dorothy, and I wanted out. I don't think the colonel was too excited to hire me, but Clare was persistent. She is my best friend, and I love her like a sister." Kit wiped her eyes quickly and smiled at Rock. "I was afraid the colonel would fire me after the altercation today, but he has said nothing.

"Are you going to the fireworks? They will start around nine tonight. We will close about eight-thirty and open back up at ten. We'll stay open tonight until midnight with snacks. The colonel said he was going to push the tables to the edges of the room so people can dance." She paused and gave Rock a quick smile. "Thanks again for your help, Mr. Beckler. I won't forget that."

Rock grinned at Kit. "It was my pleasure," he drawled.

After she hurried away, he turned his eyes to the door to watch for Clare. *So, Clare is rescuing other women who are in bad situations. Well, good for her. I am guessing that won't increase her standing around the proper women of the community though.* He chuckled to himself as he muttered, "And I doubt if she cares."

Clare was back shortly after eight with a small, excited boy by her side. His reddish-brown hair was curly like his mother's, and his large eyes were brown. He ducked behind Clare and peeked out at Rock.

Rock stood and dropped two bits on the table. He squatted in front of the boy and put out his hand. "Hello, Zeke. I'm your Uncle Rock. How are you today?"

Zeke gave him a shy grin. He stared at the small hat on the table before he pointed and asked, "Is that for me?"

Clare started to scold him, but Rock just laughed. "Sure is. Maybe someday you will want to be a cowboy like your Uncle Rock." He put the hat on Zeke's head. It was large and went down over the tops of his ears, but Zeke was delighted. He pulled it down farther and gave Rock a big smile before he ducked behind Clare again.

Rock laughed. He stood and offered Clare his arm. "So where are we going? I mean, you did ask me out."

Clare blushed and her eyes opened wide. She laughed as she took the arm Rock offered her. "I promised Zeke I would take him to the fireworks tonight. I would love for you to come along if you'd like."

The crowd was already gathering, and Clare pointed toward a small hill. "Let's sit over there. Zeke will be able to see without getting hurt."

After they sat down and Zeke ran off to play with some friends, Rock glanced over at Clare.

"I was sorry to hear about Johnny. I didn't know that until I arrived today," he said softly as he squeezed her hand.

Clare's body went still, and a shadow passed over her face. "We should never have married. We both married for the wrong reasons, and it was a difficult three and a half years." She hugged her knees as she added, "I will be forever grateful to him though for giving Zeke his name." She looked over at Rock.

"Johnny wasn't a bad man. He was just a boy who shouldn't have taken on a wife, and certainly not one with a child." Clare was silent for a moment before she continued. Her voice was soft when she spoke.

"He wanted to mine for gold—that's why we came here. He tried it for four months and decided it was too hard. I wanted him to take a riding job, but he said gambling was easier. Unfortunately for all of us, Johnny was a poor gambler. And when he drank, he was reckless."

Clare glanced at Rock before she dropped her eyes. Her voice was barely more than a whisper when she spoke.

"I couldn't make myself cry over the loss of a true love when Johnny died. I cried because I was afraid. Afraid of what would happen to Zeke and to me too." She looked toward the men who were preparing the fireworks. "I think I have been afraid my entire life."

Clare was quiet for a moment, and Rock waited for her to speak. She straightened her shoulders and took a deep breath before she gave him a quick smile.

"I am done being afraid. Leonard Cole helped me to get my job at Delmonico's, and I like working for the colonel. He is a fair man. He has even given me a room as well as a raise. And the nuns across the street are wonderful with Zeke. He is so happy." She smiled softly at Rock. "Our life is the easiest it has been since he was born."

Rock squeezed Clare's hand again and smiled down at her. "Good for you, Clare. You both deserve some happiness."

Clare didn't answer. When she glanced toward Rock, he was facing forward, and she studied his profile for time before she spoke.

"Thank you for what you did for Kit today. She is a sweet girl. I know this sounds like a strange thing to say, but Big Dorothy is a kind woman. When things were so hard for Zeke and me, she sent her mending over. It didn't amount to much, but sometimes, it was the difference between Zeke eating or missing a meal. Kit usually delivered it, and we became friends."

Clare looked away. She was silent a moment before she asked, "Did you know that Big Dorothy donates lots of money to the convent? The nuns treat the all the working girls kindly, and Big Dorothy appreciates it.

"Most of the girls on the line have the sisters watch their children too. The nuns find homes for the little ones who are given up and support the young mothers who want to keep their babies. Of course, the good sisters work to get all the women out of the brothels as well.

"In return, Big Dorother supports their school and their community projects. It's an interesting relationship." Clare giggled as she watched Rock's face.

"I'm sure some of the fine ladies of Helena would be horrified if they knew the sisters used money earned illicitly to support their works of charity!"

Rock laughed and nodded in agreement.

A loud sound came from below followed by an arch of light through the sky. Zeke jumped on Clare's lap and clapped his hands delightedly. Before long, he was sitting on Rock's lap going through his vest pockets.

Rock smiled at the happy little boy and pointed at his jacket. "Maybe you should check that one, Zeke. I think there is a lump in there."

He leaned forward and Zeke's little hand quickly found a piece of hard candy. He held it up as his brown eyes shined. Rock helped him to unwrap it, and Zeke popped it into his mouth. He grinned at Rock as syrup ran down his chin.

The show was over by nine-thirty, and the crowd began to disperse. As they walked back toward Delmonico's, Clare smiled up at Rock.

"Thank you for going with us. It was nice to have adult conversation." Her eyes were soft as she looked down at her son. "And Zeke loves his new hat." The little boy tripped, and Rock lifted him up. Zeke was asleep on Rock's shoulder by the time they arrived at the hotel.

Rock paused before they reached the door. He turned toward Clare and asked hesitatingly. "I am riding out tomorrow morning to look over some cattle at several different ranches. Would you and Zeke like to ride along?" As Clare stared at him in surprise, he blushed and turned away. "Never mind. I'm sure you have to work."

Clare touched his arm and smiled. "I would love to go. The colonel gave me the morning off since I put in extra hours today. What time should we be ready?" Clare's face was excited as she looked up at Rock.

He grinned at her and drawled, "Well, if you can be in the dining room by seven, I will buy you breakfast before we go. Do you have a favorite horse you like to ride at the livery?"

"Seven is fine as well as any horse." She lifted Zeke out of Rock's arms and hurried back to her small room. She turned once to wave and smiled as she paused at the door. "Thank you again for the lovely evening."

Rock watched her go with a smile on his face before he climbed the stairs slowly to his own room. The festivities were just cranking up in the dining room, but he was tired.

"I'm pretty sure that noise won't bother me tonight."

A Ride With A Pretty Girl

ROCK WAS UP EARLY. HE SADDLED RED AND HAD THE hostler pick a horse for Clare. He soon had them tied in front of the hotel and was seated at a small table towards the back of the room when Clare arrived. He stood and stared at her for a moment before he pulled a chair out for her. He slowly smiled as she sat down.

"I swear, Clare. You just keep getting prettier." Rock's eyes were twinkling, but the compliment was sincere.

Clare blushed a light pink, and Zeke smiled at him. The little boy climbed up on a chair and grinned at the tall man. "Hi, Uncle Rock."

Rock lifted the hat off Zeke's head and tousled his hair. "Good morning, cowboy! Are you ready to do a little riding?"

Zeke nodded excitedly and gave Rock a big grin. Clare went back to the kitchen to talk to the cook. She came back with a glass of milk for Zeke as well as coffee for Rock and her.

"I thought we'd ride out to meet with a rancher north of town before dinner. That way, I can drop the two of you in town and look over cattle at the other two ranches after dinner. Sound good?" Rock smiled as he waited for Clare's response.

Clare nodded happily. She was soon busy cutting Zeke's meat and griddlecakes when George Fox walked through the door. He tipped his hat.

"Mrs. Braxton.

"Rock, I can ride out with you for an hour or so this afternoon if that still works. I want to look Moser's cattle over anyway."

Rock agreed and the banker hurried out. Clare watched him leave and then studied Rock's face.

"How long have you known George Fox?"

Rock paused chewing as he thought. "I met him in '71. I came up here to buy cattle, and George Fox helped me broker that first cattle-buying deal. I've been banking here ever since.

"I like Fox. He's an honest man and is easy to work with. Besides, I don't need a banker hanging over my shoulder all the time, so the distance works too." He grinned at Clare before he took another bite, and she laughed.

The ride that morning was enjoyable for all three of them. Clare and Rock talked and laughed as they shared stories and memories.

Rock smiled. He enjoyed Clare's company. His heart still hurt when he thought about Suzanna, but the happy days were now more common than the sad ones. *I figure that's a good sign.*

Zeke had fallen asleep, so Rock lifted him out of Clare's saddle. He set the sleeping boy in front of him, and Zeke leaned back with a big sigh.

Rock watched Clare's face as she talked. Her eyes sparkled when she laughed. She was not only a beautiful woman, she was intelligent and caring as well. Her heart was big, and she would do anything for those she loved. He looked away. He was ashamed of himself for the way he had treated her. *Maybe it's time I apologize for that.*

"Clare, I should have said this a long time ago, but I'm saying it now. I don't think I ever thanked you for all you did for Suzanna when she was dying. I was a mess for quite a while there. I know I didn't show you much appreciation and I'm sorry."

Tears filled Clare's eyes, and she blinked them away.

"We both loved Suzanna. She was a wonderful woman and my first friend in Stevensville. I probably would have run away had it not been for her—not because I was unhappy but because it was so different from what I was used to. There is a certain sense of security in knowing what is expected of you even if it is bad. You learn never to hope because hope makes the pain of disappointment hurt even more." She smiled at Rock.

"I am happy you can smile again. You were so brokenhearted. Between the two of us, we didn't have enough joy for even one person.

"Suzanna was the strong one. She wanted to make sure that Annie and you would be all right without her."

Rock slowly nodded. "And Maggie was the glue that held all of us together. She stayed on after you left. She has never mentioned moving out, and I hope she never does. I just don't know what we'd do without her."

As they topped the rise in front of them, the O Bar Ranch spread out below them. Rock pulled his horse to a stop. "Land and cattle. There are not many things that make me happier than land and cattle."

Clare stole a sideways glance at the man beside her but didn't answer. *I wonder if Rock will ever make room in his life for another wife. He seems quite contented now.*

Francis O'Malley rode out to meet them with a smile. "Rock! Good to see you again this year. And who is this young lady? You are in Helena for less than twenty-four hours and already have a date with the prettiest woman in town!"

Rock laughed as he introduced Clare and Zeke. They visited for a time before they rode toward the cattle. O'Malley talked about his breeding program as they rode down to the herd.

"I think Angus and Hereford cattle are the future of this land. The longhorns are hearty, but they take too long to fatten. As soon as I can get some Angus cows up here, I am going to cross them with my Herefords. I've seen those two breeds crossed and I like the results." He pointed at one of the Hereford calves as it raced across the grassy valley, bucking and kicking. "I like the looks of those little white-faced calves too."

Hereford cattle were scattered all over the small valley, and Rock rode down to look at them closer. He agreed with O'Malley. Breeding was going to be more important in the days and years to come. "And I want to be among the first cattlemen to get on board," Rock commented softly to himself. He rode through the herd slowly and studied the calves. He could feel his excitement rising. He rejoined O'Malley and Clare with a smile on his face.

"I like those white-faced calves too. I think you are onto something." He looked over at Clare as his eyes twinkled. "What do you think, Clare? Think I should buy some of those Hereford cattle?"

Clare nodded and laughed. "I don't really know that much about cattle, but the calves are surely cute."

O'Malley grinned. "Let's go down to the house and see if I can take some of this cowboy's money. Maybe you can help me negotiate, Clare. Ol' Rock here is mighty hard-nosed when it comes to parting with his money."

Margaret O'Malley had made pies. The smell filled their noses as they walked into the comfortable kitchen, and Rock's stomach growled. Zeke had awakened when Rock dismounted, and he looked around the kitchen with big eyes.

Rock set him down. "Smell those pies, Zeke? That is one of the best smells out there."

Mrs. O'Malley set out pie and coffee for everyone, and the two men began to dicker. Rock bought five hundred head of young, bred Hereford cows and heifers. O'Malley would deliver the cattle to Missoula in two weeks, and Rock would pick them up there. The bank draft would be left with George Fox as they had done in the past.

It was nearly noon when they rode back into Helena. Clare's skin was flushed from the cool morning, and her eyes were bright as she smiled at Rock.

"Have a good time?" he asked

"I did and thank you for inviting me. I think I will put Zeke down for a nap. Perhaps I will see you this evening at Delmonico's for supper?"

"I'll see. It depends on how late I am and if Klaussens feed me. They usually insist that I stay for supper. We have been doing business together for five years now."

He helped Clare down and she carried the sleeping little boy back to her room. Rock sat down in a chair and had a cup of coffee while he waited for George Fox.

"I sure enjoyed my morning ride. Old George won't be as easy to look at as Clare was, but it will be nice to visit with him too."

George arrived shortly after noon. By twelve-thirty, the men had dropped Clare's horse off at the livery and were on their way out of town.

Rock was tired when he led Red into the livery. Klaussens had insisted that he eat supper with them, and it was after nine before he made it back to Helena.

The day had been a success though. He had contracted for nearly fifteen hundred head of pure and crossbred Hereford cattle. The three ranches would combine his cattle, and cowboys for all three brands would drive them to Missoula.

Rock was in Delmonico's when they opened at six the next morning. Clare greeted him with a smile and took his order. He watched as she hurried away. *Clare kind of adds light everywhere she goes. She brightens up this room.* He looked out the window and began to line his trip home out in his head. He frowned as he thought of all the work that had piled up while he was gone. He almost jumped when Clare appeared again.

"Leaving today?" she asked as she set his food in front of him.

"Yep, as soon as I eat, I am headed west to Missoula. I want to line out pens for the cattle on my way home. Thought I might run into less Indian trouble too since so many of the tribes are riled up right now."

Clare stared at Rock for a moment. She could feel tears building in the back of her eyes and she turned her head quickly. When she looked back, her eyes were red, but she was smiling.

"Thank you for taking us with you yesterday. We had a wonderful time. That is all Zeke has talked about since then. And he loves his hat!"

Rock laughed. "I usually come out once a year. I will look you up next year if you are still around." His eyes twinkled as he added, "Of course, if I was a single fellow around here, I would be trying to marry the prettiest young widow around."

Clare's face paled. "I don't think so." Her face was determined as she shook her head. "I have learned my lesson. The next time I marry, it will be for love and not out of fear."

The dining room was beginning to fill, and Clare took a deep breath as she smiled at him.

"Goodbye, Rock." She quickly moved from table to table, taking orders and visiting with the customers. When she had time to look at Rock's table again, his chair was empty. For a moment, it seemed like all time had stopped. Slowly, her mind cleared, and once again, she could hear the sounds of the busy restaurant above her beating heart.

"I miss you already, Rock. You walk in and out of my life as easily as the horses tied to that hitching rail. You enjoy my company, but you only love cattle and land.

"I should leave here. I should go far enough to never see you again. Maybe then, my heart will let you go, and I can fall in love with someone else." Clare forced herself to smile.

"That's what I'll do. I'll use the $50 I put in the bank to start my new life. I'll add a little each week, and when I get enough saved, Zeke and I will start over. Maybe in the Dakotas or in Wyoming Territory.

"Goodbye, Rock. Goodbye forever."

CHAPTER 27

Broken Hearts

ROCK RODE UP TO THE BARN AND DISMOUNTED slowly. It had been a long, warm morning, and he was already tired. Late August in the Bitter Root Valley wasn't usually this hot. In addition to the heat, fixing fence wasn't one of his favorite jobs either. Something had spooked the cattle, and they had broken through the fence he was building on Chas Boswell's and his property line. It was a rough job of sorting and then rebuilding. He rubbed Red down and turned him out into a small pasture next to the corral.

"You take the afternoon off, old fellow. I know I'd like to quit for the day, and you certainly have worked hard enough for two days." Red nuzzled his owner's shirt for the apple he knew was there and trotted out into the pasture. As Rock turned toward the house and the dinner Maggie had waiting for him, he saw a buggy coming up the lane.

He recognized the driver as the hostler from town and almost tripped in surprise when he saw who was riding beside him. A small boy had his head between the two of them and was talking excitedly as he pointed in every direction.

Rock's smile was large as he walked out to meet the buggy .

"Ike, Clare—good to see you. And look at you, Zeke! Why you are nearly grown up!"

The boy looked at Rock with serious eyes. "Uncle Rock, I don't think you know very much about kids. I am only four."

Rock laughed as he reached to help Clare down. His smile faded when she winced in pain as he put his hands on her waist. He released her, and she took his hand as she climbed down on her own.

The Clare he had checked cattle with not even two months ago was much thinner, and her face was drawn down in pain. The dark circles under her eyes were new as well, and Rock knew this wasn't a social call.

"Maggie has dinner ready. We were just about to eat if you would like to join us."

Ike paused and waited for Clare to respond. She smiled.

"That would be fine. I am hungry but I would like to talk to Rock for a bit first if you don't mind."

Rock looked at Clare in surprise as she took his arm.

"Walk with me, Rock. I need to talk to you before I lose my nerve as well as my strength." She smiled at him as she studied his face.

"Someone left $50 in an envelope at the bank with my name on it two months ago while you were in town. I was told that a man whom Johnny had loaned money had come through Helena to pay him back. With that and what I saved working at Delmonico's, it was enough to pay for our stagecoach ride down here. You don't know anything about that money, do you?"

Rock raised his eyebrows and gave her a crooked grin. He shrugged. "Don't know as I recall doing any such thing. I am kind of tight with my money, you know."

Clare laughed. She looked at him seriously as she stated, "When I first came out to your ranch to stay with Suzanna, I didn't like you. I just couldn't understand what Suzanna saw in you."

Rock's neck slowly turned red. "I reckon not. I wasn't the nicest person to you, and I am sorry for that."

"Oh, but Suzanna loved you. She told me she knew the second time she saw you that she was going to marry you."

Rock stopped and turned toward the woman beside him. Her words made his heart hurt, and he didn't know where this conversation was going.

"Clare, what's going on?"

She smiled a tired smile. "Let me finish, Rock. I have some things I need to say, and I have to say them today." Clare began to walk again.

"Suzanna was so excited when she came back from your picnic the day she asked you to the Ladies' Choice Dance. She had young men lined up just waiting for her to ask, but she asked you."

Clare shook her head. "And you barely talked. You were so quiet that it looked like a one-sided conversation to me." Clare laughed softly.

"Oh, my heart, she was in love. She saw things in you that I couldn't see. Most of all, she said you had a tender heart. That I didn't see at all."

Clare stopped and looked up at Rock with tears in her eyes.

"Suzanna was my first and best friend. I loved her as a sister, and I was devastated when she became sick. I watched how you cared for her, and for the first time, I saw the Rock that Suzanna loved." A sob caught in Clare's throat.

"And now, as my best friend's husband, I have a favor to ask of you."

Rock struggled to look at Clare. He could feel wetness in his eyes, and it pained him to show that kind of emotion to anyone.

"Look at me, Rock. Let me see the you that my friend loved. The kind man, the tender man—the gentle man."

Rock turned toward Clare. His eyes were red, and the pain in his face was easily seen. "What do you want, Clare? Why are you doing this?"

Clare laughed softly and turned to walk forward again as she slipped her arm through his.

"You know, I fell in love with you after Suzanna died. Those six months I stayed here and nursed your little Annie along with my Zeke, I fell in love with my best friend's husband."

As Rock stared at her, Clare laughed dryly. "Of course, you didn't notice. You were too busy drowning your pain in bottle after bottle of whiskey. You wouldn't have even known if Annie had lived or died those first six months let alone a sad, young woman living in your house. Thank heavens Maggie stayed on after she helped deliver Annie.

"She is the one who sent for me. She knew our babies were born close to the same time, and Suzanna's milk dried up with her fever."

As Rock stared at her, Clare's eyes opened wide. "Please tell me that you knew I was nursing Annie!"

Rock slowly shook his head. He turned his head to look away from Clare. He could feel the pain sear through his heart, and he didn't want it to leak out his eyes.

"I heard all the rumors as to who the father of my child was," Clare stated bitterly. "I know you never liked me much. I was a foul-mouthed little girl when you met me, but I wasn't loose." Clare paused and turned to face Rock.

"I used to block my door at night to try to keep my pappy's friends out of my room. I never washed my face or my hair so I would be ugly to them, and I only took baths in the creek when I knew they wouldn't be around." Clare's voice was brittle as she added, "You have no idea how awful it was for a small girl in that shack." Her face softened as she continued, "You saved my life the day you tied me to your horse and hauled me to town.

"The Macks were wonderful people. I was devastated when they were both killed two years later when their stagecoach rolled over on them. I was alone again, and I was terrified. And then, Maggie invited me to move in with her."

Clare's voice broke as she whispered, "I was packing my things when my pappy and one of his friends showed up at the Mack's house. They wanted me to go back home. Pappy wanted me to marry the man he had with him. When I refused, they both attacked me. They threatened to kill Suzanna if I didn't cooperate with them."

As Rock stared at Clare in horror, tears slid down her face. His fists clenched in rage. *I let that man go. He was in my yard, and I let him go.*

"So, I cooperated. I didn't scream. When they were done, they both left. Pappy said he'd be back in nine months to take me and the whelp home with him." Clare looked down and deep sobs shook her body. She took a deep breath before she looked up at Rock.

"I told Suzanna because I wanted her to be safe—and because she was my best friend. I made her promise not to tell, and she didn't. She kept my secret." Clare's voice was bitter when she added, "I think Maggie suspected, but most people just chose to think the worst of me—including you."

Rock's neck slowly turned red. *Clare is right. I did think she played around and got caught. I don't think I ever forgave her for her part in the killing of old Darby.*

"When Suzanna became sick, Maggie asked me to come and help. I nursed our babies and we both cried. I was broken emotionally, and Suzanna was broken physically."

Clare touched Rock's arm, and he looked down at her.

"I would have stayed, you know," she whispered. "If you had even noticed me, I would have stayed. Instead, when Johnny Braxton asked me to marry, I agreed. I ran away with him." She paused and gave Rock a sad smile.

"Johnny was a good man, but he was too young to marry. Drinking just speeded up the inevitable. He always treated me kindly though, and he cared for Zeke. I will be forever grateful to him for marrying me and giving Zeke his name—and for trying to love both of us.

"I did learn from our marriage that love has to go both ways though. After his funeral, I vowed that I would never again marry unless there was love on both sides.

"Then you rode into town. You with your big smile and those green eyes. I realized that I still loved you. How I wanted you to ask me to go back to Stevensville with you. I would have too. I had never been so happy as I was during that morning ride."

Clare laughed as she looked up at Rock. "Now here I am professing my one-sided love, and it is certainly too late for me." A large tear slid out of her eye, and she looked away. When she looked back, tears were rolling down her face.

"I'm dying, Rock. There is something terrible growing inside me. The bump you see on my stomach is a tumor of some kind. If it wasn't for Zeke, I would just let it take me. I will fight it for him though.

"There is a surgeon at St. Mary's Mission who promised to see me. I would like to leave Zeke here with you with both of us knowing that I may never return."

Rock stared at Clare in shock. He pulled her close to him as she sobbed.

"Clare, I had no idea," he grated out as he patted her back awkwardly. Then he held her away from him. "Why didn't you come sooner? Would time have made a difference?"

Clare shook her head. "The pain only became strong in the last few weeks. Before that, it was more like cramps. I knew something wasn't right, but I had no idea about the growth until last week." She looked up at him with terror in her eyes.

"Please take care of Zeke. I don't have anyone else to turn to," she whispered. "The Sisters of St. Joseph offered to take him in. They said they would find a home for him." Tears poured from Clare's eyes as she sobbed, "But I don't want my son to be raised by strangers.

"Kit offered to help too, but she has no way to provide for a young boy."

Rock pulled Clare close again and patted her back until she stopped sobbing.

She looked up at him and tried to smile. "Zeke talks about you all the time. He wants to be a cowboy like his Uncle Rock."

Rock squeezed Clare's hand. "Zeke has a home here for as long as he wants to stay. I hope you will come and pick him up when you are better, but if you don't, I will raise him as my son."

As Clare smiled sadly, Rock pulled her close to him again. He whispered, "I'm so sorry, Clare. I'm sorry I didn't see your pain or see you for the woman you are. I'm sorry I sopped my sorrow in whiskey and never thanked you for all you did for us. And I'm especially sorry you have to make a decision like this." He paused and added softly, "You know, I almost asked you to come back to Stevensville with me when we went riding. You were happy though. I thought it might be best for the two of you if I didn't bother you."

Clare looked up at Rock in surprise. Tears were still leaking from her eyes, but she laughed as she wiped them. "Finally, I see that heart that Suzanna loved!"

Rock blushed and then grinned at her. He quietly led her to the graveyard under the large tree. Snowberry, arnica, and twinflower were planted around the small tombstone with Suzanna's name. The large pine towered above the small clearing, and the smell was wonderful. Rock had made the small picket fence larger, and it encircled both Darby's and Suzanna's graves.

"All of Suzanna's favorite flowers. You did know her heart, Rock." Clare leaned forward to smell the flowers. "It is so peaceful here," she whispered as she breathed in deeply.

"If I don't make it, will you bury me here, Rock? Put me under Suzanna's tree so my little boy can visit my grave. Please?"

Rock nodded and rubbed his sleeve roughly across his face. Tears were once again trying to push their way out of his eyes, and he stopped them. He turned Clare toward the path to the house, and she looped her arm through his.

"Now tell me about your ranch and all your plans for this place. I know you have plans and probably all on a timeline."

Rock looked surprised but slowly grinned as he agreed. "I guess I am pretty predictable," he laughed. "You are right, though. I was one of the first ranches here to fence off pasture, and I fence a little more each year. We have twelve thousand deeded acres, and I am leasing eight thousand more. Water is plentiful, so that's a blessing.

"I have started to put up a little hay for winter feed. I'd like to do more, and I am finally in the position to hire some full-time hands."

They were both smiling as they came into the house. Ike glanced up at Rock, and the sorrow on his face was visible for just a moment. He masked it as he looked toward Clare with a smile.

Annie awoke just as they were finishing dinner, but she was too excited about having a friend to play with to bother with eating.

"Come on, Zeke! Let me show you my hay forts! And my new kittens and the baby calf…" Her excited voice trailed off as she rushed out the door followed by an excited Zeke.

Ike's eyes were soft as he looked at Clare.

"Well, little darlin', are ya ready to head back to Stevensville? That padre wants to see ya soon as we git back. He's hopin' to do yur surgery yet this evenin'."

Clare nodded as she took a deep breath. "I told Zeke he would be staying with you a time. He is a wise little boy though. I think he suspects there is more to what I told him."

Maggie pulled Clare to her feet and hugged her tightly. "Your little boy will be here waiting for you when you return. You just focus on getting better." Maggie's eyes were red as she hugged Clare and tried not to sob.

Ike took Clare's arm and led her outside. She wiped her face and smiled before she called for Zeke.

The little boy rushed up with shining eyes. "Mama, can we stay a little longer? I am having so much fun!"

Clare pulled her little boy close and talked to him. His smile faded, and he grabbed his mother around her neck as he shook his head.

CHAPTER 28

ZEKE

ROCK STEPPED FORWARD. "ZEKE, HOW ABOUT WE GO for a ride this afternoon? I have been thinking about getting a second pony. Maybe we will just ride over to the neighbor's ranch and look at some. How does that sound to you?"

Zeke looked from his mother to this man he called Uncle Rock and slowly nodded. He watched silently as Ike helped a sobbing Clare into his buggy and turned it quickly down the road.

Maggie held one hand over her heart and the other over her mouth, and Rock reached to pick up Zeke.

The little boy sobbed as he hung onto Rock's neck, and the big man carried him toward the barn.

"Annie, I am going to catch Steed, and then we'll take Zeke for a ride," he called over his shoulder. "Maybe we should take our fishing poles along so you can show him your favorite spot. You had better eat something though. Otherwise, you'll be hungry in an hour or so.

Annie's blue eyes were large as she looked from Rock to Maggie.

When she paused, Maggie called, "Annie, you come in here and eat. You will be too hungry to fish all afternoon if you don't have something in your stomach." She smiled at the little girl and whispered loudly, "I made bear sign. You may have some when you finish your dinner."

Annie's face lit up with excitement. She rushed to Maggie and grabbed her hand as they hurried toward the house.

"Okay, Auntie, but we have to hurry. I don't want Papa to leave me."

Rock set Zeke on a pile of hay and dropped down in front of him. Zeke's brown eyes were red as he stared solemnly at Rock. The big man waited for him to talk.

"My mama said she's sick. She is going to the doctor, but she has been sick for a long time."

Rock nodded and squeezed Zeke's legs.

"My mama's not coming back, is she? She cried like this when my papa died, when she didn't think I could hear her. She acts scared sometimes too. She is going to die, isn't she?" As the little boy began to sob, Rock pulled him close and kissed his wet cheek.

"Zeke, your mama is very sick. She is going to see if the doctor can fix her. If he can, she will be back in a few weeks. If he can't, then she will be in Heaven with the angels, but you can still talk to her." He pointed at one of the small tombstones beneath the pine tree.

"Annie's mama died shortly after she was born," he continued softly. "Annie doesn't remember anything about her—not how she smiled or how she smelled or the color of her eyes—but we talk about her every day, so Annie knows who she is. We can talk about your mama too because I have known her for a long time.

"Did you know that your mama was Annie's mama's best friend? You and Annie are almost like twins—you were born just a few days apart to mamas who loved both of you very much."

The little boy stared at Rock through tear-filled eyes before he whispered, "If my mama doesn't come back, can I call you Papa?"

Rock's heart crumpled as he nodded. He pulled the little boy close and whispered, "You bet you can. I would love to be your papa."

When Zeke's little body quit shaking, Rock set him up and grinned at him. "Now let's go find a pony for you to ride!"

Excitement flickered in Zeke's eyes, and he nodded. He slid down to take Rock's hand just as Annie came rushing into the barn with a package of bear sign.

"Look what Auntie sent with us! And we can eat them while we're riding!" She was still chattering excitedly as Rock grabbed a rope and whistled for his horse.

"Red, I know I told you that you could take the rest of the day off, but that's all changed. You too, Steed. I promise this afternoon will be an easy one though."

Rock saddled the horses quickly and grabbed the fishing poles from the barn. He didn't take the time to look for bait. *I'm sure we can find something to use there. We need to get down to Boswells or it will be dark before we get back.*

He held Steed while Annie clambered on. She almost shimmied up his front leg until she could reach the saddle horn and then pulled herself on up.

"Zeke, how about you ride in front of me?" Rock asked. "Have you ridden a horse much?"

Zeke shook his head, "No, just a few times. Mama doesn't like to ride horses by herself, and she won't ride out with all the fellas who invite her." He gave Rock a quick smile. "My mama is real pretty, and lots of fellas want to take her places. She always says, 'No.' She told me she wouldn't go riding with fellas unless they invited me along." His smile became bigger. "But she said she would go riding with you again because I asked her."

Rock's neck turned red, and Annie snorted.

"'Course she'd go riding with my papa. Everybody wants to ride with my papa. He is the best rider in these parts. At least that's what Auntie says. And she says you should only settle for the best."

Rock grinned. He lifted Zeke to ride in front of him. As they headed down the trail, Maggie called from the house, "Now don't you stay too long. Clouds are rolling in, and I don't want those little ones to be stuck out all night in a cave somewhere!"

Rock waved over his shoulder and smiled as the two children began to chatter back and forth.

CHAPTER 29

PATCHES, THE BEAR KILLER

CHAS BOSWELL ALWAYS KEPT A FEW SMALL PONIES around and was happy to sell one to Rock. He took Zeke by the hand and showed him the ponies that were available. He talked to the little boy about what to look for in a horse.

Boswell had been one of the first ranchers to settle in the Bitter Root Valley. He had moved in shortly after Darby McCune, and the two men shared work. Rock continued the relationship and always enjoyed visiting with the old cowman.

Zeke looked back at Rock. "What do you think, Uncle Rock?"

Rock studied the four ponies. All of them were gentle, but the little pinto seemed to be the friendliest. "Well, I reckon a fellow should pick the horse he likes. Which one do you think that would be?"

Zeke's smile became huge as he pointed at the pinto. "I like that one with the big spots. I would call him Patches. Here, Patches, come here, boy!"

Boswell looped a rope around the pony's neck and handed the rope to Zeke. "Here you are, son. Go ahead and lead your pony out of this corral while I will talk to your uncle about a saddle."

As the two happy children led the pony out, Boswell looked over at Rock. "That young man has a sad shadow that falls on him from time to time. He family?"

Rock shook his head and frowned. "His mother was Suzanna's best friend before we married. Clare even came out and helped when Suzanna became sick.

"She left Zeke with me while she goes the Mission for some surgery." Rock's eyes were bleak as he added, "She thinks she's dying, so I might be raising Zeke."

Boswell kicked a clod of manure and cursed under his breath.

"Tough old world, ain't it? Just a raw deal. Hard on the mama and hard on the boy." He stared across the corral and then clapped Rock on the back as he grinned. "Let's just call this horse a gift, but you are going to have to work for that saddle!"

The two men settled on $10 for the saddle, a bridle, and a small blanket. Chas tossed Rock a canteen.

"I'll even throw in that canteen for free. It's a little beat-up, but it doesn't leak." Rock chuckled and the two men sauntered toward the children.

Rock showed Zeke how to saddle his horse, and the excited little boy pulled himself into the saddle using the stirrup. The pony stood calmly while he climbed on, and the two children began to ride down the trail.

Boswell grinned at Rock as they shook hands. "Bring those kids over again sometime. I enjoy their chatter and their happy little voices."

Rock grinned and nodded. He pushed Red to a gallop. He didn't want two four-year-old children to get too far ahead of him.

When they had ridden about five miles, Annie pointed to the right. "The fishing hole is over there. Come on, Zeke! I'll race you!"

The two ponies streaked down the trail and Rock followed a little slower. They hadn't gone far when Red shied and blew hard through his nose. Rock grabbed his rifle as the stallion continued to snort loudly. "Easy, boy. Easy."

Just then, he heard Annie scream. Rock jabbed Red with his spurs and the horse lunged to a full run.

Annie was lying on the trail, and her pony was racing away. Zeke's paint horse was standing over her, facing a large grizzly that was standing upright about seventy yards to the left of the trail. Two cubs wandered out of the brush behind Rock, and he knew they were in trouble. A grizzly was bad enough, but a mother grizzly who considered you a threat to her cubs was deadly.

Rock lifted his rifle and fired three shots in quick succession as the bear dropped on all four feet and charged. The first two shots were to the chest and the third was between the eyes.

The bear's roar was terrifying, and both children were screaming as Rock shot a fourth time. The bear fell over and slid to a stop near Annie.

Patches didn't give ground. He lunged forward to face the bear with his mouth open. His neighs sounded more like angry screams.

When the bear dropped, Patches reared. He jumped over Annie and began to slam his feet into the dead bear.

Rock dropped to the ground and grabbed Annie. He caught Zeke as the boy was falling off the angry pony. Putting them both on Red, he talked quietly as he reached for Patches' reins. He pulled the pony back and stared at the little horse in surprise.

"Zeke, I think you just bought a bear killer. That's what I think."

Red was snorting and pawing the ground while Patches blew through his nose and trembled. Annie was crying, Although Zeke was quiet, his brown eyes were huge with fear. Rock lifted both kids from Red and hugged them tightly as he talked to them.

"Now, now. Just a mama bear protecting her young. Your mamas would have done the same thing if they thought someone was trying to hurt you."

The cubs were gone, and Rock muttered under his breath "I should track them down. I can't do it now and later might be too late." He didn't like to leave any animal defenseless, and cubs that small couldn't survive on their own.

Rock put both Annie and Zeke in front of him. Holding Patches' reins, he said, "Let's go find your pony, Annie. We don't want Steed scaring out any more bears today."

They hadn't gone too far when a frightened Steed met them. The pony crowded close to Red. Rock stepped down. He tied the pony's reins to Patches' saddle as he talked to the little Shetland.

"What were you thinking, running off like that and leaving Patches to fight that bear by himself?"

Before he remounted, Rock looked at both children. "You know, I think I need to come back here and skin that bear. That would make a fine rug for us in front of the fireplace." He squeezed Zeke's leg and added with a wink, "After all, it was Patches' bear!"

Both kids looked at him with big eyes. They slowly began to smile.

The conversation was lively but slowed before long. Soon, both children were asleep, and Rock had his hands full trying to keep them in the saddle.

He rode into the yard late that afternoon. Maggie rushed out to meet him. She reached for Annie, and Rock stepped off his horse holding Zeke.

"I'm headed back down the trail. We scared up a grizzly sow, and I want to get the hide before it gets torn up. I might try to track her cubs too if it doesn't get dark on me."

Maggie frowned but nodded. Grizzlies were fairly common, so if Rock shot one, that meant he believed someone to be in danger.

They carried the sleeping children inside and laid them on Annie's bed. Rock studied the room and frowned.

"We are going to need another bed in here," he stated. "A bunk bed might work well, at least for a time."

CHAPTER 30

LITTLE BEAR

ROCK QUICKLY THREW A PACKSADDLE ON HIS MULE and headed down the trail.

As he came around a bend in the trail, he saw several Indians gathered around the bear. One stood and stared at him.

Rock pulled his horse to a stop and grinned.

"Little Bear! What are my brothers doing in the land of the Salish?"

The young brave looked somberly at Rock and shrugged. "We come to hunt. Great White Father gives all tribes hunting ground—but maybe we take some Flathead horses with us when we leave," he stated seriously as his eyes glinted with humor. He gestured at the grizzly.

"You shoot bear?"

Rock nodded. "We were between her and her cubs. She charged, and I had to shoot her."

Little Bear pointed at the pack horse. "You come for meat?"

Rock shook his head. "I came for the hide, but if my Crow brothers need it to keep their families warm, it is theirs as a gift."

Slowly, more warriors came out of the trees and brush beside the trail. It was obvious to Rock that this was a war party, not a hunting expedition. He had been friends with Little Bear growing up and had even lived in his village. Even so, the large number of warriors in war paint still made the hair stand up on his neck. The Crow liked to fight and had many enemies among the different tribes scattered throughout the area—not only the Salish but also the Blackfeet, the Sioux, and the Shoshone.

Little Bear stared hard at Rock. "You still have your woman?"

Rock's face tightened as he shook his head. "She died after she gave me a child, a girl. Now I have a second child, a boy, who belongs to a friend. My friend is dying and asked me to take her son as my own. An old woman helps me."

Little Bear nodded. "We take the bear." He grinned at Rock and added, "We might eat some of your cattle if they cross our path."

Rock nodded somberly. "Only eat the young males. My mother cows are almost ready to calve." He raised his hand, "Goodbye, my brother."

Little Bear raised his hand as well.

Rock turned his horse around in the trail and a young warrior blocked his path. The warrior's face was painted, and his lance held several scalps. The young warrior appeared to be in his early twenties, but he was as large as Rock.

Rock met the warrior's stare and made no effort to ride around him. Both of his hands rested easily on the saddle horn. The two men stared at each other. When Little Bear barked an order, the brave moved his horse slightly off to the side.

"Someday we fight," he muttered in Siouan.

Rock responded softly in Siouan, the language of the Crow, "I do not wish to fight the brother of my brother, Little Bear, but if you bring the fight to me, I will not run."

The warrior looked surprised and then glared. He looked at Little Bear and then back at Rock. He desperately wanted to fight, but he dared not go against the order of his leader.

Little Bear barked another command. The warrior backed his horse away and sat sullenly on the side of the trail to let Rock pass.

As Rock rode away, he turned in his saddle and called back to Little Bear in Siouan, "The sow had two cubs. I did not shoot the young bears, and they are too small to survive."

After Rock rode down the trail, Little Bear glared at the young warrior. He reprimanded him.

"Our people are friends with White Eagle and his family. White Eagle is a great warrior. He will kill you if you fight him, and that would put bad blood between us. You would do well to hold your temper, Beaver Tail."

Beaver Tail's face held a sullen look, and he resisted the urge to look down the trail at the departing white man.

Rock didn't look back as he rode toward the ranch. When he was out of site, he reached down and patted Red's neck.

"Sure am glad Little Bear was there. I might have gotten four of them, but they would killed me for sure." He looked back at his mule and grinned as he muttered, "And then they would have eaten Old Jake!"

Still, it bothered him that a war party was in the area. It meant that other warriors would be out.

He scowled and shook his head. "I need to get some full-time hands hired, and I need to do it soon." In the past, he had hired hands two times each year for branding and roundup. The rest of the year, he pretty much worked alone unless a rider stopped in looking for work. Luckily, that did happen from time to time.

"Maybe I will ride down to Stevensville. I can check on Clare while I'm there as well."

Maggie raised her eyebrows when Rock rode into the yard with no hide, but she said nothing in front of the children.

CHAPTER 31

MAN TO MAN

MAGGIE COULD SEE THE CONCERN ON ROCK'S FACE when he came into the house.

"Supper is ready and then I would like to give these two youngsters baths." She paused as she pointed at the tub. "And that means I am going to need some water."

Rock nodded and smiled at Maggie. The older woman was an excellent cook. He had shot a deer several days ago, and the venison stew Maggie had prepared smelled delicious. Rock thought of how much the land provided for them, and his smile grew larger. *We live an isolated life, but I sure like it here.*

"Let's have Annie take one first. I want Zeke to help me down at the barn for just a bit." He brought water in for Maggie and then took Zeke to the barn.

"Zeke, I am going to ride to Stevensville tomorrow. I thought I would check on your mother while I'm there. You can ride along with me if you want, but it is about twenty miles. That is a long rough ride in a wagon. What do you think?"

Zeke looked up at Rock. His eyes were large, and his lips trembled. "What if she died? What will we do?"

Rock put his hands on the little boy's shoulders. "Then we will bring her out here and put her beside Annie's mama."

Zeke stared up at Rock. "Uncle Rock, do you think she is still alive?"

Rock dropped down in front of the little boy. He kept his hands on Zeke's shoulders as he looked into his face.

"Your mama was mighty sick when she left you here, so I don't know," Rock answered honestly. He looked away before he added quietly, "I don't know much about people, Zeke, but when I have cattle that look as sick as your mama did, sometimes they don't make it." He hugged Zeke and whispered, "But she did have a fierce will to live and a very good reason to as well."

Zeke blinked back his tears and wrapped his arms around Rock's neck. He whispered, "I hope my mama comes back. If she does, I hope we can stay here with you. I'd like to have a papa like you, Uncle Rock."

Rock squeezed the little boy tightly and cleared his throat. "We'd better get back up to the house. Auntie Mag doesn't like to be kept waiting, especially when she has lots of work to do."

Once the youngsters were in bed, Rock told Maggie about the Indians. The children had already given her a colorful depiction of the grizzly attack, and it gave her chills. However, the Indian threat was new.

"We are friends with the Pend d'Oreille. This could affect how they treat us!"

Rock nodded. "It could. Hopefully, the Crow will pass through, and nothing will come of it. We do need to be vigilant though. Always keep a revolver on you, and make sure the rifle is within reach when you are in the house."

"I am going down to Stevensville tomorrow to see about hiring some hands. I was going to take my horse, but I think I will take the wagon in case—in case I need to bring Clare back with me." Rock's voice cracked as he added, "We just as well pick up supplies while we are there." The struggle he felt showed in his eyes.

Maggie nodded. "Let's all go. This is going to be hard on Zeke, so it might be good to have me there too." She frowned before she spoke again.

"Besides, I'm not sure I want Annie and me up here by ourselves if we have Indians fighting around us."

Rock's eyes crinkled as he looked at her. He answered dryly, "Well, I'm not sure a wagon will be safer than a stone house, but at least we will all be together."

The next morning, Rock hitched the wagon. At the last minute, he saddled Red too.

"You are coming with me, boy. You are too good of a horse to lose to Indians looting and stealing as they ride through.

"Maggie can drive the wagon, and I will ride you. That will give us more room. Besides, you are more comfortable than a darn wagon any day."

Rock quickly hitched the wagon and tied the team in front of the house. His eyes scanned the trees before he opened the door to the house.

Maggie scowled at him as he stepped through the door. "If we had a milk cow, I could make gravy to go with these biscuits. Besides, with two young children, we need milk in this house." She had convinced Rock to get chickens, and now she wanted a milk cow.

Rock was silent, but he knew he had already lost the battle. He just hoped that one of the fellas he hired would be willing to milk. He might have to offer more money. *I will too. I detest milk cows.*

Then he perked up. "We do have two young ones here—it's about time they had some chores to do. A milk cow just might be a good idea."

He smiled at Aunt Maggie, and she beamed at him. She knew she had won, and she also knew just where to find a nice little cow.

Annie was excited at the prospect of going to town, but Zeke was quiet. He sat on the seat beside Auntie Mag and twisted his hands. Rock finally reached down and lifted Zeke into the saddle in front of him. Then Annie began to fuss, so Rock set her behind him.

Maggie kept her scattergun beside her on the wagon seat and Rock held his rifle across the pommel of his saddle. It might have crowded Zeke had he not been so small. As it was, he had plenty of room and could see everything.

CHAPTER 32

A Priest and a Surgeon

IT TOOK THE LITTLE FAMILY NEARLY THREE HOURS TO reach Stevensville. The kids moved to the wagon bed after the first hour. They played for awhile, but both were asleep by the time the town came into view. Maggie covered them with blankets, and they looked quite comfortable.

Maggie stopped the wagon in front of the dry goods store. Rock helped her down before he rode out to the Mission.

He tapped on the door that said "DOCTOR," and an older man with a large smile opened it.

"Padre?"

The man wore the long black robe of a priest. His eyes were kind, and he had sawdust on the long worker's apron he wore over his black cassock.

"Yes?"

"I—uh—I came to check on Clare. Clare Childs—I mean Clare Braxton."

The priest's smile became large. "Yes, it was a miracle that we were able to treat her so easily. She had several large gall stones, and the largest was blocking the opening of her gall bladder. It was quite inflamed, and the growth in her stomach didn't help.

"The first gall bladder surgery was performed last year. I studied it to become familiar with some of the symptoms. I am pleased I was able to copy that surgery. I took both her gall bladder and the tumor out. Provided there are no side effects, she is going to be just fine." He smiled at Rock.

"I'm sorry—I didn't even introduce myself. My name is Father Anthony Ravalli." His smile became a large grin, and he chuckled. "I am somewhat a jack-of-all-trades here," the priest explained as he brushed at the sawdust. "I will say that someone must have been praying for that young woman. How her gall bladder kept from rupturing, I just don't know. She is one lucky girl."

Rock stared at the man. "I guess I have never seen a priest who was also a surgeon *and* a carpenter."

Father Ravalli laughed. "I do what I can. Would you like to see Mrs. Braxton?"

Rock slowly nodded, still trying to process all the information that had just been shared with him.

The priest tapped on a closed door and opened it just a little. "Mrs. Braxton, your husband is here to see you."

Father Ravalli stepped aside as a startled Rock stared at the man. "I—I'm not…"

"Just go on in, Mr. Braxton. I haven't let your wife have any visitors, but I think a brief visit from you will be fine." The priest smiled again and opened the door for Rock to step through. He closed it behind him.

Rock's neck was red as he stuttered, "I didn't tell him that I was your—your husband. He just assumed that I was."

Clare laughed and Rock could only stare.

The woman whom he expected to find dead was very much alive. Her eyes were sparkling, and the dark circles that were under her eyes the day before had faded. Her first question was about Zeke.

"Did you bring Zeke with you? I want to see him. Is he okay? What a terrible burden I placed on my son."

Rock nodded and then pointed behind him toward the door. "I met Father Ravalli. Sounds like you were lucky."

Clare's face paled for a moment. "Very lucky. A priest who is also a surgeon *and* one who understands pharmaceuticals. Yes, if my gall bladder hadn't come out, I would have died. I was extremely lucky."

She paused and asked Rock pleadingly, "Please get Zeke for me. I know he has been so afraid."

Rock nodded. As he turned to leave, Clare called softly, "Thank you, Rock." She paused as color mounted in her face. "I know I shared more with you than you wanted to hear. I'm sorry. I just had to tell you in case I died."

Rock's face turned red, and he quickly stepped out the door. He shook his head and muttered under his breath as he rode the short distance back to Stevensville to find Zeke.

Rock left Red at the livery and walked across the street to the dry goods store. Maggie had both children with her at the counter and was buying them hard candy when Rock stepped through the door.

"Zeke! Your mother is asking for you. Let's go see her!"

The little boy dropped his candy and raced from the store. He jumped into the wagon and waited for Rock.

Maggie was puffing as she hurried toward the wagon towing an excited Annie.

"We are coming too! I didn't ride all this way in a wagon to miss seeing one of my favorite girls."

Rock drove the wagon the half mile back to the Mission. Zeke jumped down and raced inside without knocking. Rock lifted Maggie and Annie down. They all followed Zeke to the door. Rock was grinning as he once again tapped on the door.

When Father Ravalli answered, Rock's grin became larger. "Sorry, Padre. Clare's son didn't think his mother was going to live, so a happy little boy just rushed in here."

Father Ravalli laughed. "I'm glad I could help. I do like a happy outcome!" He opened the door and Rock stepped aside to allow Maggie to go in before he followed her to Clare's room.

Clare was sitting up in bed and Zeke was beside her. His eyes were sparkling with happiness, and Clare was smiling.

Annie wanted to climb on the bed too, but Rock held onto her. He wasn't sure how big Clare's incision was, but her surgery was a major one. He certainly didn't want Annie bouncing on her.

Maggie pressed Clare's hand to her lips. "When you are ready, we will bring you out to the ranch to recuperate. There is no need for you to be in Stevensville with no family around."

Clare's face paled slightly, and she looked over at Rock. He nodded and grinned.

"Zeke does have a horse out there, and I am certainly too big to ride it," he drawled.

They visited a while longer before Father Ravalli stepped in with a smile.

"Clare needs her rest, and I don't want her to pull on those stitches. You can bring Zeke back for a short visit before you leave town, but everyone needs to go."

Rock lifted Zeke off the bed and herded the two children out of the room in front of him. "Let's go eat some dinner, kids. We'll can stop back by after our wagon is loaded."

Zeke smiled shyly at Rock and the big man squeezed his shoulder as he smiled back. His heart twisted a little as he thought of the young boy leaving. He glanced over at Maggie, and she sniffed. She dug for her hankie and dabbed at her eyes.

Rock shooed the happy kids out the door, and they tumbled into the wagon, talking excitedly. Maggie was still dabbing her eyes as Rock drove towards the eating house.

"I'm so happy Clare is going to be all right. I was so worried."

Rock nodded but he didn't answer. *I wonder what Clare will do now. Surely, she won't go back to Helena. Maybe I'll see if Maggie can call in some favors. It would be nice to have the two of them closer.* His face blushed a little as he thought on that. *You are getting soft, Rock.*

They quickly found a table at the eating house, and Rock ordered milk for everyone. He lifted his glass.

"To happy endings, kids!" As his eyes met Maggie's, he added softly, "And to you too, Maggie, for always being here for us."

They were just ready to eat when Ike Clampant walked in.

"Mind if I join you? I heard the whole clan had come to town." He winked at Maggie as he talked.

Maggie beamed and everyone began to eat.

The little waitress flirted with Rock outrageously until Maggie started giggling. Annie was clueless but Zeke looked at Rock seriously.

"I think she'd like to go riding with you, Uncle Rock. She kind of acts like the fellows back home when they want Mama to ride with them."

Rock's neck turned a deep red, and Maggie laughed out loud.

"Why I believe you are right, Zeke! Should we help Uncle Rock out?"

Rock glared at Maggie as he hissed, "No, you will not! I'm sure she acts that way with all the single men who come in here. You will do nothing to encourage her."

Ike grinned. "Ya go ahead an' shovel that food down. I'll send the kids out when they finish. Maggie an' me cin take our time. We'll meet ya in the dry goods store when we're done."

Rock nodded and finished his meal quickly. He handed Maggie some money and stomped out of the eating house.

CHAPTER 33

Just Like a Real Family

CLARE WATCHED AS THE WAGON ROLLED TO A STOP outside her window. Rock pulled his hat off and wiped his forehead. He was scowling and muttering under his breath as he climbed down. At first, she was concerned. As the children jumped to the ground with smiles on their faces, she laughed.

"I think I know why Rock looks so grouchy."

Clare's first day back, she had watched the little waitress in the eating house flirt with all the men, "I'm guessing that is what has Rock so irritated.

"What a funny man. So big and so tough, yet so intimidated by women," she murmured. "I wonder why women bother him so? That and showing emotion to anyone but his family."

Her eyes rested tenderly on Zeke as the little boy reached up to take Rock's hand. The tall cowboy smiled down at him and squeezed it as they walked toward the Mission. Annie followed talking constantly, and Rock's smile became bigger.

He knocked on the door, and the two children raced back and forth as they waited for Father Ravalli.

Tears filled Clare's eyes. "What am I going to do? When I take Zeke back to Helena, he is going to be broken-hearted. He will have to leave the ranch, his pony, and Uncle Rock whom he adores.

"And that is what I prayed for. I had no idea it would be so hard to leave here when I came back."

Clare lifted the blanket and looked down at the bandage on her stomach. She was sore and stiff, but Father Ravalli was pleased with how her incision was healing. The priest had told her a few more days or even hours and her gall bladder could have ruptured. She whispered a prayer of thanksgiving and then asked for the strength to leave when it was time.

"Suzanna," she whispered, "I wish you could have stayed. Your man misses you terribly, and your little girl looks just like you."

Clare smiled as she thought about her conversations with Suzanna about Rock. She even told Clare about their first kiss.

"He was so shy and yet so completely honest," Suzanna had shared. "I have never seen a man hide his feelings so completely and then totally expose them when you least expect it. I have had lots of boys and men too try to court me, but none of them affected me like that quiet cowboy. I have fallen in love, Clare!" Clare smiled as she remembered Suzanna's face.

"Yes, you loved him, Suzanna. You saw his heart, and you loved what you saw."

Clare turned away from the window and winced as she tried to roll on her side. Her heart squeezed tightly in her chest.

"Oh, to have that kind of love." She took a deep breath and forced herself to relax.

"The Macks were the first to show me love. Thank heavens I met them. Rebecca taught me to read and write. She showed me how to be a lady, and that to be a woman was a wonderful thing. She also showed me how to be honest and loving.

"Father John showed me that men could be good and decent. I had never been around men like him before. And they both showed me love. I was just learning to trust when they died."

Clare put her fingers around the little cross she wore.

"Lord, thank you for putting those good people in my life. Please help me to find love." She paused and added softly, "If that is not to be, please help me to be strong and happy for Zeke."

Clare grimaced as she tried to pull herself up. Father Ravalli wanted her to get up and move around, but the incision pulled. Moving was painful.

She asked him if she would be able to have more children.

He nodded slowly.

"You should be fine, but I would recommend that you have a doctor present. Hopefully, there won't be any scar tissue on the inside. If there is, it could attach to something it shouldn't."

That frightened Clare. Doctors weren't always available in her area. Then she laughed.

"What are you worrying about, Clare? You were just crying because you had no one to love you!"

Clare could hear the children's voices coming down the hall. Rock knocked on the door. He leaned against the doorjamb, holding Annie's hand. Zeke rushed to Clare and threw his arms around her neck.

"Mama, can we live with Uncle Rock when you get well? I like his ranch, and Annie is fun to play with." He whispered loudly in her ear, "And then you can go riding with Uncle Rock every day!"

Clare blushed deeply and Rock ducked his head. He dug the toe of his boot into the floor as the red crept up his neck. Finally, he looked up and grinned.

"Why sure. We can all go riding. You can show your mother where Patches tried to kill that bear!"

When Clare looked up with alarm, Zeke began to excitedly tell her all about their trip to buy Patches and how brave he was. He told her how Uncle Rock had saved all of them.

He looked back at Rock, "But I don't know what happened to the hide. Uncle Rock went to get it, but he didn't bring it home."

Rock's eyes twinkled and he nodded.

"Well, some other folks needed it more, so I just let them have it. Besides, when Patches scares out another bear, we'll take his hide!"

Zeke nodded excitedly and launched into another story.

Rock laughed and stepped toward the bed. "Time to tell your mother goodbye, Zeke. She needs her rest. Ike is going to bring her out when she is strong enough to travel."

Zeke kissed his mother and slid off the bed. Clare looked up at Rock with a smile.

"Thank you so much, Rock. You have no idea the load you have lifted from me by taking in Zeke."

Rock tousled Zeke's hair. "I like having Zeke around. We needed another man in the house," he drawled, and Zeke grinned at him. He took the little boy's hand and led him out the door. As they passed by the window, Rock lifted him up so he could wave goodbye to his mother.

Clare watched them walk away. Zeke was holding Rock's hand as he chattered, and the big man was smiling down at him.

Annie rushed up behind them and grabbed Zeke's other hand. The three of them walked to the loaded wagon, and Rock lifted the children in. As the little family headed back toward the dry goods store, Rock pointed toward the window by Clare's bed. He turned the wagon to drive by as closely as possible, and all of them waved to Clare.

Clare waved back. She put her hand over her heart as she smiled.

"Just like a real family. Oh, my heart."

CHAPTER 34

SWEET MEMORIES

T HE NEXT FEW WEEKS WERE BUSY ONES ON ROCK'S Slash B Ranch. The help for the fall gather began to arrive. The sorting and branding meant long days and hard work, but Rock loved every moment. As he looked at the cattle with his Slash B brand, he felt a swell of pride.

He thought about his first trip to Helena to buy cattle. He had taken four bags of gold to the bank there and deposited them. When the teller weighed the bags and gave him a total, he stared at the number. $50,828.28. Rock had never seen that much money in his life. He kept his face blank as he walked to the hotel where the cattle buyer he had been corresponding with was staying.

Rock smiled as he thought about Suzanna's reaction to the gold. He had told her about it at the Ladies' Choice Dance. She was shocked that he wanted to share it with her.

Rock held her hand as he told her how he had come to have it. "Old Darby thought a lot of you, and I'm sure he would want this."

Suzanna stared at him for a moment. Then she smiled and stated, "You spend my share on your ranch and on cattle too. We can be partners."

Rock's heart sang when she smiled at him. Then she led him onto the dance floor. He had never danced much but found that he enjoyed dancing with Suzanna. She had him swinging her all around the dance floor by the time the dance was over. He wasn't always in rhythm with the music, but they both had a good time.

As he walked her home that night, he commented shyly, "I guess you will need to come out from time to time to check on your cattle."

Suzanna looked up at him and laughed. Then she stopped and turned Rock toward her. "Or?"

Rock's face turned a deep red as he looked down at her and then over her shoulder.

"Or what, Rock?" she asked again softly.

Rock remembered looking down at Suzanna. He could still feel how his heart beat wildly that night. Suddenly, all his shyness faded away. He knew then that he wanted this woman beside him forever. "Or we could just get married!"

Suzanna smiled and pulled his face down to hers. "Yes, Rock. Oh, yes."

Rock remembered how he felt when he scooped her up and swung her around.

He was laughing when he saw Maggie watching from her window. She smiled at them. She told Rock later she knew at that moment that Suzanna would be leaving her. However, looking at her niece's face, she could only feel joy for the happy young woman.

Rock remembered setting Suzanna down. His heart squeezed as he thought of that night. He had been almost giddy, and his smile had nearly split his face.

As they continued to the door of Maggie's small quarters behind her store, both were quiet.

When they reached the back door, Rock bent to kiss Suzanna, and that time, it was a long one. When he pulled her close, both of their hearts were beating loudly.

"We probably should make this wedding soon," he had whispered thickly.

Suzanna agreed, and the two of them went inside to tell Aunt Maggie.

Rock could still taste that kiss. He didn't realize he had stopped his horse. He was broken from his reverie by a cow charging toward him. Red snorted, and the rider to his left shouted. He cut quickly and turned the cow back into the herd.

The rider gave Rock a funny look and the gather continued.

"Sure looked like the boss was in another world for a time there," the rider muttered. "Folks shouldn't daydream when we have cattle to work, and Rock is *never* caught off guard."

John Dackenberry, or Dack as he was known, looked over at Rock again. The cowman was once again his intense self, and Dack shrugged. *Guess he's all right. Maybe somethin' is goin' on at home.*

"Better Look At Your Hole Card"

COOKIE CLANGED THE DINNER BELL AND THE RIDERS gathered around the chuck wagon to eat. The bantering was loud and often obnoxious.

Dack looked over at Rock and grinned. "I thought for a time there that you was thinkin' about that blue-eyed gal who showed up in town several weeks ago."

As Rock turned red, the men began to laugh. Some didn't know there was a new woman around, but Dack seemed to have lots of information.

"She's a looker alright. I hear she's a widow woman. Been stayin' at the Mission for a time, but she is up and around now. Word it she is headed out to some ranch to recuperate." As Dack spoke, he rolled his eyes over at Rock and the men laughed.

Rock snorted. "Alright, you darn snoops. She was Suzanna's best friend, and she lived with Maggie for a time about five years ago." He grinned at the cowboys and added, "But don't get too attached 'cause I don't think she is staying around. At least she hasn't told me she is."

The men were quiet for a moment. The arguing soon began as to who might be able to change her mind.

Rock grinned again and helped himself to more food. He moved over to talk to Chas Boswell. The two men discussed the condition of the cattle and the grass.

"You could run more cattle on your grass, Rock. You have the quality there."

Rock nodded. "Maybe, but I want to increase my herd by crossing cattle breeds. I brought in fifteen hundred head of bred Herefords this past summer. I know what the calves will look like, and I'm looking forward to that calf crop.

"The calves from those Angus bulls I brought in several years ago look like they fared the winter better than the straight longhorns. Plus, some of the heifers are now big enough to breed. Those Angus-cross calves gained better than the straight longhorns too. I guess that makes sense since the longhorns are a southern breed, and the Angus cattle originally came from England."

Rock took another bite of food and chewed before he added, "I'm going to bring in more Angus bulls and gradually cull my longhorn bulls. I have even thought of heading down to Cheyenne in Wyoming Territory to buy some mama cows. There is a fellow there who is selling pure and crossbred Angus cows. His seed stock came out of Kansas."

Boswell nodded. He liked Rock. The young man was a forward thinker, and he didn't waste time chitchatting.

"Say, did the little fellow's mama pull through? I never did hear."

Rock nodded. "She sure did. She should be at the ranch by the time we finish here. She is going to stay with us for a while until she is strong enough to travel. She and Maggie are pretty close."

Boswell grinned at Rock. "Maybe you should just marry her. Maggie won't stay out there forever, and you are going to need some help with Annie."

Surprise showed in Rock's eyes as he stared at the man. He honestly hadn't thought of Maggie ever leaving.

Boswell grinned bigger. "Old Ike Clampant is sweet on Maggie. He has been pestering her to move back to Stevensville and marry him ever since she moved in with you. I think he is softening her up, so you might want to check your hole card again."

Rock almost had to pull his mouth shut. "I sure didn't know that," he commented as the remnants of surprise remained on his face.

Boswell laughed again and clapped the younger man on his back. "I didn't think so. You don't seem to see much except what is right in front of your eyes…and not even all that unless it involves cattle or grass."

Rock grinned at the man. "That's true." Still, he was worried. *What will I do if Maggie wants to leave? And it sure isn't fair to keep her with us if she wants to get on with her life.* Rock shook his head and scowled. Change just plain irritated him.

As the men tossed out their coffee grounds and mounted up, he pushed the situation to the back of his mind. *I don't have time to ponder on it now. I will talk to Maggie when I get back home.*

Rock kept his tally book busy as they finished the branding. He was pleased with his calf crop and the condition of the cattle.

"Darby, you sure set me up with a nice ranch. Good grass, winter graze, and plenty of water. I wish you were still around to enjoy all this with me," he muttered to himself.

Rock had donated money to St. Mary's Mission anonymously, and the Jesuits were building onto their facilities. Father Ravalli was surprised when the bank draft for $500 arrived. The note said it was from a friend, but no one seemed to know who. The bank draft was from a bank in Cheyenne, and it caused quite a bit of speculation. Only a few people in town had connections to anyone in Cheyenne, and none of them knew a thing about it.

Rock didn't go to church and seemed to have little to do with the Mission. No one even considered him.

The young rancher stayed in contact with Badger McCune, and the ornery old fellow was more than happy to help him out with the bank drafts. Rock had Ike post the letters for him, so no one in Stevensville even saw Rock mail a letter. Rock chuckled as he thought about some of the stories Badger included in his letters.

Rock hadn't even met the priest when he sent his first donation. He just liked what he had heard about all the good coming out of the Mission. He wanted to donate some money and thought the Mission would be a good fit.

Father Ravalli was delighted as it meant he could add some new medical equipment as well as expand his small cow herd.

Rock didn't know where or what money he would donate this year. *Maybe I will donate it to Stevensville for a school. Of course, if I do that, the city fathers will need to hire a teacher. If she is young and pretty, she will rile up all the young men, and a replacement will be needed right away!* He grinned. *That will be their problem, not mine.* He paused and shook his head. *Naw, I think I'll donate it to the Mission again. Those priests do a lot of good work with the Indians and with other folks around here too. I have never heard of them saying no to any request for help. Besides, we owe Father Ravalli for Clare's surgery.*

CHAPTER 36

Big Changes

ROCK WAS TIRED AS HE RODE BACK HOME. HE HAD talked to Dack and two other riders about hiring on. They were going to start on Monday. He needed to build a bunkhouse, and they would help him do that if it wasn't finished by the time they arrived. They agreed to sleep in the barn until it was completed, but he wanted to get started on it right away.

He spotted Ike's buggy in the yard as he rode up. He looked around but he didn't see Annie or Zeke anywhere. Rock took Red to the barn and rubbed him down. As he turned him into the small pasture behind the barn, Annie raced out of the house.

"Papa! I missed you!"

Rock picked her up and swung her around as she squealed. As he set her down, Zeke peeked around the corner and Rock grabbed him. He tickled both children until they could hardly breathe. He set them on their feet, and each grabbed a hand as he walked to the house.

"Papa, Clare is here. She is going to stay with us for a while!"

Rock feigned surprise as he answered. "She is? Does that mean that Zeke will be staying longer too?"

Both children nodded excitedly.

As Rock looked up laughing, he saw Clare standing in the doorway smiling at them.

Where Suzanna had been short with lots of curves, Clare was tall and slender. She still had plenty of curves though, and Rock noticed they were all in the right places.

Clare stepped out onto the small stoop. "Hello, Rock. I see the greeting party found you!"

Rock laughed. "They sure did. It would be mighty lonely around here without greetings like that."

The two little ones moved from Rock to swarm Clare, and they pushed her back into the house.

Rock glanced at Maggie as he walked in. She was blushing, and Ike had an ornery smile on his face. He casually walked back across the floor and sat down at the table. Maggie was obviously flustered, and Rock laughed out loud as he looked from one to the other.

"I see I have missed a few things over the last what, four years?"

Maggie's face turned a darker red and she began muttering in Gaelic while Ike grinned and winked at her.

"Sure now, I am tryin' to talk Maggie Mae into comin' back to Stevensville with me. Looks like ya might be able to find someone to do part of what she does 'round here so mebbie she cin take some time off."

Both children stared and tried to figure out what was going on while Rock and Clare joined Maggie in turning a dark red.

Ike laughed out loud. "Here, Maggie, let me help ya lift that big pot 'fore ya drop it. My, my, I ain't never seen my Maggie so flustered."

Rock shook his head. He decided to wash up at the horse tank and Clare followed him outside.

"Did you know anything about Maggie and Ike?"

He shook his head. "No, Chas Boswell filled me in during roundup. I must be blind to live with a woman for over four years and not have a clue that she is in love."

Clare laughed out loud and cocked an eyebrow. "Ya think?"

Rock grinned at her. "I suppose you had it all figured out the first day you hit town."

Clare shrugged. "I was suspicious. Ike told me on our trip out here that he was going to ask Maggie to marry him today."

Rock looked up with shock on his face. "He asked today? Why, she could be leaving any time!"

Clare laughed as she nodded. "Yes, she could. I would offer to help, but it wouldn't look good to have a single woman living in your house unsupervised."

Rock frowned. "Surely Maggie will give me a little time to find someone." He shook his head and almost cursed. "I have no idea where to look." He added softly, "Annie will be lost without her."

Clare said nothing and it wasn't long before Maggie called them in for dinner.

CHAPTER 37

FROM THE MOUTHS OF CHILDREN

AS ANNIE FOLDED HER HANDS, ROCK DUCKED HIS head. He knew what the prayer would be. However, it was a little more specific than he expected.

"Dear Jesus, thank you for the food and for our family and for Zeke and for Ike and for Clare. Thank you for bringing Papa home safe and please bring me a new mama as nice as Clare."

Zeke added, "And please let Uncle Rock be my papa."

Clare and Rock were both quiet. Clare's face was strained as she smiled at the children. Rock showed no emotion, but his neck became redder.

Maggie cleared her throat and asked Rock how the gathering had gone.

He shared how the crossbred cattle had fared and how pleased he was with their condition. "I am going to add more black bulls and try to bring in some mama cows. I was impressed with the amount of beef still on those yearlings after a long winter. They were in better condition than the longhorns." They talked a little more about cattle, and then Rock began to eat.

Maggie and Clare talked and laughed throughout the meal, but Rock was quiet. Ike didn't talk much either. He didn't like to chit chat.

Rock finally asked, "How long will you be staying, Clare? Did the padre tell you how long before you can travel long distances?"

Clare shook her head. "Father Ravalli told me not to lift anything over ten pounds for two weeks. After that, I am to limit what I pick up. Otherwise, I can do whatever doesn't hurt." She paused and looked at Maggie. "As for staying, I guess that will depend on Maggie."

Annie looked up and frowned. "Don't you want Clare to stay, Auntie? She can sleep with me—I want her to stay."

Maggie smiled at Annie and patted her hand. "Of course I want Clare to stay. I love her every bit as much as I love you. Why, she is like one of my children too!"

Annie beamed and the children finished their meal quickly.

As they rushed toward the kitchen door, Rock hollered, "You both take care of the chickens and see if any of those heifers calved. Stay outside the fence. Check the horses too. Make sure the fence is up all the way around their pasture." The children agreed in unison and rushed out the door.

Rock looked around the table. "I think we have some things to discuss."

Maggie rose and began to stack dishes. Her muttering was once again in Gaelic, and her face was red. Ike pulled her down beside him and kept his hand on her arm.

"I asked Maggie to marry me today. I been tryin' to court her fer four years an' she kept puttin' me off. She finally said yes today. We ain't set a date yet, but we is lookin' at this fall, mebbie even yet this month."

Maggie turned to Rock as tears filled her eyes. "Oh, Rock. I am sorry to spring this on you. I just don't know what to do. I do want to marry Ike, but I can hardly stand to leave Annie. I so want you both to be happy."

Tears were leaking from Maggie's eyes, and Rock smiled at her. He rose and came around the table to lift her up.

"Maggie, you have given us four years of your life—four very important years for both Annie and me. I can't ask you to put your life on hold any longer. You will always be an important part of Annie's life, but you go ahead and make your plans."

He hugged her and added softly, "You will be hard to replace, but we will figure it out."

Maggie began to cry, and Ike put his arm around her shoulders. He offered her his bandana.

"Mebbie you'ins cin clean up tonight. I'd like to take my future bride fer a walk. 'Course, we'll invite the youngsters to come with us so's ya cin have some time to talk yur own selves."

As Ike led the sniffling Maggie out of the door, Annie came racing up.

"Auntie Maggie, why are you crying? Are you sad? Papa said that ladies cry sometimes when they are happy. Are you happy? I don't cry when I'm happy, but I sure do cry when I'm sad."

Maggie patted her shoulder.

"Annie, I am a little bit of both. Why don't you and Zeke come on a walk with us? You can show Ike where you find the best nightcrawlers. He loves to fish, but he just can't find any worms in town."

Zeke and Annie both began to talk at the same time as they raced toward the creek in front of the two older people.

"This way, Auntie Mag," shouted Zeke. "The fattest ones are on this side, and the longest ones are over there!" he exclaimed as he pointed toward the small creek that ran through the horse pasture.

CHAPTER 38

"Maybe I Should Court You"

CLARE WAS ALREADY STACKING THE DISHES, AND ROCK began to scrape the plates.

He finally looked at the woman beside him and grinned.

"You know, an easy solution to all this would be to just get married. Then both kids would get their prayers answered. I would have someone to watch Annie too. You could even cook and clean for me."

Rock chuckled as Clare's neck began to turn red and he added with a grin, "I'm just not sure what you would get out of that deal though."

Clare was quiet. She didn't respond as she carried the dishes to the wash area. Rock touched her shoulder to turn her around, and her body was tense when she looked up at him.

"If I thought you meant that, I would say yes in a minute. I know you are just teasing though. What I want is a home for Zeke, and yes, I would love to be Annie's mommy. But I want love too, Rock. I don't want a one-sided relationship."

She took a deep breath as she looked up. "If you ask me for love, Rock, I will say yes—but only for love."

Rock wrapped his arms around Clare as she softly cried. Finally, she wiped her eyes on her apron and looked up at him.

She whispered, "I'm not sure coming here to recuperate was a good idea. The kids are going to be broken-hearted when Zeke and I leave."

The pure honesty in Clare's eyes pulled at Rock's heart. He had kept it locked away for so long that he surprised himself when he took her in his arms and kissed her.

Clare started to push him away, but he pulled her tighter and kissed her again.

"Yep, the second one tasted just as good as the first one did," he drawled softly as he grinned down at her.

Emotion stormed through Clare's eyes. She slowly lifted her arms and wrapped them around Rock's neck. The third kiss was longer, and they were both a little breathless when Clare pulled back.

Rock's green eyes were sparkling as he suggested, "Maybe I should court you for a few weeks and see where this goes. It is looking fun so far."

Clare pulled back and looked up at him. "And maybe I will just play hard to get. I would like to see you work a little to win a woman over. Most of them seem to drop at your feet," she commented dryly.

Rock pulled her in for another kiss and she didn't protest.

He laughed as he released her. "You didn't start off so tough though. Maybe you need a little more practice in that area." He frowned as he added, "But I hope it's not on me!"

Clare studied his face for a moment before she laughed out loud.

"All right, you can court me. I expect it to be more than chasing me around the wash basin after supper though. I want to see your ranch. I want you to share your dreams and your plans with me." She added softly, "I want to see your heart, Rock."

Rock chuckled. "Deal. And to show you I mean it, I will even wash the dishes."

When Maggie and Ike returned, the kitchen was clean. Rock and Clare were sitting on the porch steps. Rock was talking about his ranch and Clare was listening. Her arms were wrapped around her knees, and she was watching him with a smile on her face. He put his arm in front of her as the kids came charging up.

"No jumping on Clare until she is healed up, remember? We talked about that. The doctor had to cut her stomach open and take out what wasn't working. Then he sewed her up like I do the horses when they get hurt. Now let's get faces washed and teeth brushed so you both get some sleep tonight."

Rock looked at the grinning Ike. "And you can just work for your keep, Ike. I'm starting on a bunkhouse in the morning, and I could use some help getting the forms laid for the foundation. I would like to lay some rock up around the bottom too.

"Do you want to stay over and help? You will have to sleep in the barn because you aren't sleeping with me."

Rock had converted one of the stalls in the barn to a little room and set up some bunks to get ready for the hands. It was rustic, but it was cozy.

Ike looked at Maggie and winked. She promptly blushed and he laughed. "I reckon that would be all right. I do need to put my hoss up though, an' I'd like to pull the buggy into yore barn if ya don't mind."

After the men left, Maggie hugged Clare.

"Now that face looks happier than it's been in some time. Were Rock and you able to talk some things over?" she asked with a smile.

Clare blushed lightly as she replied, "We did talk a little. We are going to try courting and see how that goes."

Maggie wrapped Clare up in her arms. "That man should have married you a long time ago," she whispered, "but I guess he had to do things on his own time. Good thing I'm getting married or he might have put it off for another ten years!"

Rock had added a second bed on top of Annie's, and that was where Zeke slept. He loved his new "high bed" as he called it.

"Look, Mama, I'm so high that I can see out of the top window!"

Clare had the children say their prayers. They were whispering as the women left.

"I ain't tired yet. Are you tired, Zeke?"

"Annie, don't say ain't. It's not a real word. It is a pretend word, and smart folks shouldn't use it. That's what my mama says. She said her pappy used it all the time, and that he wasn't a very smart man." He paused and whispered louder, "Mama said he cursed a lot too, but she won't let me curse. Sometimes I try to sneak one in, but Mama switches my bottom when I use bad words."

Both were quiet for a time when Annie whispered, "I had better tell my papa not to say ain't. Sometimes he does, but he is a real smart papa. I sure don't want folks to think he's not."

When the men came in, Maggie and Clare were sitting at the table. Maggie was embroidering another shirt for Annie, and Clare was darning a hole closed in one of Rock's socks.

He stared at her in surprise. "You can fix a sock? I didn't know socks could be fixed."

Clare looked up at him and answered dryly, "You should be more impressed with Maggie's embroidery—it takes way more skill."

Rock grinned at the two women and pulled off his boots.

As he rubbed his tired feet and toes, he commented, "Now if only one of you would rub my feet!"

Maggie threw the kitchen rag at him. "If only you would wash your stinky feet maybe they would get rubbed once!"

Rock grinned at her as he agreed.

Ike removed one of his boots quietly. He smelled it and quickly put the boot back on. Rock laughed.

"You had better put that boot on, Ike. Your feet make mine smell like flowers."

Rock washed up. He threw the water outside and rubbed baking soda on his teeth. He rinsed them and bid the women good night as he headed for bed.

He could hear them talking softly as he drifted off to sleep. *Women sure talk a lot and about all kinds of things.*

CHAPTER 39

BEAR SIGN

CLARE HAD OFFERED TO HELP MAGGIE MAKE BEAR sign after everyone went to bed. Even though both women were tired this morning, it was worth it to see all the happy faces as their little family bit into the soft doughnuts at breakfast.

It had been a long time since Maggie had anyone help her around the house. Having a helpful young woman around every day was a pleasant change.

Ike grinned at Maggie around his bear sign. "How 'bout ya go down to St. Mary's with me this mornin', Maggie Mae? I'd like to talk to Father Ravalli 'bout our weddin'."

Maggie studied Ike's face, and he winked at her.

She laughed as she nodded her head even though she didn't think a conversation with the priest was necessary. Her husband had died, and Ike had never married. There was really nothing to question in their marriage. Still, if it was important to Ike, she would go to make him happy.

"I will pack us a little picnic lunch, and you can find a pretty spot for us to eat. We had better leave soon though as we will have a good two hours or more each way." Maggie began to quickly gather the morning dishes and rushed to the sideboard to wash them.

Rock was grinning. He was quite sure that Ike had something in mind. Ike wasn't saying, and he wouldn't look at Rock. Rock thought about asking them to pick up some lumber, but he decided not to slow down Ike's party. *Maybe they could drop off an order though.*

"Ike, would you mind dropping this order off at the mill? Dack is helping out there for a few days before he heads up here. He can bring the lumber with him when he comes."

Ike nodded his head. "I cin take the wagon down—"

Rock interrupted him, "No, you just go on down and do what you need to do in the buggy. It will be more comfortable. I need to quarry some stones out of a sidehill to build the base for the bunkhouse. I have some pulled out but not enough. When I'm finished, I'll need the wagon and team to haul that rock back up here."

Maggie quickly began to prepare a meal to take with them. Ike grinned when she added a large package of bear sign. He rubbed his stomach.

"The first thing I fell in love with was my Maggie's cookin'. That an' the way ol' Paddy always smiled. I figgered if a feller could smile like that after pertineer forty years a marriage, then I needed to get me a woman like that."

Ike was teasing, but his eyes were tender as he looked at Maggie. She laughed and shook her head.

Rock helped Ike hitch the buggy before he hitched his mules to the wagon. Ike and Maggie waved as they headed down the little lane.

Rock turned to Clare. "I should be back around noon," he stated hesitantly.

Clare laughed. "I will be glad to keep an eye on Annie, and I will have dinner ready."

Rock nodded and pointed at the shotgun in the corner. "I have seen a lot of Indian sign—lots of different tracks. I think it would be a good idea to keep that close to you. And maybe have the kids play closer to the house today."

Clare's face paled as she studied Rock. She picked up the shotgun and stood it next to the washtub. "We are going to work a little on numbers today so I may keep them in the house for a while anyway."

Annie looked up with horror on her face. "Stay in the house? I have chores to do, and I don't want to look at any old numbers."

Clare laughed down at her. "Annie, I know you love bear sign. See all those little balls that we cut out of the centers of the bear sign? I thought maybe you would help me count them so we know how many you and Zeke can have. How many do you think there are?"

Annie's face lit up.

"Come on, Zeke! Let's get our chores done so we can count bear balls!"

CHAPTER 40

FIRE WOMAN

IKE WAS QUIET AS THEY DROVE DOWN THE ROUGH road. Maggie knew he had something on his mind, so she waited for him to talk. Before long, he pulled up the horse and turned to look at her.

"Maggie, when ol' Darby first come to this country, I grubstaked 'im. We was 'bout the same age. I had me a ridin' job an' had come in on a Saturday night fer a drink. There he was at the bar. New feller in town, no money, no mule, no nothin' 'cept that ornery grin. I bought 'im a drink, an' we talked pertineer all night.

"He knew his minin' business like nobody I'd ever talked to. We decided that we'd file on a couple of little pieces. We put one in my name an' one in his brother's name, but they both was his.

"He pecked 'round up in these here hills all his life. He found jist enough to pay me back an' buy his place out there. He always give me a share like we agreed. I wasn't sure I wanted to settle down, so I jist banked mine.

"Then, 'bout ten years ago, Darby hit the mother lode. He took me up there to see it." Ike shook his head. "I never seen so many gold veins in my life. Darby were a wealthy man, an' he'd barely touched what was back in there.

"He started takin' a little out an' stashin' it in different places. Then those bushwhackers killed 'im." Ike frowned and Maggie patted his arm.

"Ya know how Rock helped 'im. Well, Rock found those old deeds, an' he stopped in to see me."

He looked at Maggie with pure amazement on his face. "He give me the deed to Darby's mine what had my name on it. He said no one man should keep all he was given, 'specially what he didn't work for."

Maggie covered her mouth as she stared at him.

"Oh, Ike. I always knew my Suzanna picked a good man, but I had no idea he had given Darby's mine away."

Ike nodded. "He didn't want nothin' fer it but as I take outa it, I give to Rock like Darby give to me. 'Course, that other piece he filed on didn't produce nothin'." He smiled at the woman next to him.

"Funny how those little things cin come back to ya. I sure didn't think Darby'd find gold, but we was friends, an' minin' was his love." He rubbed his face and added roughly, "I sure miss that ol' feller."

He started the horses down the road before he added softly, "Rock had 'im a hard time lettin' go of the fact that Clare were part of Darby's killin'. I told 'im from the get-go that she were jist an abused kid, but in Rock's world, thirteen be growed enough to know right from wrong. Heck, Rock were on his own at fourteen, an' he jist couldn't quite forgive 'er."

Maggie squeezed Ike's arm. She looked off in the distance before she answered quietly, "I told Rock he should have married Clare long ago. She is a fine woman. My Suzanna was too, but she is not coming back." Maggie wiped her eyes, and a soft smile crossed her face.

"I do believe Rock is letting Clare get just a little closer. I hope they marry. It would be so much easier for my little Annie." A sob caught in Maggie's throat. "I am going to miss her so."

"Now, now, Maggie Mae. We cin come out ever' week to visit if ya want. My ol' Pete pertineer knows the way by hisself now, an' we cin make this here trip as often as ya like." He patted her arm as he grinned at her and added, "'Sides, one a these days, those kids is a goin' to have to go to school an' they'll need someplace to stay durin' the week."

Maggie's face lit up as she smiled and squeezed Ike's arm. The smile slowly froze on her face.

Painted Indians crowded in front of their buggy and pushed up against the sides. Ike cursed slowly under his breath. He started to reach for his rifle, but Maggie held his arm. She stood up in the buggy and began to speak in Siksilka, the language of the Blackfeet.

"Good morning to my friends, the Blackfeet. Fire Woman greets you along with her man, Old Grandfather."

Maggie looked each brave in the eye and began to name them. "Poundmaker, Great Elk, Stone Face, Running Horse—what are my friends doing here in war paint, so close to where I live with White Eagle and his children?"

The young warriors stared at her, unsure of what to do. One she hadn't seen rode out of the brush and pushed close to her side of the buggy. "Old Grandmother has a different man. All Smiles is no longer by your side?"

Maggie shook her head. "All Smiles was my man for over thirty summers before he went to sleep. Now, Old Grandfather is my man."

The young warrior stared at Ike. "I don't think I like this man. Maybe I will kill him and take his scalp. Fire Woman can find another old grandfather to be her man."

The young warrior held his spear near Ike's chest. The old man just stared at him. Maggie slapped the spear away.

"You should remember your manners around old ones. Old Grandfather is a great warrior. You ask your grandfather, Big Bear."

The young warrior stared at the old woman with hair the color of fire. He had always been a little afraid of her when he visited the trading post. Now she knew who he was. He tried to stare her down, but the old woman just smiled.

Maggie turned her eyes from the young man and smiled at the rest of the warriors. "I have a gift for my young friends, the future of the Blackfeet people."

She handed the young warrior beside the wagon the bag of bear sign.

"A gift from the old grandmother, Fire Woman. We live in peace here. Old Grandfather, White Eagle, two little ones, and White Eagle's woman. Our friends, the Blackfeet, are always welcome at our table."

She sat down, and Ike clucked to Pete.

The young warriors parted to let the buggy through. Some grinned at Maggie as the buggy passed.

Poundmaker watched them closely. His horse was to the side, so he didn't need to move. Still, he knew this woman. She was correct. Old Grandfather *was* a great warrior. He had heard Chief Crowfoot and Mountain Chief discuss him around their fires at night. They also talked about White Eagle.

The old woman showed no fear, and among his people, warrior women were listened to. Poundmaker's face remained stoic, but he lifted his spear slightly as they went by. Ike's slight nod was only visible to the young warrior.

When they were about a mile down the road, Ike looked over at Maggie. "Fire Woman, huh? I think they know you!" He grinned as he squeezed his future wife.

CHAPTER 41

"We Must Be Grateful"

CLARE WAS JUST FINISHING MORE BEAR SIGN WHEN the door burst open. Indians filled the room so quickly that she didn't have time to grab her shotgun. Two were carrying Annie and Zeke. The braves held their hands tightly over the children's mouths. Both were frightened, but Annie was trying to bite the warrior who held her. She kicked hard to get loose.

Clare lunged for the shotgun, but a brave grabbed her.

She pointed at the children as she glared at the warriors. "You put them down immediately. I won't have this behavior in my house."

The warriors looked toward the brave who was closest to Clare. He nodded. As the warriors dropped them, Annie kicked the man who had held her.

"You mean man! You hurt my arm!" She tried to kick him again, but he jumped back quickly. Several of the braves snickered, and the warrior glared at them.

The brave who appeared to be in charge stepped forward and pointed at his chest. "I am Little Bear. White Eagle is my brother. We come to take you away. Our people, the Crow, are at war with the Blackfeet, and the fight between us will cross this place. Some will die. White Eagle's family is my family. You come with us. We protect you."

Clare looked around at the warriors. They were all covered with warpaint and looked terrifying. One warrior stepped forward. He looked at her insolently and reached down to take a handful of doughnuts.

Clare slapped his hand. She lifted one finger.

"One. You may take one."

She put the bear sign in a bowl as she looked around the room. "One," she repeated.

Annie stepped forward and took the bowl. She walked around the room and stopped in front of each warrior. She repeated, "One."

The warriors grinned at the small girl and somberly took one. Some laughed and poked each other.

When the bowl had gone around one time, Clare handed Zeke and Annie each one. She ate the last one herself.

Little Bear laughed out loud. "We call you Bear Woman. Come."

Clare paused. "I need to leave a note for Rock so he knows where we are."

Little Bear shook his head. "He will know. Come."

Three horses were saddled and standing in front of the house. A warrior held the lead ropes to Red and Georgia. Gomer wouldn't let anyone get close to him, and a brave drew back his bow to shoot the little donkey.

Annie jerked on his arm as she screamed, "Don't shoot Gomer! He's my friend. He will follow us—just leave him alone!"

The brave looked down at the small girl.

She stood with her fists clenched and was glaring at him out of bright blue eyes. Her dark hair hung down in two small braids.

He shrugged and pointed his arrow once more at Gomer. Annie kicked him and the arrow went astray. The little donkey kicked up his heels and farted loudly as he dashed over the hill.

The braves began to laugh. The warrior whom Annie had kicked glared at her. He muttered something under his breath and mounted his pony.

The Indians led the little family deep into the Sapphire Mountains.

Clare had no idea where she was. In addition, she was terrified that Rock would not be able to find them. Still, she did her best to be brave for the children. The Indians rode in silence, so she kept the children quiet as well.

They finally arrived at a large cave. The braves signaled for Clare to get down. She slid off the horse, and the children followed her into the cave.

The cave showed the blackness of both old and new fires. It had obviously been used as a stopping point many times. Little Bear pointed at a pot in the center and then at the supplies they had taken from Rock's house.

"Cook. You feed." He waved his arm around the room of silent warriors. Clare had never cooked for Indians let alone for so many. She tried to keep her face still and began to dig in the packs.

The Indians had cleaned out their food larder. At first Clare was angry. Then she realized that had they not taken it, it would probably have been stolen or destroyed.

Georgia suddenly threw her head up and looked down the trail. She tugged at her rope with her teeth and was able to pull the slipknot loose. She raced out of the cave and down the trail. Several braves tried to stop her, but she dodged them and continued to run.

It wasn't long before Rock appeared riding Old Jake. His feet were nearly dragging on the ground, and neither he nor the mule looked pleased with the situation. Sally, the second mule, along with Georgia and Gomer, trailed behind him.

Rock quickly took stock. When he saw that Clare and the two children were present and unhurt, he grinned and walked off the mule.

Little Bear was laughing, and Rock laughed with him.

"And that is why I ride Red," he stated seriously.

Zeke and Annie swarmed Rock as he came into the cave, and he squeezed Clare's shoulder. She was so relieved to see him that she almost started crying.

Rock smiled at her. "Little Bear is helping us. He is treating us as his family. We must be grateful," he told her softly as he patted her back.

"He wants me to prepare a meal. I have no idea how to cook for this many Indians or even what to fix!" she whispered.

Rock laughed and went back outside. He untied a small deer from Sally's back and began to cut it up. The chunks of meat went into a large pot. Clare added some water.

She had expected him to rinse the meat off but realized that was neither a concern nor an option. She watched Rock for a moment and then began to mix up some biscuits. That she knew she could do.

Several times when she raised her eyes, she saw the insolent brave watching her. *He gives me chills. His eyes follow everything I do.*

Once Rock left the cave, the brave moved closer to her. He tried to touch her hair, and Clare smacked his hand with her spoon.

She shaped the biscuits as calmly as possible even though inside she was shaking. Once the biscuits were formed, she put them in another kettle she found in one of the packs. *They were certainly thorough. They didn't miss much in the kitchen at all.*

Rock was back quickly. He carried a blanket full of wild onions and herbs. He started dumping them into the kettle.

Clare found a canteen. She washed some potatoes and carrots as best she could. She set them beside the stew to add later. As she looked at all the food they were cooking, she felt a chill. *We are using too much of our winter store. What if we run out of food before winter is over?* She looked over at Rock cautiously. *That doesn't seem to be a concern for him. I need to calm down and stop panicking.* A chill went through her again though as she thought about her childhood and all the times she had gone hungry. *I guess I have never completely walked away from my childhood. I just don't want Zeke and Annie to experience the hunger and fear that were part of my early life.*

Rock went outside to talk to Little Bear and the insolent brave moved toward Clare again.

She tried to ignore him as he smirked at her. He moved closer and spoke softly. "Soon you will be my woman. I will beat you to make you behave. White Eagle will die, and you will belong to Beaver Tail."

Clare stopped what she was doing and stared at the brave. Her blue eyes flashed as she glared at him.

"I will never be your woman. I will knife you in your sleep. You will never sleep soundly with me in your tipi," she hissed.

The brave stared at her but finally moved back.

Little Bear had seen the exchange. He scowled. He didn't know what was said, but it was obvious that Beaver Tail was bothering White Eagle's woman.

Beaver Tail won't be happy until he spills the blood of my brother. White Eagle and I will lose regardless of who dies.

CHAPTER 42

THE HIDING PLACE

EACH BRAVE HAD HELPED HIMSELF TO A BOWL FROM Clare's kitchen. Some had taken spoons as well. As soon as the venison stew was ready, they filled their bowls. The meat was still tough, but they didn't seem to mind.

They stared at Clare's biscuits. Some tapped them on the floor of the cave. Others dropped them into their stew. In the end, the pot was empty, and the braves seemed satisfied.

Clare managed to scoop out some soup for the children and herself. She didn't want them to take seconds because the braves dipped their bowls directly into the pot for more, licking their fingers to clean them off.

Rock sat down next to Little Bear. They discussed the tribes who were present in the valley and the tensions between them.

The Blue Coats had forced nearly all the Indian tribes onto reservations, killed off their buffalo, and made them dependent on government rations. Unfortunately, the rations were too small and were often spoiled when they arrived. The young warriors were angry. Now, small groups of Indians from the various tribes were roaming around and looking for fights. Finding game was secondary.

"Your family should stay inside cave. Our party too small to leave braves to protect them. They should be safe if they stay hidden. We graze horses at night, and my braves watch yours along with ours."

Rock shook his head.

"I need my hay stores for the coming winter, and I don't want my house to be burned. I think I will sneak down there and make sure no one tries to burn me out." Rock didn't like abandoning his ranch, especially so close to winter.

Little Bear frowned. "White Eagle puts too much value on house. Houses are nothing, just place to sleep. You can build another."

Rock grinned at his friend. "That's true but we don't move around like you. Besides, you are tougher. I like my warm house at night."

Little Bear snorted, and the two men laughed.

"Perhaps we join you. It is good place to plan ambush if the Blackfeet attack."

When Rock told Clare that he was leaving, her eyes dilated with fear. "Rock," she whispered, "What if you don't come back? One of those braves wants to make me his woman. He said you would die, and I would be his."

Rock scowled. *And I know which one said that too.* When he pulled Clare close, he could feel her trembling.

"I'll be back, Clare," Rock whispered. "You just make sure the kids stay in here. Go deeper into the cave and see if there is a pool of water back there. You might need it to fill your canteens. I've never been back any farther than this open part so be careful." He stared toward the darkness that loomed from a partially hidden opening. "Pick a hiding spot too. Little Bear is sure you will be safe, but it never hurts to have a back-up plan. Try to walk on the smooth parts of the cave floor and leave as few tracks as possible."

Clare took a deep breath and forced her hands to quit shaking. She slowly nodded and stepped away from Rock. She looked over at Annie and Zeke.

"Come, children. Let's explore this cave and see how far back it goes."

Rock shoved a packrat's nest onto a stick and dipped it in the fire. He handed it to Clare.

"Watch for other nests as you follow that passage. You don't want your fire to burn out before you return."

He hugged each of the kids and was quickly gone. The warriors slipped out behind him. They left so quietly that Clare didn't even hear them go.

She whispered to the children, "Follow me and be quick." The three walked carefully through the dark cavern. They almost stepped on a packrat's nest, and Clare had Zeke pick it up. "We might need it before we find the back of this cave."

The main part of the cave was bowl-shaped, but a small opening led off to the right at the very back of the cavern. Clare shined her fire into the opening as she stepped forward. She kept the children behind her. Directly in front of the opening was a large hole. Clare dropped a pebble into the hole, and they all listened. The rock did not hit the bottom for a long time. Clare's hand trembled as she reached back to touch the children.

"You stay here. I am going to follow the tunnel in front of us a little farther and see where it goes. I promise I won't be gone long. Push back against the wall and don't move," she whispered.

Clare stepped carefully around the large hole and continued through the passageway. The air became easier to breathe, so she knew the cave opened to the outside. While that could provide an escape for them, it also meant that someone could come into the cave from the other direction. Clare could feel her breath catching in her chest as she forced herself to remain calm.

When she was near the back entrance of the cave, she found a square opening in the thick wall of rock. The children could crawl through the small window easily, and she thought she could fit as well. *If we need a hiding place, now we have one.*

Clare hurried back to where Annie and Zeke were anxiously waiting.

"I found a hiding place for us plus the cave opens to the outside. Now we have two secret places if we decide to hide," she told the children with a smile. "Let's pack a picnic lunch in case we need to go exploring again."

They hurried to the front of the cave, and Clare packed everything she found that showed the presence of a woman or children. She lifted her pack and led the children toward the back of the cave to take a nap. She dropped the smoldering pack rat's nest into the deep hole as they felt their way around the chasm.

She had just dozed off when she heard guttural voices at the front cave entrance. Gomer rushed to the opening and began to bray loudly.

Clare quickly woke Zeke and Annie. Signaling them to be quiet, Clare hurried them down the narrow passageway. Zeke crawled through first followed by Annie. Clare barely fit as she slid through to crouch beside them. She sifted sand over the edge of the hole and felt her way around the edge of the opening. She scooped more loose sand and sifted it over their footprints. It wasn't perfect but it might work if someone glanced in quickly.

She pressed the children against the wall. A stone jutted out and they slipped behind it just as they heard voices coming toward the back of the cave.

One of the braves had brush on a stick, and he was shining his light back and forth. He stopped right before the deep hole and moved to the right to go by the window they had climbed through. He paused and looked in. His torso wouldn't fit through the opening, but he reached his arm in and moved his light around. Another brave called, and they all rushed toward the back opening of the cave.

Clare was terrified. If the Indians looked closely, they would see that the tracks stopped at the hole. In addition, the ground outside would show that no one left the cave. She could feel panic rising in her chest. They needed to go farther down the small passageway, and she had no light to see in front of her.

She put her fingers over each child's mouth and began to feel her way in the dark. She kept one hand behind her so she could feel both children. Clare smelled the water before she reached it. She stopped and pushed the children against the wall behind them. "Perhaps no one will come in this far," she whispered to herself. *Dear Lord, please let the floor be hard enough that our tracks don't show*, she silently prayed.

Clare pulled the children against her and once again put her fingers over their mouths. The guttural voices were returning from the back entrance, and once again, a light was shown down the narrow corridor. As the light came closer, Clare's breathing became shallower.

When the light shone in front of them, she almost gasped. They were on the edge of a large pool of water. The narrow path in front of the rock they were hiding behind offered the only path around the water.

A wiry, young brave climbed through the small opening and cast his light over the water. It was undisturbed. He shined his light back and forth to take in the entire lake, but he didn't try to walk around the ledge like they had. He finally backed down the passageway and crawled out of the hole. Clare could hear them arguing as they went through the packs and destroyed the supplies.

Finally, their voices faded. Clare carefully led the children toward the back opening of the cave. Her breath was coming in short gasps, and both children were remarkably quiet. She couldn't hear Georgia or the wagon mules, so she assumed they were gone.

There was nowhere in the back cavern to hide. Clare only paused a moment before she led the children outside.

Rock, where are you? I don't know where I am or how to keep these little ones safe!

Zeke tapped her arm and pointed. Up and over where they now stood was a dark opening.

"Maybe that's another cave," Zeke whispered.

Clare picked up a stick and shoved some brush onto it. She lit it with one of the matches she had packed and led the way to the top of the large hill. After several minutes of steep climbing, they peered into the opening.

As she moved her torch back and forth, she realized they were looking down on the area where they had just hidden. They had found a third opening to the cave.

The hole on top was very small. However, the cavern opened much wider at this end than where they were before. They squeezed through the small opening, and Clare settled the children against the back wall. She held her finger over her lips and pointed toward the opening.

"I am going to try to cover our tracks," she whispered.

There were lots of crumbled rocks and sand just inside the opening. She scooped up handfuls and tossed them around on the rocks outside the opening. She sifted more sand around the opening. There were several large rocks inside the cave, and she shoved those into the mouth of the hole to make it less noticeable.

Satisfied that they were better hidden, she returned to the children.

"We can have that picnic now, but you can't talk," she whispered. "We must be very quiet."

Clare gave each some jerky and water from the canteen. *At least I know where to find water if we must stay here all night.*

She pulled her cloak over all three of them, and they finally fell asleep.

Several times during the night, she heard Indians close by. None of them climbed the rock toward the third opening nor did anyone try to come through the small hole.

Panic surged through her as she thought about Rock. *If he doesn't come back, we will have to hide from Little Bear's warriors as well as whoever else is on this mountain.* Her heart clutched in a knot. She forced herself to be calm. *Rock promised me, and he will move mountains to keep that promise.*

When daylight finally came, Clare became nervous about how open the large cavern was. It was much lighter than the rest of the cave since the opening was on top.

She repacked their small bundle of supplies and pushed the second pack rat nest onto her stick. She lit the brush torch and led the children toward the small corridor where they had originally hidden. It was terrifying to see what they had felt their way through in the dark.

Once again, she pressed the children behind her and began to inch her way around the large pool of water. Finally, they were in the small hiding place they had found the day before with the ledge in front of them.

"Let's rest here awhile," she whispered. "I am tired, and my hands are shaking too much to feel my way any farther." The torch was nearly black, and she covered it with sand to put out the embers.

Annie's eyes were huge in the shadowy cave as she stared at Clare.

"Can I sit on your lap, Clare?" she whispered.

Clare reached out her arms. She pulled the little girl onto her lap and kissed her. Zeke crowded close to her as well. Soon, the children dozed off. Clare could feel her eyelids drooping. She tried to stay awake to keep watch, but exhaustion took over and she drifted off to sleep as well.

CHAPTER 43

"Let's Go Home"

LOUD VOICES SOUNDED IN THE CAVE. CLARE recognized some of them, but she didn't hear Little Bear or Rock.

Annie started to stand, but Clare shook her head. She put her fingers over her lips and tapped them softly. Once again, a light shone through the opening, and they heard Indian voices.

Clare knew they were Little Bear's warriors, but unless Little Bear or Rock was there, they weren't coming out. She believed what Beaver Tail had told her. *I am not going to make it easy for him to take me.*

She had just decided to slip out through the back of the cave when she heard Rock's voice.

He was calling for each of them. Clare didn't want to expose their hiding place, so she signaled for the kids to be quiet as she eased them around the ledge.

She could hear the panic in Rock's voice as he searched, but she didn't answer until they had all climbed through the window. Once they were past the hole, she turned them loose.

Annie and Zeke rushed to grab Rock's legs, and Clare gave him a tremulous smile.

Little Bear was nowhere to be seen, but Beaver Tail smirked and stared at Clare. He was sitting by the fire and braiding a long piece of hair. When Clare looked at him, he held it up so she could see it was a scalp.

Clare shuddered and looked away.

Rock picked up both kids and pulled Clare into a hug. She began to shake, and Rock kissed her cheek. "You were a brave one today, Clare," he whispered. "We found Indian sign all around this cave. I don't know where you were, but it must have been a good hiding place."

Annie started to speak but Clare shushed her.

"It's our secret, Annie. You can tell your papa another day."

Clare was surprised to see Georgia and the wagon mules back in the cave.

"Gomer found them." Rock laughed as he added, "He chewed their ropes in two and led them back here. Guess he's good for something after all." He rubbed Gomer's head and chuckled. "Probably a good thing. Old Jake and Sally would have been a meal for a bunch of Blackfeet braves."

"Did they burn the house or barn?" Clare asked. "Were you able to save them?"

Rock nodded. "We saved everything. Led those Blackfeet right into an ambush. We took out several in their war party and wounded more in the first round of fighting. They tried to regroup, but we were hunkered in and had lots of cover to shoot from.

"They pulled out. They headed north and ran smack into a bunch of renegade Sioux warriors. They had a heck of a battle trying to fight their way through them." He paused and added, "It was Sioux sign we found around here. They were moving fast, so they didn't waste much time in this cave."

He studied Clare. "Good thing you took everything of yours and the kids," told her softly. "If they had known a woman was in here, they might have looked harder. We were lucky today."

Rock squeezed Clare's hand. "I think we can go on home tonight if you want. Little Bear is there now keeping an eye on things." He paused, "Unless you feel safer here."

Clare shook her head and tried not to look at Beaver Tail.

"Let's go home. I am worried though that we don't have any food stores left."

Rock shrugged his shoulders. He pulled her close and whispered, "I have all I need right here. Annie, Zeke…you." He looked up as Gomer stuck his head into the cave opening. "And Gomer."

Clare laughed out loud. "He warned us last night when the war party approached. He stood in the opening and brayed. I didn't see him then or any time after that, but he let us know that something wasn't right."

Clare glanced toward the fire and Beaver Tail smirked at her.

"May we go home now, Rock? I'd like to leave now if we can."

Both children hung onto Rock tightly and refused to let go. He carried them to the opening of the cave. Steed, Patches, and Georgia were already saddled. Rock had packed the salvageable provisions and cooking pots on Old Jake and Sally. He nodded toward the horses and chuckled.

"I don't know where those ponies were all this time. They just showed up when I arrived today. I guess they were hiding too."

Both kids climbed on their ponies, and Rock gave Clare a foot up on a nervous Georgia. He stood there for a moment looking up at her like he was going to say something. He finally turned to mount Red. He looked around at the three of them.

"Let's go home."

Rock led the little group through the mountains and back to his ranch. Gomer fell in behind the last horse, running back and forth beside them as he pleased. He finally rose on his back legs and dug in Rock's saddle bag looking for an apple. When he found one, he dropped down on all fours and happily chewed it.

Rock grinned back at Clare.

"Durn donkey. He believes he runs the place."

Clare didn't think any place ever looked as welcoming as the little rock house. Darby built it as a one-room cabin, but Rock had added three bedrooms. He also pushed out one wall to make the living area larger when he took the place over. It was quite comfortable now.

"You have done a lot of work around here, Rock. I see a big difference from four years ago."

Rock nodded. "Old Darby set me up pretty good when he passed this place on to me. The least I can do is make it better before I hand it off to the next generation."

Clare nodded as she studied Rock's profile. *He is so good-looking, and he doesn't have a clue. No wonder the women throw themselves at him.* She almost blushed as she thought of all the things she had told him when she thought she was dying. *Oh well. It is certainly too late to take anything back. Still, I wish I hadn't been so free with my words.*

Rock helped Clare tidy the kitchen before he sent her to bed. "You are worn out and probably lifted more than you should have." He gave a dry laugh.

"You were supposed to come here to recuperate. Instead, you spend thirty-six hours hiding from a bunch of blood-thirsty savages in a dark cave with two little ones to watch." His mouth twisted in a sardonic smile. "I guess I am not much of a host."

Clare laughed as she agreed. "I'd really like to take a bath, but I'm too tired tonight. Maybe you can haul some water in tomorrow. I'd like to bathe the children too."

She closed the door to the small room where Maggie usually slept. She stripped down to her undergarments and crawled into bed. *I wonder what Rock will want for breakfast. I'm not even sure what is left…*

CHAPTER 44

BEAVER TAIL

CLARE AWOKE THE NEXT MORNING TO THE SMELL OF side pork and eggs. She dressed quickly and rubbed her face with her hankie. *I just know it's dirty—I can feel grit all over me.* She had let her hair down last night and the long braid still hung down her back when she walked out of the bedroom.

Rock looked up and stared at her for a moment before he went back to mixing his biscuits.

Clare smiled at him as she went to the basin and washed her face. "I totally overslept. I didn't realize how tired I was."

Rock nodded at the room where the two children slept. "You and them too. Little Bear pulled out this morning. They are headed back up to the reservation. I sent a few cattle with them. Hopefully, they will be able to calve some of them out and not have to eat all of them this winter." He scowled as he thought of all that Little Bear had shared.

"Being forced to abandon your way of life and live on a reservation, dependent on someone else for food—it's almost too much for them.

"That's really what led to all the fighting around here. All the tribes have been forced onto reservations that are too small for their way of life. Their children are hungry and their old are dying. I'd be hankering for a fight too." Rock's face broke into a slow grin as he looked at Clare.

"How about you, Miss Clare? Are you hungry or are you hankering for a fight? Food I can handle, but I have had my fill of fighting for a time."

"I'm starving," Clare admitted. "We only ate a little jerky while you were gone. I'm sure the children will be hungry as well."

"Well, there are plenty of eggs. We'll just scramble more if we run out. Eat up. I want you healthy when you leave here."

Clare didn't respond, and Rock frowned slightly as he ate.

When she finished, Clare picked up their plates and carried them to the wash area. Rock filled the basin with hot water and set the bucket down.

He turned Clare to face him and studied her face. Then he pulled her tight. His voice was rough as he spoke.

"I was so afraid you had been taken when I couldn't find you last night. The children too."

A shadow suddenly filled the doorway, and Beaver Tail smirked at them. "I fight you for the woman. Then I kill you, and she will be mine."

Rock pushed Clare behind him as he stared at Beaver Tail.

"My brother, Little Bear, left this morning. Why are you still here?"

Beaver Tail's nose flared, and he raised his head. "Little Bear is not my chief. I do as I please. I don't go with him because I want to take woman—White Eagle's woman. Little Bear says I cannot." Beaver Tail spat on the floor. "White Eagle is nothing. I will kill you and take the woman. I will beat her until she does as I tell her. Then I will beat her because I like to beat women."

Rock's face hardened and he gestured toward the door.

"Then let us fight under Father Sun and the best of us will win. If you win, I die. If I win, you leave. You never come back, and I keep my woman."

Clare's breath was ragged. As Beaver Tail backed outside, Rock followed him. Four braves had chosen to stay with Beaver Tail, and they spread out in a semicircle.

The two large men circled each other. Beaver Tail was an inch taller than Rock and looked a little younger. Both men's bodies were hard with working muscles.

Rock's movements appeared to be awkward. Beaver Tail smirked. He wrestled often and was confident of his skill.

Beaver Tail charged Rock and tried to trip him. The rancher stumbled. He almost fell but caught himself before he went down.

Clare picked up the shotgun and checked to make sure it was loaded. She felt her dress pocket for the Derringer she kept there. Then she leaned the loaded shotgun against the inside of the doorjamb and stepped into the doorway.

Rock looked like he was losing, and Beaver Tail was confident. He grabbed Rock's wrist and turned his back to flip Rock over his shoulder in a flying mare. Rock whipped his wrist free. He grabbed Beaver Tail's wrist and put the younger man in a choke hold. As Rock bent his arm up, Beaver Tail's eyes opened wide in surprise. He grunted and tried to roll out of the chokehold.

One of the braves tossed Beaver Tail a knife. He caught it as he twisted and tried to slice Rock.

Rock hit him hard in the temple with his fist. Beaver Tail shook his head, stunned for a moment. Rock kicked the brave's right leg. As the man went down, his knife arm was twisted high on his back.

The braves all heard the bone break as Rock wrenched Beaver Tail's arm even higher. The knife dropped from his hand.

Beaver Tail grunted, and Rock flipped him on his back.

Rock hissed at the brave in Siouan.

"You fight for her so you can beat her, but I fight for her to love. She is my woman. You will leave and you will never cross the lands of White Eagle again." Rock released his hold and added, "Or I will kill you."

Rock picked up the knife the brave had tossed. He spun on his toes and threw it. The knife landed between the feet of the young brave who had tossed it. The blade went into the ground up to the handle. Rock strode toward the brave. He stopped with his face close to the young man. The Siouan words he spoke were harsh and angry.

"Crow warriors do not need help to fight. They win or lose with their own skill and power. You have embarrassed your brothers, but if you want to prove how brave you are, pick it up."

The young warrior stared at White Eagle. Little Bear had warned them that he was a great warrior, but they hadn't believed him. Little Bear told them to come with him, but they didn't listen. Instead, they followed Beaver Tail. Now they would have to ask the council if they could once again be part of the tribe, and they might not be allowed to return. He looked down at the knife and shook his head.

"I was wrong to throw the knife. I have broken the rules of my people and disobeyed Little Bear. I leave now, my brother."

Beaver Tail leaped from the ground with a roar and charged toward Clare.

Rock scooped the knife from the ground. He threw it just as Clare aimed the shotgun. She fired both barrels. Beaver Tail caught the full force of both loads and was blown backwards, nearly cut in two. The knife was embedded in his back, the tip protruding from his chest. Either the knife or the shotgun blast would have killed Beaver Tail. Together, they were strong medicine.

Clare quietly reloaded. She pulled the knife from Beaver Tail's back and glared at the shocked braves as she spoke quietly.

"I will be no man's woman unless I choose to be, and no man will *ever* beat me." Her face was pale, but her eyes were angry as she stared at the braves.

She stood in the doorway, slender and straight, as the braves mounted their ponies. One of them draped Beaver Tail over his horse, and the quiet cavalcade left the ranch.

Rock watched them go before he walked over to Clare. He took the knife from her and wiped it on the ground before he shoved it in its sheath. Her hands were beginning to shake, and he took the shotgun from her.

He pulled her close as he whispered in Siouan, "You are a woman to make many braves. A woman to stand tall in her man's home. You are the woman I want in my home."

Clare stared at him and sobbed silently. She melted against Rock, and he kissed the top of her head.

Zeke and Annie came outside rubbing their eyes.

"Something loud woke us up. Did you shoot at something, Uncle Rock?" Zeke asked.

Rock shook his head. "Nope, your mother shot a coyote. That coyote was warned but he just didn't listen. Now he won't be bothering us anymore."

Zeke looked at his mother with pride and smiled.

CHAPTER 45

"She Kinda Dresses up the Kitchen"

MAGGIE AND IKE RETURNED THE FOLLOWING DAY. They were worried, but the ranch looked peaceful. The little ones ran to meet them.

"Auntie Maggie, we were worried about you! Did you know that the Indians came, and we went to a cave, and Clare had to hide us, and then Papa found us, and we came back home!"

Ike helped Maggie down and she leaned to hug each of them.

"My goodness. It sounds like I missed a lot of excitement! Now who would like a piece of hard candy? I didn't think you would want any, but Ike insisted."

As the children jumped up and down, Maggie dug in her bags for the candy. Ike stood behind her smiling as the kids chattered excitedly.

Clare appeared in the doorway. She was wiping dough off her hands as she came outside.

"Welcome back, Maggie. Hello, Ike. I hope you didn't have any trouble getting to Stevensville. Things were kind of wild around here several days ago."

Ike looked around the neat ranch yard. His eyes finally settled on the bunkhouse.

"Where's that man of yurs? Don't look like he's been gettin' much done whilst I was gone. Guess I *will* have to stay an' help fer a time."

Rock walked out of the barn with a smile on his face.

"That would just be fine. I have all the rock hauled and I'm getting ready to mix the mortar right now. You climb down and we might be able to stack a few rocks before Clare calls us for dinner."

Ike grabbed the reins to his horse and led him to the barn while Maggie followed Clare into the house.

Clare had bread rising in the pans in a warm corner of the kitchen. The cinnamon rolls were ready to slice and a pan for them was ready. The windows were open, and the kitchen felt clean and cool.

Clare hummed to herself as she washed her hands.

Maggie studied her face and then hugged her.

"Your face is telling me that things are going well here. Is Rock finally letting you have a piece of his heart?"

Clare laughed. "He is still afraid to show me his heart, so he talks in the Crow language when he wants to say something sweet—and he has no idea that I understand everything he is saying!"

Maggie looked surprised but started to giggle. "When did you learn Siouan, Clare? I had no idea you were familiar with the Crow people."

Clare's face clouded. "My pappy had a Crow wife for a while. He just called her Woman, but she told me her name was Running Bird. She had been captured by the Pend d'Oreille, and my pappy bought her. She was a kind woman and taught me her language.

"Pappy was mean to her, and she finally ran away. She wanted to take me with her, but I was too small to make that decision. One day she was just gone. I was lost without her, and Pappy beat me for crying."

Clare's voice was soft as she added, "I despised Pappy for beating her. When he turned his fists on me, I swore that I when I grew up, no man would ever beat me again."

Maggie wrapped Clare up in her arms. "Clare, I am so happy that you were able to escape that life. And I am so pleased that you are sharing your big heart with this little family," Maggie whispered as she hugged Clare tightly.

Clare hugged her back. She smiled at Maggie through the tears in her eyes. As she looked down at the rolls, she gasped. "I need to get these sliced and into pans or they will rise too much and be ruined!"

Maggie quickly put on her apron, and the two women sliced the cinnamon rolls. They had the pan filled in no time.

Rock had butchered a beef, and it was hanging in the smokehouse. He brought a large piece of meat into the house after breakfast.

"How are you with beef, Clare? Think you can cook this up for dinner?"

Clare studied the meat and smiled at Rock sweetly as her eyes snapped.

"I guess we will have to see, won't we?" she responded. "Probably will be tough and dry, but I'll see if my cooking skills have improved."

Rock grinned at her and left the kitchen.

Clare snorted. She was an excellent cook. *Just because I didn't know how to prepare an entire deer in a cave doesn't mean I can't cook.*

When Clare called the men for dinner, they were met with fresh bread, the smell of cinnamon rolls baking, and roast with carrots and potatoes. The rich gravy was thick and dark.

Little Bear's braves had not found the small cellar where most of the vegetables were stored. Now there would be vegetables to last most of the winter.

Rock stared at the food and looked up at Clare with a grin.

"Guess my cooking skills have improved some since the last time I tried this," she commented dryly.

Maggie laughed out loud, and Ike grinned as he waved his hands over the table.

"Clare is quite the cook, Rock. If ya don't know that by now, ya cain't taste." His eyes moved from Rock to Clare, and he drawled, "She kinda dresses up the kitchen too, don't ya think? Not ever' woman cin look that purty after cookin' a spread like this." His grin became bigger, and he added, "Cept fer my Maggie," as he winked at both women.

Maggie blushed and Clare rolled her eyes as they both sat down.

Rock nodded. "She does make this kitchen look good," he agreed seriously. His green eyes were intense as he looked at Clare.

Clare could feel the pink rising in her cheeks, and she tried to push it down. She cleared her throat and spoke softly, "Fold your hands, children, so Grampy Ike can lead us in a prayer of thanksgiving."

CHAPTER 46

A Gift From Suzanna

SEPTEMBER 10 BEGAN WARM AND SUNNY. BREAKFAST was relaxed and everyone but Maggie was talking. She kept fidgeting and finally laid her fork down.

"Ike and I are getting married in eleven days. We talked to Father Ravalli, and the service will be on Saturday, September 21. We thought three in the afternoon would be good. That way, we can eat a bite afterwards."

Ike grinned as Rock stared at the two of them.

"Now don't act all surprised, boy. Ya knew this here day was a comin' an' you'ins had some time these last few days to make plans on yur end."

Annie stared at Maggie, and her chin began to tremble.

"Auntie, are you leaving? Who is going to take care of me until I get a new mama?" Tears were beginning to run from her eyes, and Rock picked her up.

"Now Annie, Auntie Maggie has stayed with us for a long time. She isn't going far. She is going to marry Ike. He is already like a grandpa to you."

He hugged his little girl as she clung to his neck.

Finally, she looked up. "What about Clare and Zeke? Clare said she would stay as long as Auntie Maggie stayed. Now they'll leave too!"

Zeke's eyes were large as he watched Annie and Uncle Rock. He climbed onto Clare's lap.

"Mama, are we leaving too? I don't want to leave. I like Uncle Rock and Annie. I don't want to go away!" He hugged Clare's neck, and his silent sobs shook her as she held him.

When both little ones had calmed down a little, Rock looked over at Maggie.

"Maggie, how about the two of you clean up and keep an eye on the kids. I would like to take Clare for a walk."

Annie sat up. "I want to come too. And Zeke. We want to go with you."

Rock shook his head. "Not this time, Annie. I need to talk to Clare by myself. We will be back to have some cinnamon rolls with you in a little while though."

Annie slid off Rock's lap and ran over to Clare. "Cinnamon rolls! You make yummy things just like a real mama, Clare."

Clare's heart melted and she kissed Annie's little face as the small girl hugged her. "Annie, how about you and Zeke be the first ones to taste the cinnamon rolls? Auntie Maggie can cut one for each of you. Maybe you can share with Grampy Ike too." Clare's face was pale as she smiled.

As the children climbed up to the table and excitedly held out their hands, Clare took Rock's arm, and they slipped out the door. They could hear Ike talking behind them.

"Maggie, why don't ya cut me that big one right outa the middle. Ya two kids pick the ones ya want too."

Rock led Clare past the barn. They walked up the hill behind the horse pasture. The trees opened up to show a little meadow. In the far corner was a rock bench surrounded by purple, blue, and white lilacs. The aroma was wonderful. Clare paused as she breathed in their fragrance.

"Oh, Rock. This is a beautiful spot, and it just smells wonderful."

Rock nodded. "I built this after Suzanna died. I like to come here and think sometimes." He blushed a little as he added, "I have never brought anyone else up here—for sure no other woman."

He turned Clare to face him. "Clare, I know I haven't courted you properly. Things kind of went haywire here and threw me off track. Now Maggie is moving out in a week and…"

"You need to find someone to replace her," Clare finished quietly as she studied his face.

Rock fidgeted uncomfortably. "Yes…but I would like you to stay even if she wasn't leaving."

Clare looked up at this man she had loved all her adult life. "Why Rock? Why do you want me to stay?"

Rock frowned. *She is trying to force me to share my feelings, and I am not comfortable doing that.*

Clare turned her face up to him. "Rock, I told you before that I would stay if I knew you loved me. That hasn't changed. I just want to hear you say those words. I don't want to live with a man who assumes I know how he feels. I want you to share your feelings with me, even if it makes you uncomfortable. That is what marriage is all about." Clare's eyes were soft as she spoke.

"Marriage isn't always about being comfortable. It is about two people sharing with each other the most intimate parts of themselves, and I am not going to do that unless I know the man to whom I'm married truly loves me."

Rock looked down at Clare intently and muttered in Siouan as he pulled her close.

"Woman, why do you make this so hard. Can't you see that I love you, that I want to be with you? I would give my life for you."

Clare smiled up at Rock and wrapped her arms around his neck as she responded in Siouan, "Was that so hard, my husband? Yes, I will marry you and fill your home with love and happiness."

Rock's face turned red, and he stared at Clare in surprise. "You speak the language of the Crow? Then I have no secrets from you. You know my heart." He wrapped his arms tightly around Clare and kissed her, gently at first and then with a passion.

Clare pulled away a little breathlessly. "Now we need to talk about a wedding date. You know I am not staying out here unmarried after Maggie leaves."

Rock's eyes twinkled. "I think both of our reputations are already sullied. You were her for four days unsupervised while Maggie was gone." He grinned down at her.

"How about we get hitched tomorrow?"

Clare looked up at Rock and laughed out loud.

"When you finally get around to things, you don't waste any time, do you? Tomorrow will be fine. I will have the children ready to drive to the Mission by eight."

As she started to turn away, Rock caught her. "I have something for you." He took a sapphire necklace from his pocket. The heart-shaped stone sparkled as the sun's rays caught its surface.

Clare drew her breath in and shook her head. "I remember that necklace. Suzanna wore it almost all the time. It needs to go to Annie, not to me."

Rock stared at the necklace and then looked away. When he looked back, Clare could see that his eyes were red.

"I found the stone as I was crossing the Sapphire Mountains the first year I rode into this valley. It was laying in a small gulley. It had probably washed out above somewhere and was pushed down by the water.

"It was so blue that it stood out on the ground. When it caught the rays of the sun, it sparkled like a star. I stopped to see what it was. I've always liked rocks, so I picked it up and dropped it in my saddlebag.

"I didn't think any more about it until Suzanna agreed to marry me. I had it made into a necklace and gave it to her our first Christmas." Rock stared at the blue stone and tears showed in the corners of his eyes.

"I was going to bury this with her, but Suzanna asked me not to. She asked me to give it to the woman who would become Annie's mother on the condition that she give it to Annie when she turned sixteen."

He smiled softly at Clare and lifted the necklace to place it around her neck. He whispered, "Maybe Suzanna knew that you would be wearing this someday."

Tears filled Clare's eyes as she touched the necklace and looked up at Rock. She stood on her tiptoes and kissed him.

"Thank you, Rock. Thank you for asking me to be Annie's mother and for sharing Suzanna's story with me. I will always remember the love this holds, and I will be proud to pass it along to Annie someday."

Rock wrapped his arms around Clare. His heart felt warm and happy. He smiled down at this woman who was going to share his life.

"I think I am going to enjoy having you around," he drawled as he released her and took her hand.

As the two of them walked into the house, Zeke shoved his last bite of a cinnamon roll into his mouth.

He tried to talk but Annie didn't wait for him. She turned her little frosting-covered face to Rock as she frowned.

"Papa, I don't want Clare and Zeke to leave. Can they stay with us forever?"

Rock dropped down in front of Annie as his eyes twinkled.

"In order for that to work, I would need to marry Clare. Of course, that would make her your new mama. What do you think of that?"

Annie's face lit up. She jumped down from her chair and charged toward Clare. Clare bent down and Annie leapt on her so hard, she almost knocked Clare over.

"You are going to be my new mama? I prayed for this every day!"

Zeke watched Annie and his mother. Then he took a tentative step toward Rock. He asked softly, "Does this mean you are my new papa? And I can call you Papa?"

Rock held out his arms to Zeke and the little boy rushed into them. "It sure does, Zeke. And that's good because we need more men on this ranch."

Zeke nodded happily as he wrapped his arms tightly around Rock's neck.

"I prayed that you would be my papa," he whispered. "Mama said God doesn't always answer prayers like we want Him to, but I think she was wrong. This is what I asked for."

CHAPTER 47

LAYING DOWN THE LAW

CLARE UNFOLDED HER BEST DRESS AND HELD IT UP in front of her. She only owned three dresses, and she saved this one for special occasions.

The fabric was soft purple with a lilac print bodice. A small lace ruffle scalloped the neckline and the bottom of the short, puffed sleeves. The neckline scooped in the front, and the fitted bodice came to a point in the center of the skirt. Clare's small straw hat had purple flowers on it, and a trail of ribbons hung down in the back. The dress buttoned in the back. Clare sighed. *Maggie will have to help me fasten this. I think my future dresses will button in the front.*

Clare found a heavy iron and set it in the fireplace to heat.

The cotton fabric would handle quite a bit of heat, but she took a tea towel from the kitchen and dampened it. When the iron was hot, she laid it over the skirt and began to press it. She hummed to herself as she worked.

Maggie squeezed her. "You are going to be a beautiful bride, Clare. Purple is your color, and I love your little hat. Where in the world did you find that?"

"A woman I knew in Helena was throwing it away. I cleaned it up and found some silk flowers one day in the trash at work. I added those as well as the ribbons." Clare laughed.

"I hadn't made this dress yet when I acquired it, so I have never worn it. I'm not even sure why I thought I needed to bring it along. I do think it will look nice with my dress though."

Maggie nodded and then asked, "Do you need to go back to Helena for anything, or did you bring everything with you?"

Clare was still for a moment. She slowly shook her head.

"We didn't have much. I brought what I thought I should keep and gave the rest away." She paused and added softly, "I thought I was dying, so I never planned to return. It was a wonderful surprise to me when Father Ravalli said I was going to live." She smiled at Maggie. "Other than one special friend whom I will miss, I have no reason to return."

Clare looked out the window where Gomer and the two children were playing.

"I want to give the children baths tonight and take one myself. I hope Rock will have time to haul some water in for us."

Maggie smiled. "And if he doesn't, Ike will. We'll put the children down after their baths, and you can take a nice soak in the tub after the men go to bed."

Clare nodded and her hand paused as she lifted the iron. "Oh, Maggie—I have wanted this for so long," Clare whispered as tears filled her eyes. "When I came here, I never dreamed my prayers would be answered."

Maggie laughed. "Well, they say God listens to children and you certainly had them going up from here for quite a while…although after you came, they did become much more specific!"

Clare looked through Annie's clothes and picked out a pretty dress. Zeke didn't have many choices, but she found a shirt and britches that had barely been mended.

When Rock came in for dinner, Clare asked, "Do you need me to wash or press anything for you to wear tomorrow?"

He looked at her in surprise. Then he disappeared into his room and came out with a shirt.

It was dark red and didn't look like it had been worn much. As Clare took it, she saw a little heart embroidered in the back of the neck. She looked up in surprise.

Rock's neck colored and he shifted his feet as he looked at her.

"Suzanna made it for me. I don't wear it much even though it's my favorite." He turned a darker red as he added, "She always put a little heart somewhere in everything she made for me."

Clare could feel her eyes becoming misty as she hung the shirt over a chair. Then a thought jolted her. *What if I am compared to Suzanna every day? What if Rock expects me to be just like her?*

Clare pushed her panic down. *Rock loved Suzanna so much, and he knew he could never replace her. That is why it took him so long to open his heart to love again.* Clare's breath caught in her chest.

Suzanna, I am so sorry your life ended so quickly, but thank you for allowing me to be part of this family you loved—your family.

As they sat down for dinner, Ike grinned at Rock. "I been doin' some thinkin'. Why don't ya take Clare down in the buggy. Maggie an' me cin follow in the wagon. The buggy 'ill be smoother fer Clare, an' mebbie she cin keep that fancy hat on 'er head." He winked at Clare and added, "The youngins cin come with us. That way they cin sleep when they git tired."

Rock looked surprised but slowly nodded.

"That will be fine. We can bring the wagon back. I thought I would pick up supplies while we were in Stevensville."

Ike looked at Annie and Zeke. "How would the two of ya like to spend the night in town? Maggie an' me bought us a little house close to the Mission. It's all fixed up an' ready to move in. I'll sleep in my little room at the livery, but Maggie is goin' to stay there tomorry night. An' she could sure use some company."

Annie looked at Maggie with big eyes and then at Rock. "Can we, Papa? I ain't never stayed in town before!"

Zeke leaned over to her and whispered, "Can't use that word, remember?"

Annie frowned but reworded her request. "I never stayed in town before. Can we please, Papa?"

Rock could feel color climbing up and circling his shirt collar. "I reckon so since Grampy Ike is so helpful and all," he answered dryly.

Clare's cheeks were light pink, but she pretended to be oblivious to what Ike was setting up.

When Zeke looked at her in question, she smiled. "Your papa already said it would be fine, Zeke."

Zeke's brown eyes shone with happiness, and he climbed onto Rock's lap. He wrapped his arms around Rock's neck. "Thanks, Papa," he whispered.

Rock smiled as he patted the little boy.

Clare pointed at the two children. "I want both of you in the house when I call tonight. We are all taking baths tonight, and you must go to bed early. Tomorrow will be a long day."

Rock's eyes began to twinkle. "How about me? When should I take a bath?"

Ike began to laugh, and Clare blushed furiously.

"I guess I didn't think about you. How do you usually take a bath?"

"Why right in the middle of the kitchen there. I usually smoke a cigar, sip a little whiskey, and sit there till the water gets cold."

Clare studied his face to see if he was joking, but she couldn't tell. "No cigar but figure out when you want to do that. I want to have the kids in bed and be out of your way."

Ike began laughing. "Layin' down the law, she is! Guess ya have a few new rules."

Maggie snorted. "You will have a few new ones too, Ike, so don't be laughing too hard!"

Ike's face showed surprise, but he grinned at Maggie. "I reckon we cin shore 'nough discuss a few rules. 'Course, I'm an easygoin' kinda feller. Takes quite a bit to fluster me." He rolled his eyes toward Rock.

"Rock on the other hand is fer shore set in his ways."

Eating was quick since Rock and Ike wanted to get back to their work on the bunkhouse. Ike headed outside and Rock paused beside Clare.

"You go ahead and take a bath when the kids are done. I'll haul in fresh water for you, and then I'll use your water. I'll work outside until you call me in. That way, you don't have to wait on me."

Clare smiled and Rock pulled her in for a quick kiss. "You and me all alone tomorrow night. Hmm. Something to think on."

He grinned as a small red spot appeared in each of Clare's cheeks. She put her hands on her hips and cocked her head.

"You convince me that you are afraid of women, and then you make a comment like that. I don't know what to think of you, Rock Beckler."

"Afraid of *most* women, not *all* women," he corrected her as he headed out the door with a smile on his face.

CHAPTER 48

Moving On

ROCK WAS UP EARLY AND OUTSIDE BEFORE THE SUN was up. He sat against the big pine and stared at Suzanna's grave.

"I'm getting married today, Suzanna. Of course, you know that already. I believe the Good Lord lets you look down and check in on us." Rock sifted some dirt through his fingers and looked up as the sun began to break over the mountains.

"Sure is a pretty morning. Just the kind you and I used to enjoy. All the colors stretching across the sky. A picture so pretty that no paintbrush could do it justice." He frowned as he looked again at the tombstone.

"I wanted to talk to you this morning and now my durn mind just stalled out on me. I don't know how to tell the woman I pledged to love all my life that I am going to pledge that love to someone else." Rock tossed the dirt on the ground.

"Why did you have to die?" he whispered. "We were happy." He looked over Suzanna's tombstone toward the rock house. His eyes were red, and he brushed them irritably.

"I was so afraid when you became pregnant with Annie. We had already lost two little ones, and you so wanted babies. I just knew it was my fault when you died. The doc told me otherwise, but in my mind, I was the one who killed you.

"I didn't want anything to do with Annie those first six months. I was so busy blaming myself that I couldn't even see the beautiful little gift you had given me."

Rock looked toward the house and frowned. "Did you know that Clare nursed Annie?" Then he smiled wryly.

"Of course you did. You asked her to. She saved Annie's life, something you couldn't do yourself. You knew you were dying, but you made sure that tiny girl there in the house would survive. And I was so busy wallowing in my self-pity that I didn't even notice.

"Now today, seven years after I tied her to a horse and hauled her to jail, I am marrying Clare and bringing her to our home." Rock picked up a twig and broke it in two.

"I love her, Suzanna. Oh, I know it's different than how you and I loved, but it is deep, and it feels good. She is strong but gentle, kind but fiery, stubborn but quick to turn her heart to help others." He laughed lightly.

"Clare is every bit as blunt as you were. I suppose that is why the two of you were such good friends. Did you know that she speaks and understands the Crow language? She caught me saying things in Siouan that I couldn't say out loud." Rock threw the crumbled stick on the ground.

"My pa was a good man, but he didn't know how to show affection. He lost all interest in us kids after Ma died. Just drank himself to death.

"Georgia was so little. I tried to help her get better when she became sick, but I was just a kid. I didn't know what to do.

"Pa just sat at the kitchen table and stared. He had a tintype of Ma in one hand and a bottle in the other. When I tried to get him to help Georgia, he looked through me like I wasn't there."

Rock was silent as he picked up another stick.

"I never told you much about Georgia. I blamed myself for her too. She was less than three years old when she died. I rocked her and held her constantly that last day, but she just faded away." He paused as he looked over at Darby's grave. "I was only ten, but that was when I started asking Little Bear about Crow medicine. His grandmother taught me how to use herbs for healing and how to find medicine. She showed me plants to use in the forests as well as those found on the prairie. I didn't ever want to be that helpless again."

Rock looked up at the sky. The sun was just peeking between the mountains, and the colors of the sky were getting lighter.

"Georgia used to follow me around. She jabbered constantly. I didn't understand most of what she said, but when I picked her up, she would give me the most glorious smile. She melted my heart just the way our little Annie does." Rock smiled softly.

"You would love Clare's little boy. Zeke has big brown eyes. He's taller than Annie. Quieter too. He loves to ride his pony and wants to be a cowboy."

Rock laughed out loud as he looked toward the house.

"I don't think Clare and I had a snowball's chance *not* to fall in love. Annie prayed for a mama every day, and Zeke prayed for a papa. When Zeke came here to stay, those little ones changed their prayers and added our names to them." He chuckled again. "It was a little awkward in the beginning. They were not only sincere—they were persistent.

"And that brings me back around to today. Clare and I will be getting married at St. Mary's Mission this afternoon. I know I have always been skittish around women—heck, you saw that right away and teased me all the time. That hasn't changed much, but with Clare, it's different.

"She is so honest with me. She just opens up and shows me her heart without hiding anything. And she has a wonderful heart, Suzanna. She is so full of love and so ready to share it. She makes me ashamed of the years that I disliked her. You always told me Clare was a wonderful person, but all I could see was that foul-mouthed girl who took part in Darby's death."

A single butterfly flitted around Rock's head and settled on his vest pocket. It worked its wings back and forth before it flew away, disappearing in the trees. The tear that had been hiding in Rock's eye leaked out.

"Yep, just like that butterfly, you landed on my heart and now you are gone." Rock wiped his eyes and stood up.

"I'm moving on, Suzanna. You will always be my first love, but I'm moving you over in my heart. Clare loves you too, and I know she will tell Annie more stories about you. Today though is a new road in my life, and I'm riding down it with Clare." He leaned over and kissed the tombstone.

"Goodbye, Suzanna. Goodbye, sweetheart."

As Rock left the little cemetery, his heart felt like it had broken free. He would always love and cherish his memories of Suzanna, but he was looking forward to a new life with Clare.

He looked at the sun. It was now over the mountains, and the tops of the trees almost looked gold.

"I'd better get my chores done or I will be late to my own wedding." He grinned. "And what if I am? It can't start without me!"

Rock strolled to the barn and led Georgia out. He stopped in the doorway. They both stared at the mountains and soaked up the morning.

"It's going to be a fine day, Georgia," he told her with a smile as he turned her out into the pasture with Red. Darby's little mare was now pregnant with her sixth colt, and Red was the sire to the last five.

Rock sold Suzanna's colt when it was two years old. It was a fine little horse colt, but his heart hurt every time he looked at it.

He sold it to a tall cowboy who liked horses. The stranger said, "George Spurlock is the name, but most folks just call me Spur. My boss down by Cheyenne is always looking for new breeding stock. I think he will like the lines of this little stud."

Rock smiled and slapped Georgia on her rump.

CHAPTER 49

CLARE'S PROMISE

MAGGIE WAS FIXING BREAKFAST. SHE SMILED AT CLARE as the young bride appeared in her purple dress.

"Don't you worry about helping this morning, Clare. I about have it done. Rock was already outside when I started breakfast. I'm sure he wanted to get some things done before the two of you left this morning.

"We'll let the kids sleep in a little. You already set out their clothes, and I can help them dress." She smiled at the nervous young woman as she helped her button her dress.

"You just enjoy this day with your man, and we will meet you in Stevensville in time for dinner." She pointed at the sapphire necklace and whispered, "Suzanna will be smiling today."

Clare touched the heart-shaped stone and smiled softly. "I think I will go for a walk. It is a beautiful morning, and I rarely take the time to walk for no reason."

She walked down to the bunkhouse and studied the progress Rock and Ike had made. The stone walls were up about two feet. Clare looked back toward the house before she studied the barn. The rock used on all three buildings looked nearly the same.

The ranch headquarters were neat and tidy. Everything was well-built, and no broken boards were seen anywhere.

"Rock sure likes things nice and tidy. I'm not surprised though. He takes pride in everything he does."

Clare could see Suzanna's tombstone from where she stood, and she walked to the little grave site. "Good morning, Suzanna." Tears filled Clare's eyes as she looked down at the stone.

"I don't know what to say to you today. Nothing seems appropriate." Clare took a deep breath and began.

"I promise to love your little Annie like my own little girl. She is so excited to get a new mama. I know you are happy for her. And Rock…I have loved Rock most of my adult life. I can never replace you, and I won't try, but I will love him with all my heart." Clare kissed her fingers and touched Suzanna's stone as she whispered, "Thank you for sharing your family with me." She jumped when someone touched her shoulder.

Rock smiled at her. "I had a talk with Suzanna this morning too." He took Clare's hand and led her toward the house. He squeezed her hand as they walked.

"This seems right, Clare. Four years ago, you helped Suzanna when we needed your help, and now you are becoming a full part of this family." He cupped her face and kissed her. Then he grinned.

"I guess it's a good thing I shot you seven years ago. Who'd a knew then that you would be my wife someday." His grin became bigger. "Or that my wife would have such a prolific vocabulary of bad words. You really let me have it that day."

Clare laughed and then looked seriously at Rock. "You saved me that day. Who knows what my life would have been like? I'm thankful I was the only little girl there. You have no idea how awful it was." She shivered and Rock pulled her close.

He smiled at her. "Well, Mrs. 'almost' Beckler, let's go see that padre. I figure we can eat in Stevensville before we head out to the Mission around one. Father Ravalli is usually available in the afternoon for confessions, so we should be able to catch him." He winked at her and grinned as he added, "Good thing we are getting married soon, or I would probably have go to confession first."

Clare's face blushed a deep red as she stared at him. "Rock Beckler!" she sputtered.

Rock was laughing as they stepped through the doorway into the house. Clare's face was still pink, but she was smiling.

She looked up in surprise as the smell of lilacs greeted them. A huge bouquet of wild lilacs was on the table. Blue, purple, and white flowers were combined in a large spray of color. The aroma was wonderful. Clare bent her head to smell them.

"I love lilacs! Who picked these?"

Maggie pointed at Rock, and he grinned.

"I thought you might want to make a bouquet or put some in your hair—or whatever it is that women do with flowers."

Clare smiled at him. She scooped up the flowers and pecked his cheek as she hurried toward Maggie's bedroom. "Give me about ten minutes and I will be ready to go," she called as she shut the door.

Maggie smiled at Rock. "She is a wonderful woman, Rock.

"Now you be sure that she buys some fabric in town. That girl likes to sew but she will spend nothing on herself. She wants to make clothes for the children too, but she has no supplies at all." Maggie looked hard at Rock. "You have no idea how hard her life was before she came here."

Rock looked surprised. He frowned as he shook his head.

"I would never tell Clare what to buy. She can get whatever she thinks we need."

"And that is what I am saying. She won't ask for anything for herself, so you make sure you get some things just for her. You make sure she has what *she* needs—and maybe a few extra things just because." Maggie was waving her wooden spoon as she talked.

Rock laughed and agreed. When Maggie waved her spoon, it was wise to sit up and take notice. She was likely to whack whoever she was talking to if they didn't.

CHAPTER 50

"Ask Me Anything You Want"

ROCK AND CLARE ATE QUICKLY AND SLIPPED OUTSIDE. The children were still asleep, and it was a perfect day for a buggy ride.

Rock had old Pete hooked to the buggy, and it was tied in front of the house.

As he put his hands around Clare's waist to lift her up, he thought of the last time he had started to lift her down from a buggy. He had felt the growth in her stomach that day and he frowned at the memory.

Clare saw him frown and glared at him. "I don't weigh that much, Rock. And if you do think I'm too heavy, just give me a hand next time."

Rock stared at her in surprise but laughed. "No, that isn't what I was thinking." He jumped onto the seat beside her and clucked to Pete as he patted her leg.

"I was thinking about the last time I lifted you down from a buggy and how I hurt your stomach when I squeezed it."

Clare's face paled a little, but she didn't answer.

Rock grinned as he stated, "We have two and a half hours in this buggy, side by side, to talk about whatever you want. Here is your time to ask me anything you want about the ranch. Finances, debt, plans… curtains…"

Clare looked over at him and her eyes opened wide. "Curtains? What do you know about curtains?"

"Not much, but women seem to like them. Tell me what it is about a flimsy piece of cloth blowing on a rod that women seem to like so much."

Rock looked so puzzled that Clare laughed out loud.

"Color. They brighten the room and can usually be made at little cost."

Rock nodded. "So, what color would you make curtains if you were to put some up?"

"Purple is my favorite color, but I think I would put red in the kitchen. You have two windows in there, and I love the one over the wash area. I can look out in the yard and see what is going on. I would make them open in the middle. That way, they could be pulled apart to see out and to let the sunshine in. Red with some little flowers—or gingham—but I like flowers the best.

"And I would paint the walls to make the kitchen lighter. It would make it seem larger and brighter too. I like things bright and open. Lots of light and sunshine." Clare's eyes were sparkling as she talked, and Rock watched her as she moved her hands.

"How about you, Rock? Do you like curtains?"

Rock grinned at her. "I don't much care one way or the other, but if it will make you happy, we will have curtains."

He studied her face as his eyes twinkled. "How about the bunkhouse? Think we need curtains out there?"

Clare rolled her eyes as she replied, "No, but make sure you have spittoons. And just so you know, I am not cleaning them out."

Rock laughed as he agreed. Then he looked at her more seriously.

"So, what do you want to know about the ranch, Clare? We have hardly talked about it at all."

Clare answered slowly, "Well, I know that Darby McCune gave you the ranch when he died. I know it is around twelve thousand acres although I have no idea how much or how big that is. I also know that you introduced Angus bulls several years ago."

When Rock cocked an eyebrow at her, she explained, "Some of the ranchers around Helena were talking about it, and I heard your name.

"My pappy was sure Mr. McCune had gold stashed here, but when I first met Suzanna, she was convinced he didn't have any money. We didn't really talk about it after that. Suzanna didn't bring it up, and it was none of my business." She smiled at Rock.

"Suzanna did tell me that she went partners with you on some cattle. She was so excited. I'm not sure if it was the idea of buying cattle or if it was just being partners with you though!" Clare's eyes were sparkling as she laughed.

He chuckled and tapped the lines on Pete's back.

"It didn't matter much. We were engaged that night and married the next month, so she would have been my partner either way."

"Just like you," he added. "We own everything together. None of this mine and yours—it is ours."

Clare was quiet as she studied her hands. Finally, she looked up at the quiet man sitting beside her. He was watching her closely, and she almost didn't respond.

"I have scraped by on next to nothing most of my life, Rock. It is okay if you want me to do that, but I would like to get some fabric to make Zeke a shirt and a little dress for Annie. I can make you a shirt if you want as well. Of course, if we can't afford it, I will patch the things we have and make them work."

Rock shook his head. "If you see something in town that you think we need, buy it. Now if it costs as much as a horse or a piece of land, then we need to talk. Otherwise, you decide.

"You run the house, Clare. I don't need to oversee what you do. I would like you to be part of the management decisions on the ranch though. If something would happen to me, you need to know how to run things on your own."

Clare was surprised as she listened to Rock. She had never heard a man talk that way before.

As she pondered what he had just said, Rock touched her arm.

"What about you, Clare? What would you like?" Rock asked softly.

Clare twisted her hands together and sat stiffly in her seat. "I really don't need anything but some needles and thread. I have three dresses and that is enough."

Rock pulled Pete to a halt. He put his arms around Clare and pulled her close as he smiled at her.

"Clare, Darby did have gold. I kept some of it and gave some of it away. In addition, I have had some good ranching years. We can afford for you to buy things for yourself as well as for the kids. And I would love to have a new shirt. I like dark green—but no little flowers."

Clare smiled at him, and Rock kissed her. As he released her and picked up the lines, he smacked his lips. "Yep, you still taste good, *and* you smell like lilacs!"

Clare turned her head so Rock could see her hair. She had woven lilacs into her hair. The purple and blue blossoms blended in with the purple of her dress and the blue of her sapphire necklace.

He sniffed them and then tried to sniff her neck.

She laughed as she elbowed him. Then she looped her arm through his and they talked the rest of the way to Stevensville.

Pete was excited to get back home. He picked up his pace the closer he came to Stevensville. The old horse acted like a colt as he pulled the buggy briskly through town. Rock didn't even have to turn him into the livery—he went there on his own.

The temporary hostler came out. He said nothing as he eyed the horse and buggy.

"Ike will be in with my wagon before too long. Have him take it up to the dry goods store before he unhitches so we can load it. And give old Pete some oats. We worked him mighty hard this week."

Rock took Clare's arm. "How about we get supplies right away? Ike should be along in a half hour or so, and then we can eat." He grinned at her as he added, "That means we have less than an hour of peace and quiet before the storm."

Rock led Clare across the street and into the dry goods store. He left her by the fabric and handed his list to the clerk.

Clare fingered some of the fabric before she walked over to where Rock was waiting.

"I'd like to add some baking soda and sugar to your list as well as cinnamon and corn meal if they are in stock."

The clerk nodded and then looked at Clare. "Anything else, ma'am? We just got some cocoa in. It's a little pricey, but a little chocolate cake is tasty now and then."

Clare paused but shook her head.

"No, but I do need some fabric if you can help me with that."

When she turned her back, Rock pointed at the cocoa and then at his pile on the counter. The clerk smiled and added a large can of cocoa powder to the provisions stacked there.

Rock followed Mrs. Hoffman over to where Clare was looking at the fabric.

She showed Rock two different greens and he picked the one he wanted. Clare decided to make Zeke's shirt the same color while Annie's dress would be pink with lots of flowers. As she handed both bolts of cloth to the clerk, Rock lifted another bolt from under the counter. The deep purple was darker than the dress Clare had on, and the fabric was a little heavier.

"Like that color?"

"I do but I don't need it."

Rock laid it on top of her pile.

"Tell Mrs. Hoffman how much you need. Better add some sewing things to that pile too. Maggie will be taking her supplies with her when she leaves."

Mrs. Hoffman eagerly showed Clare where the sewing accessories were, and she picked out what she needed. Rock watched as Clare carefully selected the bare minimum of sewing necessities.

Maggie was right. Clare refuses to get herself anything that is not necessary.

Rock felt in his pocket for the simple wedding band. Ike had a friend who worked with gold, and he helped line things out. They even used gold taken from Darby's mine. *A ring made from the ranch itself.* Rock smiled as he fingered the ring. He had thought for some time before he had it engraved. He finally settled on "For My Beautiful Clare."

The band was thicker than Rock had originally requested. The craftsman told Ike that pure gold was soft and would wear down. He suggested making it thicker to stand the daily wear and tear better. Ike had even figured out Clare's finger size when he was measuring Maggie's finger.

"Put yur finger up here, gurl. Let's see how much smaller yore knuckles is than ol' Ike's." He slid his string over her finger and kissed her hand as he pulled the string off.

"You'll always be my special gal," Ike had whispered.

Clare loved the old man. He was rough and gruff but had a heart of gold. *I wish my pappy had been as kind as Ike.* Every day, she was thankful that she was the only little girl.

CHAPTER 51

FATHER RAVALLI

ROCK HEARD A WAGON RUMBLING DOWN THE STREET and stepped out to greet Ike. Two little faces were wedged between Ike and Maggie, and they waved excitedly when they saw Rock.

Several people turned to see what the excitement was about, and Annie shouted, "My papa is marrying Clare today, and I get a new mama!"

Clare blushed as she hurried toward the wagon. She held Annie's hand as the little girl jumped down.

Zeke jumped on Rock and whispered, "And I get a new papa!"

Rock squeezed the little boy and whispered back, "Yep, and I get a new son!"

Ike rushed to help Maggie down, and they soon had the wagon loaded. Ike pulled it into the livery and threw the blankets over the provisions piled in the back. He was sure that everything would be safe, but it never hurt to cover things up.

He hurried across to Mrs. Barry's eating house and joined his family at their table.

The little waitress rushed out to help them, and the disappointment on her face when she saw Clare was clearly obvious.

Clare was trying not to laugh when Annie announced, "My papa is getting married today, and Clare is going to be my new mama. Ain't—uh—isn't that nice?"

Ike and Maggie were laughing, and Clare blushed as she smiled at Annie.

The bold waitress always made Rock want to run, but she wasn't a threat anymore. He squeezed Clare's hand and agreed, "You're right, Annie. After this afternoon, your daddy is a married man."

As the waitress hurried away, Clare commented dryly, "Well, you just broke her heart."

The look Rock gave her made everyone laugh. He growled to himself and shoved in a mouthful of food.

Clare had butterflies in her stomach and could barely eat, but Rock had no such problem. He ate his meal and cleaned up hers as well. Then, he finished off Zeke's and Annie's as they were too excited to eat theirs.

When the plates were empty, Maggie suggested they take a surrey to the Mission.

"I know the walk to the Mission would do Annie and Zeke good since they need to run off some energy, but I want to introduce Clare to my good friends, John and Nancy Owen. Fort Owen is over a mile from the Mission, and that is too far for me to walk."

Rock laughed as he agreed. "You two bring the surrey. We'll let the kids run as far as the Mission. Clare and I can follow them that far."

As the kids went racing ahead, Rock took Clare's arm.

"Nervous?"

"Terrified," she answered.

Rock looked down at her in surprise.

"What is there to be terrified about? I think it will be nice to have you around every day. I can put my cold feet on you at night, steal all the covers, and maybe even drool on your pillow."

Clare looked up at Rock and he smiled at her. She laughed and jabbed him with her elbow. Her nervousness melted away, and she squeezed his arm.

"You're right. For all you know, I snore like a freight train and hog the bed. Yes, I'm looking forward to being married to you too."

Rock studied her face, and his eyes began to twinkle.

"Hog the bed, huh? I guess that means you don't stay on your side. I think I might be okay with that."

Clare blushed as Rock grinned down at her. She muttered under her breath, "Shy man, my eye. You are quite bold and proud of it."

Rock laughed out loud. He hollered at the kids to slow down and was still laughing when they caught up.

Father Ravalli was working in the chapel, and he greeted them. Once again, he had a long apron on over his black cassock and was covered in sawdust.

He pointed up at the statues and fixtures inside the chapel. "We can't afford to spend money, so these must be made. I like to work with wood though. It relaxes me when I talk to St. Joseph."

At Rock's surprised look, Father Ravalli laughed. "Yes, Jesus' father on earth was quite the carpenter. I ask him for advice when I get stuck on something. That is his statue over there. I'm working on the baptismal font now. I use what's available, so I am doing lots of soldering."

Father Ravalli walked them around the little mission church and pointed out each saint. He was especially proud of the crucifix that hung above the wooden altar at the front of the church.

That altar was larger and more ornate than the side altars, but all were handmade. Rock was amazed at the man's skill.

"Craftsman, doctor, surgeon—is there anything you can't do, Padre?"

The priest laughed, and his kind eyes twinkled.

"Well, I have never experienced marriage nor will I, so you are one up on me there." His eyes were still twinkling when he added seriously,

"Of course, I have heard lots of stories, so if you need advice, I can pass along what I have learned."

Clare laughed along with Rock. She hadn't been to church since she had left the Macks, and she felt a strong pull. She smiled as she listened to the priest talk. The little church was very welcoming, and she liked Father Ravalli.

Ike and Maggie stepped through the door. They seemed to know the priest well, and they visited a while. Father Ravalli smiled at the young couple.

"If you are ready, let's go up to the altar. Rock and Clare, you can stand here in front. Ike, Maggie, you stand on either side." He placed Zeke and Annie beside Maggie, and they were craning their necks to ensure they didn't miss anything.

Clare stated nervously, "Father, you know I am not Catholic. I'm not sure we discussed how that could affect our marriage in any of our conversations."

Father Ravalli smiled.

"No, but Rock is, and you told me you had been baptized." He grinned at the fidgeting groom and added, "Although it would be nice to see him in church more often than weddings and funerals."

When Rock looked at the priest in surprise, Father Ravalli laughed.

"And how do I know that? We priests have our ways."

Father Ravelli was direct and to the point. He read from the Bible before he talked to them about marriage and what God expected of them.

When he was done, he made a large sign of the cross over them.

"I bless this marriage in the name of the Father, and of the Son, and of the Holy Spirit. What God has joined together, let no man put asunder." Father Ravalli paused just a moment before he added softly, "You may kiss the bride."

Both Annie and Zeke giggled as they leaned forward to watch.

Rock took Clare's face in his hands and kissed her gently. Then he pulled her close and kissed her again.

Zeke was smiling, and Annie was laughing so hard that she was almost falling on the floor.

Rock grinned at the two of them. He thought it was a fine wedding. Small, quick, and to the point—just the way he liked things.

Clare was quiet during the service, and her eyes were misty when the priest finished.

Father Ravalli shook Rock's hand and then Clare's.

His eyes were twinkling as he stated, "See—I had him pegged as the husband from the beginning. You should listen to your priest. Sometimes, he is right."

Clare laughed. "Thank you, Father. And thank you for doing my surgery. I feel wonderful."

"That's good. And let me know when you become pregnant. We want to keep an eye on that incision."

Rock's heart clutched at the priest's words. He looked quickly at Clare, but she was smiling. He frowned but forced himself to relax. *We can talk about it later. This is our wedding day, and I don't want anything to ruin it.*

Maggie grabbed Clare's hand. "Come—I want you to meet my good friends."

She hurried them to the surrey, and Ike drove them to Fort Owen. The trading post was busy with lots of rigs and horses tied in front.

Nancy saw Maggie coming and rushed to meet her. "My friend! Is it true? You will marry again?"

Maggie nodded happily and pulled Ike forward.

Nancy grabbed Ike and hugged him. "I know this man. He is a good man. He often helps us with the horses." She smiled from Maggie to Ike as she held their hands.

"When two of my favorite people decide to marry, it is a day to celebrate. Come and share a root beer with me. And who are these small children?"

Maggie tugged Clare's arm until she stepped up, and Rock joined her.

"These two are the closest Ike and I will ever come to having children of our own. Clare and Rock Beckler. They were just married today."

Nancy's eyes shined brighter. "More reason to celebrate. We will have some cake as well. John ordered some cocoa, and our oldest daughter made a cake. Come, my friends. Let us celebrate."

Clare followed Maggie and Nancy through the trading post toward the small living quarters in the back. She stopped when she heard a sharp, tinny voice that she recognized. A tight knot formed in her stomach, and she could feel her body try to shrink. Her breath caught in her throat, and she wanted to hide. Her eyes darted back and forth, and just for a moment, she was a little girl again.

"Now ya jist sit yurself down, an' don't ya move. Little girls ain't good fer nothin' so ya ain't a gonna eat today. Mebbie you'ins cin eat tomorrow an' mebbie you'ins won't."

Clare slowly turned toward the voice. She put her hand in her pocket and felt for the Derringer she was never without.

CHAPTER 52

LITTLE NORA

CLARE'S YOUNGEST BROTHER, SILAS, WAS SQUATTING beside a small girl. The child's face was dirty, and her reddish-brown hair was tangled and matted. For Clare, it was like looking in a mirror from the past. She could feel the horror rising in her chest.

"Hello, Silas. Is this your little girl?" Clare asked as she bent down beside the small girl.

Silas looked at his sister in shock. "Yur all growed up, Clarey. We thought ya moved up north somewhere."

Clare stood and reached behind her. She pulled a piece of beef jerky off the rack. She handed it to the child. The little girl looked from her father to Clare as she slowly reached out her hand.

Pappy stepped forward. He tried to knock the meat away and Clare shoved him.

"Don't you come any closer to this child. She will eat, and I will stay here until she is done," she hissed. "You are a pathetic example of what a father should be and even worse as a grandfather."

Rock was meandering through the tack section. He looked up when he heard Clare speak angrily. His eyes found her, and he strode back to where she was standing. His stomach knotted at the sight of the small girl on the floor, and his eyes were hard as he moved close to Clare.

Clare turned again to Silas. "Why did you stay with him?" she asked bitterly. "You have a little girl, and you know how he is. Leave with me today. Come to our ranch and work. You can bring your daughter with you, and I will watch her while you are working." She paused and looked around. "Where is her mother?"

Silas shrugged.

"Pappy said she done runned off. I ain't so sure. He was always pesterin' her. Either way, she's gone, an' she didn't take Nora with 'er."

Clare grabbed her brother's shoulders and pulled him up.

"Come with me, Silas. Please! You don't want your daughter raised anywhere close to that monster."

Pappy roared at Clare as he pulled his pistol.

Rock jerked her out of the way, and Pappy's shot took Silas in the chest. Rock lunged at the old man and hit him hard enough to break his jaw.

Clare was sobbing as she dropped to the floor by her brother.

Rock cursed under his breath. "The one day I leave my guns in the wagon," he growled.

"Oh, Silas. You were the only kind brother I had. Why didn't you leave?" Clare sobbed.

Silas gasped, "Pappy wouldn't—let me—take Nora. Said I could—go anytime but—but—Nora had to stay. Couldn't—couldn't leave 'er."

Nora squatted on the floor and stared at her father. A big tear slid down her face.

Silas grabbed Clare's arm. "Please—take 'er. Take 'er with ya. Don't let him have…"

Silas's grip relaxed and he fell back on the floor. Clare's face felt like stone when she stood. Her eyes were hard, and her face was white as she pulled the small gun from her pocket.

Rock grabbed her hand and turned the gun away from her father.

"Give me the gun, Clare. He will hang for what he did today. I will make sure of it. Don't do this. Give me the gun and go to Nora."

Clare's body went from rigid to shaking. She let go of the gun, and Rock handed it behind him to Ike. He held Clare as she sobbed.

Pappy roared and grabbed for his gun. He pointed it again toward Clare.

Rock threw Clare to the side and dove toward Pappy's knees. He smashed the man backwards. The bullet hit the floor, and Rock slapped the gun from Pappy's hand. His fist slammed into the old man's chin a second time, and Pappy collapsed.

Clare slowly pulled herself up from the floor. She took several deep breaths before she hurried to where Nora was cowering.

"Come, Nora. You come home with me and be my little girl." Clare dropped to her knees and tried to put her arms around the frightened little girl.

Nora looked about the same age as Annie and Zeke. She was still clutching the jerky, but silent sobs were jerking her body, and her eyes were terrified. She watched Pappy, and when the old man's leg moved, she fled. She crawled under a shelf and crouched in the corner. Her breathing was choppy and rough.

Clare knelt on the floor and peered under the shelf. "Little Nora, come to Mama Clare." Clare was trying to smile as she held out her arms.

Nora finally crawled out, and Clare picked her up.

She could feel the little girl's ribs as she hugged her. "No one will ever hurt you like that again, Nora. You are safe now," Clare whispered. "And I will make sure that you always have food." She kissed her dirty cheek. "Little Nora, I am so glad we found you today."

Nora touched her cheek where Clare had kissed her and then put her hand to Clare's lips. Clare kissed them as the little girl smiled in surprise. She pointed at Clare. "You Mama?"

Clare nodded, "Yes, Mama. I am Nora's mama."

The little girl hugged Clare's neck so tightly that she could barely breathe.

Nancy touched Clare's arm. "Come. We will wash the child and give her some clothes." She had a tub filled with warm water in no time. She grabbed some soap and sent her second daughter to find a dress for Nora.

When the women removed Nora's tattered clothes, large bruises showed all over her small body. When they touched her ribs, she winced and pulled away.

Clare carefully set her in the tub, and Nora's little eyes opened wide. She tried to stand up, but Clare shook her head.

"Bath, Nora. Wash."

All three women worked to clean the little girl. Nancy brought in a blanket and a new hairbrush when they were done. Clare stared at the brush and a sob caught in her throat. Maggie patted her back while Nancy pretended not to notice.

"I so didn't want any more little girls to experience that man's evil," Clare whispered.

Maggie put her arms around Clare and Nora. Annie stared from face to face with big eyes, and for once, had nothing to say.

CHAPTER 53

"I Married Your Daughter Today"

JOHN OWEN RUSHED INSIDE WHEN HE HEARD THE gunshots. He helped the men tie the unconscious Pappy, and they tossed him in the back of one of John's delivery wagons. They wrapped Silas in a blanket and lifted him into the back of the wagon as well.

Rock climbed in to take the lines, and Ike hopped up beside him. They headed back to Stevensville. Ike reached into Pappy's pocket and pulled out a packet of papers.

"John Henry Fohrman. Well, at least we'll know what name to call 'im when they hang 'im."

Rock was silent for a moment. "He'd better hang. Clare and Nora won't be safe as long as he's alive." Then he cursed under his breath.

"That's the last time I go somewhere without my guns. Foolish thing to do. I left my guns and my knife in the wagon since we were going to church. That old man nearly killed Clare, and he shot his own son."

Ike was quiet as Rock talked. *Rock's right*, Ike thought. *Pappy won't rest until he has destroyed both of their lives.* He nodded somberly but finally chuckled.

"Ya left yur guns to home but yur wife shore didn't. I believe ya better keep one eye on her."

Rock wasn't listening. He stared straight ahead and frowned as they drove. He stopped at the livery and pulled his guns out of the wagon. He strapped them on and shoved his knife into its sheath.

"I should have shot him seven years ago. It would have saved Clare's family a lot of grief," Rock grated out as they drove up the street.

Sheriff Hawkins met them as they pulled up in front of the sheriff's office. Rock grabbed Pappy by the collar and dragged him out of the wagon bed. He dropped him on the ground and the old man groaned. His jaw was obviously broken. Rock glared at him and pushed down the urge to kick him. He stared at the man on the ground before he looked up at the sheriff.

"There's a dead man in the back of this wagon. That fellow shot his own son when I jerked Clare out of the way. The dead man is Clare's brother, and we are going to take his little girl in."

Rock's eyes were hard as he looked at Sheriff Hawkins. He added softly, "And if the judge doesn't sentence him to hang, I am going to hunt him down myself. He has already been to my place to rob and kill. I won't have this man loose when he might be looking for Clare or that child."

The sheriff studied Rock's face and slowly nodded. He had never seen Rock mad before, but he believed the angry father *would* hunt the old man down if he walked.

"Judge Wheeler will be coming through tomorrow or the next day. I will write down what you told me. Just stop by on your way out of town to sign it. I think this is a cut and dried case. With your statement and Ike's testimony, I think we can move this along fairly quickly.

"Why don't you go ahead and take him on into the jail. I'll start on that report."

Rock nodded. Once again, he grabbed Pappy by the collar and dragged him up the steps and into the jail.

The old man began to curse, "Ya broke my jaw!" As he spit out a couple of teeth, Rock pulled back his fist. He stopped when Ike grabbed his arm.

"Leave 'im be, Rock. Let's git on back to our womenfolk an' thank the Good Lord that this here man won't never hurt another helpless little gurl again."

Rock stared from the old man to Ike and slowly nodded. He shoved Pappy into the cell and slammed the door. He started to speak but turned away. He stopped at the door and slowly walked back to the cell. He gripped the bars. His hard green eyes bored into the old man as he spoke.

"I married your daughter today. She and Nora are the only good things in your life you didn't destroy. Clare's a fine woman and little Nora has a home with us."

Rock gripped the bars of the cell so tightly that his knuckles turned white. He added softly, "And if by chance you don't hang, don't bother to run because I *will* find you. And when I do, I'll make you pay for everything you put Clare through as a child." Rock spit on the floor. "You are a disgrace to all men."

Pappy was quiet as he stared at Rock, and the big man left the jail without looking back. He stopped at the sheriff's desk.

"I think we will head on home. How long will it take you to write that up? Ike and Maggie were going to keep the kids tonight, but I'm not sure—that might have changed since we have Nora."

Rock looked toward Ike who shrugged his shoulders. "Don't matter none to us—guess that will be up to Nora an' Clare. One more so quiet as Nora won't matter, but she might not want to let Clare out of her sight."

The sheriff looked at his scratches on the note pad beside him. "Give me about a half an hour. It will be brief, but it will be complete."

Rock stared at Silas's body. "I'm not sure what to do with him."

Ike thought a moment before he pointed across the street. "Let's leave him over there. The smithy runs a burial service. He'll arrange fer a coffin. Maggie an' me 'ill make arrangements to bury 'im up yonder in the cemetery tomorrow."

CHAPTER 54

To Heal a Little Heart

SILAS'S BODY WAS LEFT WITH THE BLACKSMITH. IKE drove the delivery wagon back to Fort Owen. Rock followed him with his loaded wagon. He was anxious to get home. He wanted to look things over before dark, and he didn't want to try to navigate the rough road home in the dark with a wagon.

When they asked where the women were, Nancy pointed and replied, "They left just a few minutes ago with the children. John took them back to Maggie's new house."

Rock thanked her. He started to leave but turned around.

"And thank you for helping Clare. What do we owe you for the jerky and Nora's clothes?"

Nancy smiled as she patted Rock's shoulder. "You owe us nothing. We are all called to help from time to time, and I was glad to do so."

Rock nodded and the two men headed back towards Stevensville.

Ike and Maggie's little house was tucked back in a grove of trees. The yard had a white picket fence around it. Someone had planted multiple flower beds, and the bright spots of color could be seen from the street.

Rock looked at Ike in surprise, and the old man grinned.

"I bought this here little place several years ago an' started workin' on it. It woulda been a lot more house than this here ol' bachelor needed, but I knowed Maggie would love it if I could ever win 'er over." Ike's eyes twinkled as he laughed.

"I knowed my Maggie liked flowers, so I planted all those little beds. I showed it to 'er jist the other day, an' she was so plumb happy she jist 'bout cried." He frowned as he added, "I have never figgered out why womenfolk cry when they's happy. It's all durn confusin'."

"Women are just confusing all the way around," Rock agreed, and both men chuckled.

The children ran out to greet them when they arrived, and Ike began to pull dried apricots out of his pockets.

"Now how did that there fruit git in my pockets? Nora, ya come on over here. These two little hooligans cin share with ya."

Nora spied the basket of apples in Rock's wagon, and she pointed at them.

"Ol' Pappy eats those." She was looking around furtively as her eyes darted from place to place.

Rock lifted the little girl into the wagon bed.

"I tell you what, Nora. You pick out three apples, one for each of you kids. You pick whichever ones you think look good, and you can eat yours all by yourself."

Nora stared at the apples almost reverently, but she didn't touch them.

Rock finally picked one and handed it to her. "You can eat this one, Nora. You don't even have to share because we have enough for everyone."

He picked one for himself. "You bite apples like this," he stated as he took a large bite.

Nora smelled the apple and took a tiny bite. She gave Rock a glorious smile as she sat down in the wagon bed. She slowly ate the entire apple. When she was done, she picked two more apples and climbed out of the wagon.

She ran to where Zeke and Annie were digging outside the picket fence and handed each an apple. All three children sat in the dirt and talked as the apples were consumed.

Rock watched them with a smile. "I think Nora will probably be okay here tonight. Let's head on in to talk to the women."

Clare glanced up as the men came through the door. Her face was pale, but she gave Rock a small smile.

Rock pointed outside. "Nora seems to be fitting in all right. Are you ready to head out to the ranch? Ike said Nora can stay here if you are comfortable leaving her."

Clare started to shake her head, but Maggie touched her shoulder.

"Let's let Nora decide. I will call the children in for a cookie, and we can see what they all say."

Maggie walked to the door. She stood in the doorway with her hands on her hips and hollered, "Any kids out there who want a cookie? I have just a few, and your papa is trying to eat them all!"

All three children came bursting through the door. They charged toward the table, bumping each other as they pulled out the chairs.

Clare pointed at the wash basin as she shook her head.

Annie frowned as she studied her hands. Her fingernails were back with grit, and she had dirt smudges all over her face. She started to argue, but Rock frowned at her. Her frown turned into a full scowl, and she sat there for a moment. Finally, she climbed down to follow Zeke.

Nora wasn't very dirty, but she followed the other kids to the wash basin and watched Zeke as he washed.

He handed Nora the bar of soap. "Use this, Nora. The dirt comes off easier. Then you use this little brush to get your fingernails clean."

Nora began to scrub, and Annie joined her. As they passed the soap back and forth talking the entire time, Clare smiled. *Nora is going to be okay. There is nothing better to heal a little heart than other little hearts.*

Once again, all three children climbed onto their chairs, and Maggie handed each a cookie. Annie and Zeke began to wolf theirs down.

Nora stared at hers and carefully laid it on the table. She kept one eye on Rock and Ike as she smelled it. When they didn't do anything, she slowly picked it up.

The memories of Clare's childhood returned vividly as she watched the little girl. It was obvious Nora was not used to eating all the food that was placed on the table. Clare's stomach tightened.

She leaned down and whispered, "Nora, that cookie is yours. In our family, we all eat the same things. If Annie and Zeke get a snack, you get a snack as well. Sometimes you will need to share, but you will never be left out."

She kissed the little girl's cheek, and Nora looked up at her in surprise. Once again, she touched her cheek and smiled at Clare.

Annie was munching delightedly. She looked up as Clare kissed Nora.

"Is Nora coming to our house? Is she going to stay forever?"

When both Rock and Clare nodded, Annie jumped down and ran over to Nora's chair.

"Did you hear that, Nora? We are going to be sisters! I always wanted a brother or a sister, and now I have both!"

Nora smiled and took a big bite out of her cookie as Annie hugged her.

Rock smiled as he watched the kids. "That is what I want to talk to you kids about. Do all three of you want to spend the night with Ike and Maggie? They can bring you home tomorrow—"

"Or even the next day if we are having too much fun," Maggie interrupted with a big smile.

"All of us?" questioned Zeke. "Nora too?'

Clare nodded. "If she wants to stay, she can. What do you think, Nora?"

Nora studied the faces of the adults and the excited children. She smiled and nodded.

"I stay with Auntie and Ike." Her smile slowly disappeared, and a worried look came over her face. "You come back?"

Annie snorted. "We are their kids. They would miss us too much to leave us here."

Rock grabbed Annie and Zeke and swung them around. "You are right about that, Annie. I will miss you tonight!"

He put them down and turned to Nora. "Would you like a wild ride like I just gave Annie and Zeke, Nora?"

At first, Nora just stared at her new father. Then she gave him a shy smile and nodded.

Rock swung Nora around but not as fast as he had the other two. She was laughing when he set her down.

"Did you like to fly like a bird, Nora?"

Nora nodded and her eyes shined. "Nora likes birds."

"Clare and I are going back to the ranch to do chores." He grinned as he looked at the kids and whispered, "I might even swing her around like a bird. What do you think, kids?"

Annie and Zeke began to talk excitedly about how he would have to hold her, and Rock winked at Clare.

"What do you think, Mrs. Beckler. Would you like me to swing you around like a bird and play a little tonight?"

Clare's face blushed a deep red, and Maggie smacked Rock.

"You behave yourself, Rock. Don't you embarrass your wife before you even get her home."

Rock's grin became bigger, and he offered his arm to Clare. "Ready to go, Mrs. Beckler?"

Clare looked at the children and panic rose up in her. The only time she had left Zeke overnight was when she was sick. *And little Nora. What if she cries?*

Zeke waved as he raced outside. He hollered over his shoulder, "Grampy Ike is taking us fishing, and we are digging for nightcrawlers. Come on, girls. We're burnin' daylight!"

As the three kids tumbled through the door, Rock took Clare's hand and tucked it through his arm.

"I think that answers your worries. Let's head for home before it gets too dark."

He lifted Clare onto the wagon seat and turned the team south. He patted her hand and smiled down at her.

"This day sure didn't end up like I planned, but I'm happy we were able to help little Nora."

CHAPTER 55

A Slow Ride Home

"I'LL BET YOU LOOKED A LOT LIKE NORA WHEN YOU were that age," Rock commented quietly.

Clare looked away. Her voice was strained when she spoke.

"The first time I ever saw myself in a mirror was at Pastor Mack's home the night they took me in. Suzanna and Rebecca gave me a bath. Rebecca handed me a mirror and a new hairbrush. I recognized the women in the mirror, but I didn't know who the girl was." Clare took a deep breath before she continued. "When Nancy handed me a hairbrush for Nora today, that night flashed in front of me." She squeezed Rock's arm.

"Thank you for supporting me and taking Nora in."

Rock looked surprised. "Why wouldn't we take her in? She is little and helpless. Besides, she's your niece."

Clare's lips trembled as she stared up at him, and Rock pulled the team to a stop. He took his wife in his arms and kissed her gently before he pulled her close.

"Clare, I know I'm rough, and I don't always get things figured out as fast as I should when it comes to people. I promise you though, I will never intentionally break your heart.

"My family is my everything, and you are my family." He pulled her onto his lap, and the mules stamped impatiently as the wagon stayed right where it was for some time. Rock finally slid Clare back onto the seat and clucked at the mules.

"We are for sure going to get home after dark now." He grinned as he squeezed her leg, "But it will be worth it."

Clare turned the gold band on her finger, and Rock touched it.

"Ike mined that gold out of Darby's mine."

Clare slid the ring off her finger. She blinked away her tears as she read the inscription. She was quiet as she slid the ring on.

Rock squeezed her leg again. "Now don't you tear up on me. I just don't know how to handle women when they cry."

Clare smiled up at Rock. "I'm crying because I'm happy—because you had a ring made especially for me from gold mined on your ranch. Because you had it engraved with words from your heart and because you are such a good man. I'm crying because I'm so blessed."

She smiled as she kissed Rock's cheek, and his big heart squeezed in his chest. He cleared his throat and smiled as he looked down at her.

He drawled, "You left out one detail—you went and married a rich feller!"

Clare laughed softly as she looked up at him. "Yes, there is that." She moved closer to Rock and whispered, "But I would have married you if you had been a $30 a month cowhand, riding from outfit to outfit. I love you, Rock Beckler."

Once again, the mules stamped their feet and waited for the signal to move on. They didn't know what was going on back there, but they were certainly not used to stopping on the trail…for sure when it was getting dark.

CHAPTER 56

A Donkey In The House

IT WAS NEARLY DARK WHEN THE BECKLERS FINALLY pulled into their ranch yard. Rock drove the wagon up to the house and began to unload the supplies. Clare started to help, but he shook his head.

"I don't think you should be leaning and lifting like that. You just put things away as I bring them in. It won't take me long to unload."

Clare quickly put the supplies away as Rock stacked them on the table. Mrs. Hoffman had wrapped her fabric in brown paper. She started to carry the paper packages to Maggie's room when she realized she had four packages instead of three. She frowned as she pulled the end open on each one. When she opened the fourth one, she saw red fabric.

Clare's eyes opened in surprise as she tore the wrapping loose. Red fabric spilled out. It was solid red on top with a border of small flowers.

Rock had just brought in the last load when she looked up from the fabric. He grinned at her.

"Now how did that get in with our provisions? Sure now, Mrs. Hoffman must have given us someone else's curtain cloth."

Clare threw her arms around Rock's neck. "Thank you, Rock. Oh, thank you!"

Rock stared at his pretty wife and the small package she was holding. He wrapped her up and held her tightly. He knew she would like it, but he was a little surprised at how happy it made her. Rock smiled down at her.

"There you go, distracting me again." He stepped back.

"I have chores to do, but you hold that kiss for me till I get back. I will sure be glad to discuss that further." He grinned at her and hurried outside to take care of his animals.

Red and Georgia both nickered at him when he opened the gate. They followed him into the barn. He broke an apple and gave half to each of them. Patches and Steed raced up. They pushed by him to get in the barn first.

Darby's little mare was the last one to arrive. She was followed by last year's foal. The little filly didn't want to leave her mother, and Rock hadn't separated them yet. "Tonight's the night," he muttered as he petted her and gave them both apples.

"Hello, Lady. How are you feeling tonight? Is that foal about ready to come?" Rock asked as he felt her stomach. He lit a lantern and checked her from behind.

"It sure looks like it. I had better check you later tonight. Back in your stall you go. You too, Red. And no, you can't be in the same stall."

Rock opened the wide doors at the front of the barn and led the wagon team inside. Once they were unhitched and put away, he forked hay to all the horses. He gave all but the Shetlands and the filly oats.

"You are ornery enough without anything else to charge you up more," he told the two ponies. He locked the filly in a small stall with them. Now that he was storing hay, he didn't want any horses loose inside the barn.

Rock carried the lamp carefully outside and closed the door. He shut the chicken house door and held the lamp up to look over the yard.

"I sure am glad Maggie's milk cow was never purchased. I'd have to milk a cow yet tonight."

Gomer raced up behind Rock and butted him, knocking him forward several steps.

Rock looked around at the donkey in surprise. "What's going on with you, Gomer? Don't tell me you want to spend the night inside!"

Gomer pushed him again, this time toward the house.

Rock stared at the little donkey and slowly lifted his six-shooter out of the holster. "I need to check the house, Gomer? Well, come on then. You help me."

Rock pushed open the door to the kitchen, and Clare looked up with a startled look on her face. He signaled for her to grab the shotgun and crawl under the side cabinet. He knew she had already been in Maggie's room, so his mind was quickly processing where someone might hide in the other two rooms.

Gomer followed Rock into the house, and he immediately went to the doorway of Annie's room. His ears pricked forward as he stared.

The blanket on the top bunk moved slightly, and Rock pointed his gun toward it.

"You climb on down out of that bed. My trigger finger is itchy, so I suggest you not waste any time."

The blankets on the bed didn't move, and Rock edged his way into the room. He worked his way around to the foot of the bed and jerked the blanket off. His gun was cocked and ready to fire. He stared at the small garter snake curled up in the blankets and began laughing.

Gomer charged into the room, grabbed the snake by the tail, and whipped it back and forth. When it dropped, he stomped it and stood there trembling.

Rock stared at the small donkey. He shook his head as he scratched the donkey's long ears.

"Thanks for being such a good guard dog, Gomer."

Rock picked up the pieces of the snake and threw them outside. The little donkey followed him to the doorway and stood there until he came back in. Rock was still chuckling when he helped Clare up.

"We have a snake-killing donkey who thinks he's a watch dog," he told her as he pointed at Gomer.

Clare's heart was pounding, and Rock pulled her close. "Nothing to worry about," he whispered. "You have a furry little protector who has decided that he is going to watch over you." He looked over at Gomer.

The donkey was standing beside the fireplace. His eyes were shut, and he looked like he was asleep.

"In all the years I've known Gomer, he has refused to sleep in a barn. Now, here he is asleep in the house!" Rock grinned at his wife. "It's your call—do you want a donkey in the house who thinks he's a guard dog?"

Clare walked over to Gomer and hugged the little donkey. "Thank you for protecting me, Gomer. I feel safer when you are around."

Gomer opened one eye and wiggled his ears back and forth. He stretched out his neck when Clare scratched his head and rubbed it against her. She hugged him again.

"You go ahead and sleep in the house, Gomer. I will have Rock attach a strap to the door so you can get in and out when you want."

Rock shook his head.

"I sure never thought I would ever have a donkey in the house. I don't know, Clare." He smiled down at his wife as he whispered, "Donkeys are loyal though, and old Gomer loves you."

Clare smiled up at Rock and wrapped her arms around his neck. "How about you, Rock? Do you love me, or can you only say it in Siouan?"

Rock pulled her tighter. "I reckon I love you just as much as old Gomer does—maybe just a little more," he answered huskily as he lifted her up and carried her to the bedroom. All was quiet until Rock growled, "Good grief, woman. How many buttons do you have on this dress?"

Gomer opened one eye and looked toward the bedroom. He heard Clare laugh softly, and then all was quiet in the little stone house.

CHAPTER 57

"I Guess You Knew What You Were Doing, Lord"

ROCK WOKE EARLY AND STARED AT THE WOMAN sleeping next to him. He kissed her gently, and she smiled in her sleep. He rolled over on his back and locked his hands under his head as he stared up at the ceiling.

"Well, Lord, I guess you knew what you were doing. I just don't know how I could be any happier than I am right now." He heard snuffling outside the door, and he grinned.

"I'm coming, Gomer. Just hold your horses, and don't pee on that floor."

Rock swung out of bed and pulled on his pants. He grabbed his shirt and quietly slipped out of the bedroom. He let Gomer out, and the little donkey bucked and brayed across the yard before he disappeared into the trees.

"I never would have dreamed that Gomer would be sleeping in my house when he followed me out of the Three T. I'm kind of glad Old Man Slate didn't get him throttled that day." Rock grinned and shook his head. He chuckled as he remembered the angry rancher.

There were still hot coals in the fireplace, so Rock added more wood. He tromped outside to cut some side pork from the pig that was hanging in the smokehouse.

"I am plumb tickled that young fellow in town sold me this pig. And it was for sure easier to haul the meat than it would have been to drive a pig up here."

He took the pork into the house and laid it on the table. He grabbed the egg basket and headed toward the small chicken house. The chickens were clustered by the door, and they flapped their wings as they raced out. Several of them began pecking at the dead snake, and the rest rushed over to help. Rock stood for a moment and listened to the sounds of the morning.

He set the egg basket down and strolled down to the barn, whistling as he opened the door. He stopped in the doorway and then rushed to Lady's stall.

"Darn it, Lady, I forgot all about you last night!"

He quickly opened the stall, and the little mare nickered softly. A new colt lay in the hay. Rock reached in to pat the little mare.

"That is a fine horse colt, Lady. You are another gift old Darby left me." He filled her feed pan before he left.

The other horses nickered at him, and he began to open stalls. The ponies followed him out of the barn and into the little paddock. He studied the grass before he opened a second gate to let them graze on a different patch.

When Rock opened the gate to Red's stall, the big stallion pushed his head against Rock and nuzzled his shoulder. Rock wrapped his arm around the horse's neck. Georgia pushed in next to Red, and he patted her as well. He led the two of them out, bridled and saddled them, and left them ground tied. He looked at the busy ranch yard and grinned.

"All we need now is a good dog." His face broke into a scowl as he added, "And a durn milk cow."

Rock carried some water into Lady's stall and was still whistling as he strolled back to the house. The saddled horses followed him.

Clare was standing in the doorway, smiling at him.

He moved up beside her and pulled her close. "Good morning, beautiful."

Clare's hair was loose. It curled around her face and down her back. He turned her around to look at the back of her dress.

"I'm glad to see this dress doesn't have as many buttons as that one last night," he drawled as he grinned at her.

Clare's cheeks turned a light pink as she laughed. "So, you are saying that you don't want me to put lots of buttons on my new purple one?"

"That's what I'm saying. And in front would be even better," Rock growled as he grinned at her. They were both laughing when they walked into the kitchen.

Clare already had a skillet heating, and she took the basket of eggs from him.

"How do you like your eggs, and how many do you usually eat?"

Rock grinned at her. "I like them cooked however you feel like cooking them—and I would like five of them."

He sliced some side pork and dropped it into the hot skillet while Clare made scrambled eggs. When the meat was browned, she lifted the skillet out of the fire and cut up the meat. Then she added the eggs and stirred them together. When the eggs finished cooking, Rock lifted the skillet out of the fire and set it on the table.

He took Clare's hand and bowed his head. "Lord, we thank you for this fine day and for this food in front of us. Please keep our livestock healthy, our grass plentiful, and our family safe. Amen." His wife smiled at him, and he squeezed her hand before he released it.

"Clare, how would you like to ride out with me today and check the cattle? I haven't been around the pastures since we branded, and I would like to get a rough count."

He grinned at her and added, "We could even pack a little lunch and have a picnic if you'd like. I have a special place I take all my girls. So far, that has only been Annie, but I'd like to show it to you."

"I would love to do that. Let me put on my riding skirt. I can be ready in ten minutes."

Rock stared at her for a moment and before he asked softly, "Need any help with buttons? I think I am getting pretty good at them."

Clare laughed as she shook her head. "No, I don't. Maybe you can clean up here while I change. Otherwise, you are going to get a late start." Her cheeks were pink, and he almost followed her into the bedroom.

Rock grinned as he scraped the plates. *I like being married. It is nice to have a companion and someone to tease.* He stacked the dishes in the wash basin. Then he rubbed the skillet with a pumice stone before he went outside. He leaned against the door and looked out over his ranch. *It is going to be a beautiful day for a ride.*

When Clare joined him, he turned her around to look at the mountains. "This is my favorite time of the day. So quiet and peaceful. I love the colors of the morning when the sun is just breaking over the mountains."

Clare nodded. "It has always been my favorite time as well."

Rock slid his arm around her. He was pushed away when Gomer shoved his head between them.

Clare looked down at the little donkey and laughed.

"Good morning, Gomer. Thank you for checking up on me." The little donkey rubbed his head against her side and stayed between them.

Rock looked down at him and shook his head.

"Gomer, if I had known how jealous you'd be, I would have left you up north at the mercy of Old Man Slate." He gave Clare a leg up, and they rode down the valley.

Gomer watched them go. He brayed a couple of times, ambled over to the barn, and was soon asleep.

CHAPTER 58

SMITTY

AS THEY RODE, ROCK POINTED OUT HIS PROPERTY line along with the best grass. He also showed Clare the areas he was haying.

"My brand is the Slash B, so anything with that mark belongs to us. I keep adding a little more fence each summer, but it's a long process." He waved his arm to the south.

"Our land is all on this side of St. Mary's River and runs south of here for about twelve miles. That lease for eight thousand acres I told you about will connect with ours on our south boundary line." Rock grinned and added, "I want to introduce you to the old fellow who owns that land today." When Clare looked at him quizzically, Rock shrugged.

"Smitty's been telling me ever since Suzanna died that I needed to marry to give Annie a new ma. He said I was too crotchety single." Rock laughed. "I know he'll approve of you."

As they rode, Rock made notes in his tally book. Clare noticed that he seemed to recognize the cows. She watched quietly. She finally commented, "You seem to recognize your cattle. How can you tell when there are so many? They all look alike to me."

Rock chuckled and nodded.

"I don't have names for them, but I can usually pick my cows out of a herd. Besides, all the momma cows are branded.

"See those black spotted calves? I added some Angus bulls two years ago. I brought them in from England. Long boat ride for them, but see how much more flesh those Angus crosses are carrying than the longhorns? They can handle the cold weather well too. Their hair coat is thicker, and being black, they seem to stay warm easier." He pointed at another group of cattle. "All those little red, white-faced calves are out of the cows I bought up by Helena when you and I went riding."

Clare watched Rock as he talked, and she smiled as she listened. *He loves this life—he truly loves what he does.*

Rock pointed down the valley to a little ranch house. It was surrounded by trees, and the grass stretched out in front of it as far as they could see.

"That little spread down there is Smitty's. He plans to sell his cows at the end of the summer, so we should have his land to use for winter graze. If he ever decides to sell, I'm hoping he'll give me first chance to buy." Rock turned his horse into the little valley. "Let's go see if Smitty's home."

As they rode up to the ranch house, a dog raced out to greet them. A grizzled old man hollered from the barn, and the dog trotted back toward the house.

Rock reined his horse in and grinned at him.

"I see you found yourself a wife, and a right purty one to boot." The old man put out his hand to Clare.

"Come on down off that horse and tell me what you saw in this hard-hearted cowboy that made you want to marry him."

Clare accepted Smitty's hand and slid off her horse. She looked innocently at Smitty as she answered sweetly, "Why, it was his smooth-talking that won me over. He just has a way with words, especially around women. He's as smooth as honey."

Smitty choked on his chewing tobacco, and Rock scowled as his neck turned red.

Clare laughed before she added sincerely, "Rock finally showed me his heart, and I liked what I saw. My name is Clare, Mr. Smitty. It is nice to meet you."

Smitty looked up at Rock. "I like her. You make sure you treat her right 'cause I'll be ready to swoop in and take her off your hands if you don't."

Rock stepped off his horse and moved up beside Clare. He put his arm around his wife and gave her a squeeze as he grinned at the old man. "We've been married a day, and so far, she seems to like me."

Smitty grinned at Clare again and offered her his arm as he turned her toward the house.

"Come on in. I went ahead and drew up the papers. I think we can both agree that I am offering you a fair deal." He turned his head to look up at Clare, and his grin became bigger. She was almost four inches taller than the grizzled old man, and he winked at her.

"So where are you from, Clare? How did you meet this sour cowboy."

Clare looked seriously at the old man, and Rock's neck turned red. *Honest to the letter. She is going to tell him the truth.*

"Let's just say I didn't have the best upbringing. When I met Rock, he didn't approve of my behavior. He tied me to a horse and hauled me to town. I'm quite sure neither of us would have guessed that we would marry someday!"

Smitty stared at Clare and slapped his leg as he began to laugh.

"Are you that sassy little gal the sheriff locked up—the one with the colorful vocabulary?"

It was Clare's turn to blush, and she did. She nodded as she replied, "I'm the one, I'm sorry to say."

Smitty's eyes became serious. "Rebecca Mack was my niece. I was at their house a few times shortly after they took you in." His old eyes became soft as he added, "She loved the living daylights out of you."

Clare's eyes filled with tears, and she nodded. "The Macks were wonderful people. I owe them everything. Rebecca taught me to read and write. They taught me what love was and how I could become a new person. They showed me I didn't have to stay the hurt and angry child that I was." Recognition slowly filled Clare's eyes.

"I remember you now! You had a full beard then, mostly black with just a little gray—and you told stories of how your father traveled with the Lewis and Clark expedition across this area.

"I had never been anywhere, and your stories were so exciting. I used to dream of being part of an expedition like that and traveling around to see the world."

Smitty smiled at Clare. He stretched up and kissed her cheek. "You grew into a fine young woman, Miss Clare. I always said you would."

He turned to Rock, "You really did lasso a fine little filly, Rock. I don't know how you won her over, but you married a good woman." He patted Clare's hand and led her into the cool house.

Rock followed quietly, a small frown on his face. *How is it that even this old codger saw Clare as fine and good while it took me seven years?*

CHAPTER 59

The Contract

SMITTY HAD THE CONTRACT LAID OUT ON HIS kitchen table. Clare stopped to look around the room before she sat down.

"Did you make your furniture, Mr. Smitty? The craftsmanship is incredible."

"I did make some of it, but the nicer pieces were made by Father Ravalli. He is quite a fellow. Doctor, surgeon, wood carver, artist, priest—why the man can just about build or fix anything. He was out here several times when the missus was alive. He gave her that rocking chair over there on one of his visits. She gave him a couple of bred cows every year, and he always appreciated it."

Clare studied the beautiful rocker. It was simple and sturdy, but the workmanship was exquisite.

The old man took a beautiful rosary out of a small wooden box. His eyes were soft as he held it. He handed it to Clare.

"He made this for my Mary when she was ailing, and it gave her comfort. He said he made it out of deer horn. I used to tease her that she would wear it out the way she smoked those beads. She never did though, and she prayed with it every day.

"Mary's been gone now nearly ten years. I can still see her sitting there with those little beads rolling through her fingers and her lips moving. Always gave me a little peace to see her pray."

Smitty looked out over the valley. His voice broke a little as he added, "I never was much of a praying man, but my Mary liked to pray. I always told her that she prayed enough for the two of us."

Clare and Rock were quiet as the old man roughly wiped his eyes. He looked hard at both of them.

"And that is why I'm selling this place. I'm darn lonesome out here. We never had kids so there is no one to pass it on to." He grinned at Rock but addressed Clare.

"Old Rock here pulled me out of a few tight spots over the years, so when I decided to sell, I figured I'd offer it to him first." He winked at her. "Your man is kind of tightfisted with his money when it comes to spending, but he gives his share away."

Rock stared at the old man. *Now how did he know that? Why, I've learned more about Smitty in the last ten minutes than in the seven years I have known him.*

Smitty laughed out loud at the look on Rock's face. He patted the table as he leaned over it. "Take a look at this contract, Rock, and see what you think."

Rock studied the contract. He finally looked up at Smitty. "I thought you were going to sell your cattle this fall and just lease your land."

"That was the original plan, but I am going to sell this place. I ain't going to stock it myself anymore, so I just as well let some other feller take it over. As far as the cattle, we can go partners. If I sell the cows, you will need to buy more to replace them. Besides, what am I going to do with that much money? Put it in the bank and let that banker make money off my hard work? I just as well help you out.

"I'll sell off the oldest and the meanest cows. You and me can partner on the rest. That way you don't have to buy a bunch of new stock, and I can keep my finger in the pie." He winked at Clare again.

"I'm moving down to Stevensville. It won't take me much to live on. You buy the land and give me thirty percent of the calf crop on the cows I leave here until I die—or until they do—and we'll call it a deal."

His old eyes twinkled and he added, "That and a meal or two Clare here puts on your table. I had some of her cooking when she was a youngster. I'm betting it's even better now…and bring those kids by to see me now and then."

Clare hugged the old man. "We will be glad to, Mr. Smitty. The children can always use another grandfather."

Smitty's smile became bigger as he looked at Clare. "The name is Alexander Newton Schmidt. You can call me Andy but not where folks can hear. I'm known around these parts as Smitty, and I don't want to confuse nobody."

Rock stared from Clare to Smitty. The contract was more than fair—in fact, it was generous, and Rock was surprised. He was even more surprised though by how the old man opened up to Clare. *That tight-lipped old codger just spilled his guts all over her, and they both liked it.*

Smitty glared at Rock and snorted. "Now don't go looking at me like that. I know I went soft when I wrote this up, but like I said, you helped me out of some tight spots. You have been a good neighbor over the years. Besides, Darby was a fine man, and he was my friend."

Rock added a line to the contract for Clare's name, and they both signed it. Smitty made some coffee, and they visited for nearly an hour. As they were leaving, Clare took Smitty's arm.

"How about next Sunday? Why don't you come up for supper? We will plan to eat around five so you can get home before it gets too dark.

"Come up early though. Any time after two will be fine. Maggie and Ike Clampant are marrying the day before so we might spend the night in town."

Smitty agreed. As the young couple rode out of his yard, he rubbed his stubbly jaw. "If I'd a known he was marrying that little gal, I'd have sweetened the pot even more.

"Sure am glad that old pappy of hers hung. The judge showed up last night, and they hung him at seven. He was a buckin' and a snortin' all the way up to the gallows, but he hung all right. And good riddance."

Clare smiled at Rock as they left.

"What a delightful old man. The children are going to love him. Isn't it exciting that neither you nor I have parents, and yet our children are going to have grandparents around them?"

Rock smiled at this woman who had just become his wife. Their horses were close to each other and he stopped Red. As Clare looked at him in surprise, he reached over and lifted her across his saddle. He wrapped his arms around her and kissed her gently as his eyes studied her face.

"Clare, I don't know how I could have been so blind to not see you as the woman you are. Heck, even that crusty old man saw through you. I'm sorry for that."

Clare's eyes were soft as she smiled up at Rock. "You were hurting, and I was mean. It's okay, really it is." She lifted her hand to touch his cheek.

Rock looked at her intently before he lifted her back onto her horse. He commented dryly, "I think I had better leave you on your horse or this trip home is going to take way too long."

Clare laughed. "And I think that shy guy act is just that—an act."

Rock grinned as he shook his head. "You are quite the woman, Clare Beckler."

As they rode back toward the ranch, Rock talked about the bookwork the ranch required. "That is the hardest part for me to get done. I have to move all my notes from my tally book to the ledger. When I get in the house at night, I am usually too tired to think. Then I end up spending an entire day in the house doing bookwork just to catch up.

"Just like this next bunch of cattle coming in. I bought fifty more Angus cows to run on Smitty's place. I need to tally their first cost and mark down when they calve. If they have trouble calving, I note that too.

I like to keep records so I can see what cows I need to cull and which ones are throwing nice calves."

Clare smiled as she listened.

"I can record your notes, Rock. I love to work with numbers. You just tell me what information you want to record, and I will take care of the books. I kept Maggie's books at the store when I stayed with her. It was just one year, but she had me doing everything by the time I left."

Rock looked surprised and then pleased. He moved Red closer to Georgia as he grinned at Clare. "You know, this marriage venture is looking better all the time."

Clare laughed and pointed down the trail. "You behave yourself, Mr. Beckler. There are men up ahead, and your current behavior might not be considered proper."

Rock looked down the trail and his eyes narrowed.

"Move to the other side of the trail, Clare. Those boys' cinch irons are black which means they've likely been doctoring brands."

CHAPTER 60

CATTLE THIEVES!

CLARE'S BREATH CAUGHT IN HER THROAT. THE ONLY protection she had was the small Derringer. She pushed her hand into her pocket as she moved to the outside of the trail.

Rock turned Red at an angle. He blocked the trail but was still facing the approaching men.

"Howdy, boys," he drawled. "Out checking cattle today?"

The two men looked up quickly. They glanced at Clare, but their eyes shifted quickly toward Rock. They held their horses still as they faced the man in front of them.

One of the horses started moving sideways and Rock pulled his gun. "Drop your guns. You are on my land, and I can see you've been doctoring brands. Who do you work for? Answer quick because I am fresh out of friendliness."

The rider on the right put his hands in the air. He carefully lifted his gun out of his holster and dropped it. Rock swung his Colt to cover the second man.

The second outlaw paused, and the first outlaw cursed at him.

"Pete, drop that gun. We're guilty an' you know it. Don't shoot this feller for defendin' his land."

Pete studied his partner. He muttered under his breath as he carefully removed his gun and flung it to the ground. He slowly lifted his hands above his head.

Rock pushed Red closer. "Now start talking before I forget that I am a peaceable man."

Clare clenched the small gun in her pocket as she looked around. She was afraid there were more men than just the two on the trail.

Pete growled, "Nobody! We don't work for nobody. We just wanted to brand a few head so we could make a little extra money at roundup."

Rock studied the two men. He didn't believe they were working alone, but there was no way he could prove the man was lying either.

A stick cracked behind Rock, and he thumbed back the hammer on his Colt. He pointed it at the first man who sat with his hands locked around his saddle horn.

"Tell your buddy behind me to drop his gun or you are a dead man," Rock ground out.

A voice sounded behind Rock. "I have my rifle pointed at your woman. Drop your gun and turn around."

Clare slid sideways on her horse as she slammed her spurs into the startled Georgia. The little mule shot forward and hit Pete's horse as she raced for the brush beside the trail.

The outlaw behind them fired. He missed Clare and grazed Pete's shoulder as the man tried to control his horse.

Clare slid to the ground beside the trail and rolled into the brush.

As Georgia raced forward, Rock hit the ground and rolled. He swung his gun toward the brush behind him. When the startled man leaned forward to take a second shot, Rock shot him.

Pete's horse was spinning, and the rider was trying to get it under control. Rock turned his gun back to the two men in front of him. His voice was cold as he spat out the words, ""Get off your horses."

As the two men stepped down, Rock lunged to his feet and knocked both men to the ground.

He looked toward Clare. She appeared to be uninjured, but she tripped as she pushed her way through the brush.

"Are you all right? You weren't shot, were you?"

Clare shook her head. Rock started to say something. Then he growled to himself and turned his attention back to the men in front of him.

He threw his rope over the branch of a large tree and made a noose. The two men looked at the noose in horror and started to protest. Rock grabbed the closest one and jerked the noose over his neck. He hoisted the man onto his horse and tied his hands in front of him.

Looking up at the man, Rock stated quietly, "You'd better start talking before I smack this horse. I've wasted all the time I am going to with you fellows."

The second man frowned. He shrugged and was about to speak when Pete started hollering.

"It was just a job! We was told to brand anything we found without a brand with a Slash BB or a Sleepy A. That first brand would cover a Slash B, so we was to rebrand any of those cows we come across."

Rock stared at the man a moment and then asked, "Who owns the Slash BB?"

The man's face went white. "If I tell you, I am a dead man."

Rock's face was hard, and his eyes looked like pieces of hard green glass.

"And if you don't, you die now." He took the piggin' string off his saddle, uncoiled it, and lifted his hand to whip the outlaw's horse.

"Stop! Have mercy, man! It was Jip Johnson down in Stevensville. He just come up the trail with a herd of cows. They have mixed brands on 'em, an' he figgered he could add a few head to his herd. It was just a ridin' job, I swear it."

The man on the ground stood and threw his hat down in disgust. He looked up at his partner.

"We knew it was wrong, Pete, an' we signed on anyway. We're rustlers as clear as day, an' there ain't a thing we can say to change that." The man looked up at Rock.

"My name is Dally, Dally Long, an' my partner is Pete Thompson. The feller back in the brush there is the one who hooked us into this deal. His name was Long Lewis. We run into him in the saloon in Stevensville. He could tell we was hard up. We was tryin' to mine an' spent the last six months up on top. Yesterday mornin', we rode into town an' headed for the saloon to spend our last dollar. He bought us drinks an' offered us this job." Dally's voice was soft when he added, "We knew it was wrong, but we did it 'cause we was hungry. An' here we are."

Rock pulled the noose off the rustler and rewound his rope. He tied it to his saddle and pulled the rope off Pete's hands.

"Where did you push those cattle? Do you have them penned somewhere?"

Dally pointed behind him. "There's a box canyon back that way. Another feller is keepin' an eye on 'em."

"I'll tell you what we are going to do. We are going to round up all the cattle you branded in the last two days and drive them into Stevensville. Then, we are going to talk to your Mr. Johnson and get this all straightened out."

Pete rubbed his neck and stared at Rock. "You ain't goin' to hang us?"

The outlaw on the ground looked up at his partner with disgust.

"Shut up, Pete. Just shut up."

CHAPTER 61

"I See You Found My Cattle"

ROCK WAS SCOWLING WHEN CLARE JOINED HIM ON the trail. He frowned at her again and started to speak. Finally, he just shook his head.

He pointed Dally and Pete down the trail. "You fellas ride in first and we'll follow. Just know that one of you will have a rifle pointed at his back, so don't try to be heroes."

Once the two men rode down the trail, Rock turned to Clare. "What were you thinking? You could have been shot!"

Clare looked at him coolly, and little red dots appeared in her cheeks. "As I recall, Mr. Beckler, I had a gun trained on me, so I could have been shot either way."

Then she laughed ruefully and added, "And as far as what I did, it was total reaction. I guess I still have a little of that small, wild girl inside me—I just didn't intend to fall off!"

Rock looked at Clare in surprise and slowly grinned. He reached over and squeezed her shoulder.

"Well, wild girl, let's catch up with those fellows. If you can still use a rifle, I'll give you this one. I don't want you to ride up with me and get caught in crossfire."

When Clare nodded, Rock handed her his rifle. His hand closed over hers and he squeezed it.

"Stay back and stay out of sight. Only shoot if you have a clear shot or if it looks like I'm in trouble."

As they came to the crest of the hill, Rock flicked his finger toward the side of the road. Clare turned Georgia into the brush to the right of the trail. The little mule picked her way delicately through the brush and up the side of the hill. Clare lay down over the saddle to stay as quiet as possible.

They finally came to a little clearing overlooking the penned cattle, and Clare slid down. Pete and Dally were visible along with a third man who carried a rifle.

Clare lay down behind a large rock and balanced her rifle as she sighted it in on each of the three outlaws. The hair came up on her neck when she saw a fourth man squatted behind a rock on the side of the opposite hill. She looked down where Rock was riding and could see that the outlaw's position was not visible to him. Her eyes narrowed as she sighted in on the squatting outlaw.

Voices carried up to Clare, but they were muffled. She only caught part of the conversation. Pete and Dally were silent and kept their hands on top of their saddle horns. The hidden outlaw quietly shifted his position and stood to take aim at Rock.

Clare squeezed the trigger, and the man rolled down the small hill. He slid to a stop in front of the remaining outlaws. The third outlaw stared at the dead man and looked up the hill toward Clare's position. She nicked his hat with a bullet for good measure, and it sailed off his head.

He threw his gun down and began to holler. "Sakes alive, mister. Tell whoever you have shootin' up there that there ain't gonna be no trouble here. I'll take my chances with a jury over the itchy finger that feller has!"

Dally turned to look at the outlaw Clare had shot.

"Who was that? There was only sposed to be the three of us workin' this job."

"Jip sent him out this mornin'. He thought the two of ya might go honest on 'im an' light a shuck outa here. That feller was to be Jip's insurance." The man paused and spat in the dirt. "Guess that insurance didn't work out so good."

Clare mounted Georgia and rode down the hill to join the riders on the trail.

The third man stared at her and cursed softly as he stared at Rock. "You had yore woman shootin' at me? It's just durn scary when a woman cin shoot like that."

Rock grinned at Clare as he agreed. "Yes, it's best to not cross her. The roots of her raisin' pop through from time to time."

He gathered the rifles from all three men. The best two were stashed in the rifle boots on his and the dead man's saddles. The third rifle was broken over a rock. He dropped their six guns into his saddle bags. When he reached for the reins of the dead man's horse, the third man spurred his horse and disappeared into the brush.

Rock hollered, "If I see you again on this ranch, my wife will cut you down!" He winked at the startled Clare before he turned back to the remaining outlaws.

"Pete, throw those dead men over their saddles, and hand their reins to Clare. Then you open that gate and let's start these cattle. It will take us at least three hours to get them to Stevensville, and I want plenty of daylight left when we get there."

As the cattle filed out of the box canyon, Rock studied them. Several small calves were caught up in the gather, and he could hear the mama cows answering as the calves bawled.

"Let those calves go. Their mamas are all branded so we don't need to worry about them." He glared at Dally and Pete.

"You know a calf that small would die without its mother. You fellows weren't too particular what you threw that brand on."

Dally ducked his head, and Pete said nothing.

Rock's scowl became bigger when some of his crossbred pairs filed out. "I may not wait for the judge. I just might hang your boss myself," he muttered.

The cattle were tired when they finally arrived in Stevensville. Rock's green eyes were hard, and anger glinted from them as he watched his cattle move slowly up the street to the holding pen at the end of town.

He had pulled up as they entered town so that only the two outlaws were trailing the cattle. He watched the street closely for the man who had orchestrated this steal.

A tall, pompous man in a white hat stepped off the sidewalk as the cattle trailed by.

"Good job, boys. I see you found some of the cattle we lost on our way up here. Just pen them at the end of the street, and we'll move them out to join the herd afterwhile."

Rock rode Red toward Johnson. He turned his horse so close that the man tripped as he stepped backwards. Red followed him, and the lines of the man's face hardened down as he stepped onto the boardwalk.

Red stopped with his nose almost against the man's chest. He shoved him backwards with his head.

Johnson cursed and raised his hand to strike the horse. He paused when he looked into the hard, green eyes behind the gun that was pointed at him.

CHAPTER 62

An Angry Rancher

ROCK FLICKED HIS THUMB OVER HIS SHOULDER. "Your cattle?" When the man nodded, Rock continued. "You must be Johnson. Jip Johnson?"

Again, the man nodded, his eyes narrowing as he studied Rock.

People were gathering on the street, and the noise of the crowd was growing louder. Rock dropped his gun in his holster and rested his hands on his saddle horn. He looped one long leg over his horse's neck and relaxed in the saddle.

"Those Slash BB and Sleepy A brands could cover quite a few brands in this area including my Slash B. Besides, I didn't know anyone but me had Angus bulls," Rock stated quietly.

Jip Johnson swung his large head toward the street as a string of cows with black and white crossbred calves filed in front of him. He could feel the panic rising in his chest, but he pushed it down. He had pulled this steal many times, and he wasn't going to let one lousy cowboy stop his deal.

He waved his hand carelessly. "Oh, you know cowboys. They probably just swung too wide of a loop. That Dally fellow had to get his name somehow."

Rock studied the man. A deep anger was pushing its way up. *I had better rein myself in or I am going to shoot this man where he stands.* He slowly nodded.

"How about we sort them once we get to the pens? Then, we are going to pull out one that you claim. We'll skin it in front of all these folks. If that brand has been reworked like I think it has, we'll just go ahead and hang you today."

Rock's voice was quiet and deadly. Another cowboy stepped out of the crowd and moved up beside him. Rock turned to the cowboy.

"Dack, why don't you take a couple of boys and peel off about twenty-five head of Johnson's herd. They are out north of town a couple of miles. Bring them in here, and we'll check a few of those brands too."

Sheriff Hawkins stepped forward. His voice was deceptively soft as he spoke.

"I'll go with you, Dack. Meet me at the livery, and we'll ride out together."

Jip Johnson looked around at the group of men and women gathered there. Realization hit him suddenly. He had picked the wrong town.

Rock's eyes were hard, but he grinned at the man in front of him.

"Your jig is up, Johnson. Why don't you go ahead and grab that gun? Let's see if you can beat me. I mean, I am in an awkward position here."

Clare stared at Rock in horror. She didn't have any idea how fast he was, but he was in no position to draw. She pulled Georgia back and lifted her rifle out of the boot. Her voice was soft as it cut through the quiet street.

"Mr. Johnson, my husband will likely kill you if you go for your gun, but I believe you should stand trial for what you have done. You drop your guns, and that includes the arm gun you think you can use. I guarantee I won't miss at this distance."

Rock's face was hard as he slowly turned his head to look at Clare.

Clare's eyes became large. *Rock doesn't think I have faith in his shooting abilities.* As her face became pale, Rock laughed and turned to address the town.

"Have to watch my wife, fellows. She has a short fuse and an itchy finger." He looked hard at Johnson.

"Go ahead," he stated softly. "Try any gun you want, and let's get this over with."

Jip Johnson looked around at the clustered townspeople and cursed under his breath. He could tell by their faces that the trial would be fast and deadly.

A rope snaked over his chest, pinning his hands against his sides. Dally's horse kept the rope pulled tight, and Johnson was jerked from his feet.

"Let me help ya out here, Mr. Beckler. I'll jist drag this feller down to the jail, an' he cin think on his behavior till the sheriff gets back."

Pete roped Johnson's feet, and the two cowboys dragged the cow thief down the street to the jail. Dally eased up on his rope. When Johnson jerked his arms up, the rope snapped around his neck. His eyes became large, and he gagged as he pulled at the rope. Pete said nothing as he kept the rope on Johnson's feet taunt.

Dally eased on the rope just enough for the man to take a few ragged breaths. "Jip," he said softly, "I ain't been a perfect man all my life, but I was never a cow thief.

"Now I might swing at the end of a rope, but I guaran-dang-tee you, Pete an' me won't go first. An' we won't go alone. I know some of yore riders, an' I will get them to testify as to where yore herd was picked up.

"Y'all are done stealin'. Ya sealed yore fate when ya thought ya could steal from a new town in Montana Territory. Ya figgered folks here was too stupid to know the difference." He stared at the gagging man on the ground as he shook his head.

"What is it about ya big rollers that ya think y'all are so much smarter than ever'body else?" he asked with disgust.

He flipped the rope to loosen it from around the outlaw's neck, and Pete dragged the man into the jail. Pete lifted a rope off the wall and slid it around Johnson's legs as he removed his own. Dally grabbed Jip's shoulders, and Pete hoisted his feet up to tie them on an upper bar leaving Johnson's shoulders barely resting on the floor of the jail. Dally swung the cell door shut as Johnson screamed for them to cut him down. Dally grinned at his friend.

"That'll give 'im a little taste of what's to come."

Pete scowled as he looked at his riding pard.

"For us too, ya know. No way are we gettin' off here."

Dack, along with the sheriff and his group of cowboys, was back shortly with twenty-five head of cattle. Some of the brands were easily identified as worked over while other cattle would have to be skinned to know for sure. The sheriff addressed the group of citizens gathered in the street.

"Most of the brands in that herd appear to be worked over. I'm guessing they picked up cattle all the way up here. Now either he is expecting a buyer—and that's doubtful since it is mostly a young, mixed herd—or he was planning a land grab as well."

He looked around and added, "I need some cowboys to go out there and sort those cattle. Drive them in here so I can get all the brands recorded. I want all Johnson's hands in here to list those brands. They can testify against their boss too so get moving."

Sheriff Hawkins turned to Rock. "You look those animals over in the pens. If they are yours, take them home. We have enough witnesses here that we don't need them for evidence. There is nothing to eat here, so get them back on your range."

Rock nodded. "Clare should stay in town. It's been a long day already. I can't get these tired cows home by myself though. I'd like Dally and Pete come on back to the ranch with me."

The sheriff studied Rock with his wise eyes. "Are you saying that those two fellows work for you?"

Rock grinned as he looked at the startled men. "That's what I'm saying. It's hard to find good help around here and harder to keep them. Dack starts on Monday, but I want these boys back on the ranch if you don't need them here."

The sheriff's hard eyes moved from Rock's face to the blackened cinch rings on Dally's and Pete's saddles. His eyes moved up to stare at the two men. The two riders were quiet as they studied their horses' ears.

Sheriff Hawkins slowly nodded. "I reckon I know where to find them if I need to talk to them." He waved toward the corral and growled, "Now get those noisy animals out of town."

CHAPTER 63

DALLY AND PETE

DALLY AND PETE WERE QUIET AS THEY MOVED THE cattle down the street. The animals were thirsty, and the three men let them drink from the horse troughs as they pushed them through town. The tired cattle were moving slowly but they picked up the pace when they reached familiar pastures.

Finally, they were near enough to the rest of the cattle. The men stopped their horses and eased back to let the cattle graze.

Rock studied them. "We probably walked ten pounds or more off them today, and none of it necessary," he growled as he shook his head.

Dally's face was red when he looked at Rock.

"Mr. Beckler, I'm not sure why ya said what ya did back there, but Pete an' me want ya to know that we appreciate it."

Rock looked hard at the two riders.

"I'm not sure why I did either. I don't typically give fellows a second chance. I'm more of a right and wrong man. I believe you two boys are mostly honest though, so don't make me regret taking a chance on you."

As they rode up to the ranch headquarters, Dally looked around with approval. The buildings all had stone foundations that went up about three feet. Everything was neat and tidy. It was apparent that Rock took pride in what he owned and what he worked with. The bunk house was about half done, so the two men assumed they would be sleeping on the ground.

Rock pointed toward the barn.

"One of the stalls has been made into a temporary room. I'm too tired to cook tonight, but breakfast will be ready at five-thirty tomorrow morning."

As he turned toward the barn, Dally called, "Boss, we can finish up here. I'll take yore hoss. I think we can figger out what to feed the livestock an' shut up the chickens too."

Rock waved his hand at them and walked slowly toward the house. A small donkey came rushing down from the hills and raced up to nuzzle the tired man. He looped his arm around the donkey's neck. The two men watched in surprise as the donkey followed their new boss into the house.

"Sure never figured him as a feller to keep an ol' donkey as a pet," Dally muttered.

Red snorted at him and bared his teeth.

Dally turned to look at the big horse and chuckled.

"Sure now, we won't go talkin' 'bout the boss that way. Come on, big feller. Let's rub ya down an' get ya some oats. I'd say y'all are some important 'round here."

The little mare and her colt raced up and Pete caught them. "Sleep in the barn, do ya? Well, that ain't a bad plan."

Pete penned her away from Red, and the two men caught the old wagon mules. Once everything was penned, they found the stall that had been converted into sleeping quarters.

"I've slept in worse bunkhouses," Dally commented as he pulled off his boots.

Pete lay back on his saddle and stared up at the hay loft as he chewed a stem. "Now why do ya spose the boss said we worked fer 'im? He don't know us, an' we sure did deserve that noose." He added softly, "An' I thought Smith was a dead man when he took off."

Dally shook his head. "I don't know. Mebbie he stepped outside the law his own self once or twice, or mebbie someone give 'im somethin' he didn't earn." He shrugged and added, "I don't really care. I'm just pleased we didn't hang, an' we have a ridin' job to boot."

He looked over at Pete. "He is goin' to be mighty pleased when he finds out how handy y'all are with buildin' things!"

Pete grinned at his partner. "An' mebbie he'll even git ya a milkin' cow when he finds out how much ya like to milk."

Dally nodded slowly. "I do like to milk cows, 'specially Jerseys. Good temperament an' lotsa cream in their milk."

Talk trailed off as the two men grew tired. Pete thought about his folks in Oregon, and Dally wished he had someone waiting for him somewhere.

CHAPTER 64

HANDY COWBOYS

THE MEN STARTED ON THE BUNKHOUSE AS SOON AS breakfast was over, and Rock *was* impressed with Pete's building skills.

When Clare arrived with the children around ten that morning, she was pleased at how much more of the bunkhouse was completed.

As Rock helped her down, both Annie and Zeke began to maul him.

"Papa," asked Annie, "When can we stay with Auntie Maggie and Grampy Ike again? We had so much fun! And Nora had fun too, didn't you, Nora?"

Nora smiled shyly. She froze when Rock picked her up but slowly relaxed when he set her on the ground.

As Rock lifted Clare down, he swung her around.

"Welcome home, sweetheart. This house was sure quiet last night!" he whispered as he squeezed her.

"And that's why I only spent one night in town," Clare whispered back as she laughed.

She clapped her hands. "Come children, let's change clothes and get your chores done." She slid her eyes sideways toward Rock as she tried to keep from laughing. "Your papa's milk cow is being delivered today."

As Rock stared at her, Clare laughed and shrugged her shoulders, "Talk to Maggie. It was a wedding gift."

Dally looked up hopefully, "Is it a Jersey? I hope she's a Jersey!"

Clare looked at Dally in surprise. "You know milk cows, Dally? I'm not sure what breed it is. Maggie said it is gentle and makes lots of cream. Does that sound like a Jersey?"

Rock turned full around and stared at Dally. "Tell me you like to milk cows!"

Dally nodded happily. "I do like milk cows and Jerseys in particular. I always thought it would be fun to have enough milk cows around to sell a little milk an' make some cheese an' butter. Puddin' too an' buttermilk for breakfast."

Rock clapped Dally on the shoulder as he grinned at the young man.

"Dally, if I had known you liked to milk, I wouldn't have let you go to town yesterday for fear Sheriff Hawkins would keep you! Let's work on this bunkhouse until Clare calls us for dinner. Then we need to figure out a stanchion to hold that cow. She will need to be milked tonight, and we need someplace to pen her."

Rock was still smiling when Clare called them in to eat. She looked from him to Dally and laughed.

"You just made yourself invaluable, Dally. Rock knew a milk cow would be coming at some point in time, and he *hates* milk cows. Now eat up, both of you, and welcome to the Slash B."

Clare filled the men's plates followed by those of the children. She smiled at Nora as she set a full plate in front of her.

Nora watched carefully to make sure Zeke and Annie also had food. Only then did she begin to eat.

Zeke took several bites before he looked up at Rock with big eyes.

"Sheriff Hawkins is going to hang that cattle rustler today. How do you hang somebody, Papa?"

Rock put his fork down as he studied the faces of the three children. They were all watching him as they waited for an answer.

"Hanging is something that you do to very bad men. It's another way to make someone die."

Annie nodded excitedly.

"I wanted to stay and watch, but Mama Clare said we needed to come home."

Rock looked at Annie seriously.

"There is nothing fun about watching someone die, Annie. And your mama was right to bring you home. I hope you never have to see someone hang. Now let's don't talk about that anymore. Your mama worked hard to make this meal. Let's enjoy it."

Dally and Pete stared at their plates as they ate, and Clare's face was pale as she picked at her food. As much as she had despised her father, it made her sad to know that he had also hung.

She looked up from her plate and smiled at the children.

"How about you help me plant a garden today? Maybe your papa will spade the ground so we can put some seeds down. Wouldn't that be fun?"

Rock smiled at Clare and squeezed her hand.

As the two new hands trudged back toward the bunkhouse, Rock picked up a spade and a large hoe. He followed Clare out behind the house to Maggie's vegetable plot. He began to spade the ground. Clare followed him with the hoe, breaking the clods into small chunks.

The kids squeezed the clods to break them and dug in the dirt for worms.

Rock left the happy group when he was done and headed back to the bunkhouse. Pete was ready to start on the roof and was laying out wood for the trusses. "How big of a pitch do you want on the roof to make sure it drops the snow?"

Rock looked around at the barn and the house. Both had been built before he came and their roofs worked well.

"Angle it like the barn. If you can handle that, Dally and I will work on that stanchion."

Dally walked through the barn. He chose a small end stall. It was too small to pen a cow but was adequate for milking. Rock left Dally there and headed back to help Pete with the trusses. By evening, the trusses were in place, and the roof was taking shape.

Rock was pleased. He slapped Pete on the back. "One more day of working like this, and we just might be done."

CHAPTER 65

A Milk Cow For Dally

AS THE THREE MEN PUT AWAY THEIR TOOLS, A stranger rode in leading a cow. She was dark brown with a nearly black head, especially around her eyes and nose. Her small hooves and tail were also black. Her head was feminine, and her dark eyes looked friendly.

The man held out the lead rope, and Rock pointed toward the pleased Dally.

"She likes to kick, that one does. The old man thought you might need these kickers. And a milk bucket too in case this was a surprise!" He dropped a set of kickers and a bucket on the ground. The small chains fit around the cow's back legs to keep her from kicking as she was being milked.

He hollered over his shoulder as he left, "Maggie and Ike said to enjoy your wedding gift. They will see you at their nuptials on Saturday.'"

Clare laughed as Rock stared at the man's parting back in surprise.

"I guessed you had forgotten. Today is Thursday so it is the day after tomorrow." She nodded toward the nearly completed bunkhouse. "I'm sure you will have that done by tomorrow night," she added as she smiled at her husband.

Dally and Pete were late coming in for supper. Just as Rock pulled the curtains aside to look out the window, they carried a small bed into the house.

Pete smiled at Nora. "We thought ya might like to have yore own bed, Nora. Now, if yore mama an' papa can find ya some blankets, ya will be sleepin' fine an' soft tonight."

Clare's eyes were soft as she looked from Dally and Pete to Nora. The men set the little bed in the children's room, and Clare unrolled a small cotton mattress. Rock leaned against the doorjamb and smiled at all of them as Nora touched the bed.

"For me?" she asked as her big brown eyes sparkled. "Just for me?"

Rock scooped her up.

"Just for you, Nora. Your mama will put some blankets on it, and you can sleep there tonight." He smiled at the tiny girl and kissed her cheek as he set her down. She touched her cheek and returned his smile.

Rock cleared his throat and left the room. Looking at Nora was like looking at Clare as a child.

"Let's all get in here and eat before this food gets cold," he called roughly. As everyone gathered at the table, Rock started to lead the family in a blessing. However, the children took over.

Annie began, "Thank you, Lord, for supper and for my new mama and for Nora—"

Zeke interrupted. "And for my new papa and for my sisters." The table was quiet for a moment and then Nora added softly, "And for Dally and Pete."

Rock looked around the table at the happy faces. His throat was tight as he squeezed Clare's hand. He added, "Amen."

The children were soon talking excitedly. It turned to loud arguing until Rock had to quiet them down.

"Now you kids know you don't yell at the table. After you eat your food, you can go outside and play for a while. Maybe next week, I will hook up a rope so you can swing out over the creek and drop into the water."

The noise level ramped back up again but decreased as the kids rushed to finish their meal. As they hurried outside, Clare called after them, "You may play for just a little while. Then, you need to come in and help me with the dishes."

Rock grinned at the two men as they held out their plates for seconds.

"Enjoy this, boys. Dack is bringing a cook with him on Monday so you only get to eat Clare's food for a few more days. That's another reason that the bunkhouse has to be finished."

The meal was finished quickly, and the outside chores were completed. Dally came in with a full bucket of milk.

Everyone stared at it in awe. Clare looked up at Dally and smiled as she took it from him.

"Thank you, Dally. Is she the type of cow you had hoped for?"

As he grinned and nodded, Clare pointed at the milk. "It is nice and clean. Did the kickers work to keep her feet down?"

Dally laughed. "I didn't need kickers. I introduced myself to her and we had a little talk about what we each liked and expected. I think I'll call her Grace after a sweet little gal I knew a long time ago." He looked around the room.

"Goodnight, kids. Y'all sleep quiet tonight now, ya hear?" Dally was smiling as he backed out the door.

Clare sang softly as she strained the milk into large jars. When Rock came in, she showed him the full jars. "Look at this, Rock. Oh, all the things I can make with fresh milk and cream!"

Rock smiled at his wife's happy face. He set the milk bucket aside and pulled her close.

"You smell like lilacs," he whispered as he sniffed her neck. He felt the back of her dress. "And not too many buttons either."

"Rock!" Clare hissed. "The children will hear you."

He turned toward the bedroom where all three children were all laying on Nora's bed as they talked excitedly.

"I don't think so. They are busy with their own conversations."

He grinned again at Clare and then frowned as he looked at the milk. "How are you going to keep that from spoiling? You can't leave it out overnight, can you?"

Clare shook her head. "No, we'll lower it into the well. The coolness of the water will keep it fresh. Tomorrow, we will have cold milk for breakfast and warm bread with fresh butter for dinner." She could see Rock calculating the amount of milk they were going to get each day.

"And if a little of it goes bad, the chickens will be happy because they love curdled milk." Clare smiled excitedly and added, "I saw a large can of cocoa in our supplies. Sour milk also makes excellent chocolate cake."

Rock stared at his wife and shook his head as he grinned. "If I had known how handy you were, I might have chased you a long time ago."

Clare's hands paused as she screwed the lids down tight, and a blush climbed up her neck.

"How about you lower these into the well and then take a bath in the creek. I prefer to sleep with a clean man."

Rock studied her face for a moment. As the blush continued to rise, he grinned and nodded.

"I believe I will do just that," he agreed. He grabbed the jars and was back quickly for a bar of soap and his razor. He strolled out of the house with a smile on his face and a whistle deep in his throat.

Clare washed all the children. She had them brush their teeth with soda and salt before she scooted them off to bed.

Rock came in just as she was tucking them in and he joined her in the small room. "Name one thing that you are thankful for, kids. Zeke, you start tonight."

Zeke looked around the room and smiled. "I'm thankful for having a mama and a papa."

Annie added, "Me too, and I'm thankful for Steed."

Nora smiled and said, "I'm thankful for my bed."

Rock looked at Clare as he squeezed her hand. "How about you, Mrs. Beckler? What are you thankful for?"

Clare kissed each of the children and smiled up at Rock. "I'm thankful that God hears and answers prayers."

"And I am thankful for everyone in this room—and for Gomer," Rock stated.

Gomer brayed from the doorway. The noise level escalated once more from the small beds as the children called, "Good night, Gomer!"

The little donkey backed out of the doorway and went back to his spot between the door and the fireplace. His head dropped close to the floor, and he was soon asleep.

Rock kissed each of the children and followed Clare into the kitchen.

She set out her supplies for a chocolate cake before she let Rock lead her to the bedroom.

Gomer flicked his ears and opened one eye. All was quiet, and he soon went back to sleep.

CHAPTER 66

Fresh Butter and Chocolate Cake

ROCK WAS WHISTLING SOFTLY WHEN HE WALKED INTO the kitchen the next morning. He grabbed a large knife and headed for the smokehouse. As soon as he opened the door, Gomer pushed him aside and rushed out. Rock shook his head.

"I need to put a latch on there that you can open, Gomer. I think maybe you would like to go outside earlier than we get up."

Clare had the skillet heating when Rock came back into the house. He set the meat and the knife on the table and nuzzled her neck as she tried to crack the eggs.

She was giggling and Rock was laughing when Dally and Pete knocked on the door. Clare backed away from Rock and waved the knife at him as she pointed at the door. He winked at her and hollered for the men to come in as he sat down at the table.

Dally and Pete looked from one to the other and grinned as they sat down. Clare blushed furiously and quickly sliced the meat into the hot skillet.

Rock shifted his attention to the men in front of him. "We are headed into Stevensville tomorrow for a wedding. I'd like you fellows to stay here. I think it best that you do not spend a night on the town until the rest of the hands get here."

When Pete and Dally nodded, Rock continued, "I'd like to finish that bunkhouse this morning. When it's done, we will ride around some of the pastures so you can see the layout of the ranch.

"I'd want you to put up more fence while we're gone too. I'll show you the boundary line I'm working on."

Clare soon had the meat browned and was whipping up eggs. When Rock looked up, she smiled at him.

"Cold milk would sure be good this morning."

Dally rose quickly. "I will plan to bring the milk in every morning, Mrs. Beckler."

Pete followed him out, and the two men drew the milk up. They carried the cold jars back into the house.

Clare's eyes lit up with excitement at the amount of cream on top of the milk. She skimmed it off before she whipped the small pieces into the milk. She poured a foamy glass of cold milk for each of them.

The milk was cool and sweet. Even Rock had to admit that it was a nice addition to breakfast.

Breakfast was barely over when Clare put the cream in the churn to make butter. The heavy cream soon separated into buttermilk and butter. Clare set the buttermilk aside to use in her cake. She was humming to herself when Annie wandered into the kitchen, rubbing her eyes.

"What are you making, Mama? Is that butter?" she asked in excitement.

"It sure is. I need to rinse all the buttermilk out of it and then we'll add a little bit of salt. Would you like to wash your hands and help me?"

Annie nodded excitedly and rushed to wash her hands. Clare put some cold water in a bowl and dropped the lump of fresh butter into the water. She showed Annie how to squeeze and rinse the butter, changing the water several times until it remained clear. Then she sprinkled the blob of soft butter with a little salt and had Annie work it in.

"Look at that, Annie—now we have buttermilk *and* butter to use in our cake!"

Annie was fascinated as she watched Clare mix up the cake. When Clare slid the messy bowl across the table for Annie to clean out, the little girl was delighted.

Rock set a big bucket of fresh morning milk down just as Annie finished licking off her fingers. When he saw the empty breakfast plate, he grinned and shook his head.

"Cake batter before breakfast? I don't know about your new mother, Annie."

Annie held up the sloppy spoon. "Lick this, Papa. Mama Clare makes yummy cake!"

Rock pulled his finger through the batter and rolled his eyes in delight.

"Think that will be done by dinner? And maybe some frosting on it too?" he asked hopefully.

Clare nodded happily and began to clean up the baking mess. She quickly strained the milk and poured it into jars for chilling. She sent the full jars outside with Rock.

"We need to start some bread, Annie. We want it done in time for dinner. Warm bread with fresh butter—I can't wait."

The little girl was covered in flour by the time the dough was prepared. Once it was rising in the bowl, Clare had Annie clean up and she began to wash dishes. The other two children appeared, and Clare sat all of them down for breakfast. Their eyes were large with excitement as Clare pulled the cake out of the oven and set it on top of the stove.

"Now hurry to finish your chores. When you are done, we will make frosting to go on that cake."

As they rushed through breakfast, excited little voices reached the men working outside. The smell of the cake wafted through the air, and the men raised their heads to sniff the inviting aroma.

Clare's bread was in the oven by eleven. When she called the men in for dinner, fresh bread was on the table.

Each child's face was covered in chocolate frosting as three happy children helped clean out the frosting bowl. Clare's eyes were sparkling, and she held up a finger for Rock to taste.

He smacked his lips and asked with a grin, "Now who wants to thank Papa for marrying Mama so we can have cake and bread to go with our beef stew?"

Happy voices filled the room, and Rock's grin became bigger. He kissed his pretty wife and wiped a smudge of flour off her cheek.

Dally and Pete grinned as the children talked and laughed with their dirty little faces.

Clare was smiling as she set the food out. She cut the warm bread and handed a thick slice to each person. The fresh butter disappeared quickly as it was slathered onto the warm bread. The children watched in amazement as it melted before their eyes.

Rock rolled his eyes and almost moaned in delight. "Sure am glad I married a good cook," he commented as he winked at Clare.

"We finished the bunkhouse this morning. Beds will have to be made and a table added, but the building is done," Rock stated with pride.

Clare looked at Dally and Pete in surprise. "That certainly went faster with the two of you helping." She leaned to look out the window.

"It is a beautiful building, right down to the chimney. You fellows will be nice and cozy this winter."

Pete and Dally thanked Clare for dinner and headed outside to hitch up the wagon. The fencing supplies were soon loaded in the bed of the wagon.

Rock followed them. He looked back at Clare as he reached for the doorknob.

"We will be on Smitty's land building fence. We'll work until late afternoon before we head back up here. I'm taking Red, but Gomer will be here. He will let you know if anyone is coming, so keep the shotgun handy. The rifle is loaded there by the door too."

Clare could feel her chest tighten, but she forced a smile. *It is silly to be afraid when Rock isn't around. We are completely safe here.*

She followed Rock to the door and waved as he rode off. The house was quiet. *I have just a little free time. What shall I do this afternoon?* Her eyes settled on the red fabric, and she felt a small thrill.

"I believe I will start on those curtains this afternoon. They won't take me long and will add so much color to this room."

CHAPTER 67

ROBBERS AND THIEVES

CLARE WAS ENGROSSED IN MEASURING AND CUTTING the curtain fabric when Gomer brayed loudly. Her heart skipped a beat, and she rushed to the door. Gomer was trying to herd the children toward the house. Clare cupped her hand over her eyes and squinted to see down the lane.

Six dusty, rough-looking men were riding toward the house. She swept the rifle up.

"Kids! Come in now." Clare's voice was sharp, and the kids looked up in surprise. "When Gomer tries to herd you, pay attention to him."

As the three grumbling children shuffled inside, Clare pointed toward her bedroom. "Go in there and shut the door. Don't come out until I call you."

All three children stared at Clare, and Nora began to shake. Clare kissed Nora's cheek and smiled at the children. "Don't be afraid. I just can't see who these visitors are, so I don't want you outside."

Annie's and Zeke's eyes opened wide, but all three filed silently into the bedroom and shut the door.

Clare stepped into the doorway and cocked the rifle. Gomer stood close to her, and Clare could feel the little donkey trembling. She hoped he wouldn't charge the group of men. She didn't want him to get hurt.

She touched his neck and whispered, "Thank you for being my protector, Gomer."

The riders pulled their horses to a stop in front of the house. Gomer brayed and showed his teeth at the surprised men.

Clare said nothing. She shifted her rifle to train it on the one who seemed to be the leader, and her hands were steady.

The leader kept his hands on the saddle horn as he spoke.

"Ma'am, we'd like to water our horses and get a drink if that is all right with you. We are powerful hungry too if you could give us a bait of food."

Clare looked at the Wells Fargo saddle bags on the man's saddle and shook her head. "I won't refuse a man or animal water, but I won't feed a thief. You boys get your drinks and head on out."

Some of the riders shifted uncomfortably while others ducked their heads.

Clare let her eyes settle on each one before she added quietly, "Or you can drop those money bags here, and I will make sure the law gets them. I'm guessing you are being chased as worn down as your horses are."

The leader looked surprised. He turned in his saddle and studied the men behind him.

One cowboy spoke up, "Let's leave it, Black. I never robbed anyone in my life, and I don't much like how it makes me feel. I think I would rather take a chance on a rough riding job than do something like this again."

Several of the men nodded in agreement, but one young man exclaimed, "Like—!"

As he started to curse, one of the riders slammed a fist in his stomach. When he leaned over, coughing, the rider who had punched him grated softly, "You don't curse in front of a lady."

Clare noticed that one of the riders was holding tightly to his saddle horn and appeared to be bleeding.

"Did you kill anyone in this robbery?"

Black shook his head. "No, my little brother is the only one who was shot. He needs a doctor, but we aren't familiar with this area."

Clare pointed her rifle at Black. "Get your brother down and bring him into the house. Let me look at his wound." She looked over the rest of the outlaws.

"The rest of you, make up your minds. Will it be fresh bread, beef, and chocolate cake or are you going to keep that money?"

The riders stared at her as she stepped aside for Black and his brother. She set the rifle down and followed them into the house. She pointed at the children's room and hurried to throw a quilt over Nora's small bed.

"Put him on there," she directed.

As she leaned over the man, her body went still. Her voice was furious when she spoke to the man they called Black.

"He is just a boy! A fine brother you are to get him into a mess like this."

The boy's face was drawn down in pain. He tried to smile though.

"Don't be mad at Black. He told me I couldn't go with him till I was fifteen, but I didn't want to wait three years. I sneaked away and managed to get myself shot. It was my fault, not Black's."

Clare moved the boy's hand and saw a wicked wound in his side. She patted his arm and turned to Black.

"Have one of your men draw a bucket of water and get it heating. I need to clean this wound.

"Zeke! Annie!" A bedroom door opened, and three little faces peeked out. Clare's voice was sharp as she pointed toward the trees.

"Find some moss and hurry back here as fast as you can. Nora, you get some clean rags out of the kitchen."

Clare looked down at the boy and smiled. "What is your name, young man?"

The boy's blue eyes showed his pain. He whispered, "They call me Tuff, but I don't feel so tough right now. Am I going to be all right?"

Clare smiled at him again and patted his arm. She turned to Black. "I need some whiskey or alcohol of some kind. Do your riders have any?"

Black nodded and turned toward the door.

Clare knelt on the floor by Tuff.

"I need to treat your wound, and the alcohol is going to burn. I am sorry to hurt you, but it is inflamed and must be cleaned."

The riders looked up as Black came outside. The three men on the left had thrown their Wells Fargo bags on the ground while the young man on the right was stuffing money into his saddlebags. He tossed the empty Wells Fargo bag on the pile.

Black looked at him and pointed down the lane. "You'd best get out of here. That posse will be here in a few hours. Head south and don't shoot anybody!"

As the young man spurred his horse down the lane, Black muttered under his breath, "Little hothead. He almost killed a man back there." He shook his head as the rider whipped his horse and yelled at the tired animal.

"He will never make it out of these hills alive. He'll run that horse in the ground and get himself lost."

Black looked up at the three cowboys. "Guess you can take the lady's offer on that food and then you had better ride out of here. Blend your tracks into some cattle tracks and hole up for a while. There are lots of caves in these Sapphire Mountains."

Black pulled a bottle of whiskey out of his saddlebag and drew a bucket of water. He carried them inside.

Clare looked up and stared hard at Black for a moment. "You can't help him here. Ride out with or without your saddlebags."

Black slowly shook his head. "It's too late for me. I'm a wanted man all over the West."

Clare studied his face. She shook her head as she replied, "Then maybe you had better turn your life around for your brother. He obviously worships you, and you are leading him down the same path."

She looked down at the boy. "Bite down on this stick. I am going to pour whiskey into that wound, and it is going to hurt."

Tuff pinched his eyes shut as the alcohol burned his raw flesh, but he didn't make a sound. When he finally passed out, Clare quickly poured more whiskey in and around the open wound.

Clare chose some herbs from her stash in the kitchen and mixed them with hot water to make a paste. She smeared the paste around the wound.

Annie and Zeke rushed in with moss and Clare laid it on the wound. She tied a clean rag around the young man's waist and led Black out of the room.

She made a quick pack of food and took it outside for the three cowboys. As she handed it to them, she looked seriously at each rider.

"Stay out of trouble. If you are free this fall, come back this way for fall gather. I will see that you have a place here for the winter."

The men looked at her in surprise as they took the food.

The tallest one quietly thanked her and the other two chimed in. They turned their mounts east and headed higher into the mountains.

One turned around. He raised a hand to Black who waved in return.

Clare picked up the saddlebags and stacked them on the porch. She turned to Black and cocked an eyebrow. "What is it going to be? A meal or another man's money?"

Black stared at her for a moment and finally grinned.

"Ma'am, you are sure a wise one even though you are young and pretty. I think maybe you were raised around some tough men."

Clare nodded and answered sincerely, "I was, and thank heavens I was able to get away from that life.

"Walk away, Black. You are a good man at heart, and this path only has one end. Make a change today. I will nurse your brother back to health. He can stay here until you send for him."

As Black stared at her, Clare added quietly, "I have a soft spot for children, but I will not have this ranch used as a haven for outlaws."

Black slowly nodded. He took the pack of food that Clare handed him and dropped his Wells Fargo bags beside the others. He pointed his horse east.

Clare called after him, "Come back this fall for that riding job!"

Black turned his horse and saluted her before he disappeared into the trees. The horse Tuff had ridden followed him.

Clare let out a ragged breath before she hurried to the bedroom where Tuff lay. All three children were peeking through the door, and Clare shooed them out.

"You can all go outside and play now." She paused and looked at each of them sternly. "But when that sheriff and his posse ride in, I want you back inside."

CHAPTER 68

BLACK'S LITTLE BROTHER

ROCK AND HIS RIDERS DISMOUNTED IN THE RANCH yard just in time to see the posse riding up the lane. He looked at them in surprise and frowned as he walked out to meet them.

"I am Sheriff Beacon. I'm from up north in Missoula County. My county borders Idaho Territory, and we had a bank robbery yesterday."

As Rock talked to the sheriff, the tracker scouted around the yard. The children had all run up to the house when Clare called and were now inside. They reluctantly followed Clare into her bedroom. Annie was whispering about crawling out a window, but Zeke ignored her.

"Six horses, Sheriff. They split and rode three different ways."

Clare walked out of the house and pointed toward the Wells Fargo bags. "I believe that is what you are after, Sheriff. I'm not sure how much was stolen, but I'm guessing most of it is here."

Rock stared at Clare in surprise while the sheriff dismounted and checked the bags. He looked up with a puzzled look on his face. "One bag is empty, but there is a little more money in the rest of the bags than was taken!"

Clare shrugged. "Everyone has good in them, Sheriff. Guess those fellows were just tired of being outlaws."

Sheriff Beacon looked at Clare carefully and asked, "I don't suppose you got a good look at those fellows?"

Clare's face was cool as she replied, "I don't make it a point to associate with outlaws, Sheriff. What they looked like was of no importance to me."

The sheriff was quiet for a moment. He finally swung his hand toward the men. "Let's go home, boys. No one was able to get a good description of those fellows, and we have our money back. I'm calling off this chase."

He tipped his hat to Clare. "Ma'am."

Sheriff Beacon rode around the small donkey. He grinned at Rock.

"I'd say that little donkey thinks a lot of your wife."

Rock nodded as he laughed. "He sure does. He also thinks he's a dog and likes to sleep in the house. No one goes in or out without his permission."

The sheriff laughed along with Rock, and the posse rode slowly down the mountain.

Rock looked around. He leaned down to look closer at the kitchen door. He touched the doorjamb where a streak of blood showed.

"What happened here? I know the kids are all right because you are calm, but whose blood is this?"

Clare pointed toward the kids' bedroom.

"There is a young boy in there who was shot. I told his brother I would nurse him back to health. Other than that, just some young men who made bad decisions and tried to make it right."

The children came bursting out of the bedroom, all talking at once.

Rock caught "food or money, cake and saddlebags." He put his arm around his wife as he grinned down at her.

"I don't know, Clare. I leave you alone for a few hours. While I'm gone, you tame wild outlaws and get them to give back stolen money. You even persuaded the toughest sheriff in Montana Territory to abandon his chase and take his posse home."

Clare rolled her eyes. "They weren't outlaws—they were just young cowboys who made a wrong turn. And I told them to come back this fall. I said you would make a place for them here if they stayed out of trouble."

Rock choked as he stared at Clare. She smiled sweetly at him as she batted her eyes.

"They can be my half of the fall hire. After all, you did say you wanted me to join you in management decisions."

Rock shook his head and began to laugh.

"Clare Beckler, you are going to keep me on my toes. Let's go check on your patient and see how he's doing."

Nora was sitting on the bed beside Tuff, and she had a clean cloth on his forehead. As Clare and Rock walked in, she looked up. Her little face was worried.

"He's sick, Mama."

Clare hurried to the young man's side. When his eyes opened, she smiled at him.

"Hello, Tuff. We bound your wound. It is quite large though, so you are going to have some pain."

Tuff's face was flushed when he looked up at her. His eyes moved to Rock, and he smiled.

"Rock, I haven't seen you since I was a little tyke. Black told me I would be in good hands here."

Rock was startled when the young man spoke. He squatted by his side, and his eyes showed his surprise as he stared at the young man's face.

"Tuff? What is Black doing mixing you up in a bank robbery?" Rock's face pulled down in a scowl as he waited for an answer.

Tuff's face lost its smile as he slowly answered.

"Things have been kind of tough the last year or so, and the last rancher we worked for refused to pay us. He said some of his cows disappeared, and he blamed it on the riders. We didn't take them, but he fired us anyway and refused to pay our wages.

"Black and the other fellows thought about stealing his cattle. We decided to rob the bank instead since it had his name above the door.

"No one was shot except me. In fact, no shot was even fired. I was hit while we were riding out of town."

Rock was quiet as he listened to the young man. His face was hard, but he slowly nodded.

"Let's check that wound and see what you have going on."

He loosened the rag and pulled back the moss. He stared at the wound for a moment.

"I think we need to get a doctor up here. I will send one of the boys."

As Rock left the room quickly, Clare smiled at Tuff.

"Now don't you worry. Father Ravalli is one of the best doctors around—for both body and soul."

Tuff nodded weakly as he closed his eyes. Clare patted his arm and took the cloth that Nora held.

"I will bring you a pan of water, Nora. Dampen it from time to time and sponge Tuff's face to keep him cool." Clare kissed the little girl as she whispered, "You have a kind heart, Nora."

Rock walked back into the house as Clare was filling a pan of water. His face was worried, and she felt her stomach knot.

"What is it, Rock? I know the wound in his side is large, but did you see something else?"

Rock nodded grimly.

"I think he is bleeding internally. Blood is seeping from somewhere, and that's not good. Dally is riding for that priest doctor, but he may be too late."

As Clare's face crumpled, Rock pulled her close. "We can't do much other than keep him comfortable," he whispered. "He shouldn't even have any water if we can hold him off. Sponging his face is a good thing. We'll let Nora continue that. Maybe Tuff will feel the love in her little heart. That could do him a lot of good."

Clare nodded. She wiped her eyes and carried fresh water back to the bedroom for Nora.

"Tuff, would you like me to read to you? Or maybe sing to you? It might help you to relax. I would like you to go to sleep if you can."

The young man looked up at Clare and nodded as he whispered, "I'd like a song if you don't mind. My old ma used to sing to me when she put me to bed. That's been a long time ago, but I'd like it just fine."

Clare knelt by Tuff's bed and began to sing. She started with "Home on the Range" and moved to "Amazing Grace." She held Tuff's hand as she sang.

Tuff squeezed his eyes shut tightly as he listened. Slowly, his body relaxed, and he was sleeping by the time she finished the third verse of "Amazing Grace."

Nora looked up at Clare.

"Can I stay, Mama? I think Tuff needs me to stay."

Clare nodded and kissed the little girl. "I think that would be fine, Nora. You can sing to him too if you want."

As Clare left the room, Nora's little voice lifted in "Swing Low, Sweet Chariot" and Clare smiled through the tears in her eyes.

"What a sweet little heart Nora has," she whispered.

CHAPTER 69

KITCHEN-TABLE SURGERY

DALLY WAS BACK THREE HOURS LATER WITH FATHER Ravalli.

The kindly priest hurried into the small room and leaned over the young man. Nora had fallen asleep beside Tuff with her face resting next to his. Tuff's breathing was shallow. His face was flushed, but he was asleep.

Father Ravalli gently lifted Nora off the bed and handed her to Clare. He unwrapped the wound and stared at the seeping hole.

"Let's move him to the kitchen table. I need a firm surface to perform surgery. It needs to be scrubbed down first though." He paused and smiled at Clare. "And I'll scrub it again when we finish. Now start some water boiling, Clare. You can assist me. Just hand me the instruments I need when I ask for them."

The priest's actions were quick and sure. He quickly treated the clean table with something he carried and gave Tuff some chloroform. He then sterilized the skin around Tuff's wound.

Father Ravalli rolled the young man on his side and studied his back. Then he made an incision and began to probe for a bullet. He tied off a vessel that was bleeding and examined the opening closely, carefully checking to make sure none of Tuff's organs were damaged.

The bullet was pressed against the skin in Tuff's back, and the priest removed it as well as any metal shards that were left behind. Once he was satisfied that no more could be done, the priest stitched the incision shut. He once again sterilized the wound.

Father Ravalli hardly talked as he worked. When he was done, he signed a cross over the young man and bowed his head in a prayer.

He smiled as he looked up.

"Clare, you are a wonderful assistant. I could use your help with all my surgeries." He gestured toward the boy. "We have done all that we can. Tuff is in the Lord's hands now. Give him tiny sips of water but no food until tomorrow. Try to keep his fever down. If he becomes hot, bathe his chest and head." He handed her two small jars.

"Give him this medicine twice a day, and rub this ointment on the incision. Most of all, make sure your hands are clean when you treat him. I will ride out in a couple of days to check on him."

Clare's lower lip was trembling.

"Will he live, Father? Rock was afraid he was bleeding internally."

Father Ravalli smiled at Clare as he patted her arm.

"I believe he will. I was concerned when I saw where the bullet had entered, but it was evidentially shot from a sidearm and at a distance. Had it been a rifle, he wouldn't have made it." The priest frowned slightly and added, "He was shot twice. Luckily, a rib deflected the other bullet. I would say the Good Lord was with him on both of those shots."

Relief flooded over Clare's face.

"How do we pay you, Father? Do you prefer cash money or beef? We will be glad to do either one."

Father Ravalli's face melted into happy creases as he smiled at her.

"Live beef is always welcome, but pay whatever you can afford. And let's talk to that husband of yours about coming to church. I would like to see him when I look out at my congregation."

Clare laughed as she nodded. "I would like that. I'm not sure Nora has been baptized, so maybe you can do that this weekend. I will see if Rock will let us spend the night with Maggie and Ike after their wedding so we can go to church on Sunday."

Father Ravalli nodded. He lifted the young man easily off the table and carried him back to the bedroom. He gently laid him on Nora's bed and pulled a quilt over him. He touched his head again as he said a silent prayer and followed Clare out to the kitchen. He quickly cleaned the table and gathered his instruments.

Rock stepped into the house and shook Father Ravalli's hand.

"Would you like something to eat before you go?"

The priest shook his head. "No, but I will plan to be here in time for dinner on Monday," he responded with a grin. "And I told Clare that I would like to see you at Mass more often."

Rock's face colored a little, but he nodded. "I will work on that. With all these little ones around, I need to set a better example.

"How about I cut out a couple of bred heifers and send them down tomorrow? I know you like beef for payment."

Father Ravalli nodded his head.

"That will be just fine, Rock." His grin became wider as he added, "And once you get those black cows established, you can send some of them my way to help me do the Lord's work. I liked what I saw on my ride up here."

Rock laughed and agreed. He shook Father Ravalli's hand again, and the priest headed down the trail on his large mule.

Rock was grinning as he watched the priest ride away.

"I think the Good Lord enjoys men like that priest. He can build just about anything, cure most ailments out there, operate in the most primitive of conditions, and make a fellow donate way more than he intends. Yep, he sure does the Lord's work well."

Clare looked up hopefully at her husband. "Does that mean we can spend the night with Maggie and attend Mass on Sunday?"

Rock smiled down at Clare as he squeezed her.

"That would be fine. I'm sure Maggie and Ike will be glad to have us, and the kids will be excited to spend the night again.

"I think I'll have Dally and Pete drive those heifers down. I wasn't going to let them go into town, but they have been working hard. I'll give them tomorrow night off so they can have a few beers while they are there."

Nora was sitting beside Tuff again and was singing to him. She smiled brightly at Clare and Rock when they walked into the little room.

"He's getting better, Mama. He smiles sometimes when I sing so I know he likes my songs."

Clare kissed Nora's cheek. "Nora, you are such a sweet little girl. Your kind little heart will help Tuff heal. I'm sure he does like it when you sing.

"Why don't you let us know when he wakes up? We can't give him any food today, but we can give him little sips of water."

They quietly left the room. Clare frowned as she looked back toward the closed door. "I don't think Tuff should be left alone while we go to the wedding. Do you think you could send Dally and Pete down this afternoon with the cattle? Then one of them could stay closer so Tuff can be checked on while we are gone."

Rock slowly nodded. "That would work. We'd better round up those cattle right away since it will take them over two hours to get down there. Let's eat a quick bite, and then I'll help them cut out three or four head of heifers."

When Clare looked at Rock in surprise, he shrugged.

"I know that is overpayment, but like I said, Father Ravalli has a way of making a fellow want to give more than he intends."

Rock sniffed the air and looked sideways at Clare. "I sure could use some fresh bread and butter tonight. Maybe my wife can whip that up while we are gathering the cattle."

Clare laughed and nodded her head. "Maybe she will as long as her husband promises to get water in here tonight so everyone can bathe."

Rock winked at her as his eyes twinkled.

"That sounds like a fair trade. Too bad our tub isn't bigger—we could take one together to save water," he drawled as he tromped outside.

Rock looked back and chuckled when he saw pink move up Clare's neck. He was still grinning when he hollered at his hands.

"Dally! Pete! Get your horses saddled. We are going to cut out a few head of cattle for the Mission. You boys can spend the night in town as long as you are back home by eight tomorrow morning."

Annie came running into the house.

"Mama, can we help Papa round up cattle? He said we could go if you said it was all right!"

Clare almost said no as she wiped a smudge of dirt off Annie's cheek. She looked at Annie's hopeful face and laughed. She kissed her quickly.

"That will be fine, but you tell your papa I want you home before dark to take baths."

Annie rushed out the door, hollering excitedly to Zeke.

"We can go! Quick, let's catch Patches and Steed so papa doesn't leave us behind."

The five horses were quickly saddled, and the riders headed out of the yard. The children were chattering excitedly to Dally and Pete while the two cowboys laughed. Rock swiveled in his saddle and grinned as Clare watched from the doorway. He waved his hand before he turned around.

Clare placed her hand over her chest and waved back at him. Her heart thumped loudly beneath her hand.

"There goes my everything. Dear Lord, bring them safely back to me." She smiled as she turned into the house. She paused to listen to Nora's singing and added, "And little Nora too. Please help her tender heart to help heal Tuff."

CHAPTER 70

BLACK

CLARE SANG SOFTLY AS SHE KNEADED THE BREAD. IT was rising in the pans when Gomer brayed and rushed up to the house. She quickly grabbed the shotgun and swung the door open for the little donkey to come inside.

Gomer stood quietly beside her as he watched the trail. Before long, a man appeared. Clare recognized Black. She set the shotgun down and stepped outside with a smile on her face.

"Good morning, Black. Step down and come in."

Black dropped the reins to his horse at the hitching rack and stepped down.

Clare could see the exhaustion in the man. She smiled at him again.

"Tuff is doing much better. Come, we'll look in on him."

She softly opened the bedroom door. They could both see that Tuff was resting quietly. Once again, Nora had fallen asleep with her head next to his.

Black looked at Clare in surprise and she smiled.

"Nora has been his personal nurse ever since you brought him here. She sings to him, and they both fall asleep." Clare looked tenderly at the little girl before she looked up at Black.

"I think her little heart is helping him to heal."

Black nodded slowly and turned back toward the door.

Clare pulled out a chair by the table and said softly, "Sit down, Black. You look like you could use a rest. Eat supper with us tonight, and you can spend the night in the bunk house."

Black's face tightened. "I'm not sure your husband would like that," he answered as he dropped tiredly onto a chair.

Clare sat down at the table and looked at Black directly.

"How long have you known Rock? I am guessing for some time the way the two of you act."

Black nodded tiredly. "We grew up together. Our places were about five miles apart, and we were together all the time. Our folks were good friends too. After Rock's ma died, his pa just kind of shriveled up inside. He started drinking heavy and quit working his ranch. Rock's little sister, Georgia, was two or three, and Rock took care of her.

"Rock started cooking all their meals so they could eat. He ate some with us, but he always had a powerful pride that he carried around. He refused to take charity."

Black paused and smiled as he looked over Clare's head. "He was my best friend, and I loved him like a brother. I still do.

"When Georgia became sick, Rock was frantic. He was only ten at the time, and he didn't know what to do. Their pa was no help. He just sat at the table and drank while he stared at a picture of their ma. He didn't pay any attention to those kids." Black frowned and shook his head.

"Rock held Georgia almost constantly those last days. He begged his pa to do something, but his old man just…" Black shrugged. "Rock finally took her to the Crow encampment and asked their medicine woman to help her. It was too late though. Georgia died, and Rock blamed himself.

"He moved in with the Crow people after that. Little Bear was like a brother to both of us, and his family took Rock in like he was their own. Rock studied Indian healing with the old medicine woman, and he knew all the healing herbs around here when he left four years later."

Clare's heart tightened in her chest. *Rock blames himself for so many things that he couldn't possibly control. How difficult to watch your little sister die and feel so helpless.*

"Did you leave with Rock?"

"Naw. My folks were good people. My pa wanted me to take over the farm, but I wanted to cowboy. Rock came back about two years later. He'd heard that his pa had died. He wanted to see what was left of the place. His old man lost everything, so he pulled out a few days later. I left with him, and we rode together for about four years." Black drew his hand across his face and took a deep breath before he continued.

"Rock and me was pards. We only hired on at ranches that needed two hands. Rock was always a top hand with horses and cattle, and I was pretty good with cattle. It usually worked out for us. Then one day…" Black's voice faded away and the planes of his face hardened down.

"We worked one winter for a mean old shyster. We stayed out in his line shack and about starved to death. If we hadn't hunted, we would have. I wanted to eat some of his beef, but Rock said if we could shoot deer, we'd leave the beef alone."

"When we came in that spring, the boss cut our wages in half. He said that was for all the beef we ate. 'Course Rock and me were both mad.

"Some of the fellows planned to steal his cattle. He shorted all the boys every chance he got, and they decided to get even. I wanted to join them.

"Rock refused. He said he wouldn't become a cow thief because of the greedy old—because of a greedy boss. He went up to the house and had a talk with the old man. That talk was loud and involved some punching. In the end, the boss paid us our full wages. Rock didn't know that I'd run off some cows the night before. When he found out, he was furious.

"We parted company that day, and I lost my best friend. Rock doesn't have much tolerance for bad behavior…even less for dishonesty, and I'd broken all his rules."

Clare nodded and laughed softly. Black looked at her in surprise.

"I received that same wrath from Rock the first time I met him. He tied me to his horse and hauled me to Stevensville. Turned me over to the sheriff. I was thirteen, and my brothers had killed the old man who lived here. It took Rock seven years to forgive me for being with them."

As Black stared at her, Clare put her hand on his.

"Rock has a tender heart, but he hides it. Apologize to him, and I will talk to him as well. You can't move Tuff for a while yet. You just as well stay and work for us until that time." Laughter bubbled out of Clare, and her eyes sparkled as she looked at Black.

"Rock wants me to be part of the management decisions here. I will tell him I just hired our foreman!"

Black's face turned a deep red and he shook his head.

"No, I won't be the cause of a fight between the two of you. I'll come back when Tuff can travel and—"

"Nonsense. I'm sure Rock has missed your friendship as much as you have missed him. You let me worry about how to handle Rock.

"Now tell me about Tuff. How did he come to be with you?"

CHAPTER 71

"Are We Staying?"

ROCK WALKED INTO THE KITCHEN JUST AS CLARE asked Black about Tuff. He looked from one to the other, and his face drew down in hard lines. Black turned red as he started to stand.

Clare stood and pointed at Black. Her eyes were glinting, and her chin was pushed out in a manner Rock had come to recognize.

"I invited Black to stay here until Tuff is ready to travel. I told him he could stay in the bunk house and work here until then."

Rock frowned as he looked from Black to Clare.

Black stepped forward and shook his head.

"I told Clare I didn't think that was a good idea. If you'll let me stay the night though, I'd like to see Tuff before I take off. He's asleep right now."

Rock nodded. "That would be fine, but then—"

Clare glared at him, and Rock felt his neck turning red.

Black cleared his throat.

"Rock, I'd really like to talk to you outside if you can take the time. We have a lot of things that need to be said."

Rock's scowl became deeper, and his face hardened down as he stared at his old friend.

He caught Clare's face from the side of his eye and glanced toward her as he continued to frown.

"Just a few minutes, Rock. What can that hurt?" Clare asked softly.

Rock grunted and turned out the door. He walked toward the small cemetery and waited for Black to catch up with him.

"Black—"

"Rock, let me say my piece. Then, you can say what you want."

Rock's face was hard, and his green eyes glinted as he took a deep breath. He slowly nodded.

"I've done some things these last years that I'm not proud of. I knew I'd made a mistake when we ran off that first bunch of cattle. The second bunch was easier. After that, it just seemed like that was the person I had become.

"I really didn't think I could ever go back, not until I talked to your wife the day we brought Tuff here. She told me I could change. Since then, I've given it a lot of thought.

"I don't want Tuff to become what I am. I'm going to take Clare's advice. The posters out there don't have a very clear picture of me. If I was to shave off this beard and stop using the name Black, I'm not sure anyone would know who I was."

Rock stared at his old friend in surprise, and Black shrugged.

"You are the only one who knows my real name is Steve Jackson. I could even go by the name you all called me when we wore short pants."

Rock's eyebrows shot up in surprise and he laughed. "You hated it when we called you Stub."

Black nodded his head somberly.

"I never much liked being short, but I reckon there are worse things." He grinned at his old friend. "At least I'm not as ugly as you in the morning!"

Rock looked at this man who had been his best friend for nearly half his life, and something hard broke inside him.

"I'm sorry I didn't give you a chance back then to make things right, Black. I threw your half of our wages on the ground in front of you and rode out." Rock scowled as he added, "Even now, I can guess how the boss would have handled it if you had come clean.

"Clare has shown me that people can change, and I know she expects me to give you that chance." He put out his hand to Black as he grinned.

"Welcome to the Slash B, Stub. It will be good to have my old pard around again."

When Stub reached for his hand, Rock wrapped the smaller man up in a bear hug. Then he knocked his hat off and rubbed his head roughly.

"Let's go back in the house so you can tell Clare how Tuff came to be with you. I'm guessing your folks passed away, but don't tell me yet. Clare will make me repeat every word if she doesn't hear if from you." Rock's grin became bigger. "She's a sassy one, my Clare is."

Stub's eyes glinted as he nodded.

"She has to be if she is going to put up with you. Someday, I will tell her how you came to get the name of Rock. I'll bet she doesn't even know that your real name is Jamison Worthington Beckler!"

Rock's face turned red, and he growled, "And she had better not hear that name either."

Both men were laughing as they came in the house, and Clare could feel the tension drain from her chest.

"Clare, I don't think you have been formally introduced to our newest hand. Meet Stub Jackson."

Stirring could be heard in the small bedroom, and Tuff appeared in the doorway. He was holding his side and had a huge smile on his face.

"Black! We are staying? That would sure be fine with me."

A tousled head of reddish-brown curls appeared under his arm, and Tuff smiled down at the little girl. "Nora here is a fine nurse. She even sings to me."

Stub reached for his little brother. His voice was rough as he stared at the young man and held onto his shoulders.

"Tuff, it is sure good to see you smile. Yes, we are staying, but Black is gone. We are starting over here with a clean slate. Your brother will now be known as Stub Jackson, just like he was when you were a little squirt…as soon as I get rid of this beard."

Rock looked away. He tried to scowl to cover his feelings, but the look on Clare's face made him smile.

She had no problem letting her joy show as she smiled at the two brothers.

"Stub, Tuff—welcome to the Slash B." She kissed Tuff's cheek and shook Stub's hand. Humor showed on her face as she looked from Rock to Stub. "And later we'll see about the rest of that hiring proposition we discussed, Stub."

Rock looked confused, and Stub stuttered as he looked down.

Clare laughed as she pushed them toward the door.

"Go finish up outside so we can eat early tonight. Remember, everyone needs to take baths. And, since Dally isn't here, someone is going to have to milk that cow!"

Stub slid his eyes sideways at Rock as they went outside and tried not to laugh.

"Milk cow? I sure never thought I'd see the day that you'd own a milk cow."

Rock glared at him and the scowl remained on his face.

"You know it wasn't my idea. Aunt Maggie and Ike gave it to Clare and me as a wedding gift. They knew Clare wanted a cow. Of course, they knew I didn't, but that really didn't matter.

"Dally, one of the new hands, offered to do all the milking. He even milks her without kickers. He's gone this evening though, so someone else will have to milk." Rock grinned as he added, "I will say the fresh milk and cream has been a nice addition though."

Stub nodded somberly. He turned his head away as he grinned, and his chest shook as the laugh he tried to hide leaked out of him.

"Rock, I never thought I'd see the day. You are a whipped man."

As he folded over, Rock shoved him. Stub fell over, still laughing.

Rock grinned at his old friend. He reached down his hand and pulled Stub up.

"You know, Stub, it's the little things—crazy little things make women happy. I don't understand Clare at all, but milk cows and curtains make her happy. Shoot, if that's all it takes, I reckon I can go along."

"She's a good woman, Rock. Sure better than some of those gals who used to chase you. Remember the one who chased you when we worked on that ranch in Idaho Territory? We were running our horses for all they were worth. We were barely eighteen, but she intended to marry you if she had to drag you back."

As both men laughed, Stub added, "I thought you should have let her catch you. Her daddy had the biggest ranch in those parts. I told her, 'Rope me! I'll go back!' but it was you she wanted. 'Course, you were scared to death." His eyes were twinkling as he jabbed his old friend.

"And folks wander why I'm leery of women. They can be just plain scary, and their minds work kind of like a beetle running circles around a cow patty. Their reasoning process is all twisted up. I never have been able to track with them.

"Clare is blunt though. She doesn't play mind games with me, so we get along. I can't follow her all the time, but sometimes, I figure it out."

Stub was quiet for a moment. His voice was soft when he spoke.

"I heard about your first wife. I was passing through Stevensville right after she died. I heard you weren't doing too good, and I really wanted to stop in." Stub dug the toe of his boot in the dirt as he looked up at Rock. "I just didn't think you'd want to see me, so I rode on. I didn't even tell anyone that I knew you."

Rock's face grew still as he looked toward the small tombstone. He nodded.

"It's just as well. I was on a six-month drunk, and I wasn't talking to anyone." He nodded toward Annie. She was digging by the corral with Zeke.

"Suzanna died shortly after Annie was born. Clare was her best friend, and she came out to help. She'd had Zeke just a few days before Annie was born, and she nursed both babies." Rock took a deep breath.

"That was a hard time, but it all worked out. I sure wouldn't have guessed that Clare would be my wife one day though. We married about a week ago, and I'm just plain happy." He grinned at Stub.

"Now let's go get that cow in so *you* can milk her."

CHAPTER 72

"You Have Any Family?"

DALLY AND PETE DELIVERED THE SLASH B CATTLE TO Father Ravalli at the Mission, and the priest was delighted.

"I sure appreciate these cattle and you fellows too for delivering them. Be sure to thank the Becklers for me.

"You be safe now and keep an eye out for trouble. Lots of strangers passing through here this week." Father Ravalli shook each of their hands. His eyes twinkled and he added, "There is always room in our church for two more cowboys if you would like to join us on Sunday."

Dally was startled. He glanced quickly at Pete, but his friend was focused on his horse's neck. Dally stammered an answer, and the two riders turned their horses toward Stevensville. Rock had paid them, so they had a little money in their pockets.

Pete was looking forward to a night on the town, but Dally had an uneasy feeling. He couldn't shake it as he followed Pete toward the town's only saloon.

The Star Saloon was hopping on Friday night as they pushed through the doors and up to the bar. They each ordered a beer and leaned their backs against the bar while they surveyed the room.

Dally studied the patrons. He frowned at his partner and drank his beer quickly.

"I'm thinkin' we should just mosey on back to the ranch tonight. It'll be dark before we get there, but I think it might be a little safer than spendin' the night in town."

Pete stared at Dally for a moment. He drained his beer and slammed the mug down. Dally dropped some money on the bar, and the two men walked out.

They looked longingly at the eating house but mounted their horses instead. Gunfire sounded in the saloon as they loped out of town.

Soon, the shooting spilled into the street. A horse whinnied as it raced down the street. The riderless horse passed Dally and Pete as it raced south down the trail, away from the shooting.

Pete grinned at Dally. "There was a time when I woulda argued with ya, but ya have an uncanny way of tellin' when trouble is goin' to start."

Dally was quiet for a time. His voice was soft when he answered.

"I recognized some of those boys. Did ya hear what the feller said who was dealin' cards? He said, 'I am innocent!'"

Pete stared at his partner. "But the Innocents Gang was broken up, an' Henry Plumber was hanged in '64! This is '79. None of those fellers would be around anymore."

Dally shrugged. "Nobody knows for sure who all was in that gang. They hung twenty-two supposed members plus Henry. I ain't so sure though that all those fellers was guilty or if they even caught ever'body.

"Regardless, we made it out 'fore the shootin' started, an' I'm durn happy about that. That ol' sheriff would love to have a reason to throw us in jail, and we'd be out of a good job."

Pete studied Dally and slowly nodded as he stared at the trail in front of them.

The two men had met on the Double Diamond Ranch six years before and had become good friends. When Dally decided to move on, Pete rode with him.

Pete constantly wore a grin and was still wild and reckless when he drank. Six years ago, he had been wild and reckless all the time. His blond hair was curly and clung tightly to his head. He was of average height and had the bowed legs of a rider who had spent most of his life in the saddle. Pete's blue eyes twinkled constantly, and he was always looking for ways to rattle Dally. He wasn't particularly handsome, but the women liked him because he was funny. Since Dally didn't talk much, Pete was compelled to talk even more.

Dally was a little taller than Pete and much quieter. He liked to think, and the two men often rode for miles with only the sound of Pete's voice. Dally's brown eyes were windows to his soul, and his gaze was clear and steady. He combed the dark brown hair that curled up around his hat every morning and washed it in the horse tank every night. He kept his gear and his gun impeccably clean, and he took a bath as often as possible.

Pete once commented, "Dally, ya jist took a bath last week an' we are chasin' cows tomorrow. What do ya want to take a bath for again tonight?"

Dally would only grin at his partner and drawl, "One of these days, we are goin' to meet a nice little gal. I'll be able to talk to her first 'cause y'all will smell so bad that she'll make ya ride downwind."

Pete snorted, but it did make him think. For nearly a month, he took a bath every week. Of course, they didn't meet any girls, and Pete soon went back to his old ways.

As the two men rode along, Dally frowned and looked over at his partner. "Do you have any family, Pete? Like folks that miss you and wonder where you are? Neither of us ever gets a letter. I know I don't have any family, but what about you?"

Pete looked down at his horse and stroked its neck before he looked at his friend. "I have folks or at least I did when I runned off. My pa was a good man, but he didn't like me runnin' wild, an' I didn't like his rules. One night, I come in drunk, an' he walloped me good. I swung back an' we fought it out right there in the kitchen. My ma was a cryin', an' my pa was madder than an ol' bull. He beat me good." Pete laughed ruefully and shook his head.

"I'd never seen my pa that mad before, an' I sure didn't know he could hit that hard. I was fifteen an' purty sure I knew ever'thing.

"The next mornin', I packed up my few things an' rode out. My ma was cryin' in the doorway, an' my little sis begged me not to go. The old man jist stared at me an' didn't say a word. That was seven years ago, an' I ain't heard a word from 'em since. 'Course, I ain't written 'em neither."

Pete stared down the trail. "My little sis would be seventeen now." He grinned at Dally. "I'll bet she's good lookin' too. She was always a cute little gal. Sassy too. Mighty sassy."

Dally was quiet and Pete waited for his friend to talk. Finally, Pete asked, "So what about you? What happened to yore family?"

Dally stared at the mountains as he sifted his horse's mane through his fingers. His voice was bleak when he answered.

"Ma and Pa died on the trail headed west from Missouri. Pa always wanted to be a cattleman. He was tired of trying to scrape out a livin' on our little farm. He finally convinced my ma to go West.

"We joined a wagon train headed for Oregon Territory. Then the sickness came. It went through that wagon train like a ragin' fire. Finally, the folks that wasn't sick packed up an' left the rest of us—jist left the sick folks there to fend for themselves.

"We had hardly any food an' no men strong enough to hunt. I was ten an' was one of the few who didn't get sick. I took Pa's ol' gun an' went out ever' day to try to get some meat. Pa would only let me take one bullet. My pa was a thrifty man. That's the way we hunted at home too.

"He always said, 'If ya cain't drop it with one shot, then a second bullet probably won't help ya neither.' I brought back somethin' ever' day but not near enough to feed seven wagons of sick folks." Dally's face drew tight, and he scowled.

"Then folks started to die. It seemed like we buried four or five ever' day." Dally stared down again at his horse's mane.

"Little Grace Miller was only four. Her folks both died the third day after the healthy wagons left. I brought her over to our wagon. Ma seemed to be doin' better, an' she was a comfort to Grace.

"Grace was a sweet little gal. Blondest hair I ever did see, an' blue eyes so big they looked like little ponds in her face.

"Folks kept dyin', an' before long, only five of us was left."

Dally took a deep breath. His face was bleak when he looked at Pete. "Then Pa died, an' Ma passed two days later. The last old man was mighty sick. Before he died, he told me to burn the wagons after he passed an' him too. He said to head southwest till I found a town.

"After he died, I did just that. I loaded up what little food I had found in the wagons an' tied it on one of the mules. I hid Grace a ways off in some bushes, an' I set those wagons on fire. They lit up like seven big torches, an' I'll never forget that smell. I had emptied the water barrels around the wagons, so the grass only sizzled. 'Course, there wasn't much grass left 'round there anyhow. That fire had plenty of fuel in those wagons though.

"Once ever'thing was burnin', I put Grace in front of me on an ol' work hoss an' off we went. I wouldn't let her look back neither."

Pete stared at Dally as he talked. He had known his friend for six years and had never heard him tell this story. *No wonder Dally don't talk much. I guess I wouldn't neither if I'd been through all that as a kid.* Pete was almost ashamed of himself for not writing his old Ma. *She's likely worried sick thinkin' of me.*

Dally looked out over the trail and smiled as he talked about Grace. "She was such a brave little tyke. She tried so hard not to cry. I told her it was alright to cry though. I said, 'Cryin' is jist a way for the sad to leak outa yore heart. Ya go ahead an' cry.'

"We finally made it to Manhattan, Kansas. Folks there was surprised to see us ride in. It seems the wagon train had been through there 'bout a week before, an' the wagon boss said we'd all died." Dally frowned and shook his head.

"I used to promise myself that if I ever ran into any of those folks that I would give them a piece of my mind. An' that wagon boss…I wanted to hurt 'im.

"The townsfolk wanted to put both of us on the Orphan Train that was goin' through there. It had just come into town a few hours before an' was leavin' that evenin'. At the last minute, a couple passin' through town come forward an' adopted little Grace. She cried like crazy when they took her outa my arms, but I couldn't do nothin'. I was jist a ten-year-old kid, not old enough to be on my own let alone take care of a little girl. I begged that family to take me too, but they said they couldn't afford to take in a big boy like me.

"I was shoved onto another train an' on I went to Cawker City. I was adopted by a nice old couple an' stayed with 'em for five years." Dally stopped talking. He slapped his reins against his saddle several times before he continued.

"They died when a prairie fire went through. I got the horses outa the barn. The missus said to take 'em to the creek an' stay there. She an' her man were goin' to try to save the house an' the barn." Dally frowned again and shook his head.

"They didn't make it. The wind changed direction an' brought that fire right in on 'em. I buried what I could find of those good folks an' rode out.

"I left a note for whoever might come by sayin' I took the horses. I figgered they'd have wanted me to have 'em." Dally paused and looked at Pete somberly.

"I headed north an' met y'all."

For once, Pete was quiet. He had never heard his friend talk so much at one time. In fact, for as long as he had known Dally, the cowboy had never said as much as just now.

Pete reached over and squeezed Dally's shoulder. "I ain't cried since I left home, but if ya keep a talkin', I'll be bawlin' like a baby!" He wiped one eye with the back of his hand.

"I shore am glad we met. Ya are the best pard I ever had," Pete said roughly as he grinned at the man next to him.

Dally slowly smiled as he scratched his horse's neck. He grinned back at Pete.

"It ain't been such a bad life. Kind of a rough start but it's good now."

Pete nodded. His curiosity was stirred, and he had to ask a question.

"What happened to little Grace? She'd be a growed woman by now. Did ya ever write her?"

"We wrote back an' forth for several years before those old folks died. I sent 'er one last letter after the fire. I told 'er what happened to the folks who took me in. Francis an' Kathryn Eilert. Fine people.

"I don't know if Grace got that last letter though. Her letters to me all burned in the fire, so I put the address on as best I could remember.

"I said I was headed north, an' I'd write again when I was settled. 'Course we ain't been in any one place too long, an' I never did send that letter I promised her."

Pete's blue eyes began to twinkle. "I tell you what. I'll write my folks if you'll write to that little gal. Let's see who gets an answer first. Now let's pick up the pace an' see if we can get back to the ranch while this moon is still shinin'."

CHAPTER 73

A Quiet Evening

CLARE HAD THE KIDS BATHED AND IN BED BY SEVEN-thirty. Rock had talked Stub into milking the cow, and both men were laughing as they came in the house.

Tuff was sitting at the table. His eyes sparkled as he watched his brother. *I haven't seen Black this happy in a long time,* he thought as his brother tousled his hair.

Rock took one look at the brown water and brought in fresh water for Clare's bath.

"Think you can handle the bunkhouse tonight, Tuff?" Stub asked. "I'm guessing Clare doesn't want those kids woken up tonight since it's so quiet in there."

"Sure, Black—I mean, Stub. Mrs. Beckler fed me with the kids, so I'm ready to go any time."

Clare set the food in front of the men and asked Rock, "What time to you want to leave in the morning? I want to have everyone ready."

Rock grinned at her. "Let's just take it easy. The wedding isn't until the afternoon, so we'll make it an easy day. Pete and Dally should be home by eight, and I'd like to talk to them before we leave." His grin became bigger.

"Maybe I will even let you sleep in, and I'll fix breakfast for the men."

Clare's eyebrows went up. A slow blush started up her neck when Rock winked at her. She hurried to the stove and busied herself scraping pots and banging pans.

When the men finished eating, Stub helped his brother to the bunkhouse. Clare sent a stack of blankets with them, and the house was nearly silent when they closed the door.

Rock soon had water heating. He looked at the tub and then at Clare. "Do you want to take a bath in here or in the bedroom?"

Clare blushed slightly as she answered, "I think the bedroom would be best. With all the men around, I'd like a little more privacy."

Rock carried the tub into their bedroom and filled it with hot water. He was just getting ready to tease her when he heard riders outside. He frowned as he grabbed his rifle and opened the door.

"Dally! Pete! What are you doing back so early?"

Clare couldn't hear their response, but she grabbed a pan off the stove. She handed it to Rock along with some plates.

"Give this to them. I'm guessing they haven't eaten since they are home so early."

Once Rock carried the food outside, Clare shut the bedroom door. She quickly undressed and slid into the tub. The water felt wonderful, and she soaked until it began to cool. Rock was just returning when she grabbed her nightclothes. She was buttoning her nightgown when he opened the door.

"Everything is fine. There was trouble brewing in town, and Dally decided to leave early." He smiled at Clare. "I sure am glad we hired him. That boy has a good head on his shoulders."

Rock brought in more water and soon had it heating over the fire.

Clare hurried to clear the dishes. She was washing dishes and jumped when Rock's breath tickled her neck.

"You sure smell good, Clare. Did you use some of that fancy soap you were trying to make?"

Clare turned to face her husband as she nodded. "I added some crushed lilac to it. It is subtle, but it's pleasant."

Rock wrapped his arms around her as he grinned. "You have added a whole new dimension to this ranch, Clare. I sure am glad you talked me into marrying you."

Clare rolled her eyes as she smiled up at Rock. Her heart was happy, and it belonged completely to this man.

She kissed him gently and whispered, "The water is boiling. I need just a little for my dishes, and you can have the rest. I'll clean up here while you take your bath."

Rock's smile became bigger. He was whistling as he poured water into her basin. He carried the rest to the tub.

The water was soon splashing, and Rock was whistling "Buffalo Gals, Won't You Come Out Tonight?"

Clare smiled as she listened. When she finished her dishes, she blew out the lamp and tiptoed toward the bedroom door.

Strong arms grabbed her as she tried to slip through. She almost screamed but began to laugh when Rock scooped her up. He swung her around as he sang, "And dance by the light of the moon."

CHAPTER 74

"Don't Be Afraid, Sweetheart"

THE CHILDREN WERE UP EARLY, WHISPERING AND giggling, as they tried to slip into Clare and Rock's bedroom.

Rock put his arm over Clare and caught them as they attempted to jump on the bed. He grinned and asked, "Who is ready to go to a party today?"

"We are! We are!" they screamed as they jumped up and down.

Rock grabbed all three of them and ran around the bedroom as the kids screamed even louder.

Gomer brayed and charged out the door. Rock had put a strap on both sides of the door so the little donkey could let himself in and out of the house. Now, he came in whatever time of night he chose and was usually gone by morning.

Clare climbed out of bed and quickly dressed. Rock was on the kitchen floor wrestling with all three children, and it looked like they were getting the best of him. She clapped her hands, and they looked up.

"I am making flapjacks for breakfast, and you need to get your chores done. Today is Auntie Maggie's and Grampy Ike's wedding. Chop, chop, chicken mop!"

Rock groaned as he rose from the floor. "You saved me. They are getting harder to control."

Clare laughed as she looked at her husband. His hair poked out in every direction, and heavy stubble covered his face.

She laughed again and pointed at the mirror. "I think you had better find your comb and a razor. And then, we should trim your hair. You will scare the new hands if they see you this morning."

Rock grinned at her as he pulled his fingers through his hair. He was soon dressed and shaved.

"I'm going to line out the men. We can head out any time after we eat breakfast."

Breakfast was a noisy affair. Clare fed the children first and sent them outside. When the men came in, she placed the second round of flapjacks on their plates.

Dally brought the milk in, and Clare handed him a glass of cool buttermilk. He smiled and drank it slowly, savoring every drop. He had mentioned to Clare that he liked buttermilk, and she made sure he had a glass every morning. The quiet cowboy took his chair. He always washed before he came in for breakfast.

Pete soon appeared. His hair was wet, but he didn't bother to comb it. Dack followed Pete in. His clothes were brushed and his mustache was trimmed. Even though he had known Rock the longest, he was nervous about eating in the presence of a lady. Once Stub and Tuff arrived, they all sat down. Rock began to line out the day.

"Stub, you are in charge. Make sure that line of fence we have been working on gets done. Dack knows where our boundary lines are. And check on old Smitty. Dally and Pete can show you where he lives. See if he needs any help moving to town. If he does, leave one or two men there."

"We'll be back Sunday afternoon. You boys are on your own for meals until then. You are welcome to use the kitchen but make sure you leave it clean. We have a cook coming out on Monday along with a few more hands, so we'll have a full crew here by Monday night. Clear your gear off those empty bunks because they will all be full. And when Cookie gets here, don't mess with his gear."

The men ate quickly and filed out of the house. Each thanked Clare. They were all a little sad that she would no longer be feeding them. Her meals had been something they looked forward to. They hoped the new cook's food would be as good, but none were too optimistic.

Clare put on her good purple dress and Rock groaned as he helped her with the buttons. "Not all these buttons again. I think I am going to hide this dress."

She laughed at him and twisted away when his hands strayed. "Yes, I think the next one will have buttons *I* can reach."

Rock's eyes began to twinkle, and he chuckled as he left the house. "I think we will save that conversation for later."

Clare shook her head and followed him to the wagon.

Three excited little voices called back to the hired hands as the wagon disappeared down the lane.

Clare set a basket down by their feet and Rock sniffed. "I smell lilacs. Did you make some soap for Maggie too?"

She nodded happily. "I did. I put together a little basket for them. Some soap and some doilies I tatted along with a couple of dish towels. It's not much but I think Maggie will like it. Of course, whatever makes Maggie happy, Ike likes."

Rock grinned as he agreed. "That's how it works for sure."

After an hour on the trail, the children began to slow down. Before long, all three were asleep in the back of the wagon.

Rock's face was serious as he looked at his wife.

"Clare, there is something I have been meaning to ask you. Does Father Ravalli think you are going to have trouble birthing babies?"

Clare's face showed her surprise as she looked at Rock. She slowly shook her head.

"He said the scar tissue from my surgery could possibly cause problems. He wants to see me if I become pregnant just to keep an eye on it."

When Clare saw the fear in Rock's face, she touched his arm. "I'm sure I will be fine, Rock. I had no problem with Zeke, so that is the only thing we need to watch."

Rock was quiet for a time as he looked straight ahead. His voice was soft when he spoke.

"Suzanna and I lost two little ones before Annie was born. One of them was early on, and that was hard enough. The next one was…was clearly a little boy. That one was terrible hard on Suzanna. It broke my heart twice—once when I held that small child who would never see life, and a second time when Suzanna cried." He took a ragged breath. "I don't want to do that again, and I sure can't bear to lose another wife."

Clare kissed Rock's cheek and scooted closer to him. She pulled his arm around her.

"Rock," she whispered softly, "Some women have trouble birthing babies. I am not one of those women. Even though Zeke was my first, he was an easy delivery. Don't be afraid, sweetheart. We will fill our house with little feet, and I will be fine."

Rock looked down at her, and Clare could feel the tension slowly flow out of him. He pulled her close and kissed the top of her head.

"I'd sure stop this wagon and do a little spooning if we didn't have sleeping kids back there," he whispered.

Clare smiled at him.

"I do love you, Rock Beckler."

CHAPTER 75

ONE PRAYER AND TWO ANSWERS

ROCK STOPPED THEIR WAGON IN FRONT OF MAGGIE'S house around ten that morning. The kids were once again awake and piled out of the wagon screaming for Maggie and Ike.

Maggie rushed outside to greet them as they all talked at once. She finally turned a puzzled face to Rock.

"Who are Tuff and Stub?"

Rock grinned and nodded at Clare.

"Clare made some new hires while I was gone. I think they are going to be good help. I just might make Stub my foreman. I put him in charge while I was gone so we will see."

As Maggie looked from one to the other in surprise, Clare rolled her eyes.

"Stub and Rock have known each other since childhood. Rock is very aware of Stub's ranching and foreman skills." She smiled sweetly at Rock as she added, "I did tell Stub on the first day though that I thought he would be a good foreman."

Rock's eyes opened wide in surprise. He shook his head as he chuckled.

"I tell you, Ike. I have to work mighty hard to stay in front of Clare. I think with a little encouragement, she would just take over!"

Ike's old eyes shined as he hugged Clare. He nodded as he agreed with Rock.

"Didn't I tell ya that ya shoulda married 'er sooner? Shore now, ya know I was right."

Maggie had three empty baskets in her hands, and she handed one to each child. "Your Grampy Ike made these last night out of peach cans. See how he split the sides down and wove shaved wood through those slits? He made the handles out of some old wire he found out back. Now, I want you to take these baskets over to those two flower patches and fill them up with flowers.

"Zeke, you are in charge of the scissors. Be sure your sisters only take flowers from those two beds. Cut the stems about an inch long." Maggie pointed at the flower beds and held up her fingers to show them the length. "Don't mash them down but make sure those baskets are full. We are going to take them to the church with us."

As the excited children rushed toward the flower beds, Clare followed Maggie into the house. The older woman's face was flushed, and she seemed to be out of breath.

"Why I believe you are nervous, Maggie," Clare teased as she smiled at this woman who was both a mother and a friend.

"Aye, I am at that. I nearly fainted from nervousness when I married Paddy, and I'm feeling the same way today. My Ike is such a good man. He wanted to marry me four years ago. I knew little Annie needed me though, so I turned him down. I barely let him court me these last four years, and I sure didn't think he would wait. Ah, but he is a persistent man, my Ike is." Maggie smiled at Clare as her eyes watered.

"When you came back, we were both hopeful that Rock would fall in love again. He did, and now look at the two of us. One prayer fulfilled two wishes, and we both have good men in our lives."

Clare hugged Maggie tightly. Her eyes were watering as well. *Maggie is right. We are both lucky women.*

Rock slowly backed out of the doorway as he growled to himself, "I never will understand why women cry when they're happy. I don't like tears, and happy ones are even more confusing."

Ike sauntered up to stand beside Rock and heard the younger man growling to himself. He nodded but his eyes twinkled.

"Females is a confusin' lot, but us menfolks seem to like bein' confused. We jist keep a walkin' right back in."

"And why is that? What is it about women that we just let them mess with our heads all the time?"

Ike laughed out loud as he thumped Rock on the back. "It's jist the way the Good Lord designed things. Some of his designs make no sense, but they all seem to work."

The two men walked toward the children. The kids had cut every flower from the two designated flower beds. Annie was pointing at a third and Zeke was arguing with her. Rock grinned.

"I think Maggie was wise to give the scissors to Zeke." Rock pointed at the butchered plants and the mangled flowers in the little baskets. "What are you kids doing with all those flowers?"

Nora held her basket up for Rock to see. "Auntie Maggie said we could cut all the flowers here and put them in our baskets. I am saving some for Mama's hair."

Rock squatted down in front of Nora as she talked. Her little eyes sparkled as she showed him her flowers.

"And which ones did you pick for your mama?"

"Well, purple is her favorite color, so the purple ones are for her. Do you think she will like them, Papa?"

Rock's heart was just a little squishy as he hugged Nora.

"I'm sure she will love them. Now what about Auntie Maggie? Think she would like some flowers in her hair?"

Nora looked up at Ike, and he nodded his head seriously.

"Your Auntie Maggie sure does love flowers, an' I don't believe anyone has ever given 'er flowers fer 'er hair. I think she'd like that jist fine."

Nora studied her basket before she raised her big eyes to Ike.

"What colors do you think she would like?"

Ike scratched his head.

"I believe yellow an' orange be her favorite colors, but I reckon any flowers ya give 'er would be jist fine."

Nora beamed at the two men. Soon three little heads were discussing and digging in their baskets for all the right colors.

Rock smiled as he stood.

"The three of you get on in the house and see if Auntie Maggie and Mama need any help with dinner. Grampy Ike said Father Ravalli moved the wedding time up since there is a funeral this afternoon. That means we need to eat soon."

As the kids rushed into the house, Rock turned to Ike.

"Who is being buried? You said there was a funeral, but you didn't say who."

Ike scowled and shook his head. "A rough bunch of miners come through this week. There were a fight in the Star Saloon last night, an' the son of a rancher were shot. The kid warn't involved, but he got hit by a stray bullet. Two of the miners be in jail an' John Ketchum pledged revenge fer his son if they ain't hung.

"Glad none of yur boys stayed in town. There be lotsa shootin' fer a while there."

Rock nodded slowly. Dally hadn't given him many details last night. He just said he could feel trouble, so they rode on home.

"Two of the boys delivered cattle to the Mission, but they didn't stay long. They went into the Star, had a quick beer and left. Dally can foresee bad situations, and he walks away. Now Pete—he's another story. If he sticks with Dally though, he'll be all right."

When the men walked into the house, the kids swarmed Clare and Maggie as they tried to shove flowers into their hair. Maggie's head almost looked like a pin cushion, but she loved it.

There were only three purple flowers and each child stuck one in Clare's hair. She hugged them and was laughing when she caught Rock's eye.

Rock could feel his heart squeeze in his chest. *Clare is a wonderful mother.*

He moved up beside her and pulled her close as he whispered, "Mrs. Beckler, you sure look pretty today, and you smell good too."

Clare laughed but was soon pulled away by the kids as they showed her where she needed to sit.

The little group ate quickly and loaded in the wagon for their ride to the Mission.

Annie swung her basket around and sang loudly all the way. She lost most of her flowers before they ever arrived at the church. When she started to cry, Zeke gave her some of his. All three children were smiling as they jumped out of the wagon.

Nora held her basket carefully. She lifted the flowers to her nose, one by one, and smiled as she smelled each of them.

After Zeke climbed down, Ike handed him a little pillow where Maggie's ring was tied.

"Now ya have an important job, Zeke. Ya make sure nothin' happens to Auntie Maggie's ring. When I give ya the signal, ya bring it up to me.

"And ya gals, when I wink at ya, you'ins need to walk toward the back of the church. Ya drop all those flowers on the floor, all the way from the front to the back. Just toss 'em around as ya walk."

Annie nodded excitedly but Nora frowned. "Won't folks step on them? I don't think we should throw pretty flowers on the floor."

Ike grinned at her and winked as he whispered, "I tell ya what, Nora. Once all the folks leave, ya jist go on back in an' pick 'em all up. I'm sure Father Ravalli would like ya helpin' him to clean up."

Nora smiled happily and Rock grinned. *Ike is a wise old grandpa even though he never had any kids of his own. A mighty sharp old fellow.*

CHAPTER 76

NORA'S SPECIAL FRIEND

FATHER RAVALLI GREETED THE HAPPY FAMILY. HE shook Rock's hand as he smiled at him.

"Thank you for the cattle. Two of your riders delivered them yesterday. I told them to be careful when they left. I hope they made it home okay."

Rock nodded as he answered, "They did. Thanks for the suggestion. They had a drink and left before the trouble broke out. Dally is cautious, and he keeps Pete out of trouble."

The good priest laughed and moved on to greet the Owens.

A few more townspeople arrived as well as some of Ike and Maggie's Indian friends. Soon, the little church was full of smiles.

Father Ravalli began promptly at one. Clare had never been to a Catholic Mass before. Although all the standing and kneeling confused her, she thought it was beautiful.

Nora was staring at a statue on the side altar. Finally, she pulled on Clare's dress.

When Clare leaned over, Nora pointed at the statue and whispered loudly, "I know that lady. She is my friend."

Clare looked down in surprise. "What lady, Nora? There are no ladies seated up there."

"*That* lady, Mama. The one up *there*."

As Clare stared from Nora to the statue of the Blessed Mother, Nora continued, "I don't know her name but when I was at Pappy's house, sometimes she would come and visit me. She let me sit on her lap when I was afraid."

Clare was silent as she looked into the little girl's innocent face. Nora's eyes were shining, and Clare smiled.

"Her name is Mary, and she is a wonderful person to have as a friend, Nora. See the man on the cross? She is his mama."

Nora stared at the crucifix. When she looked at Clare, there were tears in her eyes. "I'll bet she cried when the mean men did that to her son. She is a nice mama."

Clare kissed the little girl's cheek. As they both faced forward, Clare looked again at the statue. She didn't understand what Nora thought she had seen, but she was glad it gave the little girl comfort. Clare smiled at the beautiful statue and turned her eyes toward Father Ravalli.

Annie was trying to tie the strings on the ring pillow in knots, and Zeke finally slapped her hand. She started to cry, and Rock picked her up.

"Maybe you had better pick up your flowers, Annie," he whispered. "They are all over the floor. You won't have any to drop when we're done if you aren't more careful."

Annie slid down and began to stuff the flowers into her basket. Nora helped her, and soon, only a few mashed petals were left on the floor.

Zeke watched Ike carefully. He almost ran to the altar when the old man waved at him. Auntie Maggie tweaked his cheek before he walked back to his seat with a big smile.

As Ike and Maggie made their vows, Rock put his arm around Clare. Finally, the service was over, and the organist began to play loudly.

Ike winked at the kids, and the girls scrambled out of their seat. Annie promptly dropped her basket, and Rock helped her pick up the now-wilted flowers.

Annie skipped down the aisle and threw the flowers everywhere. Some of them hit the guests. A few of the people ducked while others tried not to laugh.

Nora followed and dropped hers one at a time. She stopped and looked at each one to make sure each blossom landed correctly. If it didn't, she turned the flower over.

Maggie and Ike soon caught up with her, so she quit dropping flowers and took Maggie's hand. She skipped happily beside Maggie down the aisle and out of the church.

When people moved to congratulate Maggie and Ike, Nora rushed back into the church and began to pick up the flowers. Annie and Zeke followed her. Soon, most of the flowers were again in their baskets.

Nora walked to the front of the church and stood under the statue of the Blessed Mother. She stared up at the beautiful young woman.

Father Ravalli stopped beside her and looked up at the statue as well. "Do you know who that is, Nora?"

The little girl nodded her head quickly. "Her name is Mary, and she is my friend. And that is her son. I think she cried when the mean men hurt him because she is a nice lady."

Father Ravalli looked down at her in surprise and then smiled.

"Would you like to have a picture of Mary just for you? I can paint one for you if you would like."

Nora's eyes lit up with excitement. "Oh, yes. Then I can talk to her whenever I want!"

Father Ravalli laughed as he took Nora's hand. "Well then, that is what we will do. I will bring it out with me on Monday when I check in on your young friend. What is his name? The young man you are helping take care of?"

Nora took the hand the priest offered her and talked to him as they left the church.

"His name is Tuff. He is much better. He sleeps in the bunkhouse now with his brother, and sometimes, he walks without anyone helping him. His brother's name is Stub, and Stub loves Tuff a lot. I'm glad they came to our house. Stub and Dally and Pete and Dack are my friends too. Sometimes, they play with us. They tell us stories and rope us when we run."

Both the priest and the small girl were smiling as they came out of the church.

After Nora ran off to play, Father Ravalli smiled. He nodded in her direction when he stopped beside Clare and Rock.

"Are we baptizing Nora after Mass tomorrow? I believe the Good Lord has something special planned for her."

Clare nodded happily, and Rock smiled as he watched Nora play with Zeke and Annie.

"She's a mighty sweet little girl. We're happy she lives with us especially since her start was so rough."

They talked a bit longer before Father Ravalli hurried inside to prepare for the funeral.

CHAPTER 77

A Contented Man

BY THE TIME ROCK HAD HIS FAMILY LOADED IN THE wagon, the baskets of flowers were mashed and full of dirt. That didn't stop the kids from loving them though. They threw flowers all the way back to Auntie Maggie and Grampy Ike's house. Then Zeke announced they were going to use the baskets to hold their worms.

Clare caught all of them and made them change their clothes before they rushed outside to dig more holes. Grampy Ike had pushed little sticks in the ground to mark where they could dig, and there were lots of places marked.

Maggie had ordered some fresh lemons for the occasion, and the adults enjoyed fresh-squeezed lemonade as they watched the kids play. Maggie was beaming and Ike's blue eyes were sparkling.

Rock pulled Clare down beside him on the porch swing and they all relaxed as they enjoyed the warm afternoon.

The small creek in front of the house bubbled and sang as it flowed toward St. Mary's River. Stevensville was a bustling town, but here on the edge, it was quiet and peaceful.

Rock stretched out his long legs and pulled Clare a little closer. He grinned at his friends.

"Life is nice and quiet here, Ike. I am sure glad you bought Maggie this house. Now, we can all come to see you and stay as long we want."

Maggie smiled at Rock and kissed Ike's cheek. "You just come whenever you want, and you leave those precious little ones here from time to time too. I miss those children terribly after a week or so."

Ike grinned at his new wife. "Now Maggie Mae, ya know it's only been a few days since they was here.

"But she's right," he agreed as he looked over at Rock and Clare. "Ya drop 'em off whenever ya want."

He winked at Clare as he added, "An' fer sure when the next one comes along."

A slow blush began at the base of Clare's neck and moved up to her face. Rock laughed. He kissed his wife and whispered softly, "And we will keep working on that." He settled back against the swing and crossed his legs. His family was healthy, the cattle were fat, and love had opened his heart again. He tipped Clare's head to rest on his shoulder and closed his eyes.

Rock Beckler was a contented man.